SLEEPERS

CLANCY WEEKS

AVALON PRESS

Acknowledgements

As a first novel, the people responsible for this book making its way into a reader's hands are legion, but I would like to point out a few who made this possible. First up would have to be my editor/ friend/sounding board/therapist (because every writer needs one of those, right?) Jae Mazer. An author in her own right, she has been instrumental in pushing me to finish what I start. A bit of a nag, really.

Next are all those editors who made it a habit of rejecting my work. Seriously, without those people I likely would have never worked to improve. C.C. Finlay at Fantasy and Science Fiction in particular writes the nicest rejection letters. Insightful, to the point, and often quite helpful.

Last, but definitely not least (if I may use the cliché) is my family. Molly, the best wife a writer could have, never reads my work, doesn't really like science fiction, and sometimes thinks all I do all day is stare at the wall. What she *has* done, is give me the time and freedom to write. That's not a small thing in a world where two incomes are practically required. My son, Leo, has been an inspiration. The kid can crank out fifty story ideas before I've booted my computer, and constantly bugs me to finish so he can judge the quality for himself.

PART ONE

The evening hangs beneath the moon
A silver thread on darken dune
With closing eyes, and resting head
I know that sleep is coming soon
Upon my pillow, safe in bed
A thousand pictures fill my head
I can not sleep my mind's aflight and yet
my limbs seem made of lead

"Sleep"—Elvis Costello

CHAPTER 1

March 24, 2015

N[O MATTER WHAT ANYONE SAYS], jet–lag is real. The jet–lag experienced traveling from Kazakhstan to Atlanta, Georgia was the worst in Jack Montgomery's opinion. Arriving too late to check in at the CDC, he took a cab the twenty–five miles to his single–bedroom apartment outside of Sandy Springs. By the time he unlocked his door and tossed his bag and briefcase on the battered leather sofa, it was 2 am and all he wanted to do was fall into bed and sleep for a week. The case bounced once, fell to the floor and spilled its contents. Two pages of his preliminary report stared up at him, peeking from the pile of papers. Both pages were photographs of children asleep in their hospital beds. Round angelic faces poking from beneath slim covers, some clutching fuzzy stuffed animals. Asleep for nearly three months, they were among the first of those suffering from "encephalopathy of unknown etiology"—otherwise known as "we haven't a fucking clue."

Jack ran a hand through his hair and blew out a long sigh. *Bed's gonna have to wait.* He walked to the bar, pushing several unopened moving boxes out of his path, and poured three fingers of bourbon into the nearest glass. Stumbling back to the sofa, he set his drink on the second–hand IKEA coffee table and knelt to gather the weathered canvas case and the report.

The trip was a waste of both his time, and the Center's resources. Not because it wasn't important, but because no one knew what the hell to do about it. The doctors and nurses on the ground had everything covered. "Everything" consisted of keeping the patients comfortable and the IV's flowing. Without a clear cause, everything was considered. The uranium mines in nearby Krasnogorsk were ruled out as an environmental cause because no one there suffered from the malady. One by one, the researchers eliminated infections, poisons, viruses, biotoxins, and pretty much everything else they could think of. Regardless, twenty-five percent of the residents of Kalachi—most of them children—were suffering from a severe case of "you're fucked".

Sleep wasn't going to come easy tonight, even with the jet-lag. Jack reached for the remote and turned on the television, hoping late-night infomercials would do the trick. Instead, he was greeted with a breaking news report. He took a long sip of his drink, then listened to another disaster in the making as he turned the wedding band on his finger.

"Once again," the bottled-blonde newsreader said with forced gravitas, "the Germanwings Flight 9525 crashed 62 miles north-west of Nice in the French Alps in an apparent act of suicide by the co-pilot."

"Great. We not only have to worry about the planes and terrorists, but now the even damn *pilots* are trying to kill us." He surfed the channels, hoping to find something a little cheerier to watch, finally landing on an *X-Files* marathon.

* * *

The morning light streaming through the window was so bright it buzzed, vibrating his brain like the inside of an angry beehive. Jack sat up, holding his head as the buzzing grew more insistent. The gauze clouding his mind cleared enough for him to locate the source of the noise. He grabbed the cell phone from his briefcase, bumping his head on the coffee table and spilling the remainder of his drink. "Son of a bitch!" he said. The liquid soaked into the carpet, spreading like an infection, and he watched it grow before turning away and answering the phone.

"Morning, Mason," he said, rubbing his temples.

"Morning, buddy," Mason said, unnaturally buoyant for so early in the day. "How come you didn't call me for a ride from the airport when you got in?"

"It was pretty late. I didn't want to put you out."

"Of course," he said, "what else could it be?"

"Don't start, Mason," Jack said. The comforting friend routine was getting stale. It would be so much easier if everyone just let him be.

"Okay, okay," he said. Jack imagined the man holding his hands in front of him for protection. "I was just calling to see if you were coming in today. You know... to work?"

"What time is it?"

"Quarter to one."

"Shit!" Jack jumped from his seat, barking his shin on the coffee table that was now apparently trying to kill him. "God–*damn* it."

Mason laughed. "Don't sweat it, Jack," he said. "Sally said to take your time. She knows the trip was hard on you." Not as hard as *Sally* was when she was in a mood. Nominally his superior, his position was fluid enough she often had to ask rather than order. When she *did* order, though, it wasn't pretty. At all.

Jack looked down at the pictures, holding the phone to his ear with one hand and scrubbing his head with the other. "You have no idea, Mace."

"Well, anyway... Sally said to take the rest of the week off and come in fresh on Monday."

"Wow," Jack deadpanned. "A whole two days off. I'm honored."

"You're forgetting today is Wednesday."

"No, I'm not. But since it's past noon, today's already gone any-way."

"*That's* the spirit!" Mason laughed again. "How about we meet up for drinks after *I* get off work, and you can tell me about your trip?"

"I don't think—"

"Not taking no for an answer, buddy." His tone softened, and he said, "Seriously, Jack, you need to do something besides work. Start living again."

Jack looked around his apartment at the bare walls and the un-packed moving boxes, both mostly untouched since the day he signed the lease almost a year ago. "Sure, Mace. I'll see you at Jimmy's around six. You get to pick up the first round."

"Deal."

Maybe it's time, Jack thought as he hung up, walking to the larg-est stack of boxes. The one on top stared up at him like the children he spent so much time with the last five weeks, forlorn and lifeless. The label on the side read "photographs." He frowned, picked it up in trembling hands, and placed it in the corner of the room closest to the door.

That one would be last. It had to be. *I'm not ready*, he thought.

He wondered if he ever would be.

* * *

Jimmy's was a noisy place on the slowest of days, but Wednesdays were unique. The back room was devoted to an especially boisterous version of Trivial Pursuit that included teams, cheerleaders, and betting. The front was a frenetic mix of pool, parties, and piano. Most nights the musician was female, young, and pretty; tonight, however, a rotund man with long hair and a graying beard pounded the keys into submission. There was an abandon to his playing, fat fingers hitting more keys than intended at times, offering a simple elegance to his delivery. When Jack first walked in, he was greeted with a discordant—and in his opinion, more beautiful—rendition of Leonard Cohen's "Hallelujah". The man's voice was both grating and powerful, and choked when he came to the lines:

And it's not a cry that you hear at night

It's not somebody who's seen the light

It's a cold and it's a broken Hallelujah

"I hate that song," Mason said as he slapped Jack on the back and sat next to him at the bar. "Same thing over and over again. Never goes anywhere."

Jack turned, shook his head. "I think that's the point," he said. " It's about the futility of life."

"Whoa," Mason said, popping a handful of peanuts in his mouth. "A bit early in the evening to go all philosophical and morose, don't you think?" Jack winced as Mason spoke, watching the man's hand dive into the bowl of complimentary nuts. Jack never ate those. Working in the field for the CDC's Global Health Center taught him the dangers of communal food sources; and besides, they were liberally doused with hot sauce in order to get the patrons to buy more drinks. In Mason's case it worked like a charm.

"If you'd seen what I had..." Jack began.

"Yeah, I read the preliminary report you filed," Mason said, shaking his head. "Sounded rough." He brightened a bit, and said, "On the up side, Sally took your advice and is sending in a second team and some serious equipment."

"Won't help," Jack said, lifting his beer to take a drink. He stared at nothing while he drank, imagining the pure, dreamless sleep those people endured. *What did it feel like?* he wondered. *How is that any different than death itself?*

"But you said—"

"I know what I *said*. What I'm saying *now* is that it won't help."

Mason watched him for a second. "Jesus, Jack. Talk about morose." He waved at the bartender for a beer, then handed the woman his credit card to run a tab. He grabbed the bottle by the neck, took a swig, and said, "Let's get a booth so we can scope the ladies without looking like creepers." As he rose from the stool, he pointed at the nearest empty table. "That one looks good." He winked at Jack and waved his hand. "Full view of the room." Mason lead the way a few steps, then turned back. "And no more talking about work," he scolded, wagging a finger in Jack's face. "I get enough of that *at* work."

"Deal," Jack said, and followed him to the table, grabbing a menu from the bar on his way. "I don't know about you, but I could go for some wings."

"More of a leg-man, myself," Mason said, laughing at his own joke. Jack noticed Mason did that a lot, and had for as long as he had known him, going all the way back to college. Mason was tall and thin, but his presence filled a room like no one else Jack knew. Loud to the point of *almost* being bellicose, he had a knack for making any gathering more fun. He was the perfect counterpoint to Jack's staid seriousness. Especially lately.

Mason surveyed the room while Jack checked the menu. Both actions were pointless. The bar was lousy with regulars, and Mason had already hit on most of the attractive women—and been shot down—over time. Jack knew the menu by heart, and could write it out longhand if required. *At least with my nose buried in the menu, I don't have to listen to endless questions about my mental health.*

Mason stopped pretending to look at women and turned his attention back to Jack. "So... how are you doing? *Really.*"

"No," Jack said, waving his hand in front of Mason's face.

"No, what?"

"No, as in 'we're not doing this now', no." He had grown impatient with everyone trying to help him. There was nothing anyone *could* do to help.

"Jack, it's been a year—"

"Ten months, twelve days, and two hours." Jack's eyes narrowed and he took in a slow breath. "I know *exactly* how long it's been, Mason. I don't need anyone to remind me." He rubbed the back of his neck, feeling for the scar. "I have an empty apartment reminding me every goddamn waking moment of my life!"

"Calm down, man," Mason said, his voice soothing. He reached across the table and placed a hand on Jack's shoulder. "I'm just trying to help. That's all."

"I get it, Mace. You're trying to help, Sally's trying to help, Jenna and Bill are trying to help. The whole goddamn *world* is trying to help, but the only person who can help me is *me*." He finished by pounding his fist once on the table, rattling his bottle. It danced to the point of tipping, but he snagged it with a deft swipe of his hand before it fell. A few of the regulars turned their way, but the rest ignored them. *Everyone's wrapped up in their own shit*, Jack thought. *They don't need mine, too.*

Mason pulled away, and leaned back. "Fine, I get it," he said. "Not another word tonight." He crossed his heart with the bottle still in his hand. "I promise."

Jack watched him with one eyebrow cocked, then sighed and took a long drink. "So..." he said, pointing with the neck of his bottle, "how about that one over there?"

Mason turned to where the bottle pointed, squinted, then shrugged. "Nah. She turned me down last week."

"Woman's got good taste, then." Jack tried on a smile to see if it fit. *Tight, but not uncomfortable.*

Mason clinked bottles with Jack and grinned. "Damn straight."

* * *

With a long weekend to fill, Jack considered driving the two hours to Greenville where his brother Bill and his wife Jenna had the perfect life with their two children. As a police detective, Bill had a certain amount of flexibility in his schedule, and was certain to make time for a visit, but Jack knew the questions and concerns were sure to come up. Last night with Mason was almost more than he could bear, and an entire weekend of sad, sincere faces would drive him to drink.

He swirled the glass in his hand. *Okay,* he thought, *drink more.* He grabbed the remote and turned on the TV, then reached for the stack of mail he retrieved from the hold bin at the post office. Large enough to choke an elephant, most of it was junk. And bills. Always bills. The medical bills were the worst, most arriving months after he thought everything had been paid. The first one of those had a balance high enough to make him laugh out loud. "Might as well just ask for eighty *bazillion* dollars," he said. "It would be just as likely to get paid." He touched the long scar on his left arm that was the object of that particular bill. "Would have been cheaper just to take it off."

There were twelve more just like the first, all from different doctors and specialties—five were names he didn't recognize. Odds were they had just been standing near his door and had spoken to the real doctors once, giving them an excuse to sign his chart and try to take a slice. As far as he was concerned, used car salesmen were more honest.

Another late notice from the landlord, but since he already put a check in the mail, he threw that one away. The letter from Mark and Betsy he set aside unopened. Like the photographs in the corner, he would get to it later. In the middle of the pile was a letter postmarked from Kazakhstan dated two days *before* he arrived in that country. *Odd,* he thought. There was no return address, and he couldn't imagine anyone there who knew he was coming. The envelope had come open at some point during transit, and was resealed with tape. If he were a prominent figure in the government he might take it directly to the FBI for a once-over and let them open it, but he was neither that important nor that paranoid. Jack ripped the letter open at the end, extended his arm, and shook the contents onto the coffee table.

A standard A4, coarse-grained sheet of paper, folded twice, fell out and fluttered down. Jack held the open end up to his eyes, but there was nothing else inside. He set the envelope aside and carefully opened the letter, flattening it on the table. Handwritten cursive letters, formed by a thick soft-leaded pencil, lay there accusing him in English—*I know who killed your wife and daughter.*

"So do I, asshole," he said, grabbing his drink and downing the remainder in a single gulp. "*I did.*"

* * *

"It's not working, daddy," Riley said, kicking the back of his seat.

"Sorry sweetheart. It's probably just locked up." He turned his head just enough to see her pouting in her car seat, "Do you know how to reboot it?"

"She's four, Jack," Beth said beside him, shaking her head, "not one of your tech geeks at work."

"Hey, the kid knows more than I did at her age," he protested, accompanied by the sound of Riley pounding on the tablet's screen.

Beth turned all the way around in her seat, and said, "We'll be at nana and pawpaw's soon, baby. You can wait a few minutes."

"Too long!" More pounding.

"Ugh, fine," his wife said, unbuckling her seatbelt. "I'll come back there and see if I can fix it."

"Just have her hand it to you."

"It's strapped to the back of your seat, remember," she said with a heavy sigh. Crawling between the front seats, one knee on the center console, her ass was beside Jack's head. He remembered that perfect ass was the first thing he saw the day he met her, and, truth be told, the first thing about her he fell in love with.

He smiled and reached across with his left hand to slap it, but never finished the motion. The truck, a big red four-wheeler with the knobby tires high school boys in Georgia loved so much, slammed into his side of the car. Not his door, of course. That would have been a blessing. No, it hit Riley's door full-on, folding the car nearly in half before rolling it over. Coming to rest in the ditch upside-down, the horn stuck blaring a single soulless note, Jack winced in pain as he turned toward his wife. Her lifeless eyes stared straight at him, marking him like a witness in a murder trial.

Riley wasn't even crying. Such a good girl. Brave, like her mother. Millimeter by agonizing millimeter, he continued turning—contorting his body to see behind to his daughter. His beautiful, perfect little girl. A foot, attached to an ankle, attached to a leg, attached to...

He woke screaming, sweat flowing from every pore in his body. Flailing his arms and legs, the dream releasing him reluctantly, he swept the three empty liquor bottles off the table next to the sofa. They fell to the carpeted floor with a trio of thuds.

Jack sat up, the screams replaced by sobs, and he hugged his knees to his chest while pulling his hair with one fist. He rocked in his seat and cried for several minutes. It was comforting in its way—familiar as an old pair of shoes. "It wasn't my fault. It wasn't my fault."

A mantra as old as his pain, he would repeat the refrain until he almost believed it.

"The asshole ran a stop sign. Happens every day. It wasn't my fault. It wasn't..."

What would his friends and family say if they saw him like this? Would they worry more, or be impressed by his ability to hold it together as well as he had? *What the fuck does it matter, anyway?*

Everyone told him it would get better. It didn't. It only grew more distant. The pain of loss did not lessen, it did not get easier. It was there in an instant, hammering on the door to his brain whenever he remembered his daughter. Remembered her...

"At least the son of a bitch had the decency to die," he said, his voice stronger now that he was fully awake.

Cops said he was asleep when he hit us. He sleeps forever now. Good goddamn riddance.

Jack picked up his cell to check the time. *3 am.* He set it back on the table, and the phantom letter grabbed his attention again. He lifted it, turned it over, then back, looking for anything that might hold a clue as to who wrote it. *What's the point, anyway? Everyone knows who killed my family.*

"Mark Wilson Peters, Jr.," he said aloud, the sound of his voice mocking him. "He had help, though."

He threw the letter to the table, then stood on shaking legs. The pins in his left leg were hurting, and he rubbed it while he walked to the bar. Almost empty, it still held enough to keep him numb at least through Saturday. Sunday he would set aside for recovery before returning to work on Monday.

Until then he belonged to Jack Daniels.

CHAPTER 2

THE LIGHT TURNED GREEN AND JACK TWISTED THE THROTTLE, feeling the engine's power rumbling through the seat and up his spine. The bike, an old Yamaha Road Star, was now considered mid-sized, but the throaty growl from the pipes told another story. He bought it used not long after he quit his physical therapy. Everyone thought he was nuts, knowing the only reason he wasn't already dead was the cage of metal that surrounded him in the car. Worse, in their minds, was his refusal to wear a helmet.

Damn thing is just there to keep your face pretty for the post-mortem identification.

He would rather feel the wind on his face as he sped down the highway, knowing that any wreck serious enough to leave him paralyzed would kill him outright. *That way, no one has to make a decision. No plugs to pull* that *day—no sir.*

Weaving through traffic on his way to work each morning was an act of defiance to the gods, a big middle finger to any that dared to interfere in his life. Not that he believed in a god, anyway. Not anymore. *Or ever again.* Those days were gone, along with Beth and Riley, buried under mounds of moldy earth.

A driver, no turn signal, carelessly drifted into his lane, and Jack pressed the horn with this left thumb. He was rewarded with a middle finger of his very own. Jack removed the baffles from his pipes the first week he had driven the thing, knowing bikes were all but invisible to most drivers. Two weeks and three near-misses later, he replaced the stock horn with a cool set normally found on semi-trucks. Sometimes he pulled up next to lazy drivers and lay on the horn, but that occasionally frightened them so badly they swerved or hit their brakes. These days he settled for bumping it once to let them know they were idiots.

He passed another motorcycle going the other direction and waved. It was the one biker tradition he'd adopted after taking up the habit. *Like we all belong to the same club.* Volkswagen Beetle drivers used to do the same thing when he was a kid, and he had taken to doing it when he acquired an old fuel-injected '76 model in college. *Right before I met Beth. She* loved *that thing.*

Thinking of Beth, he smiled and twisted the throttle harder, feeding the 1600cc engine to speed around the hapless driver. He smiled and waved at the woman as he flew by, then slowed to a stop at the next light. She fumed, drumming the fingers of one hand on the wheel as she held a cell phone to her ear with the other. When the light changed, he opened it up and left a ten-foot trail of rubber on the road behind. He flew by a cop at the intersection, obviously invisible to him as well.

Two more blocks, and he turned right on CDC Parkway, leaving the idiot and the cops behind. Once on the campus he slowed to posted speeds. His coworkers already thought he was suicidal; there was no point in having them think he was a danger to them as well. He gunned the engine as he drove past Sally's car, setting off her car alarm. He smiled, then pulled into his space next to Mason's beat up old Ford Ranger. The truck's door opened just as he turned off the bike.

"Morning, Jack," Mason said, looking him over from head to toe. "You look better than I expected." He gave Jack a half smile, then reached back in his truck to grab the book-bag he used as a briefcase. He slammed the door shut and turned to wait for Jack.

Jack stepped off the bike and retrieved his own case and lunch from the saddlebags. "Feel better than *I* expected as well," he said with a brave grin. The truth was, other than the ride in, he had felt like shit all morning. His breakfast consisted of little more than dry toast, and he wasn't sure if the rumbling in his stomach was hunger or a harbinger of something worse.

"Don't get me wrong, Jack... you still look like shit." He shook his head as he began the walk to the building, "And don't fool yourself into thinking Sally won't notice, either."

Jack fell in beside him, and said, "Don't much care what she notices. I do my job, and that should be enough."

Mason laughed. "Right." He stuffed his lunch up under one arm, then threw the other around Jack's shoulders. "You go ahead and keep thinking like that... see how far that gets you."

* * *

Sally—looking like a short, squat vulture—was waiting for them when they walked into the suite of offices that served as the Center's headquarters. At just under five feet tall, no one would call her petite. Compact and round, her energy fairly crackled from every pore of her body; and as she stood in the hall blocking the doorway with her arms crossed over her ample chest, she surveyed them both with pursed lips and a disapproving eye.

"Have a nice long weekend, did we?" She began tapping her foot as her eyes narrowed.

"Per your orders, ma'am," Jack said, offering her a slight tilt of his head. "All rested and ready to go."

"Mm-hmm," she said, shaking her head. Relaxing her arms, she walked around the two men, allowing them to enter the offices. As she passed Jack, she said, "You smell like a distillery."

He chuckled and said, "Then my money wasn't wasted."

Sally continued to walk away, but added over her shoulder, "I want your final report on my desk by noon, Jack."

"Consider it done, Ms. Jackson," he called after her. Mason punched him in the arm to keep him from making it worse.

"C'mon, Jack," he whispered, "let's get to work before she finds out we suck at our jobs."

"Heard that," she said, "and I already know."

Jack shook his head, laughing quietly, and entered the over-sized linen closet they generously called an office. As a contract employee, the fact that any space was allocated at all meant they thought he was valuable, just not enough to put in a salaried position. He didn't have the required string of letters after his name, regardless. Jack was just *really* good at what he did. Mason called him the "Leap-Meister" for his almost magical ability to see outside the box. Jack considered himself an above-average diagnostician. If he had a medical degree, he would've been even better. *Not a chance in hell I'm going back to school, though*, he thought as he placed his briefcase on his tiny desk.

He sat in his overstuffed leather chair—the only nod to comfort in the whole office—and pulled the slim file from inside the case. Logging into the system from his computer, he downloaded the raw files that made up the preliminary report from his personal cloud account. The Center—Sally especially—frowned on his use of outside services, but the creaky government systems were just too unreliable in his opinion; they simply weren't practical for use in the field. He preferred thumb-drives or a direct connection from his laptop, but those options were strictly forbidden. When he offered this as a compromise, Sally reluctantly gave in. He was a notoriously slow typist, and she was impatient.

The first file he imported was a zipped directory of hundreds of pictures he had taken at the hospital. While his computer chugged away at extracting them, he left to fetch coffee to help him power through the morning. When he came back to his desk, mug in hand, the folder on the screen was full of photo thumbnails. Most of the shots were in the rooms where the children slept, nurses tending to their patients as doctors looked on with concern. Some were of the work areas behind the scenes—rapidly emptying supply closets, over-full laundry areas, harried janitors, and weary administrators. Parents and other family members constituted a whole other category, and were in a different file.

He would have to take a whole day to go over every photograph to select the right ones for his final report—Sally's deadline be damned—but he couldn't help staring at them now, seeing each one with fresh eyes. Most were similar enough to pass as duplicates. In one of them, several of the nurses conferred with a doctor while a man—a parent, presumably—stood close by. Jack couldn't see the man's face, or the worry he knew must be there, as it was obscured by the dark gray fedora the man wore. He was standing just behind a nurse, leaning in slightly with his head down, his hands stuffed into a dark overcoat. In another picture, the same man hovered over a bed that held a small girl Jack assumed must be his child. Two frames later, however, the man was at yet another bed. Then another, and another. Jack flipped through all the pictures rapidly, the same man in over a third of them, standing by as many as twenty different beds. *Why didn't I notice this guy before?* he thought. *Maybe he's an administrator or something.* That wasn't likely, though, as Jack was sure he and his interpreter had spoken to all of the management.

Jack downloaded the file with the pictures he had taken of the parents. After more chugging by the old computer, he opened the folder and clicked through each shot. The man was not prominent in any, but could be seen hovering in the background of a few. At no time was his face in full view for Jack's lens. Another folder yielded similar results. This time, the subjects were the staff, and while the man was visible in many of the shots, he was never the subject. In one sequence of pictures, Jack had captured doctors and nurses rushing to help a patient who had coded, and the man was at the far end of the room standing—then kneeling—beside another bed. A chill ran up Jack's spine as he flipped through the pictures, watching the man pull something from his pocket and lean toward the little girl asleep there. In the next frame he was standing again, placing whatever it was back in his pocket. In the last frame he was gone, only a sliver of his coat captured in the doorway to mark his passing.

Jack ran a shaking hand through his hair and leaned closer to the monitor. Zooming in on the previous picture, even as the shot pixelated, he could easily make out the shape of a syringe.

* * *

"You ready for lunch?" Mason stood in Jack's doorway, leaning just inside against the jamb.

"Uh... what?" Jack looked up from his workstation, his concentration shattered by the question. "What time is it?"

"Eleven thirty." Mason checked his cell phone, "Or close enough to count."

"Son of a bitch," Jack said, shaking his head. "There goes Sally's deadline." *How did I lose over three hours just looking at pictures?* "So far all I've done is catalog my photos."

"Well, she'll deal," Mason shrugged. He shook his lunch bag at Jack. "Shake a leg, man. I can hear it going bad in here."

"Hey, before we go," Jack said, looking over the top of his monitor at him, "can you take a look at this and tell me what you think?"

Mason lowered his lunch at the look on Jack's face, walked into the small office and around to the other side of the desk.

"Right here," Jack said, tapping on the screen.

Mason leaned closer and squinted. "Looks like one of the doctors is drawing blood." He turned his head to Jack, "So?"

"Look again."

Turning back, Mason's brow furrowed, and he pursed his lips, then his eyes widened. "Since when do doctors wear hats and trench coats in a hospital?" He shook his head, "Who the hell wears a *fedora* anymore, anyway?"

Jack leaned back in his creaking old chair, letting out a long breath he didn't know he was holding. "Pretty much what I was thinking." He swept through a number of pictures for Mason while he spoke. "At first I thought this guy was a family member, but he's in way too many shots and by too many beds. He's not in any of the staff or administrator shots, either, other than in the background."

"So... you've got some mystery man drawing blood in the middle of a busy hospital ward," Mason said, tapping the screen. "You got any with his face showing?"

"Not that I've found so far," Jack said, shaking his head. "And that can't be a coincidence, Mace. I have *hundreds* of shots here, with him in almost half."

Mason tapped the screen again with his forefinger, his nail clicking repeatedly. He stood back, blew out a long breath, and shrugged, "Can we at least discuss it over lunch? I'm starving."

"You go on ahead. I have another couple of files to download, and there might be something in there," Jack said, head already down and fingers typing."

"Ah, hell, Jack. I've seen that look before." Mason shook his head and started for the door. "If you're not down there in ten minutes, I'll send someone after you."

Jack grunted, but was no longer paying attention.

Mason shook his head again and left.

* * *

"Ba-*Bam*," Jack yelled in Mason's ear as he slammed the print onto the table. Everyone in the little dining hall started, then settled back to their meal once they saw it was only Jack. Most government employees were jumpy these days. Jack's dad would have called them "skittish". The world had changed a lot, though, in the fifteen years since Old Man Montgomery last walked the fields. That was what all the farmhands called him. The foreman once confided to Jack that it was a well-known fact the Old Man was just fine with his men working about a half a day—and he didn't care *which* twelve hours they chose.

He grinned at the old joke. Jack had taken a lot from his dad, the concept of a full-day's work for a full-day's pay being the only one that stuck. He liked to think of himself as a "plugger". The kind of guy who stuck with something until it was done, come hell or high water. In this case it had, indeed, taken only ten minutes—give or take ten—to find a picture with the Shadowman's face. It still wasn't very clear, but Jack was sure there wasn't one better.

Mason picked up the picture with one hand and continued eating with the other. "This the best you got?"

"Yeah," Jack said, sliding into a chair across the table, "there doesn't seem to be a better one."

"Does it help you ID the guy?"

"Only from an elimination standpoint." He grabbed one of Mason's fries and nibbled while he spoke. "I know for a fact now that he's not staff, or one of the administrators. He's also not one of the government officials I spoke with, either."

"Then I've only got two questions," Mason said. Jack looked at him, waiting for him to go on. "One, why is some guy drawing blood from these patients, and two... what are we supposed to do about it?"

"Well... the least we can do is alert the authorities over there," Jack said, scratching his chin. *Oops... forgot to shave this morning.*

"No, Jack," Mason shot back, "that's the *most* we can do." Jack started to protest, but Mason held up a hand. "Check with Sally on this one, but we don't really do anything unless invited in by the country in question. Local cops aren't usually keen to have outsiders come in and tell them how to do their jobs."

The wind taken completely out of his sails, Jack realized he was getting worked up over something that wasn't his business. For a moment, all he saw was the need to act; to do something other than guesswork and information gathering. *That's a sad substitute for meaning in your life, boy-o,* he thought. There were any number of explanations for the Shadowman's actions, and they did not have to be nefarious. He could easily be an investigator much like himself, working for the government of Kazakhstan directly. The problem with that, though, was there normally a get-to-know-you meeting with everyone on the ground so people didn't step on one another's jurisdiction. *Maybe he's freelance, working for a single government official.* But who... and, more importantly, why?

"Earth to Jack," Mason said, snapping his fingers in front of Jack's face. "Are you gonna eat, or what?"

"Maybe later," he said, standing. "I need to finish up the report so I can get this to Sally by the end of the day." He snagged another fry from the greasy paper boat. "After that, it's her problem."

* * *

"Montabaur?"

"It's in Germany," Sally said, sitting behind her desk and the mountain of paperwork that regularly claimed that territory for its own. On some days all anyone saw of her was the top of her head with its tight matting of graying hair.

"Yeah," Jack said, "I know that. I just don't know what's going on there that's within our mandate."

"Probably nothing," she said. "There are some nervous senators worried about the recent spate of pilot suicides. Specifically, suicide by crash."

"I'd hardly call two in the last few years a 'spate'."

She picked up a sheet of paper, "Four in the last two years alone, with a casualty count of four-hundred and twenty-three."

"Still," he sighed, "that's within statistical norms, and, near as I can tell, not a medical problem." He shook his head, "Plus, I just fucking got *home*."

"There's no call for profanity, Jack," she said, narrowing her eyes and shaking a finger at him. "We all do what we must." Her face softened. "Did I fail to mention 'nervous senators'?" she said, tilting her head up at him. Jack was a good kid, in her opinion, but sometimes he made her work too damn hard. His mind wanted not only answers, but *evidence* for those answers as well. *I think that's why he's had such a hard time accepting the death of his family*, she thought. *Without answers, there was nothing for him to accept.* His appearance was the most obvious outward expression of that state of mind. His work ethic and attention to detail were as strong as ever, but he no longer threw himself into a project the way he once did. Sometimes—like today—he tried to use

18

his superpower to talk her *out* of an investigation. *Not today, though.* Her superiors made that perfectly clear.

"Shit, Sally... *Germany?*" He was pleading with her now, but her hands were tied.

"You don't have to leave today, but you need to be there by the end of the week." She shrugged, "Besides, it shouldn't take long. You're just there to give the guy's apartment the once-over and check for anything external that could have triggered his suicidal tendencies. Those go back a few years, by the way, so it's unlikely there *was* anything external."

"But if I want to do it right, I need to trace down every lead." He shoved his hands into the front pockets of his jeans and sighed. "That could take weeks."

"Don't do it right, then. Do it quick and come home." They both knew Jack could never do that, but sometimes he needed reminding.

"Fine," he said. "Get Barbara to schedule a flight for later in the week." His shoulders slumped. "I need to hold my mail again and take care of a few other things." He turned to leave.

"Good work on your report, by the way. Even if it *was* late."

He shook his head and chuckled softly as he walked out of her office.

That boy needs a rest, she thought as he left. But if I don't keep him busy, there's no telling what he will do.

* * *

"Tough luck, Jack." Mason came straight to his office as soon as the word filtered down to his lab. He sat on the only clean corner of the desk.

"Oh well," Jack said. "It's not like there's much to do at home, anyway." Sitting at his desk again, he was methodically clicking through the pictures of the Shadowman. He had found every one that showed even a part of the man, placed them all in a single folder, and sorted them by date and time. Going through them in sequence told a story without a plot, but as near as he could tell, the man had visited every single bed in that particular ward. *And no one seemed to notice him coming or going—or even acknowledged his presence.*

"So, did you see the casualty list of the crash?" Mason picked up the baseball from the little stand on Jack's desk. He casually tossed it from hand to hand as he spoke. "Small world... there were three passengers from Kazakhstan on that flight."

"Not so small, Mace. Statistically, such an event was almost a surety."

Mason leaned down and whispered, "I love it when you talk dirty." They both laughed, breaking the tension, and Mason placed the ball back on its stand.

Jack grabbed a stack of mail from his inbox and leaned back, crossing his legs as he put his feet up on the desk. "Should probably go through these and get anything important out of the way before I leave." Two letters in, he dropped his feet to the floor, and sat up so fast the stack fell from his lap and the chair tipped precariously. His hands shook as he held the slim envelope, staring at it with his mouth agape.

"Jack," Mason said, as he stood and walked around to Jack's side of the desk, "what's wrong? You look like you've seen a ghost."

Jack ran a hand through his hair and waved the letter at Mason. "Open it. I can't."

Mason took the letter, turned it over in his hands a few times, then checked the postmark. "Hey, it's from Montabaur. That's a pretty big coincidence. Maybe this is the same letter Sally got asking for help."

"Check the date."

"March 23rd. So?"

"That's a full day *before* the crash, Mace."

Mason's eyes narrowed, then grew wide. Now *his* hands shook as he tore the envelope open and pulled the coarse-grained paper from within. He read it, lips pursed and brow furrowed. "I don't get it."

"What's it say?"

"Just, 'Mr. Peters did not kill your family.'" He turned the paper over several times, much as Jack had done with the one in his apartment. "What the hell does that mean?"

Calming the tremor in his hands, if not his voice, Jack took the letter from Mason and said, "It means I'm going to Germany for more than just a plane crash."

CHAPTER 3

*D*RIVING THE LONELY STRETCH OF HIGHWAY AT NIGHT, *it seemed even his headlights gave up after only a few feet in their attempt to pierce the darkness ahead. The cabin of the car was unusually silent, and he strained to hear his own breathing. There was no road noise, either, but a soft sound—a single pitch—gnawed at his brain, insisting to be heard. The sound grew in both volume and intensity, but instead of searching for the source in front where it surely lay, he turned his head to look behind.*

Riley, his only daughter, looking like pictures of her mother at that age, sat quietly strapped in her car seat with her head turned, staring out the window. Her yellow dress, the one her mother had picked out only hours before, was brighter than anything else in the car, making her look like a porcelain doll. Jack watched in horror as that porcelain cracked under the sustained pressure of the sound, and she turned her mangled and bloody face toward him.

"Who killed me, daddy?"

Jack woke with a start, gasping for air. He brushed the sweat-soaked hair from his eyes, then scrubbed his face with both hands. He reached behind, pulled the little pillow—also soaked—from where it had fallen, and tossed it onto the next seat. The cabin of the plane was quiet; many of the passengers were sleeping as he had been only moments before. For an intercontinental flight, there were a remarkably large number of empty seats, affording him the luxury of an empty row all to himself. He reached up and pressed the call button, and a strikingly beautiful attendant appeared almost instantly.

"Can I help you, sir?" She made it sound like an offer for sex. *Was that part of the training?* he wondered.

"I'd like a bourbon and rocks, please."

"Certainly," she said, then turned and walked away. He leaned out and watched, remembering how Beth used to point out such women to him, secure in the knowledge that he could appreciate beauty without straying. If she had been a guy, Beth would have been the perfect wingman.

Returning with his drink, she knelt beside his seat and handed it to him with a small coaster already underneath, making sure to brush her perfectly manicured fingers over his. She looked up, batted her eyelashes a couple of times, and asked, "Will there be anything else?"

Nope, he thought, now she's definitely flirting.

"The drink's enough for now," he checked her name tag, "Amber." He looked up into emerald eyes, the deep green irises stopping his heart like a punch to the chest. "I'll call if I think of something else." He smiled, remembering to breathe.

She smiled back, brushed a spray of stray hair over her ear, stood, and turned to leave. She stopped and looked back over her shoulder. "Just tap the button and I'll be right here," she said, and glided away.

There was a time, before Beth, he would have leapt at the opportunity, but not anymore. He spun the simple band on his finger a few turns, and grinned. There was also a time when a wedding ring was a clear signal to stay away, but these days it was more of an attractant to young women. If he really wanted the advances to stop, he would take it off, but he still couldn't do that. In his heart he was married, and probably always would be.

The seatbelt sign overhead lit with a soft ping, then the captain spoke over the intercom, informing everyone the flight was on time and would be landing in Frankfurt soon. "Soon" was relative in the airline industry. Jack knew he probably had about an hour before the passengers were allowed to deplane, so he pulled his tablet from the magazine pouch and opened the files about the area where he would be working. It was his first trip to Germany, after all.

* * *

Jack could have driven a government car from the airport to Montabaur, but the Cologne-Frankfurt high-speed railway promised to take him the eighty kilometers in under thirty minutes. Besides, he didn't feel up to braving the roads in an unfamiliar country. If he'd brought his bike, he might have decided differently.

Riding the train was a comfortable experience, even if the countryside flew by too fast. It was nothing like the trains in the US. This was a fast, quiet, and safe ride, even smoother than the flight in. He missed the sound of wheels as they clackety-clacked on the rails, though at this speed it was more likely to sound like a drum solo. Jack closed his eyes and nestled back against his seat, the gentle sway of the car lulling him to sleep as it took its long sweeping turns.

"Hello again."

Jack's lids snapped open and he looked up, directly into the deep green eyes of the flight attendant.

"Amber?" he said.

"You remembered," she winked. "That's a point in your favor." She pointed to the empty seat next to him. "May I?"

He hesitated, a million thoughts raging to be heard, and her smile faltered. "Oh, uh... of course," he said, finally, patting the seat. Amber placed the small travel bag she carried under the seat, then folded herself, ass first, into the empty space. Jack couldn't help himself, smiling as she sat.

She turned to him, brushing her auburn hair over an ear. "In Germany on business?"

"Yeah, I work for the CDC's Global Health Center."

"A doctor?"

"Oh no," he said with a chuckle. "I'm not smart enough for that. Field work, mostly." He leaned closer. "I'm their canary."

"Pardon?" she said as her brow furrowed.

"Canary in the coal mine," he said, leaning back. "I go in first as a general investigator, looking for things a doctor might not think of."

"Oh," she said, "that sounds interesting." Her tone said otherwise.

"Not really, but thanks for trying." He smiled again, both lapsing into an uncomfortable silence for a moment. Finally, he stuck out his hand and said, "My name's Jack."

"I know," she said, taking his hand and shaking it lightly. "I read the passenger manifest."

"Do you live in Germany?" Her face scrunched up—which he had to admit to himself was cute—and he quickly added, "It's just your accent is decidedly *not* German."

She laughed. It was a hearty, throaty laugh, unconcerned with either propriety or discretion. It was a laugh both unconventional and comfortable. It reminded him of Beth.

"Oh, no. I have a flight attendant friend who lives here, and when our downtime schedules work out, we trade apartments."

"That's got to be the most interesting vacation idea I've heard yet," he said, nodding his head.

"Well..." she said, smirking, "I think I get the better end of the deal."

"How so?"

"I live in Atlanta."

His first instinct was that it was an amazing coincidence, but his brain quickly calculated that thought out of existence. The flight originated in Atlanta, after all, so the odds of her living there were quite high. *Still...*

"How long will you be visiting..." she began.

"Montabaur," he replied. "It's open-ended, but I hope to not take more than a week or two."

"Oh my," she said with mock concern and a smile. "My apartment is near there. Anything I need to be worried about?"

"I doubt it," he said, scratching his chin. "I'm here mostly to calm my boss's paranoia." He cocked his head, "Or, I should say, *her* boss."

"Ah," she said, holding her hand up like a traffic cop, "don't get me started on *bosses*."

"Mine's pretty good as bosses go," he said, thinking about Sally patrolling the building like a bulldog. "If you screw something up, she'll hunt you down and let you know right quick." He shrugged and said, "But if you do something outstanding, she does exactly the same thing. You always know where you stand with her."

"Sounds like I should be working for her."

The train slowed, and a recorded voice announced Montabaur station.

"That's my stop," Jack said, a little sad, and a little surprised to discover that fact. As the train rolled to a stop, he stood and gathered the case. Amber stood as well, looking for something, then smiled as she reached out and plucked the pen from his pocket. She grabbed his hand, turned it over, palm up, and wrote.

"Here is my Twitter handle. I don't have a phone that works over here, so this is the best way to reach me." She looked into his eyes, holding him dumbfounded in place. A slight and lopsided smile creased her face, she said, "If you have any free time this week, we should get together for a drink."

So many emotions churned inside him, even his stomach was doing a mambo. *She's beautiful and willing, but I am just not ready yet.* His head was swimming, and now, standing so close, he felt the heat of her. The scent she wore wafted in delicate tendrils, tickling his nose. He breathed her in without a thought, and his cheeks flushed.

I can't, he thought. Reluctance pulled him in both directions at once.

He held up his left hand and showed her the ring, "I'm sorry, but I'm married."

Her smile grew, crinkling the corners of her eyes, and she said, "No you're not. But it's cute how you use that as a shield."

"But—"

Amber stood on her toes, gave him a light kiss on the cheek, then stepped back to give him room. "Seriously, Jack, you need to get out and have some fun while you're here." She moved aside so he could get to the aisle, and winked. "Besides, it's not like I'm inviting you into my bed. It's just drinks, silly."

"Okay... maybe I will, then," he said, still not sure which way to go. He stepped into the aisle and walked toward the exit, looked at his hand, and said, "Maybe I will." He waved at her and walked off the train.

Great, he thought, now I have to get a fucking Twitter account.

When he was outside, he looked at his hand again, noticing for the first time her handle included her last name. His knees grew weak, threatening to buckle completely, and he leaned on a bench for support.

Riley.

* * *

"I am not really an interpreter, Mr. Montgomery. I just know more English than the others at the station."

Rutger chauffeured Jack through the streets of Montabaur to the home of Andreas Lubitz, the co-pilot of the ill-fated Flight 9525. While Jack wanted nothing more than to go straight to his hotel and fall into the bed waiting for him, it was still daylight, and there was no sense wasting it. With luck, he might discover something today, and wrap up his investigation before the weekend.

"I thought English was a de facto second language here," Jack said.

Rutger smiled and asked, "Did you take a foreign language in school, Mr. Montgomery?"

"Yeah, Spanish. And the name's Jack."

"Do you remember any of it, Jack?"

"Um... not really, no," he said, shaking his head. "Point taken."

"I spend a *lot* of time watching American television. *Cheers* being one of my favorites as a kid," he said with a more than passable Boston accent. *Now that's just wrong,* Jack thought. *I can't even do that.*

"Then you'll be more than helpful, I think. But please, don't do the accent. It's a bit disturbing when I *know* you're German."

Rutger laughed. "I promise. No more accents."

"It's just that the first time I heard Hugh Laurie speak with a British accent it really threw me. It sounded weird after so many years of watching *House.*"

"*Ach so!*" Rutger said. "I *love* that show," he said, sounding like Gregory House.

"Stop it," Jack said, but was now laughing with him.

"Here we are, I think," Rutger said, pulling the car to a stop across from the large home Lubitz shared with his parents. The construction was a simple hipped-roof design that was—much like what Jack knew of Andreas—completely nondescript. There were reporters and police milling about, both inside and outside the taped-off areas, but no neighbors as far as Jack could see. A couple of the homes facing Lubitz's had their curtains pulled slightly askew, a face peeking out here and there, but curtains quickly fell back into place. Rutger shifted the car into park and killed the engine.

Jack pulled the camera from his bag, checked the charge, and opened the door, exiting his side at the same time Rutger did from his. Jack smiled as he shook his head. *We look like partners in a buddy cop movie.*

He stood back and took pictures of the home and neighborhood, getting every possible angle, then walked up to the police tape. A large officer stopped him before he could cross the line, with a palm in his face and a single *nein* from his lips. Rutger stepped between them, spoke briefly with the man, then ushered Jack past the barrier and the line it guarded.

"I notice you didn't even show him a badge," Jack said.

"He knows me, *and* that I outrank him," Rutger said with a wink.

Jack raised an eyebrow, now curious. "Just what *is* your rank?"

"Polizeioberkommissar. Senior Inspector, or what you might call a 1st Lieutenant detective in your country. Normally we wear a uniform with rank, but my role right now is more informal."

"I had no idea they were sending someone so senior as an interpreter," Jack said. "I feel like I should be driving *you* around."

Rutger laughed. "I fear we would end up in Spain if you were driving," he said. "No offense intended," he added with a wink.

"None taken," Jack said. "I know my limitations." As they neared the house, the front door burst open and several officers exited carrying boxes. Reporters of every nationality rushed to ask their important questions but were ignored. A single official stopped to address the press, and Rutger listened intently for a time while Jack tried to pick out the two or three German words and phrases he knew. It was hopeless, and he waited for a translation.

"He says they found no suicide note, but located something of significance which is being taken in for testing. He hopes it will provide clues to what happened with Mr. Lubitz." Rutger frowned and his brow furrowed. "That is all," he said.

Something of significance, Jack thought. *An ominous phrase if ever I heard one.* He knew that only about one in six suicides left a note, but something as big as this surely merited one. *Whatever it is, I'll find out tomorrow when we go to the station*, he thought, following Rutger into the house.

* * *

Jack entered his hotel room after what seemed like an eternity of a day. He had been up for nearly twenty-four straight hours, and all he wanted to do was crawl into that great big bed and cover himself from head to toe with the fluffy comforter. First, though, he needed to place his phone and tablet on charge and connect to the hotel's wireless network. His phone hadn't had a good connection all day, and since it hadn't pinged once, he knew he must be missing some emails from the office.

His stomach reminded him that he hadn't eaten since the plane, so he dialed room service and ordered a sandwich, then pulled his chargers and plug adapters from his bag, and plugged in each of his electronic devices. Once the tablet booted, he logged into the hotel's connection, and almost instantly was hit with a barrage of emails. Each was sorted into the various folders he used to keep everything organized—one in his brother's folder, one routed to Mason's, and thirteen to Sally's. Spam filled up, as usual, but he deleted those after a single glance to verify they were all, indeed, spam. The one from Mason had an attachment, so he opened that first, expecting the latest internet meme to brighten his day.

Jack,

I had Vanessa, a friend of a friend at the FBI, take a look at your Shadowman pics. She's a bit of a savant when it comes to photo analysis, and she's got this really cool program to combine a bunch of fuzzy pics into one clean one. Don't ask me how it's done, but the result is attached to this email. Vanessa's already done a facial recognition search on the FBI database. No hits, I'm afraid.

– Mason

p.s.—I think I've got a shot with her! ;)

Jack smiled. He had met Vanessa at a party, and unless Mason was willing to undergo a sex change operation, he actually had *no* chance with her. *I should probably tell him, but it will be more fun watching him find out for himself.*

Shaking his head, he opened the attachment, and was greeted with the stark face of the Shadowman in more detail than he expected. *He looks a lot like Patrick Stewart,* he mused. Not the cool and cerebral Picard or Professor X version, but more like the one in *Moby Dick*. Angular, severe, and a bit creepy. The man was seventy if he was a day, and there was a gray shadow of stubble on his sunken cheeks. It was the face of a man at a job long past his expiration date, but determined to finish nonetheless. The eyes, still shaded by the hat, were empty dark orbs with neither iris nor sclera; the program clearly did not have enough information to extrapolate, and it made the face that much more frightening. Jack wondered how he never noticed such a man in his presence, and his skin crawled at the thought.

"Thanks, Mason," Jack said with a sigh. It looked like sleep wasn't going to come easy this night, either. *Fortunately, there's a cure for that.* He set the tablet aside and walked with purpose to the mini-bar.

* * *

The station house was a beehive of activity when Jack and Rutger entered the building, various officers headed out for the day while others bent to the impossible task of investigating the suicide angle of the crash. If Lubitz had intended his act to cause major disruption in the daily lives of his community, he couldn't have done a better job. Not knowing the language, to Jack, everyone sounded angry with one another. For years he maintained everyone in the world should learn Esperanto as a common language. *Listening to the people in this building today, I'm now more inclined toward Klingon.*

Rutger spoke with several men as they walked toward what Jack assumed was the man's office. The last few conversations grew quite heated, with Rutger snapping orders to several underlings.

"Anything wrong?" Jack asked.

"In my office," was the response, and Rutger stopped at a door, holding it open for Jack to enter. Once both were inside, he walked around his desk, pressed a button on the intercom, and said a few words. He sat, and Jack found a nearby chair and pulled it closer to the desk, sat, and waited. "We have a small problem," Rutger said at last.

Jack opened his mouth to ask a question, but a young officer burst in, breathing hard.

"Mr. Montgomery, this is Oberwachtmeister Izzak Kohlberg," Rutger nodded at the man. "Oberwachtmeister, would you please tell our guest why everyone is so excited this morning?"

The poor man stood at attention, his eyes darting from his superior to Jack, then back again.

"It's okay, Izzak, he is a guest of the government."

"Sir," he began, nodding at Rutger, then at Jack, "the evidence that was signed in last night is no longer present in the building."

Jack tilted his head, not quite understanding. "Where is it?"

"We... do not know."

"But—"

"That will be all, Izzak," Rutger said. The man hastened out the door, closing it as quietly as he could, though clearly happy to be dismissed.

Once he was gone, Jack turned his attention back to Rutger and said, "Do you often have problems with evidence going missing?"

Rutger snorted, and said, "I'll assume you are joking, Jack." He drummed his fingers on the surface of his desk for a few seconds, then said, "I cannot imagine why someone would want to steal evidence in a *suicide* investigation, but I assure you, we *will* find out."

Jack's interpreter-slash-driver was gone, and in his place sat a *detective*.

* * *

The bar was both better lit and much quieter than Jack's usual haunt, and he checked his watch for the fourth time as he waited. After the fiasco at the station, he needed to both unwind *and* unpack the day's events. His first suggestion to Rutger had earned him a sideways glance and a smirk.

"Of *course* we have surveillance cameras in the station," Rutger had said, still drumming his fingers on the desk, "but for some unknown reason, they went offline after twenty-two hundred."

An entire surveillance system doesn't just happen to go offline, Jack thought. Not in a police station.

What was in the damn box that was so important? No one was saying, and Rutger had told Jack he didn't recognize the officer who carried the box out of the house that morning, either. It seemed to Jack the only reason the evidence made it to the station at all was the presence of so many television cameras. Regardless, he still didn't see a reason to be here; it wasn't a CDC concern, in his opinion. *More importantly, how is this connected to my letters, and are my mystery pen pal and the Shadowman one and the same?* He grabbed his drink and swirled it around, watching the light refract off the crystal and ice, then said under his breath, "Someone's gaslighting me, and I don't like it one bit." The next time he saw Rutger, he might have to mention the letters.

As he lifted the drink to his lips, a voice behind him said, "I see you started without me." Amber stepped around the table and pulled out her own chair before he could stand. "What are you having?"

"Bourbon," he said, placing the tumbler on the worn wooden surface. He waved for a waiter.

"Oh, no," she said, shaking her head, "that will never do." She looked up at the waiter, just arriving, and said, "*Altbier*, please, with a large squeeze of lemon." She nodded at Jack, "He'll have one as well." The waiter nodded once and scurried away.

"You know," Jack said, grinning, "in *some* countries, ordering for someone means you're engaged."

"You just made that up," Amber said, flipping her hand at him.

"Guilty as charged," he said, laughing.

The waiter arrived with their beer, and Amber lifted hers toward Jack. "Cheers," she said, then they clinked mugs and drank.

Oh, so that's what beer is supposed to taste like, he thought with a satisfied smile. I could get used to this.

Amber drank for a long time, finally placing the mug back on the table, wiping her mouth, and tilting her head at him. "So," she said, "what's got you drinking the hard stuff so early in the day?"

He frowned, holding the mug in both hands. "A day filled with more questions than answers, I'm afraid," he said.

"Tell me about it."

He shook his head, now pursing his lips. "It's still an official investigation, I'm afraid, and—"

"And you *can't* talk about it." She nodded once. "I get it."

"Here's what I *can* tell you," he began, without knowing why. "Someone's been sending me letters regarding events in my personal life, and I'm pretty sure the person writing them is tied to *this* investigation somehow."

"Well... that sounds ominous."

"Either that, or someone is playing a particularly heinous joke at my expense."

"If you're investigating the Germanwings crash," she said, her mouth a hard line, "I wouldn't call that a joke."

Even as her face grew hard, his softened, and he sighed. "No, I guess not." This date—if he could call it that—was already spiraling out of control, much as the day's events had. Putting aside his fatigue and frustration, he was simply not ready to date again. *Not this soon.* Worse was the realization flirting came so easily to him with this woman, and, because of that more than anything, he felt as if he were cheating on Beth.

"Why so sad?" she said, her voice dragging him from his internal despair.

Jack stared at his beer, turning the ring on his finger, comforted by its weight. "That's a conversation I'm not ready to have, yet."

"Oh," she said, watching him fiddle with the band. "Well... how about we order something to eat, then. I'm starving, and I'm sure you haven't had time for a meal, either."

Jack brightened. "That sounds—" His phone buzzed. "Just a sec," he said, and pulled the phone from his pants pocket. *Rutger. Damn.* "Hold on, I have to take this."

"Duty calls," she said, waving him to continue.

He smiled an apology and pressed the answer key. "Yes, Rutger?"

"We have something from an external camera you should see," the man said, a restrained excitement in his voice. "Can you tear yourself away for a couple of hours?"

As good an excuse as any, he thought.

He covered the phone with his free hand and lifted his head to Amber, saying, "I'm afraid I have to cut this short. Rain check?"

"Certainly," she said with a wry grin. "I understand completely."

Jack tilted his head at that for just a second, then dismissed it. "I'll be there in twenty minutes," he said to Rutger. He stood, finished off his beer, then took out his wallet. He dug inside for a ten Euro banknote and tossed it on the table to cover the drinks. Amber raised an eyebrow, and he pulled out another ten just to play it safe. Shaking his head, he pulled another forty out, tossed it on the table, and said, "For dinner."

She gathered up the last two bills and handed them back. "I'll take care of my own meal, thank you." She grinned, and added, "Save your money. The next one will cost you *much* more by way of an apology."

He said his goodbyes and hurried out before he could change his mind. Walking with a singular purpose toward the door, he never noticed the man sitting alone at a table in a darkened corner. The man crossed his legs and set his hat on the table, watching Amber finish her beer.

* * *

"Right... *here*," Rutger said, tapping the screen displaying a fuzzy image of the station's back entrance. The footage, he told Jack, came from a storefront across the street, the camera pointed their way by a fortuitous installation error. The night scene from the recording was inky-black, and the resolution of the video was not very good, but there was a light in the entry strong enough to at least see clear shapes. There was no mistaking the image of a tall man in an overcoat and fedora emerging from the doorway. Cradled in his arms was a cardboard box.

It can't be, Jack thought, his hands shaking as he looked at the paused image. He reached out and touched the screen, tracing the man's likeness from hat to boot. *What is the connection? Who is he working for?* There was more going on here than a simple suicide, or even a sleeping sickness three thousand miles away. *How is this man getting in and out of secure facilities without anyone noticing?*

"Jack," Rutger said, leaning toward him, "are you okay?"

Without taking his eyes from the screen, Jack fumbled for his phone. He glanced at it only long enough to find the copy of Mason's email from the day before. He opened it, even as he turned his eyes back to the screen, and showed the picture of the Shadowman to Rutger.

"Look familiar?" he said.

Rutger drew back, the photo having the same effect on him it had on Jack. He leaned closer again, alternating between the photo and the video of the station. "Who is he?"

"Haven't a god damn clue, my friend, but he's involved in more than just this little theft."

"Can you forward this to me?" Rutger said, still examining the Shadowman's face. "I think it's time we get in touch with Interpol."

"You won't find anything," Jack said, sitting back in his chair and crossing his legs.

"Why do you say that?"

"FBI's already come up snake-eyes, and with everything we've seen him do so far, I'm betting he's government-issue." Jack looked up at his new friend and grinned at his confusion. "Maybe not *our* government, but clearly *somebody's*."

CHAPTER 4

As jack suspected, interpol was no help, but now they had their ears on, things could change overnight. The decision to hang around for another week—maybe more—was easy, especially since he had little more to do than conduct interviews. That left him a lot of free evenings, and he spent most of them with Amber. She was right about the next meal being expensive, her dinner order ensuring his apology was well-expressed. They had already been out together three times, and he still hadn't made any overt romantic overtures other than a light peck on the cheek at the end of the evening. She never seemed disappointed or made advances either, so he naturally assumed the relationship was platonic. Either that, he thought, or *she's as broken as I am.*

At Düsseldorf University Hospital, where Lubitz had been diagnosed with mental issues, Jack hoped to find enough evidence to tie this up in a neat enough bow to call the case closed. *Still, why would the Shadowman be interested in this case at all?* That one question gnawed at him, telling him over and over this was going to be neither simple nor short. What frightened Jack most was the connection to Kazakhstan. *But is there a connection? If the Shadowman is an independent contractor, his presence at both could be a simple coincidence.*

But Jack didn't believe in coincidences, especially when someone was sending him letters that seemed to be tied to both cases. Occam's razor should help him slice through the tangle of possible explanations to find the one that was true, only there *were* no explanations. Not yet.

"A penny for your thoughts," Amber said from the driver's seat of the rental car.

"What?" he said, roused from his reverie for the first time since they entered the main road to Düsseldorf. "Oh, I'm sorry. A lot on my mind, I guess."

"No doubt."

Jack had asked her to drive on this trip because, he told her, "I don't know the roads, *or* the traffic laws." The truth was he planned to use her in his investigation. All official channels had crapped out in their quest to open Lubitz's medical records, but Jack knew a truism: *everyone* opens up to a pretty woman. The more beautiful, the more relaxed and forthcoming the response. Looking at her now, he guessed the real trick would be to get them to *stop* talking. It didn't hurt that she also spoke German like a native—at least it sounded like it to his ear.

"I'm uncomfortable with this whole thing," she said.

"Don't worry. You'll do fine."

Amber glanced across the car at him, then turned her attention back to the road. "I'm not concerned with how I'll *do*, Jack— making people comfortable is kind of my job. I'm just not sure this whole thing is *right*."

"We're not stealing anything, or breaking in, or hurting anyone. We're just gonna get some old guys to say more than they probably should," he finished, a saccharin-sweet smile on his lips.

She bit her bottom lip, then said, "Are you sure this will work?"

"Only if they're human."

* * *

Jack followed Amber up the steps inside the hospital, the black pencil skirt she wore hugging her curves and accentuating the sway of her walk, driving him to distraction. With her hair tied back in a black ribbon, the perfect pair of hipster horn-rims perched on her nose, and the crisp white buttoned-down shirt, she was the exemplar of a secretary-slash-translator. Tying the hair had been her idea—her thought was that freeing the wavy tresses at just the right time would have a disarming effect on most men. Most *being* all, *of course,* Jack thought with a wide grin.

How does she climb stairs in those heels? he wondered, marveling at the required balance and grace. Beth had been equally adept, but preferred the comfort of worn sneakers over heels. *Especially heels like those.* The four-inch spikes would make a lovely weapon, if Amber so chose.

"Stop watching my ass," she hissed.

"Can't help it," he whispered. "Okay, I *can*... I just don't want to." She chuckled but said nothing more.

At the top, a woman waited, clipboard held to her chest like a shield. She looked to be about Jack's age, and nearly a head shorter than Amber. Her raven-black hair was also tied back, but in a severe and uncompromising bun. The rimless half-glasses perched on the end of her nose were strictly for reading, and hovered over a lemon-tight mouth.

Amber reached the penultimate step and stuck out her hand. "Guten Tag, Arzt Friesenhäuser," she said.

"Guten Tag," the woman said with a nod, never taking her hands off the clipboard to return the greeting.

Undeterred, Amber dropped her hand to her side and continued, "Ich heisse Amber Riley, und dies ist mein Arbeitgeber, Jack Montgomery."

Jack, listening for his name, took the cue and offered his own hand. This time, Dr. Friesenhäuser relinquished her death-grip on the clipboard and shook it.

"Nice to meet you," she said with a wry grin and an amused tilt of her head. "Tell your interpreter we won't be needing her services today." She shook her head. "Such as they are," she sneered, peering over the top of her glasses.

"I think she got the message," he said. Beside him, Amber fumed, but to her credit kept the cheerful smile. *If they were men, this would be called a pissing contest... and already over with.* The look in Amber's eyes said this was *far* from over. He opened his mouth to speak, but the doctor beat him to it.

"Ms. Riley can visit the cafeteria while you and I chat," she said, her head facing Jack while her eyes were locked firmly on Amber. "No need to bore her with our conversation."

And there it is, Jack thought. He had seen this more than once during his marriage. There were women, usually intelligent, who were simply insecure in the presence of beauty. Beth's rivaled Amber's, and she experienced the same hostility—*especially* when he accompanied her. Worse, she was often dismissed out of hand as a "bimbo" by such women *because* she turned heads. Sure, he knew women like Amber had it easy in many aspects of their daily lives because their looks opened doors most women never knew existed, but there was this flip-side as well.

"That's okay, Jack," Amber said, sounding more gracious than he knew she felt, "I may do some exploring." She winked at him, turned to the doctor, and said, "It was lovely meeting you," and walked away.

Jack watched her for a few seconds, then grinned back at Dr. Friesenhäuser, and said, "Your office?"

"Follow me," she said. "I'm not sure what you hope to discover, Mr. Montgomery."

"Jack, please."

"Very well, Jack. You may call me Claudia, but the question remains."

"I know you can't give me any details of the man's medical history, but I was hoping for some insight."

She slowed, and tilted her head, then said, "I fear those are one and the same." Stopping at a door, she gestured for him to lead the way.

Jack entered the large corner office, tastefully decorated with minimal furniture. There was, however, a fully-stocked "I love me" wall behind the large wooden desk. These were always on display when dealing with upper-echelon military, government officials, and anyone else occupying the rarefied atmosphere of leadership. It seemed narcissism respected no national boundaries.

He took a seat in front of the desk, leaned back, and crossed his legs with casual indifference. The doctor walked around the desk, pointedly *not* looking at the display of photos on her wall, and sat. She steepled her hands in front of her face, and said, "As I have said to everyone else, I am legally obligated to keep Mr. Lubitz's records private."

"Obligated to whom?"

"Mr. Lubitz, of course."

"I'm sorry if I sound insensitive... but isn't he dead?"

Her face creased in a thin smile, and she said with deliberate pace, "That is correct, and since releasing his records requires his permission..." she put her hands in the air and shrugged. "You can see the dilemma."

"Can't his family give permission?"

"Of course, Jack, but this is Germany."

He pursed his lips and stared quizzically.

"We do *not* talk about our infirmities in this country, Jack. *Especially* those of a mental nature." She spread her hands flat upon the desk and shook her head. "I am afraid you'll get nothing without a court order, and that will take a *long* time."

"So," he began carefully, "you are *confirming* he had mental issues."

"I did no such thing!" she sputtered.

"The implication is—"

"You may *infer* whatever you like, but I will confirm nothing."

* * *

Amber wandered the halls, still seething at the way she had been treated. *She thinks being a doctor makes her better than me. I've got a job to do, though,* she thought, frowning, *and I should probably stick to the plan.*

"Sind Sie verloren, Miss?"

She spun around to confront the voice behind, thinking, *No, I'm not lost,* and stopped with the words frozen to her lips. The man was old by her standards, but he was in amazing health. *This guy is serious about his workouts.*

"Nein, ich bin nur für die Psychiatrie," she said without thinking. She didn't even know if German hospitals *had* a psychiatric ward, but a shot in the dark was better than no shot at all.

"Oh, das ist eine Etage höher," he said, smiling.

Of course it's one floor up. That's where I was headed when Nurse Diesel sent me away.

"Danke," she said, and started back toward the stairs. Walking away, she felt the man's eyes on her ass, much as Jack's had been earlier, but this was more of an assault. *Men are men, everywhere I go.*

At the top of the stairs she searched until she found the nurse's station, where a single male nurse sat filling out a form. *This is more like it.* Close to her age, he was the type of man she rarely had trouble with. Shorter than average, his nose was tucked into his task as if it were the only thing in his life. *And it probably is,* she thought, noticing the lack of a wedding ring on his hand. He looked up as she approached, his over-sized ears threatening to take him airborne, and his eyes widened.

This is gonna be all too easy.

* * *

"I understand, doctor, you have your reputation to uphold," Jack said, "but I need to wrap up an investigation I should never have been a part of. I'll take your refusal to deny as a positive answer to my question. For the purposes of my report, that is." He smiled and waited.

"I think you are twisting my words for your own ends, Mr. Montgomery."

"Guilty as charged," he said with a laugh. "I just need something to satisfy my boss so I can go home." He pantomimed typing, and said, "Mr. Lubitz was suffering from a presumed, though" he nodded toward her, "*unconfirmed,* mental disorder that may have led to his suicide."

"I will confirm only what your partner already knew—Mr. Lubitz was certified as unfit for work that day. The rest is restricted, and only available to his immediate family."

"Pardon me... did you say *partner?*"

"Yes," she said with an exasperated sigh and a wave of her hand. "He was here only moments before you arrived. I assumed he was one of yours."

"Can you describe him?" Jack said, afraid of the answer.

"Of course. Such a man leaves an impression, does he not? He was tall, in his seventies, and wore a long coat and a hat—both of which he declined to remove."

The Shadowman was here, and moments ago. Is he still in the hospital? Jack's head was swimming, drowning in the possibilities. Amber.

"Dr. Friesenhäuser, the only person with me today is Ms. Riley. That man might be with the police, but he is certainly not part of *my* investigation." He stood and started toward the door when a light knocking came from the other side. Amber opened the door before

40

either of them could respond, and said, "Mr. Montgomery? We have that appointment at fifteen hundred, and we'll have to get moving if you want to be there on time."

There was an urgency in her voice that went far beyond the fake deadline. Jack took the hint and slapped his forehead. "I completely forgot, Ms. Riley," he said with mock surprise. "Thank you for reminding me." He nodded to the doctor. "I apologize for cutting this short, Dr. Friesenhäuser, but we really must be going."

"Certainly, Mr. Montgomery, it was nice meeting you," she said, clear confusion on her face. She stepped around her desk to take his hand, looking him dead in the eye. "Are you *sure* the other man was not with you?"

"Positive, doctor. Check the sign-in sheet at the front desk if you don't believe me." He knew there would be no name for the man there, nor would there be surveillance video of him walking the halls. Amber was fidgeting in the doorway, ready to bust with some kind of news, but he knew it had to wait until they were out of the building and safely in the car. "Shall we?" he said to her, and freed his hand from the stern little woman. He nudged Amber ahead as they exited the office and hurried out of the building.

* * *

"How did you get this?" Jack asked, thumbing through the pictures on Amber's phone as she drove back to Montabaur. She had refused to tell him what her excitement was about until they were on the road.

"Oh, you know," she said with a bright smile, batting her eyelashes, "I can be very be persuasive when the need arises."

"I bet," he said, bending his head back to the display.

"The file was already on the desk when I got there, so I only needed the poor little boy to leave me alone with it long enough get some shots." She shrugged, "It was actually pretty easy."

"Translation—you got him worked up enough he had to excuse himself for a little alone time."

"I wouldn't put it so crudely, but," she grinned like an evil doll, "yeah."

He stopped on one of the pictures and zoomed in. "It says here Lubitz hadn't been able to sleep for the past five years because he was afraid he was going blind."

"Kind of like my desk nurse," she laughed.

Jack snorted. "He was also treated for suicidal tendencies." There was some stuff about ordering blood tests, but the results weren't on the first few pages he saw, and weren't likely to be of interest, regardless. He looked up at her and said, "That, right there, is the end of my investigation." Satisfied his part in this was over, he leaned back, relaxing for the first time in a week. He blew out a breath and thought about how he would spin this to Sally. She might be satisfied, but those above her in the food chain might not. *At least it's over for me, and I can go home.* There was also the mysterious letter-writer to consider, but nothing had jumped out at him during the course of the investigation of Lubitz. It could all be an incredible coincidence, after all. *Still,* he thought, *what was the Shadowman doing at the hospital? He must have been looking for something he didn't find in the evidence box. Either that, or tying up loose ends...*

"Oh shit!" he said, louder than he intended. Sitting up quickly, he fumbled for his cell phone.

"What's wrong?" Amber said, her face a mask of confusion.

"Nothing... I hope," he said as he dialed the doctor's number. It rang far longer than a hospital phone ever should, and when someone finally answered, he heard many voices in the background.

"Hallo?" said a quivering voice definitely *not* belonging to Dr. Friesenhäuser.

"Dr. Friesenhäuser, please."

There was a long pause, then the voice on the other end broke into sobs, and the background noise grew louder, as she said, "Der Arzt ist tot."

"Shit, shit, shit..." he said, banging his phone on the car seat, his voice shaking as he ended the call. "GodDAMNit!" He knew enough German to understand that phrase.

"Jack," Amber said, her voice full of worry, "what's wrong?"

He dialed a new number.

"Jack...?"

"Dr. Friesenhäuser is dead."

"What? How?" She watched him dial, and said, "Who are you calling?"

"Rutger," he said as he hit the send button. "I'm willing to bet my life savings she didn't die of natural causes," he held the phone pressed firmly to his ear as his hands shook, "and we were probably the last people to see her alive." He pulled a card out of his wallet, ran a finger down the list, then said to Amber, "Turn around. We need to go back to Düsseldorf."

"Back to the hospital?"

"No... the Consulate." She tilted her head, and he said, "I don't know if we are in any trouble, and I don't think they can keep us from the cops for long, but it might be enough to get Rutger here before things go completely south."

* * *

Rutger climbed the steps of the consulate in Düsseldorf, wondering how things had gotten so out of hand. He knew Jack had gone to see what he could find at the hospital, but he never suspected there was any danger. Even not knowing the man long, he still couldn't picture him *murdering* anyone. Especially not how it had been done. *A stiletto to the base of the skull is an assassin's method, and Jack is no assassin.* Before leaving the station, though, he did take a look at Ms. Riley's records, and other than a few traffic fines, there was nothing there. They were either both exactly what they appeared to be, or very, *very* good at hiding who they really were.

His superiors were not happy with this turn of events, nor his involvement by invitation of the Verdammt *suspect*. Rutger was told to tread carefully—*Hmmpf, as if I didn't know that*—and sent on his way. The unspoken caveat was *don't come back without them.*

Wearing his dress uniform, he was ignored as he entered the building, but now a small man wearing large eyeglasses accosted him.

"Polizeioberkommissar Brieske?" To Rutger, the man looked like a small nervous dog begging for a treat.

"Yes," he offered his hand, "and you are?"

"My name is Dixon Brill, assistant to the Attache in Düsseldorf," he said, taking Rutger's hand in soft fingers to shake it lightly.

"Secretary. Got it," Rutger said, already dismissing the minor functionary. "Where are Jack and his companion?"

"First, you must understand no arrests are to be made within this compound—"

"I am here to arrest no one, sir. This is to be a friendly conversation." He leaned into the man's personal space, adding, "for *now*."

Brill leaned so far back he stumbled a step. Recovering, he looked up at the expression on Rutger's face and swallowed hard. "Follow me, please." He turned on his heels and walked away without another word.

Gott, beschütze mich vor kleinen Männern mit großen Träumen, he thought, eyes rolled upward.

The walk was blessedly short, Brill stopping in front of an office door with no nameplate. He knocked, and a booming voice—*Not Jack's,* Rutger thought—beckoned them to enter. When he stepped through the opened door, Jack was seated on a leather sofa across the room being watched by a Marine MP. Another man, round and red-faced, sat at a large desk near a curtained window. Jack, for his part, looked glad to see him. Ms. Riley, however, was not with him.

"Hello, Jack," Rutger said, forcing a smile. Jack returned the smile, but the other man scowled. The Marine did not move.

"Hiya, Rutger," Jack said. "Fancy meeting you here."

"You were the one who invited me."

"I did, at that," Jack said, scratching his chin. "Okay, boys, give us the room."

"I'm sorry, Mr. Montgomery," the fat man said, "but I cannot allow you to be interviewed by law enforcement without legal representation."

"I'm not being interviewed. Right, Rutger?" he said with a wink. "This is just two old friends commiserating about their day at work."

"This is unwise, Mr.—"

"And completely off the record, sir," Rutger added. "If need be, we can schedule a formal interview at the local station for another time."

The man behind the desk looked hard into Rutger's eyes for a moment, then turned to the MP and tilted his head. The MP shrugged almost imperceptibly, and the large man said, "Fine. We'll give you guys some time alone." He shook his finger at Jack. "Please don't say anything stupid we can't untangle later."

"Gotcha," Jack said with a snap of his hand in salute. "No admissions of guilt."

The other man sighed, shook his head, then struggled out of his chair and left, the MP close on his heels. After the door closed, Rutger walked over to the desk and sat on a corner. "All right, Jack, what's this all about?"

"The Shadowman was at the hospital," Jack said, "and I think he killed the doctor."

"A doctor *and* a desk nurse," Rutger corrected. "The question is why."

"Damn." Jack stood and began pacing. "He was there, I know it. Of course, you won't find evidence on the video surveillance, or on any of the sign-in sheets. I think that's why he killed them." He turned to Rutger, his eyes moist. "They were probably the only ones who had any personal interaction with him. He needed to hide the trail."

"Why was he there in the first place? He already had all the evidence from the apartment."

"Not all of it," Jack said. "There is something in the hospital files on Lubitz." He pulled Amber's phone from his pocket. "And I think I know what it is."

* * *

The old man shuffled toward the large blue mailbox, a coarse envelope gripped in one gnarled hand. His fingers, worn and callused, knuckles as big as walnuts, flexed painfully as he grasped the handle and pulled the door open. He hesitated, holding the letter in stasis between here and there—between nothing and everything. *Maybe this one will be enough.* He tilted his face skyward, the sun driving hard radiation down on a soft leathery face framed by fluffy white hair and punctuated with eyebrows like Andy Rooney. He smiled, a thin line between creased lips, in hopeful anticipation.

He was a coward. *Always was, I guess. Always will be, too. If I was any kind of man at all, I would go see him in person.*

Sighing deeply, he inched the letter deeper into the yawning maw of the box. "For Mark," he said, releasing the letter into an uncertain future. The page, filled with a flowing cursive written in pencil, wrapped in an envelope covered with the location spell known as an address, stamp slightly askew, fluttered down and down into

45

the dark to seek its new owner. He released the handle, shattering the silence with a creak and a clank, and shuffled out into the chill air and warm early-morning sun in Spring Hill, Tennessee.

CHAPTER 5

H E HAD NO NAME. It had been taken from him over seventy years ago, along with his family, home, and life. Alone on the darkening street, he tried to remember the pain of that loss, but couldn't. Emotions were irrelevant, now. There was neither love nor hate, need or want. There was only the plan, and his part in it. Walking to his rental car, soles clopping on the brick in a regular rhythm, he looked forward to the long drive back to the airport in Frankfurt. In the car, away from the Others, the voice in his head was his and his alone.

An old woman stepped onto the sidewalk from the stoop of a building, and he stopped to allow her to pass, holding the door for her as she smiled up at him. He adjusted the hat on his mostly bald head, pulling it lower in front to shade his face. There were lines there having nothing to do with age, and he had always been a private man, regardless.

He didn't enjoy his part in the plan, but neither did he shy away from it. *Enjoy* held no meaning, anyway. *I do what I do because it is* necessary, he thought. That phrase became a mantra from his very first mission. Shoving a gloved hand into his coat pocket, he felt the *device* there, and its presence comforted him. In the other hand he carried the patient file retrieved from the hospital, decorated with a fine spray of blood. He had read just enough to know it was the one he sought. Reading and evaluating information was not *his* job. The copper taste in his mouth had already faded, and he breathed in the crisp, clean air to rinse the stench of death from his nostrils.

The plan proceeds. As it always has.

He opened the car door, folded in with a smoothness defying his years, started the engine, and pulled into the early evening traffic. There was no luggage, not even a toiletry bag in the vehicle. He had everything he needed on his person when he traveled. The road was damp from a recent rain, giving it a red-orange sheen under the nuclear fire of the setting sun. The same life-giving sun which would one day engulf the earth a billion or more years from now, boiling the very seas from the crust to fling the ash into the ocean of night. But he wouldn't be alive to see it.

He hoped.

* * *

Jack recognized his error as soon as he held out Amber's cell phone. *Nothing to be done for it but bluff my way through*, he thought. As Rutger stepped closer, Jack thumbed through the pictures of the lab report. "I have a copy of Lubitz's blood-work, and there's something you need to see."

Rutger leaned in, and said, "How did you come by this?"

Jack ignored the question, plowing ahead. "Note the toxicology and the presence of heavy metals." He leaned back and said, "That's just not normal."

"Would the presence of these account for his suicide?"

"Possibly, I'm no doctor, but I don't think it's a high enough level to explain his sudden shift." Jack zoomed in to a single data point. "Plus, there's the gold."

"That's nothing," Rutger said, stepping back and waving his hand. "I know people who take gold for their arthritis." He shook his head. "Stupid, if you ask me."

"But it's the *proportions* of these elements that concern me. Much of this isn't part of any medical treatment I know, and there is no evidence Lubitz had access to them in either the workplace or his environment." Jack sat again on the sofa. "This is an extremely complicated cocktail of metals and toxins delivered in exacting proportions," he said. "For several, one side effect is encephalopathy."

"Um..."

"Inflammation of the brain," Jack said. "One symptom of encephalopathy is coma."

Rutger stared at him a few seconds, then the light came on in his eyes. "Ah," he said, "your 'sleepy sickness'!"

Jack nodded, "I've been looking for some connection between these two events ever since I received that letter I told you about." He knew Rutger still didn't buy the possibility of a connection, but he at least played along.

"And you think this is it?"

He shook his head. "I don't know, but it's the best lead I've had so far."

Now Rutger stood, and *he* paced in front of the desk. "I assume you have guessed the file at the hospital has vanished," he said. Jack knew exactly what that meant, but said nothing, content to watch Rutger pace. Putting hand to chin, the detective walked a few steps, then walked back to stand in front of Jack. "I will need that phone for evidence," he said, pointing.

Jack hesitated, and said, "How about I just email the photos to you." He grinned, "I kinda need this," and slid the phone back into his pocket.

Rutger eyed him for a few seconds, clearly considering his few options, and said, "Fine, but you and your companion will have to come back to Montabaur with me." Narrowing his eyes, he added, "And I will need both passports until my superiors are satisfied you had nothing to do with these murders."

"Amber is pretty shaken up by all of this," Jack said, hoping he wasn't pushing things too far, "so I would rather we follow you back in our rental." He shrugged, "It's only rented for the day, anyway, and I'd rather not run up the tab."

Rutger seemed on the edge of protesting, then sighed and said, "Agreed." He leaned forward, placed a hand on Jack's shoulder, and said, "Jack... how much do you really know about this *Amber*?"

* * *

Amber sat in a straight-backed metal chair in a small interview room not far from the office where Jack and Rutger were meeting, her leg bouncing a rapid staccato. Staring at the door, she chewed on a fingernail, ignoring the damage to her expensive manicure. She had been told to wait there while Jack talked to the police, and while she was grateful to be left out of it, no one bothered to update her on *anything* so far. She stood, smoothed her skirt, and started toward the door, then changed her mind and walked back to her seat. Sitting, she checked her nail, then switched to another.

When the door burst open, she jumped like a coiled spring. Jack walked through with a police officer in tow. *Oh shit*, she thought, *this is it.*

"Amber," Jack said, much calmer than she felt, "this is Detective Brieske," he gestured to the man behind him. "He would like you to give him your passport." He was looking at her funny, like he was trying to communicate something with his eyes, but for the life of her, she couldn't guess his intent.

"Um... okay, but what about my—"

He interrupted her with a glare, saying, "We're to follow him back to Montabaur, where we will be free while they clear this all up."

Phone, she thought. Finally understanding, Amber closed her mouth with an audible click.

"I urge you to not attempt to leave the country, Ms. Riley," the detective said, clear menace in his eyes. His face softened, and he said with a slight smile, "I am sure we will, as Jack said, 'clear this up' rather quickly."

"I hope so," she said, an uncontrollable quiver in her voice. "I have a flight scheduled for Monday."

Jack spun his head to her, surprise in his voice. "So soon?"

"I'm afraid so, Jack." She laughed, more nervous than amused. "It's not like they give us a lot of time off, you know."

"You may want to extend your stay, Ms. Riley," Rutger said. "I cannot guarantee either of you will be allowed to travel by then."

"This just gets better and better," she said, shaking her head. The good news, she thought, is no one's talking about an arrest right now. Jack could probably get the CDC to bail him out and get him home, but Delta surely wouldn't do the same for me. Indeed, they were more likely to simply terminate her on the spot. "This isn't going to make the papers or anything, is it?"

Rutger shook his head. "Not in the middle of an investigation."

Jack smiled at her in sympathy. "I'm sure the detective will let you know if you need to, uh," he made air quotes, "call in sick." He looked at Rutger, smiled, then hooked an arm for Amber to take. "Shall we?" he said.

She took the offered arm in her own, practically pulling Jack out of the room. "I've been ready to go since we got here."

* * *

The little rental car was becoming their personal cone of silence. Jack grinned, remembering the old *Get Smart* reruns he watched as a kid. At least in this one, there was no chance of being overheard.

"They know the doctor was alive when we left because of the testimony of her secretary," he said. Amber was driving again, but this time it was more to give her something to do rather than his concern about his driving skills. She was a nervous wreck, talking a blue streak the whole time they were with Rutger. *Never say anything to a cop*, his daddy used to say. *Even when they're trying to help you, one wrong word can turn their attention on a dime.*

"So... there's nothing to worry about," she said.

"There's also the issue of the desk nurse. The one you got those files from." He faced her, and waited for her to look in his direction, "I never left the doctor's office—also according to the secretary—but *you*... you can't account for your whereabouts at the time the boy was murdered."

The car swerved slightly as she turned to face him. "You don't think *I*—"

"No, I don't," he said quickly. "But they don't know you... and Amber, it's their *job* to be suspicious."

She released a heavy sigh. "I guess you're right," she said. "What I don't understand, though, is why you wouldn't let me ask about my phone."

He pulled it out of his pocket and held it up. "I wasn't thinking when I showed the file to Rutger," he said. "Having those on *your* phone might be a bit incriminating since the only place you could have gotten them was from the nurse." He tilted his head and shrugged. "So I let him believe it was mine."

"Well, I *would* like it back at some point."

"My plan is to send the files to my phone, then send them to Rutger from there." He scrunched up his face, and said, "I hope he doesn't analyze the email header too closely. I'm pretty sure that's the extent of my spoofing abilities."

She smiled and nodded at him, flipping the turn signal at the same time to change lanes. He watched her move through traffic like a pro, sliding between cars to keep up with Rutger who seemed to be making no attempt to keep them in sight. *It helps that we all know where we're going.* More than once, though, he had to use his imaginary brake when she ventured too close to the bumper of the car in front of them. When he took his eyes off the road to look at her, she was driving one-handed while chewing on a fingernail.

She caught him watching her and took her hand away from her mouth. "Are we in danger, Jack?"

"I would be lying if I gave you an unequivocal 'no', but my best guess is that we are not." He reached across to pat her hand, saying, "We were just in the wrong place at the wrong time. *Maybe* if the killer knew we had copies of the files, he might come looking for them. Even if he did, once we hand that over to the cops, there's no point in hurting either of us."

"What if that just makes him angry?"

"One thing I'm sure of, Amber, is this guy's a professional." He shook his head, and said, "Professionals don't take things personally, and they don't kill for fun." *If I say it hard enough, even I will believe it,* he thought. *The truth is, I don't know what the fuck is going to happen.* "There's one other thing I know."

"What's that?"

"I know what the bastard looks like."

* * *

Mason Hill stepped away from the lab table and ran a hand through his hair. Ignoring the analysis he was working on, he zoomed in on the photo of a lab report Jack sent him that morning. *This is just crazy,* he thought. *There are enough rare earths and heavy metals in this man's blood to kill him outright if they were all gathered in a single organ.* It didn't make any sense. Something tickled the back of his brain, though, so he walked to his desk and lifted the lid on his laptop. Opening a browser window, he searched for information on the list of elements, alone and in various combinations. One of the elements, Boron, got an odd hit, referring to something called titanium alpha-borozene.

Borozene, he thought, scratching his head. *I've heard that word somewhere.* Spiraling outward in his search, he hit on the use of a theorized nano-structure used to store and transport hydrogen. *Or possibly other elements?*

Was this some new form of poison delivery? That didn't quite jibe with the list of elements in his hands. Sure, in large enough concentrations, many of them were dangerous—even fatal—but none of them were an outright poison in such small quantities. The levels weren't high enough to even nauseate an average man.

"Something's hinkey," he said, still rubbing his head. Pulling the thick curls down to the bridge of his nose, he chuckled. "Man, I need a haircut."

"I've been telling you that for over a week, Dr. Hill." Sally stood in the open doorway, arms in their usual position crossed over her chest. She was making *that face*. The one that appeared every time she caught him off-task.

"Which," he said with a smile, "the haircut part or the hinkey part?"

"The hair," she said, dropping her arms to her sides and entering the lab. "What's this about 'hinkey'?"

He held up his phone, "Something Jack sent me doesn't add up."

She snorted once, and said, "What about Jack ever does?"

"It's this toxicology report on Lubitz," he said. "I don't know how it all could have gotten into his system, and I *sure* don't know the reason it's there in the first place. There's no logic to it."

She stepped closer to get a better view of the phone's screen, and said, "Is it possible the sample was contaminated, or was there an error in the analysis?"

"I don't think so," he said, shaking his head. "They ran it twice over a two-week period with two different samples."

"Hmmm," she said, taking the phone from his hand. She flipped through several pages of the report.

"That's not even the worst part," Mason said.

She looked up at him, face scrunched. "What's that?"

"The strangest thing is that the numbers are *exactly* the same for each sample. Like, five significant digits, the same." He pulled at his hair and leaned back against his desk, "I mean, there should have been *some* variation, either up or down, right?"

"I would think so," she said, nose buried again in the tiny screen. "What's your initial assessment, then?"

He shrugged. "I think it's part of a delivery system—for what, I don't know."

"Why so complicated? There are any number of ways to deliver drugs or poisons."

"This would appear to be a *targeted* system. It's for delivering a payload to a specific point in a specific organ. My guess is the brain."

"To what end?"

"Well, we know Lubitz's end..."

"What, a *suicide* drug?" She shook her head and snorted again. "That seems a little far-fetched, even for Jack."

"That's *my* assessment, not his." He smiled grimly, and added, "Though I guess he would agree with me."

She handed the phone back to him and crossed her arms. "Well, please don't mention your conclusions to him," she said. "I don't know how far off the rails he would go with such information, but you can be sure it wouldn't be pretty." It was the first real show of concern Mason had seen on her in a long time, the last time being in the hospital after Jack's accident. *She's a mother to us all*, he thought. He smiled, thinking, *And a* mother *to us all.*

"Something funny?"

"No," he said. "I was just thinking you should bring Jack home. Maybe send a team to take over for him."

"Oh, I sent him that message before I came down here," she said. "I don't know about a team, though. This doesn't fall within our purview anymore."

That's true, he thought. *We only do diseases, and this is definitely* not *a disease.* But he wasn't sure if Jack could let it go that easily.

"We're going to put all this in a report—including Jack's 'Shadowman'—and forward it to the proper authorities," Sally said, as if sensing Mason's thoughts. She smiled and rested a hand on his shoulder. "After that, I'm giving both you and Jack some time off." He tilted his head, eyes narrowed. "Jack needs some R and R, and *I* need someone to keep an eye on him," she said.

"He's not gonna like that."

"That's why I'm not making it a request." She dropped her hand and walked toward the door, saying over her shoulder, "I'm giving you two weeks to clean him up."

"But that's—"

"Figure out a game plan, Dr. Hill," and she was gone.

Game plan? Jack was a borderline alcoholic with a nasty case of PTSD. There *was* no two-week game plan for such a walking disaster. Sally either knew that and didn't care, or she didn't believe Jack was as far gone as everyone else did. *I don't think he's that far gone, either, but it's still gonna take more than two fucking weeks.*

"Hmmph," he said, "two *years*, maybe." He shook his head and sat back at his computer, looking at the web-page describing the borozene cage. "Let's see just what kinds of things can be stuffed in there."

* * *

Afraid to go back to her apartment alone, Amber practically begged Jack to stay with her. He suggested his hotel, but she demurred, there being only the one bed. "There is a separate guest bedroom at the apartment," she told him. "Plus," she said, trying to sweeten the deal, "I can cook."

"Oh, well, that's different," he said. "I haven't had a home-cooked meal in..." his face fell as he trailed off. "Well, a while."

She threw her keys and purse on the side table in the entryway, and Jack followed her into the living room. It was unusually large and open for an apartment, with the main room separated from the small kitchen by only an island. To her eyes, she had always thought it was more modern American than old European.

"Would you like a bourbon on the rocks, or maybe a beer?" she said.

"Bourbon is fine, thanks." Jack walked around the room inspecting various items, stopping at the mantel over the small fireplace. He picked up a little picture in a brass frame. Electric blue eyes stared from a dimpled face framed by blonde curls. "Is this your friend?" he said, waving the frame.

"Yes," she said, preparing his drink at the well-stocked serving cart, "that's Gretchen."

"Pretty," he said without much enthusiasm, and replaced the picture on the mantel. He wandered a few more seconds, then sat on the far end of the sofa. Amber grabbed a beer from the fridge for herself and met him at the sofa with his drink in hand. "Thanks," he said, taking the crystal tumbler from her. He took a long sip and nodded approval as she sat beside him.

Taking a long drink of her own, she watched him swirl the glass in his hand. "Been a hell of a day, hasn't it?"

He clinked his glass against her bottle. "Fuckin' A," he said, then took another long sip, nursing it.

Amber kicked off her shoes, crossed her ankles on the low coffee table in front of the sofa, and leaned back against the cushion, stretching her back. She smiled inwardly as she caught him watching her breasts. He wasn't obvious about it as most men were, only chancing a sideways glance. She had to give him credit for that. He was a sweet man—caring and fun, with just a hint of sadness in his eyes. And always respectful of her space. Nothing like the boys she usually dated.

Oh, sweetheart, she thought in her mom's voice, that's the excitement of the day talking. Sitting this close to her, and he was still twisting that wedding ring on his finger. Face it—he's broken, and you don't have the time or energy to fix him.

Even though the beer was only half empty, she set it on the table and turned to face him. "I'm beat," she said. "I think I'm gonna turn in for the night." He doesn't even look disappointed. "The guest room is just down the hall when you're ready."

He set his drink down. "Yeah, I think I'm ready, too," he said, hesitation in his voice.

Amber stood, then looked into his eyes. It was all over, then, and she was on top of him before she even had a chance to think about it. Didn't want to think about it, as her mouth searched out his with laser-like accuracy, pinning him beneath her. She grabbed handfuls of his hair, holding his face to hers, and he kissed her back with a ferocity that frightened her. Reaching around, he encircled her in a desperate hug, holding her so tight she could barely breathe. She pulled on his hair, drawing his head back, and began working her way down his neck. Letting go, she fumbled with the buttons on his shirt, moving as swiftly as her fingers would allow, while he pulled her shirt from where it was tucked into her skirt. His shirt now open, she buried her face in the thick matte of hair on his chest, kissing his nipples erect.

Working lower, she felt his erection grow beneath her, and she ground her hips against him to help it along. An animal sound of hunger and desire escaped his throat, and he reached inside her shirt to unhook her bra. Jack, one arm still around her, worked the other underneath a leg, stood, and flipped positions. Now she was on her back and he was on top, kissing her neck and ear. His manhood ground against her, searching even through the heavy cloth for an entry. Before she could unzip the side of the skirt, he stopped.

Jack, breathing hard and sweating, pulled back to look deep in her eyes. The hint of sadness she saw earlier was now a thundering wave crashing against the back of the haunted orbs staring at her, forming deep pools in the corners.

"Amber," he croaked, shaking his head, "I'm sorry. I..."

She reached up with both hands and cradled his face, and said, "I know, Jack. I know." Pulling him close, hugging him like a child, she rubbed his back, whispering, "It's okay, it's okay. I know. You're still married." He buried his face in her long hair and sobbed.

CHAPTER 6

JACK WOKE TO THE SMELL OF EGGS AND BACON. He was still on the sofa, but sometime during the night amber had propped his head with a soft pillow and covered him with a warm blanket. While she busied herself in the kitchen, he sat up and scrubbed his head with both hands. The freight train that ran over him the night before left a throbbing headache as its only mark. *I didn't drink that much. What the hell?* He looked over at the serving cart, thinking, *Maybe a little hair o' the dog...*

He stood on a toddler's legs, ambled to the cart, and picked up a bottle of scotch.

"What are you doing?" Amber asked, knife in hand, a newly-sliced pineapple in front of her.

"I need a pick-me-up," he said, reaching for a tumbler.

"*Need* and *want* are two completely different things, as my daddy would say," she said, looking down her nose at him.

"Your daddy sounds like a smart man," he lifted the bottle toward her, "but I need this."

She slammed the knife on the counter, and said, "You may *want* that drink, Jack, but what you *need* is breakfast."

He tilted his head, setting the tumbler and bottle back in their places. "You're angry."

"No, I'm not," she said with an amazing calm. "I don't know you well enough to be angry about anything you have or haven't done." Her voice, hard and bitter up to this point, now softened. "What I am, is *concerned.*"

"Why?" he said. Not *about what*, but why. That was a distinction as fundamental as want versus need, and without understanding why he asked, he nevertheless needed to know. A lifetime of self-doubt and a year's worth of pain rolled into a single question. *Never ask a question you don't want the answer to.*

"Why am I concerned?" Amber screwed up her mouth, her brows furrowed.

"Yes," he said, moving toward the island. "You said it yourself—you don't know me well enough to be angry. How can you know me well enough to be concerned?"

She opened her mouth to speak, closed it, and shook her head. "You're *trying* to pick a fight with me."

"No, I'm—"

"Don't deny it, Jack. You want me to get angry and throw you out." She crossed her arms over the *Star Wars* t-shirt she wore, and said, "I'm not playing that game." She picked up a fork and turned the bacon that was sizzling in the skillet, rescuing a couple that were close to burning. "I *don't* know you, Jack, but I *want* to," she said. "I'm concerned because you seem hell-bent on keeping that from happening, and destroying yourself in the process."

"I just needed... *wanted*... one goddamn drink this morning, and—"

Amber shook the fork at him, a single slice of bacon dangling limply from the end. "Don't take that tone with me, young man."

He stopped and stared at her, his mouth still open. She could have been channeling his mother, but the effect was so comical he couldn't help himself, and he burst out laughing. The look of consternation on her face only made it worse, and he doubled over as his laughter became almost maniacal. Amber watched him for a few seconds, and, no longer able to contain herself, joined him. Having trouble breathing, Jack sat at the small wrought-iron kitchen table beside the island. Still laughing, Amber sat across from him, pulled the bacon from the fork, bit off half, and offered him the rest.

As she chewed, he took the remaining half from her and popped it in his mouth. He smiled, this time because of the burst of flavor from the bacon. "Incredible," he said, savoring the small piece, anticipating more.

"I sprinkle a little brown sugar over the top as it cooks," she said, grinning. "A trick my dad taught me. Though you wouldn't believe how hard it is to get brown sugar around here."

"Probably no worse than bacon," he said.

"This is actually Bauchspeck. The American smoked bacon is too expensive. When you can find it, that is." She stood again and went back to tending her cooking. She grabbed the handle of an omelet pan and expertly flipped the egg. "Over easy?"

"Sure," Jack said. "Or medium." He shrugged. "However it comes out, really." He reached back and snagged another piece from the plate. "This is pretty much all I need," he said, and shoved the whole slice into his mouth. *This is better*, he thought. *Hell, anything's better than discussing last night.*

Sliding the first egg onto a plate, she cracked another and dropped it into the pan. He watched her cook, remembering the Sunday mornings when Beth would make breakfast for the three of them. Riley, impatient as always, demanded the first egg out of the skillet, then complained it was too hot. He would lean across the table, cut it up for her, and blow on it to cool it off. She always ate all her bacon first, sometimes forgetting the egg completely.

"Juice is in the fridge, and there's coffee brewing. Get us a bit of each, please, while I finish up."

Jack dried his eyes before she could see, and stood to do as she asked. He made it back to the table, mugs of coffee and glasses of juice precariously in hand just as she set the plates down.

"Here," she said, taking the mugs from him, "let me help you."

"Thanks," he said, sitting, and taking another piece of the bacon. "This looks delicious." He chewed, staring at nothing, and the two of them ate in silence for a while.

Chasing the last bit of egg around her plate with a piece of toast, Amber sighed, stopped, and said, "I *do* want to know you better, Jack." She looked up at him with those large emerald eyes, concern, longing, and, above all, *fear* lingering on the end of her long lashes. There was a whole universe of emotion behind those eyes, and he wanted nothing more than to dive in and lose himself there.

Instead, he reached for his wallet.

He pulled out a picture, slid it across the table, and tapped a finger lightly upon the fading emulsion. "That's my family," he said.

"My wife, Beth, and my daughter..." he choked, and had to clear his throat, "Riley."

"*Oh*," Amber said, her hand covering her mouth as her eyes grew wide.

"You want to know me?" he said, the skin on his face so hot it threatened to split like an overcooked sausage. "I'm the reason they're dead, Amber. Or at least I thought I was." He shook his head. "Everything's changed, and while there might be someone else responsible for their deaths, what will *never* change is the fact that *I* was behind the wheel when it happened."

Amber reached across to cover his hand with hers. "Jack, you—"

"No!" he said, pulling away. "It was *my* job to keep my family safe, and I fucked it up." He pushed away from the table and stood, taking the photo and carefully sliding it back where it belonged. "Look... you didn't sign up for this shit, and I'm not gonna drag you through it, either." He hooked a thumb toward the bathroom. "I'm gonna call a cab and grab a quick shower," he said, still breathing hard. His face softened and he took a deep breath, letting it out slowly—*controlled.* He leaned down and kissed her on the cheek, saying, "Thanks for... breakfast," turned his back, and walked away.

* * *

Rutger sat in his office with the photo of the lab report on his screen. The morning sun was just peeking above the horizon outside his window, and he had already been at his desk for two hours. On the surface in front of him were the typed interview notes and statements from the previous day's fun. *Jack's in the clear*, he thought, *but Ms. Riley is another story.* The coroner's report couldn't place the time of death for the nurse within a range that would *categorically* rule her out as the killer. All the events were stacked too close together.

Rutger reached into the small container of the nurse's personal effects and pulled out a cell phone. The droplets of dried blood on the screen indicated it had been in view at the time of the man's death, but no one in the department had been able to unlock it to see if there was anything useful in its memory. The *manner* of death—again, the stiletto—indicated a professional, but there was nothing in Ms. Riley's background that led him to believe she was an assassin, professional or otherwise. Interpol had nothing on her, either. She was, by all accounts, exactly what she appeared to be, and nothing more.

He grabbed the mug of lukewarm coffee from his desk and leaned back in the chair. It complained like an old man as it settled on rusty springs, and he considered all the information at hand. Jack was convinced both deaths were the work of his mysterious Shadowman, and Rutger couldn't deny the possibility. That meant the missing file was in that man's possession, along with the evidence from Lubitz's home. The blood report from the hospital did, indeed, show abnormalities that *may* explain Lubitz's suicidal actions. *Oh, and this was likely the same Shadowman who had previously appeared in Kazakhstan.*

The only real question was, how did all this fit together? It was a puzzle full of pieces all the same size and shape, with no edges to start from.

His computer pinged, indicating an incoming email. It was from Jack. Opening it, he read,

Rutger,

Just got this from a friend in the states. I know you said to keep this between us for now, but it's my job to report this stuff. Anyway, he's got some conclusions about the blood work you need to see.

– Jack

Opening the attachment, Rutger was presented with a report from a Dr. Mason Hill. In it he described a fantastical notion of nano-structures capable of delivering a payload—drugs, toxins, poisons, whatever—to a *targeted* position in a single organ in the body. There was no hard data to support this analysis, but it contained a large list of references from scientific journals.

Wunderbar! he thought. Ein weiteres verdammtes Stück des Puzzles.

The press was already breathing down their necks to tuck the whole affair into bed, and now he had to consider this wild hypothesis as potential evidence. Rutger opened a browser window and searched the web using the terms in the report from Dr. Hill. *Looks like today will be devoted to reading*, he thought with a shake of his head.

A rap at the door, and a young officer poked her head in.

"Polizeioberkommissar Brieske?"

"I'm busy," he replied, more annoyed than he realized.

"I am sorry, but there is a man here who insists he speak with you."

"Ja, natürlich." He stood to greet the newcomer, but his eyes widened, and he gasped when the man was ushered in.

* * *

Thunder shook the apartment walls for the fourth or fifth time since he woke, and Mason rolled over to check the clock. Instead of a steady blue, it was pulsing rhythmically. *Shit*, he thought, *power's gone out again.* The grid servicing his neighborhood was always crapping out even at the best of times, but thunderstorms brought out the worst in the creaky system. Light flashed through his window, casting crooked shadows in stark detail. The thunder crashed two seconds later. Reaching for his phone on the nightstand, he checked the time. *2 a.m. Son of a bitch, I'm never getting any sleep.*

The time difference between Atlanta and Germany meant he had to wait a while longer for a response from Jack, and Mason had never been very good at waiting. *My own damn fault for sending it so late last night.* Sure, Sally warned him not to stir Jack up with what he'd discovered, but to be fair, he *was* drunk when he sent the email. *I'm sure Sally will be* fine *with that as an excuse,* he thought with a chuckle. Light flashed, an effulgent flare, but the rumble arrived later and more muted. The storm was headed elsewhere, leaving only power outages in its wake. *This time.*

The wind was waning, and the cracking and creaking from the stressed joints in the structure faded. *Even the* flooring *is crying tonight.* Unusual, but not unheard of.

Another noise from the wood floors, this one not in time with the wind, and he sat up. Mason strained his ears, listening for what had sounded like a careful step in the hallway, but no other sound came. Lightning briefly lit the room, shining a dim light through the open door into the hall.

Nothing. Jack's damn Shadowman has me spooked. He punched the pillow a couple of times then flopped over on his side, hoping to catch a few winks before the sun rose.

The front passed him by, a low and long growl trailing the receding storm, fading to a purr, and even the rain had stopped.

* * *

"Rutger called while you were in the shower." Amber stood near the sofa with his phone in her hand. "He asked if we could both come in this morning."

"Did he say why?" Jack said, fully dressed, but still toweling off his head.

"Only something about new information," she said. She bit her lower lip, then said, "He seemed pretty cryptic."

"Did he sound angry or concerned?" Not that it mattered. If they were in any real trouble, there was little Jack could do about it.

"No, but he did sound amused that I answered your phone so early in the morning," she said with a wry grin.

"Ah," he said with a nod. "I guess I know what *he's* thinking." He looked her over, still in the t-shirt and shorts she likely slept in. It beat his rumpled shirt and wrinkled slacks by a country mile. "Cab's gonna be here soon. You should probably get ready if you want to share."

"Well, I bathed last night," she said, pulling her hair up to tie it back, "so I'll just get some jeans and a pair of sneakers on, and meet you downstairs."

"Fair enough." He caught his phone as she tossed it to him, and watched her walk to the bedroom. Her legs, long and toned, flexed gracefully as she padded away on bare feet.

"Stop looking at my ass," she said over her shoulder.

"I wasn't... cross my heart," he said, making the requisite motion. Her laugh followed her out of the room. Checking his pockets one last time, he couldn't find his wallet. A quick search found it on the kitchen table, opened to the picture of Beth and Riley. He grabbed it, stuffed it into his pocket, and walked out of the apartment.

Jack stood on the street just outside the doorway, waiting for the cab. The street was damp, but he couldn't remember hearing storm during the night. *Of course, I was pretty much dead to the world*, he thought. Amber was already putting up with more than he was sure she had bargained for in this relationship. *If it is a relationship.* Jack sighed, tapping his foot and checking the time on his phone as he turned first to his left, and then his right in search of the cab.

The email from Mason he forwarded to Rutger this morning *should*, Jack hoped, take this whole thing out of his hands. This affair was now far beyond his mandate, and he wanted nothing more than to get on a plane and go home to some routine. *Maybe not exactly the same as before, though.* He shook his head, frowning. *Yeah, that's what I need—a whole* new *rut.*

And that was it, he realized. His life since the accident had been one long, lifeless rut. Drag himself off the sofa in the morning, work all day, the bar after, then more drinks at home until he passed out, and start it all again the next day. Jack recognized the signs of depression in himself, but recognizing it and *doing* something about it were two *very* different things. *I need help.*

The beige little car in front of him honked, shaking him out of his introspection. Still on the watch for a bright yellow cab, he completely forgot most of them in Germany were this disgusting color. How he missed the sign on top, he couldn't guess. He leaned down to the open window. "We're waiting on another passenger," he said to the driver.

"No, we're not," Amber said from behind. She walked past him, opened the door, and folded in using the exact same motion he had found so endearing on the train. This time, her faded jeans, tight in all the right places, complemented her movement. She wore no belt, but the shirt was tucked in tight, and her hair was pulled back in a pony tail. And even without a speck of makeup that he could see, she was still more beautiful than any model.

Yep, he thought, way *better than I look right now.* The stubble on his chin, the bags under his eyes, and the disheveled clothing made him look positively *homeless* next to her. He ran one hand through his hair in a weak attempt to comb it into submission.

"Are you coming?" she said, waving him in.

"Oh... yeah," he said, and piled in beside her, clumsy as a new puppy.

"Address, please," the driver said without turning his head.

"Koblenzer Street 15," Jack said, and the cab accelerated without warning, slamming his head against the headrest.

"You get used to it," Amber said with a playful laugh. "Still... I walk most everywhere while I'm here," she leaned over and whispered, "just to be on the safe side." The driver pressed harder, and wove the car through the light morning traffic like he was running the Indy 500.

"Amber..." he began, not quite sure what to say, or even where he was going with the conversation.

"So," she said, interrupting his thought, "why do you think Rutger needs to see us?"

"Uh... offhand, I'd say it has something to do with the email I sent him this morning," he said, glad to have something to talk about that didn't involve last night.

"The stuff from your friend?"

"Yeah. I didn't understand any more of it than you did, but it's clear there's something important there." *That's the understatement of the year. If Mason's right, someone's got an agenda, and they don't seem too concerned with collateral damage.*

"You seem troubled," she said, biting her lip. "Be honest, Jack... are we in danger?"

"No," he said, shaking his head and doing his best to sound sure, "I am sure we are not." *Not* we, he thought, *me.* After he left Germany, any part she played in this was over; it was far from over, though, for him. He would do what he always did—keep pulling at the thread until the knot unraveled and the mystery was revealed. *If I was in this to make friends, I wouldn't be very good at the job.*

The cab screeched to a halt in front of the police station, tossing them around, *Star Trek* style. Jack paid the fare, thanked the driver, then he and Amber exited the rolling death machine as quickly as they could. As the car shot away from the curb, Amber laughed. "I should be used to the idea of sudden death by now," she said.

"Hell, if you think this was bad, try taking a cab in Beijing."

"No thanks," she said. "This is quite enough excitement, thankyouverymuch."

They both turned to walk into the building, but as Jack reached for the door, it opened, pushed from inside by a tall man.

"Entschuldigen Sie mich," the man said, scowling, and passed them without waiting for a response. His eyes, red and sunken, scanned the horizon, ignoring the two people he nearly ran over.

Jack shook his head, grabbed the door, and said, "Dude needs to slow..." The look on Amber's face erased whatever thought was to come next. Her hand was to her mouth, eyes wide in horror, and all color had drained from her face.

"Amber," Jack said, releasing the door and holding her up by the shoulders, her knees buckling, "are you okay?"

"That... man," she stammered. "It's *him*."

* * *

Birds, Mason thought. *That's it?*

He searched for nearly an hour on Jack's computer, looking for a correlation of some event—*any* event—to the postmark on the letter in front of him. Jack had asked him to keep an eye out for any more letters from his "pen-pal", and, sure enough, Mason found one in Jack's letter pile this morning. The postmark was dated two days ago from Spring Hill, Tennessee, so he sat at Jack's computer to look for anything out of the ordinary in that area for the past two days. Nothing presented itself, so he worked his way backward to March 2nd, and a story of a hundred or so dead birds found in the middle of a road there.

"Fucking *birds*," he shook his head. "Is that all ya got?"

"Is that all *who's* got?" Sally, as usual, stood in the doorway, appearing as if by magic.

Someday, Mason thought, I'm gonna ask her how she does that. Not really sure I want to know, though.

"It's another letter for Jack," he said, holding the page up for her to see. She walked to the desk and plucked it out of his hand.

"And you think this has something to do with birds?"

"Not really. There was a short-lived mystery about dead birds falling from the sky near where that letter originated, but an update cleared it up." He grinned up at her, "Some pizza delivery guy claimed responsibility for the avian mass murder."

She eyed him over the top of the letter. "So, there's no event attached to this one."

"None that I can find," he said, looking back at the monitor.

"What do you make of the note, itself?"

He took the page from her hands, reading it for the fifth time.

The crash that took your family away was an accident, but the man you know as Mark Wilson Peters was not responsible.

I am. And for that, I am truly sorry.

"Normally," he said, "I would think we have a confused individual who is trying to take responsibility for something he didn't do."

"And now...?"

"Oh, that might still be the case, but this person is involved in *something*. It's also clear he's leading Jack around by the nose—to what end, I can't yet figure out—but I'm going to find a connection to Spring Hill before I say anything to Jack about this letter."

"Maybe we should just hand everything over to the FBI," Sally said. "This is, after all, the kind of thing they do."

"No," he said, shaking his head with conviction. "You're forgetting the Shadowman." Mason flattened the letter on the desk in front of the keyboard. "Jack thinks, and I agree, he's some kind of government agent. Do *you* know who he works for?"

"That's just speculation, Mason. He—"

"When was the last time Jack was wrong about a hunch?" he said, one eyebrow raised. "It's why you hired him in the first place."

"Point taken."

"Without knowing which agency, or hell, even which *government* this guy calls boss, I think we should keep this in-house as much as possible," he said. "For now."

Sally gave him *the look* that said better than words she thought he was being reckless and stupid, and he couldn't completely disagree with that.

"It's okay, Sally," he said, trying to reassure her, "I've got someone I trust who might be able to help."

"Oh? Who would that be?"

"Jack's brother, Bill."

"The cop down in Greenville?"

"Detective," he corrected.

* * *

Amber sat in Rutger's office, holding a glass of water in a shaking hand. She took a slow drink, almost spilling it before grasping the glass in both hands.

"His name is Klaus Burghoff—Diedrick's twin brother," Rutger said. Jack stood next to Amber, a comforting hand on her shoulder.

"Diedrick is...?"

"Was, actually," Rutger said. "He was the murdered desk nurse." He turned the file on his desk so Jack could get a better look at the deceased.

Jack understood, now, some of the reason for Amber's near-catatonia. The men were identical twins, right down to their choice of hairstyles. *Still, her reaction is a bit over the top.* She recognized the man right away, but had only been *told* of the brother's death, rather than witnessing it herself. Even before Rutger told them about Klaus, she might have just assumed the initial report was wrong. *I know I would have.*

"Why was he here?" Amber said, her voice shaking almost as much as her hands.

Rutger smiled down at her, sympathy in his eyes for the poor girl. "As the only known family, he was the first contacted about his brother's death. He showed up this morning with a pretty strong piece of evidence about your involvement." Amber jerked, her head snapping up from the spot on the floor she had been watching. "Or rather, *lack* of involvement, I should say."

Jack watched all this with a strange detachment, like he was watching a play. Here was the good cop, slowly building a case from fragments, and over there was the suspect with no motive for the crime. Between them was Jack, the confused friend who is convinced *everyone* is wrong.

"What do you mean?" Jack said, sitting on the arm of the sofa beside Amber. She leaned into him, and he wrapped an arm around her shoulders.

"Diedrick was on the phone with Klaus when he was killed," Rutger said like it was a revelation. Jack raised an eyebrow like he was trying to divide two thirty-digit numbers. Seeing this, Rutger added, "About five minutes *after* the secretary saw you two drive away."

"Are you sure?" Amber said.

"Diedrick's phone verifies it, and we have already checked the records with the carrier." He reached into his top drawer, withdrew their passports, and tossed them on the desk. "Looks like *both* of you are free to go home."

Jack didn't approve of the way Rutger emphasized "both," but he wasn't about to raise a stink about it, either. Without leaving Amber's side, Jack leaned over and retrieved the little booklets. He pocketed his own, then handed Amber's to her. "So... what now?" he said.

Rutger shrugged. "Now I guess we all have our jobs to do." He pursed his lips, opened his mouth to speak, then closed it again. Jack waited for the other shoe to drop. "Um, Jack, my superiors aren't stupid. They have a good idea how I got the information on Lubitz's blood tests." He stood and straightened his uniform. "I have been asked to inform you that your presence here is no longer required, and to *suggest* you return to the US at your earliest convenience," he said. He nodded at Amber. "You, as well, Ms. Riley."

"But—" Jack began.

Rutger stuck out his hand, and said, "Please keep me informed of anything you discover regarding this case." He leaned in close as Jack shook his offered hand, and added with a sad grin, "I will do the *same*, of course."

CHAPTER 7

Amber couldn't fly back until the following Monday, but Sally requested Jack return ASAP. Her tone left no room for argument, but he was weary of this investigation, anyway. It was beyond both his domain and his abilities. When there's nothing you can do, best to do nothing. Other than the letter with the Montabaur postmark, nothing in Germany connected his pen pal to events there. Just another dead-end.

Jack stifled a yawn, and reached for his suitcase as it passed him on the carousel. He pulled the strap over his shoulder, lifting his briefcase from the floor beside him. With his free hand, he opened his cell phone to call Mason for a ride, thought better of it, and closed the cover. He slipped it into the pocket of his jacket and walked through the exit to the passenger pickup area where he waved for a cab.

"Should I follow, or do you want to ride with me?"

Jack turned to the voice. "Mason?" he said, tilting his head. "What the hell are you doing here?"

Mason stepped away from his truck. "I like to watch the planes land," he said, rolling his eyes. "What do you think, moron? I'm here to pick you up." A cab pulled up to the curb, but Mason waved it off. "I'm cheaper than those guys anyway," he said, grinning. "Plus, I'll even let you ride in the front."

Jack rolled his eyes right back at his friend. "You only *have* a front, dumbass."

"Oh yeah," Mason said, drawing out the last word. "Toss your shit in the bed and let's go already."

Jack lifted his suitcase into the bed but kept the briefcase with him when he crawled in the truck's cab. He had to pull hard to slam the door shut, the latch not having worked properly in over a year. The driver's side door cried out in pain on rusty hinges, and the worn shocks groaned as Mason settled into the driver's seat. Jack shook his head, saying, "Are you ever going to replace this rusty old thing?"

Mason snorted a laugh. "Are you kidding?" he said, rubbing the dashboard. "Betsy here is the longest relationship I've had with a woman."

"You are one weird bird, you know that?"

Mason kissed his fingers and placed them lovingly on the dash. "Don't you listen to him, baby."

"You know, Mace, if you treated *actual* women like that..." Jack said with a grin.

"Sshhh... You're gonna make her jealous!"

"Agghh... Just drive," Jack said, waving his hands.

Mason started the engine which, Jack had to admit, ran smoother than his bike, and ground the gears into drive. Mason steered into the main exit lane, saying, "How about we stop for a drink or two before I get you home."

"Nah," Jack said, "I'm pretty beat. I think I just want to crawl into bed."

"Too many on the flight in, huh?"

"Not really." The truth was he had had *none* and still didn't know why. Every time the serving cart passed, he *thought* about asking for a drink, but never did. Not once.

Mason watched him, but said nothing more about it.

Jack yawned, the bright morning sunlight confusing his senses. His father had been the same. Each time they traveled on vacation—driving across the country, never flying—his dad insisted they leave hours before sunrise. And each time, someone had to take over just as the sun crested the horizon, as the sight instantly put his father to sleep. *Most likely due to all those years of the Old Man beating the sun out of bed every morning*, he thought. Why the habit extended to *himself*, Jack never understood.

He leaned against the door and allowed his mind to drift away, comforted by the rhythmic slap of wheels rolling over jointed pavement. The siren-call of the open road beckoned him to leave everything and just... *go*; put the shattered remains of his life in the rear-view mirror and watch it shrink to nothing, hauling his empty husk from one foresaken place to the next.

It all goes away, he thought. In seconds, he was snoring.

* * *

Sunlight muscled its way through the heavy wine-colored curtains of Jack's apartment, bleeding light onto the floor and casting soft shadows around the room. Jack sat up on the sofa, ran a hand through his shaggy hair, and squinted toward the only window in the room. *Must be at least 2 in the afternoon*, he thought. *I've been asleep for over twelve goddamn hours.*

He remembered trying to rouse himself several times, but each attempt failed, and sleep dragged him back into its warm embrace.

"Coffee," he said, and as he stood, the thin coverlet fell from his legs. He walked into the kitchen, stretching and yawing, and grabbed the container where the coffee beans lived. He knew it was empty before he opened it, but looked inside regardless, hoping for a different outcome. "Well, shit," he said, setting the canister down in disgust. "Only one thing left to do." He reached into the fridge and pulled out the last can of soda. "Caffeine is caffeine," he said, shrugging. He popped the top and returned to the couch, taking a long drink as he shuffled. Within two steps he stubbed his big toe against a box.

"Son of a bitch!" he said, and hopped over to the nearest chair. He sat there for a time, rubbing the offended digit and scanning the room for other booby traps. The boxes were everywhere—a minefield of memories. Some open and half empty, while others—like the one in the corner—still sealed tight. All were dented from multiple toe strikes, and each had been moved many times over the last year, like a Minecrafter's *feng shui.*

Maybe it's time, he thought, shaking his head. He took a long drink from the can, set it on the island, and stood. He looked around the room, pursed his lips, then sighed. Jack reached for the box that attacked his toe. "Looks like you volunteered to go first," he said, tearing it open. The tape made an oddly satisfying ripping sound, and he smiled as he peered deep inside at the treasures there. One by one he freed the coffee mugs from their paper cocoons, setting each on the island to bask in the warm glow of an afternoon sun.

* * *

"What do you want me to do with this?" Bill Montgomery said, looking at the envelope in the plastic bag.

"I don't know," Mason said. "Can't you guys check it for fingerprints or something? I bet there's some DNA on the seal where he licked the glue."

Bill shook his head, laughing. "You've been watching too many of those procedural shows on TV, Mason. If we're real lucky, we *might* get a partial print from somewhere on the envelope or the letter. Unless the author is in the system, though, we won't get any hits. And that seal," he pointed, "is peel and stick—no saliva required."

"But—"

"Why are you bringing me this, anyway? I'm sure this is more of a job for the FBI."

Mason looked at his shoes. He wasn't sure what he should tell Bill about his worries there. *Gonna come off sounding like some conspiracy theory nutcase*, he thought. Bill already saw him as a bit of an oddball. No sense adding fuel to the fire.

"Oh, you know," he said, shrugging his shoulders, "if it isn't related to drugs or homeland security, they're not really interested these days."

"And you thought you'd just make the two-hour drive on the off-chance I would help you out." Bill leaned over his desk, "Why didn't Jack come to me himself?"

"Well, uh... that's the sticky part," Mason said, leaning away to fall into the chair. "Jack doesn't know about this letter yet."

"Doesn't...?" Bill said, then his eyes opened wide as he straigtened. "That letter is clearly addressed to Jack, so, *just* as clearly, you have already tampered with the US mail." He shook his head and sighed, looking more annoyed than angry. "And now you want to drag me in as an accomplice after the fact? The tampering charge *alone* could get you a five-year pass into a federal amusement park."

"I didn't think..." Mason began, then swallowed hard.

"No, you didn't."

"So, you can't—"

"Even *if* we found anything, we couldn't use it to build a case— whatever *that* would be." Mason knew the stupid look on his face was a question all its own. Bill sighed and shook his head. "There's

76

no evidence chain, Mason, so there's no way to be sure there was no contamination in the collection process."

"Oh," Mason said, and slumped back in his chair.

Bill snorted once, and said, "Cheer up. As long as Jack doesn't file a complaint, and I forget I ever saw this thing, you've got nothing to worry about."

"But what about what's *in* the letter, Bill?"

Bill waved his hand. "Someone's confused, or playing some kind of sick game," he said. The big man leaned forward, the chair creaking under the stress. "If the kid hadn't died the next day of his injuries, he would be in jail right now," he finished by pounding the desk once with his fist. "We had the right guy, Mason. There's no one else to blame."

"They rarely throw kids in jail for falling asleep at the wheel, even if someone dies."

"I never bought that 'falling asleep' crap," Bill said, making air quotes. "There was some pretty strange stuff with his blood work, and me and the prosecutor figured he was high on something."

"I never heard anything about that," Mason said, raising an eyebrow.

"Ah, well, since the boy's records were lost, the family's lawyer managed to keep that part out of the news."

"The records were..." Mason's mind wandered over the possibilities, but it still sounded like another cheesy conspiracy theory. Even in *his* head.

"Yeah, some sort of computer snafu. A whole bunch of files went bye-bye that night." He plucked the baggie off his desk and dangled it in front of Mason's face. "Take this to Jack or burn it. Either way, I can't do anything with it." Bill relaxed, slouching back in his chair. "Personally, I'd do the latter. Jack needs a break from all this, and this letter is sure to stir him up all over again, if you know what I mean."

"Yeah," Mason said, taking the letter, "I'm afraid I do."

* * *

Jack stood back and looked around the room. *Damn sight better than it was*, he thought with a satisfied sigh. There were empty boxes piled up by the door waiting to be broken down and hauled out to the dumpster, and still little in the way of furniture, but the living-slash-dining area was organized. All the pots, pans, and dishes were in their correct locations, the kitchen counters neat and tidy. He nodded once and fell onto the sofa, exhausted. His bedroom and the bathroom still needed addressing, and all the trash would have to go next, but now the place looked "put together" as his mom would say.

Except it *wasn't* complete. There were still no pictures on the walls. The box of framed photos of his former life sat in a dark and solitary corner, calling to him. Not loud enough to demand attention—*yet*—but he heard it. The box was one of many—the rest living with other bits of himself in a ten by fifteen storage shed—and was the only one that mattered.

"I'll get to you when I get to you," he said, an unreasonable anger, thick as blood, rising in his chest. He grabbed the remote from the coffee table and snapped on the television. The evening news was on, the somber newsreader talking about yet another mass shooting in Fort Hood, Texas. *The world is coming apart*, he thought, *but the politicians don't seem to care.*

He turned the television off in disgust and stood again. Jack had converted one corner of the kitchen counter into a passable bar, and he walked in that direction. Before he got far, his stomach growled its extreme displeasure at being ignored for an entire day. He laughed, shook his head, and patted his stomach. "All right, all right... just calm down." Except there was nothing in the apartment that even *resembled* food. Jack sighed, grabbed his keys, and headed for the door. The only question was, fast food or grocery shopping?

He almost made it to the door before his cell phone rang. Not recognizing the number, he took a chance and answered anyway.

"Hello?"

"Hey, Jack."

"Amber? I thought your phone didn't work in Germany." He was smiling as he spoke, though if pressed, couldn't say why.

"I'm here in Atlanta," she said with a touch of impatience. "You *do* know it's Monday, right?"

"Um... yeah. Forgot what day it was." He fumbled for his keys while he opened the door.

"Nice cover. What you *meant* was you forgot what day I was coming home." He could almost see her smirking at him through the phone.

"Hey, I was just headed out to get lunch—"

"I think you mean supper."

"Yeah, whatever," he said as he stepped outside and closed the door. "I going to get something to eat. Would you like to join me?"

Amber hesitated for only a second, but Jack understood that silence before she responded. "I think I'm going to go back to my own bed and recover for a few days."

A few days? he thought. *I thought she was back at work.* Something was wrong, but he knew better than to pry—at least over the phone.

"That's okay, I understand jet lag," he said, trying to sound upbeat. "How about you give me a call when you're refreshed. Apparently I have been placed on a forced vacation for the time being, so anytime's good for me." He walked down the stairs to where he had left his bike parked. Someone had stolen the canvas cover while he was away, but at least it hadn't rained today.

"Sure," she said, yawning. "I'll call you tomorrow or the day after."

"Great, I'll talk to you then," he said. He started to say goodbye, but she had already hung up. His mood, while not exactly buoyant before, had now taken a decided turn for the grumpy. *Something's wrong, and she's not ready to tell me yet.* Jack mounted the bike, jammed his key in the slot, and fired up the big engine. He grinned in spite of his mood, and was on the road before he realized that he had already decided not to grocery shop by taking the bike.

* * *

Amber closed her phone and dropped it into her carry-on. She took a shuddering breath and walked in sullen silence to the terminal's exit and the waiting cabs, dragging her rolling luggage behind.

"You're not *fired*," her supervisor had said while placing a comforting hand over hers. "Just suspended until you can get trained and placed on a new route." The woman was sincere in her empathy for Amber's plight, but as in any large company, the standard response was still "My hands are tied, sweetie." It was all Amber could do to hold herself together until she left the office.

The government officials in Montabaur didn't just ask her to leave, they effectively banned her from the country. Delta was, of course, willing to go along. *They're a good corporate neighbor, after all,* Amber thought, spitting the words in her head.

It was all so *stupid.* Especially what she had done. Even at the time, she had recognized that, but it hadn't stopped her.

Distract him, the man in the hat had told her. Something in his eyes left her cold as he placed the crisp bills in her hands. Those eyes were dead, even when he smiled. And he did that a lot while talking to her that night after Jack left the bar, like he was trying on a human face for the first time just to see if it fit. At first it felt like stealing when she took his money. She liked Jack, and didn't need more motivation, but the man insisted.

Distract him. Not into her bed—he made it clear that was unnecessary—but she knew she would anyway. And he never told her *how* to distract Jack, or from *what.* At first she thought just spending time with him was enough of a distraction, but once Jack told her what little about his investigation he could, she knew she would have to do something big.

And then the file was just *sitting* there, open and alone, waiting to be read. So she took a few pictures. What was the worst that could happen? *A scary man might want to kill me, and, oh yeah, I got fired.*

She wasn't sure which she feared more.

Maybe worst of all was that she had lied to Jack almost from the beginning. *Not* lied, *actually. More like omitted.* She should have told Jack about the man who approached her in the bar after he left, and that the wraith was *in the hospital* that day. He had brushed past her going in the opposite direction after she'd left the nurse's station, and the chill she felt as he smiled and tipped his hat had made her skin crawl. She hugged herself, rubbing her shoulders to wipe the memory clean.

That poor boy is dead, and I still *haven't said anything to Jack.* She stepped through the terminal doors into the world. The sounds and scents of the Atlanta evening swamped her senses, leaving her foundering, searching for safe harbor. *It's too late. Telling him now will only make things worse.*

She was grasping at straws, attempting to justify not coming clean from the start. If she ever wanted anything real to happen with Jack, she would have to tell him everything—she knew that. *And if I want it to end right now, well... telling him everything might accomplish that, too.*

She waved a cab over, opened the door, and climbed in the back while the cabbie hustled out and tossed her luggage into the trunk. "Avalon Ridge apartments," she said to the driver as he settled into his seat.

"Have you there in a jiff," he said, checking her out by way of his rear-view mirror.

"I'm in no hurry." As the cab pulled away from the curb, she rested her head against the window and watched the terminal disappear. She sighed as silent tears ran tiny rivulets down her cheeks.

* * *

Tuesday morning broke early for Jack, and he dove head-first into getting the other rooms in shape. Starting in the bedroom, he assembled the bed and covered it with clean sheets and a blanket. He took a while to find the pillowcases, but now they were on as well. The hard part was filling the tall-boy dresser and organizing the closet. His clothes were scattered among two piles—one dirty and one clean—beside his bed, the bathroom floor, and several boxes around the apartment. Just deciding what he could fold and put away, and what needed laundering took much of the morning.

The stack of empty boxes near the door looked like an avalanche had trapped him inside. He attacked them with a knife, and soon had them flattened and neatly stacked. He stood back, surveyed the room, and smiled. There was a satisfaction he always felt when assessing a job well done. *It might take me forever to get started, but I always finish*, he thought. He remembered telling Beth once, "If I said I'll do it, I'll do it. You don't have to nag me every six months about it." She laughed, but he was only half-kidding.

Already past noon and he still hadn't eaten, but the tentative rap on the door told him he might have to wait a little longer. He grabbed a dishtowel from the island and wiped his hands clean, then walked to the door and opened it. Mason stood in the doorway, head bowed, pizza box in one hand and the other holding up a plastic bag with paper inside. *Not just paper... a* letter.

"I'm sorry, Jack," he said. He stepped through the open door and handed the bag to Jack as he passed, saying, "We need to talk." Walking straight to the sofa, he dropped the pizza box on the coffee table and turned to face Jack.

Gathering his wits after the abrupt intrusion, Jack closed the door. He held the letter to his face, getting a good look at what he already knew he would find there, and said, "Nice to see you, too, Mace." He raised an eyebrow. "Now, what's this about?"

Mason sat on the sofa, leaning forward and wringing his hands. "Don't be mad, but that letter came for you a few days ago, and I took it to Bill—"

"Bill? My *brother* Bill?" Confusion mixed with anger, a volatile cocktail of emotions at the best of times. "Wait—you said this came in a few *days* ago?" His eyes narrowed as he stood over his friend. "How come I'm just finding out about this now?" Mason opened his mouth, but Jack stopped him with a wave of his hand. "And why is it opened?"

Mason closed his mouth and pursed his lips as his brow knitted. "All perfectly reasonable questions," he said, almost whispering. "Sally suggested I not show it to you until you got back. Hell, Bill said I should *burn* it without showing it to you." He grinned up at Jack like a puppy waiting to be praised for crapping on the tile instead of the carpet.

"So," Jack said, every word measured and restrained, "what you're saying is that everyone's seen this but me." He threw the letter to the coffee table. "A letter, by the way, addressed to *me.*"

"Um..." Mason began, a multitude of excuses fighting to exit his mouth before he gave up. "Okay... you got me there," he said with a shrug.

Jack felt the heat rising inside his chest, frustration, fear, and anger competing to see who could stoke the flames highest. He closed his eyes and thought about... *Amber.* He had reached for Beth, as he always did when things were bad, but knew in his heart that would only make this worse. Instead he found Amber, waving that fork of limp bacon, telling him to calm down, and he laughed. He shook his head, and sat on the arm of the sofa as all the tension bled from his body.

Mason, squinting and leaning toward him, said, "Are you okay?"

"Yeah," he said, "pretty good, actually."

Mason opened the box and smiled, grabbing a slice. He turned, taking in the room. "Hey, who cleaned up around here?" he said, pausing mid-bite.

* * *

Jack flipped the last pizza bone into the box and relaxed against the back of the sofa, full for the first time in two days. *Overfull is more like it*, he thought, rubbing his belly. Mason had long since finished his half, and was busy polishing off his soda. Neither said much about the letter, both having ignored its existence during the uneasy détente surrounding the meal.

"Okay," Jack said, "so tell me about the letter."

Mason set the bottle down and belched. "It was on your desk Friday morning, and since you had me keeping an eye out for another one, I... you know, sort of... opened it." His eyes widened and he tilted his head. "Hey, I just realized the Shadowman and your pen pal can't be the same guy after all."

"Why's that?"

"Unless he's some kind of wizard, he can't be in two places at once, and that thing," he tapped the letter with a greasy finger, "was mailed from Tennessee the same day the Shadowman was killing two people in Germany." With a self-satisfied smile, he reached up and scratched his head, then leaned back and relaxed. "Anyway... it's the same as the others, but a bit more personal in tone, I think," he said with a shrug. "This guy really thinks he's responsible for the accident and is looking for forgiveness."

"Yeah... I don't think so," Jack said, rubbing his chin. "If he wanted forgiveness, he would do that in person. I don't know where he is, so I can't give him any." He lifted the bag from the table and pulled the letter from inside. "It's more than that, Mace. He wants me to *look* at something."

"I don't know what," Mason said with a shake of his head. "I've been searching the news for events around Spring Hill for the past few days, and going back to the beginning of March. Nothing."

Something clicked in Jack's head, a set of tumblers falling into place. "Why the beginning of March?" he said with little interest in the answer.

"Some weird bird catastrophe," Mason said, waving his hand. "Nothing like what we're looking for."

Jack walked the conversation back a few steps, listening for another click. *March, no. Birds, no. Spring Hill... Spring Hill, Tennessee!*

"Son of a bitch!" he said and jumped from the sofa. He strode across the floor to the box of photos that still lay in the corner. More specifically, to the *letter* resting on top. He grabbed it and waved it in the air at Mason. "Spring Hill, Tennessee!" he said. Mason looked at him like he'd lost his mind, but Jack was more aware than he'd been in months. "This is a letter from Mark and Betsy Peters, and the post-mark is Spring Hill, Tennessee."

"That's the, uh... kid's parents, right?" Mason threw an arm over the back of the sofa. "What are they writing to *you* for? Besides, didn't they live in South Carolina near your mom and dad?"

"I don't know," Jack said, looking down at the scratchy hand-writing. "I never opened it."

"Well...?" Mason looked up at him, expecting something.

What have I been waiting for? It's just a letter. But it was far more than that. It was everything he wanted to forget sealed tight in a thin paper envelope. He wanted it to stay there forever, but now, opening this envelope, reading their words, might be the only thing between him and the truth of what happened that night.

Jack tore the end and pulled the letter from the envelope's embrace. He sat on the sofa beside Mason, who had already cleared a space on the table, and opened the letter flat. It was a single page, written in ink with the same scrawl as the envelope. Jack guessed the author was Mark, Sr.

Mr. Montgomery,

I wish there was something I could say that would make things better, but I know things will never be better for any of us. That my Mark killed your wife and daughter is without question, but he did not do this intentionally. For the few hours he was awake in the hospital, he was so full of remorse for what he had done he was inconsolable. He died knowing he caused the death of two of God's creations, and the pain he put you through.

I don't ask forgiveness from you, as I know how I'd feel in your position, but I also don't think he was at fault. Mark had, only a couple of weeks before, visited Middle Tennessee State University to sign his letter of intent, and was staying with his Aunt and Uncle here in Spring Hill. Mr. Montgomery, more than a dozen kids in this town fell into a deep sleep within days of the accident, and all of them were at the same event in town before it happened. Something is wrong here, and I am looking for answers. No one seems to care.

Please, Mr. Montgomery, I know you work for the CDC. Help me find out what really happened to my boy and your family. Betsy has not been the same since the accident, and I feel that knowing it wasn't Mark's fault would go a long way to helping her.

With all God's love,

Mark Peters

Mason watched Jack wipe his eyes dry, and said, "Do you believe the nerve of this guy? I mean, his son kills—"

"Mason... shut up." Jack read through the letter a second time, hoping the words would change, but they refused. *Sleeping sickness. Suicide drugs. Spring Hill, Tennessee. That's what my pen pal wants me to see.* He shook his head, clearing the web and tangle of unconnected information. He turned to look his friend in the eyes. "You didn't go back far enough, Mason. That letter from my pen pal is not tied to some future event, but to the accident that killed Beth and Riley." This is what Jack did, time and again, seeing the forest *and* the trees, then mentally clearing them all away to find the one piece of rotten fruit in the middle of the thicket.

"So what does that mean?"

"It means the Shadowman is part of this—part of the accident," his voice grew dark and dangerous, "and I'm going to find and kill the bastard if I can." Mason's face was ashen, his eyes white orbs with pinpricks for pupils. "First, though," Jack said, slapping his friend on the back, "we're going to Spring Hill to find my pen pal."

PART TWO

Beyond the door there's peace I'm sure
And I know there'll be no more tears in heaven

"Tears in Heaven"—Eric Clapton

CHAPTER 8

"Hey, I thought we left Georgia before we got to chattanoo-ga," Mason said from the passenger side of jack's car, one hand wrapped around a sandwich, a large soda held tight between his legs.

"We did." Jack said with a grin, knowing what was coming next.

"Then why did we just pass another sign saying, 'Welcome to Tennessee'?" He punctuated the question by shoving most of the sandwich in his mouth.

"This section of Interstate 24 dips back into Georgia for a few miles. You would know that if you had been paying attention, Mr. Navigator."

"Are we still pointed in the right direction?" Mason asked around the sandwich as he chewed.

"Yeah," Jack said.

Mason wiped his hands together in front of his face, and said in a gruff voice, "Qapla'!"

"Have I mentioned yet that you are one weird bird, Mace?" Jack said, shaking his head.

"Once or twice," Mason said with a laugh. He grabbed the soda and took a long drink, then pulled one leg up to cross over the other. "Any ideas on what we do once we get there?"

"I guess we'll start by finding Mark and Betsy." He glanced at Mason, saying, "I want to hear the details from them before we start poking around in the lives of the other families."

"I've been thinking about that, Jack. Don't you think it's possible that it's all just a big coincidence?"

"I might... *if* I hadn't been led *specifically* to that event." He shook his head, "Nope, there's something there."

"Okay, but I've also been thinking that maybe the Shadowman and your pen pal could still be the same guy."

"How's that?"

"He could have had an accomplice mail the letters for him, right?"

"Well," Jack said, "just off the top of my head, I can see three things wrong with that theory. One, it's overly complicated. Why bother? Two, the Shadowman has had at least two opportunities to speak to me in person but hasn't." He grinned at his friend, and said, "Most of all, these guys are working at cross purposes. One is cleaning up after each event and snipping off loose ends, while the other is doing his best to aim me at them."

"I wouldn't say sending you cryptic letters is 'doing his best', but I get your point."

* * *

The pain starts in his arm, crawling up from below the elbow, below the numbers, up and up. Fire and ice lances through his veins, slithering beneath his skin to seek refuge in his brain. He wants to scream but is unable to do more than breathe. His mouth tastes of metal, and... berries. He is not allowed to blink. The doctor whistles a soft tune as he adjusts his bottle-thick eyeglasses and probes the boy's flesh.

Always whistling.

Thunder rolls outside the walls, shaking dust loose to fall into his unblinking eyes, and the doctor rinses them clean with cold water before continuing his invasion.

The doctor stops whistling, and says to someone the boy cannot see, "This one will do. At least the treatment has not destroyed his mind." He stands and wipes his hands on his smock, "If he survives the night, I will begin phase two."

"What about the brother?" a stern and uncaring voice says from behind.

"The twin died hours ago," the doctor says, nodding in a direction the boy cannot see. Unable to move, a single tear leaks from the corner of one eye, sliding down the side of his face to pool in his ear.

Another thunderclap, this one more intense. Closer.

"We must leave soon, doctor," the man behind says. His voice betrays him. It shakes ever so slightly, and the boy hears him swallow hard.

"You may leave whenever you wish, Sturmbannführer Ruhstadt," the doctor says. "I will stay and complete my work."

"Of course," the officer says. Heels click, and boots pound a receding rhythm.

"Do not worry, little one," the doctor says, leaning close enough for the boy to smell his foul breath. "I will stay with you." His head snaps to the right. "Dieter!" he barks.

"Yes, doctor," a young man says, leaning over the boy.

"Take this one back to his bed," he nods toward the other, "and send that one to the furnace." He leans in again, kindness in his face as he smiles. "This one is special, Dieter. Look at his eyes... each a different color, and so clear!" He stands straight. "When all this," he waved around the room to the world at large, "unpleasantness is over, you will do great things, little one." He spins on his heels and walks away.

Dieter leans in close after the door closes, and whispers, "I am so sorry." He looks around, fear and pity playing across his face. "This will all be over soon. I promise."

It wasn't, though. It was just beginning.

He woke with a sharp intake of air as he was parking the car. They did this to him often of late, setting him on a course and turning off his mind while his body performed a pre-programmed function. He no longer minded that level of control, accepting it as his lot, but the memories bubbling to the surface like a foam-filled sea of dreams were disturbing—actual events in his life re-lived in stark detail, with all the pain, hope, despair, anger, and fear replaying in the heart of a six-year-old child.

The doctor was dead, now. He looked down, thinking, *Drowned by these very hands.*

He killed the engine of the rental car and checked his surroundings. *In America again.* That was clear from the street signs and the clothing people wore as they passed by on the sidewalk ahead.

Dieter is alive still, and always a step ahead.

But not for long.

* * *

"No, mom," Amber sighed into the phone. "I'm just on vacation for a while. No biggie." *Wow, I almost believed it that time.* Her mother meant well, but the constant questions about her job were making her feel worse. *As if* that *were possible.*

"Are you *sure* there's not more to it than that? I know *I* was scared half to death about that pilot crashing his plane—"

"Mom, seriously... I'm fine. I decided to take some time and see if there's something else I'd like to do."

"Like go back to school?"

There it is. Her mother made no secret of the fact that she wanted nothing more than to see her one and only daughter finish her degree. At twenty-six, Amber knew it wasn't too late, but the truth was she *really* hated school. Dropping out after her sophomore year was the best decision she ever made, and none of her family understood. Of course, what she understood now after a few years in the working world was that a large part of her hatred stemmed from never picking a major. Nothing ever jumped out at her the way it did for her friends; nothing grabbed her and wouldn't let go. Not like travel did.

"I've thought about it," she said. Placating her mother had become a full-time job. *It's easier than arguing, at least.*

"That's good, sweetheart," her mother said. She sighed a little, a lingering sadness crawling through the phone. "Your daddy would have been proud of you for finishing."

Amber wanted to say she never said she was going back to school, *wanted* to tell her mother to stay out of her business, but couldn't in the face of that sigh. She and her mother had both been too young to lose the only man in their lives, and the years since had been a constant struggle for Amber to keep her mom from falling into a crippling depression. Amber had been far too young for *that* as well.

"Hey, mom? I've got another call coming in," she lied. "I'll call you back later, okay?" Another lie, but the conversation was destined to be over soon anyway, as it would descend into a maudlin retelling of lives gone wrong. They usually ended that way, and usually with her mother sinking into an abyssal pit of self-pity. *Better to nip it in the bud*, she thought.

"Sure, dear," her mother said with false cheer. "Call me when you can."

"Love you," Amber said, and hung up without waiting for a response. She dropped the phone to the bed where she had been laying since arriving home. She looked at the cell, considering a call to Jack, but shook her head, thinking, *My depression has only gotten worse since I got back. He has his own demons dragging him into the pit.*

Another excuse. The truth was she didn't want to talk to *anyone* right now. *Not until I can at least drag my ass out of this bed.*

She reached for the glass of ice water she had brought with her to bed last night. Now room temperature, with beads of sweat on the outside and pooled on the nightstand, she picked it up to take a sip. Behind the glass was the old black and white wedding picture of her mom and dad. Both were smiling with a childish energy, full of hope for the future. She set the glass down and lifted the frame, brushing her fingertips over the image of her father.

"I wish you were here," she said, whispering. "You always knew what to say to make me feel better." And when words had failed him, he often just pulled the covers from her bed, leaving her cold and shivering until she decided to get moving.

"Life is about being in constant motion," he would say. "Dead things just lay there."

Amber smiled, a thin line that almost lifted the corners of her mouth, if not her mood. She set the photo on the nightstand, and in one quick motion—*like pulling off a bandage*—tore the covers off and threw them to the floor.

"Time to get moving." She knew her daddy was nodding his approval.

* * *

"Oh, *hell* yeah!" Mason turned his head like it was on a swivel. "Turn around, turn around!"

"What is it, Mace?" Jack checked his rear-view mirror but couldn't see anything meriting more than a casual glance.

"One street back," Mason said, an odd gleam in his eye. "*Barbeque.* Some place called Jack of Hearts." He stretched his mouth into a big stupid grin. "I think the name is some kind of omen."

Jack shook his head as he slowed to execute a u-turn in the middle of Main Street. "Damn, Mace, you nearly stopped my heart. I thought you saw something important."

Mason narrowed his eyes. "Barbeque is *always* important, my friend. Never forget that."

"Whatever," Jack said with a wave of his hand. "Didn't you eat, like, two hours ago?"

"Yeah, but it's supper time, and I didn't see you have anything earlier."

"You got me there," Jack said. He turned the wheel again at Maury Hill Street, pulled up to the restaurant, and killed the motor. Mason leaned against his door, one leg folded underneath him, tapping on his smartphone.

"The internet says to order the brisket," he said, snapping the cover closed. "Never question the internet, I say."

Jack shook his head. "Yeah, like the stuff about our reptilian overlords, I suppose?"

"Hey... those guys are real. You don't want to fuck with them," Mason said with a grin.

"You know, Mace, some day someone's not gonna know you're kidding, and have you committed," Jack said, opening the door. He stepped out of the car and poked his head inside. "I want a ringside seat for that. A fun time will be had by all."

"Laugh it up, fuzzball," Mason said, a fair imitation of a young Han Solo. He got out of the car and opened the door to the restaurant. "After you, your highnessness."

Jack sighed. *Now I'm going to have to listen to an hour or more of "Han shot first" bullshit.*

After they ordered and paid, they carried their trays to one of the thick wood tables and sat. Mason dug in without preamble, the large sandwich in front of him disappearing as if by magic. Jack had only taken a few bites of his before Mason was wiping the sauce off his mouth with a paper napkin.

Mason threw the napkin to the table and belched. "Awesome. Best I've had in years," he said, patting his stomach.

"How would you know?" Jack said, smirking. "It didn't stay in your mouth long enough for your taste buds to activate." He took another bite of his sandwich, chewing slowly, savoring the flavor. *It is pretty awesome*, he thought. "You should slow down and enjoy your food, buddy."

"Nah, it's just fuel. You forget I grew up the baby in a family with four brothers and a sister. If you didn't eat fast, you didn't eat at all."

"I wouldn't know what that's like. Bill was my only sibling, and my mom and dad emphasized sharing." Jack laughed and said, "I think I was sixteen before I had a pair of shoes that Bill hadn't worn first."

"Hell, Jack, you think I didn't do hand-me-downs?" Mason snorted. "Bitch, *please*," he said, then took a long drink from his soda. "So... what's your plan of attack? What's our first move?"

Jack took a bite of his sandwich and chewed, thinking about that. The truth was he had reacted on impulse after reading the letter. Until Mason asked, he hadn't thought much beyond coming to Spring Hill. Acting on instinct was what he did best, but he had to admit that it wasn't *always* the best option. Sometimes you had to plan. *Especially when* not *planning can get you killed.*

"I don't know," he said, swallowing. "I guess we could plug the address into the GPS and drive over there to surprise them." He looked over Mason's shoulder to nod at the man approaching their table. "Or, we could just meet with them here at the restaurant."

"Jack?" Mark Peters called from the cash register, a tray in hand, his wife shuffling behind. "I never dreamed you would actually come," he said, hope breaking both his voice and Jack's heart. "Are you here to help?"

Jack stood, offering the man a seat and pulling one out for Betsy. "I'm here for answers, Mr. Peters." He nodded at Mason. "We'll see if that helps or makes things worse."

* * *

Six weeks was an unusual amount of time between death and funeral, but Jack had spent all of that in the hospital recovering from the surgeries to repair his injuries. The two most visible were the brace on his neck and the cast on his left leg. He sat alone in the front pew, his leg stretched out in front and the wheelchair folded beside. Jack stared at his life sealed tight inside two ornate boxes of metal and wood. The world around him faded, an ephemeral swirling mist whose only solid objects lay directly ahead.

Everyone agreed the caskets were a beautifully matched pair, much like their occupants had once been. Family members passed by *tsk-tsking* at the sheer waste of two lives, turning their heads in weepy empathy to where Jack sat alone in his misery, a few whispering to others about his appearance. All lingered at the shorter of the two closed caskets—one closed in sympathy, but this one in sheer *necessity*—and patted Jack on the shoulder as they made their way to seats far from the grieving husband and father. No one sat near. None dared.

Jack didn't care. He was thankful for the space, and preferred the cold flask in his coat pocket for company. Refusing pain medication from the start, he convinced a kind-hearted nurse to supply him with what he needed. The man, Jack was sure, now regretted that decision. Too far gone to worry about propriety, he lifted the flask to his lips and took another long swig as family and friends walked past him shaking their heads.

"Fuck you," he whispered. That defiance in the face of their sorrow comforted him in some twisted way, and he gathered strength from it, searching for more. A man and woman shuffling to the display offered him what he craved. It took him a few seconds to place their faces, but he recognized them from the hospital. They had intruded *there* as well.

"What the hell are *you* doing here?" he shouted, not realizing he had stood. He was hobbling forward before he could stop himself, the cast cracking under the strain, and with his good arm grabbed the man by the lapels of his suit. He shook the man with feeble strength as the woman cried, and several mourners scrambled to stop him before he did something worse. "You have no right!"

"I'm sorry Mr. Montgomery," Mark Peters said, holding his hands up in surrender. "We only wanted to pay our respects."

Jack released him and drew his fist back, but Mason grabbed his arm from behind and held it firm. "Don't, Jack," he whispered in Jack's ear. "You know Beth wouldn't want this."

"Fine," he said, relenting but not relaxing. "Just get them the fuck out of here."

Mason pulled Jack away from the parents of his family's killer and placed himself between. "Maybe you should leave," he said to Mark.

"I understand," he said, head hanging, hat in hand. "Just know we are sorry for your loss."

"Shut up! Just. Shut. Up." Jack spit each word, a cobra's venom of deadly accuracy. "I didn't *lose* anything. Your boy *stole* them from me." A crowd of mourners gathered around them now, some nodding in anger while others wrung their hands. Mason stood at the center of this critical mass, one hand splayed on Jack's chest and the other inviting the couple to leave.

The man nodded and said, "Come on, Betsy. We should go."

As they started out, the people parted before them, a gauntlet of angry faces. Betsy stopped and turned, her voice breaking. "We've all lost something, Mr. Montgomery. Only a month ago, we buried—"

"How *dare* you compare your loss to mine!" Jack yelled, slapping Mason's hand away. Several of the gathering, including Mason, stepped back from the hurricane-force winds of his fury. "Here," he said, tears streaming down his cheeks, and grabbed a wreath of flowers. Fire exploded along the scar on his left arm as he threw the wreath at the couple, and bellowed, "take these to your boy's grave. May he rot in Hell!"

Betsy sobbed as the wreath hit her, and she staggered back into her husband's arms. Anger, red hot, flushed Mark's face, but he said nothing. His mouth a tight line, he gathered his wife to him and ushered her out the door.

"Maybe," Jack yelled at their backs, "if you had raised your boy right, *none* of them would be dead right now."

The air pressure dropped as everyone gasped, but Mark and Betsy only hesitated a step before leaving the sanctuary.

Jack, weeping and dizzy from the pain, stumbled back to his seat and grabbed his flask. He sat with a heavy thud and took a long drink. "Show's over folks," he hollered, then wiped his eyes with the sleeve of his suit. "Sit your asses down and let's get this shit over with."

* * *

"I was hoping you might help, but the last time we saw you—"

"I wasn't myself then," Jack said. "I apologize."

"No need," Mark said, waving him off. "Betsy and I talked about it at length on the drive home that day, and agree we might have acted much the same." To his right, Betsy nodded, but said nothing. "We were wrong for showing up. It was insensitive and selfish."

"And in the past," Mason said. "Let's all agree to leave it there."

"Done," the two men said together.

Betsy leaned close to Mark and whispered in his ear, patted his leg, then turned back to her food.

97

"You'll have to excuse my wife," Mark said, hesitating, sadness in his voice. "As I said in the letter, she hasn't been herself since the accident."

"Trust me, Mr. Peters," Jack said, "I understand completely."

Mark took a bite of his sandwich, chewing in silence for a time. "As I mentioned in my letter," he said, setting the sandwich down, "something happened here the week after the accident, and no one's even looking into it."

"You said kids here fell into a deep sleep. What were the circumstances?"

Mark looked toward his wife and pursed his lips. An unspoken question passed between them, but she took no notice. He shifted his gaze back to Jack. "One of them was a nephew about our son's age," he said, pushed the plate away, and propped his elbows on the table. "All the kids had been at a party a couple of weeks before, and the doctors figured they had a delayed reaction to some bad drugs."

"That's just stupid," Mason said. All eyes turned to him. "There aren't any drugs I know of with such a delayed reaction," he shook his head, "and definitely none that would have the exact *same* reaction on all the kids who took it."

"Well, seeing as all but one of them recovered within a couple of days, no one cared enough to dig any deeper."

"All but one?" Jack said, the wheels turning in his head.

"Young girl named Becky," Mark nodded. "She was out riding her horse and took a header when she jumped a fence." He picked at his plate, eating a fry. "They declared her brain-dead and took her off the machine the next day, farming out her organs like an a-la-carte special." Beside him, Betsy sniffed once and wiped her eyes. "My guess is she fell asleep in the middle of the jump, but those types of injuries aren't unknown around here, so no one bothered to see if she had been at the same party."

"She was?" Jack asked.

Mark shrugged. "Of course, or I wouldn't have brought her up."

That's the key! Jack thought. *Motherfuckin' Shadowman has messed up big time... I hope.* He looked at Mason, who was nodding back with electricity in his eyes, having reached the same conclusion.

"Mark," Jack said, then took a deep breath, "I think we can help." Betsy looked up from her meal for the first time, a prim smile on her lips. He reached across the table and placed a comforting hand on hers. "I'm going to share with you why I believe your son wasn't at fault," he said as tears welled up in the woman's eyes. "But first I need to ask you something."

"What's that?" Mark said, his voice cracking.

"How well do you know Becky's parents?"

CHAPTER 9

*D*IETER IS HERE, THE OTHERS TOLD HIM. Not near, or in the area. *Here.*

Here still covered a lot of territory, as the building was quite large. There were too many exits and not enough time to cover them all. *I will have to find the security office, and that means more deaths.* Murder was a distasteful business, and the Shadowman's mouth drew into a hard line as he touched the stiletto in his pocket. He would do what he must.

For once he walked a hallway clear of people, but he knew such luck wouldn't last. He didn't believe in luck, regardless. *Luck is not what brought me to you, Dieter. That was simple carelessness on your part.* The old man—older, even, than *he* was—grew sloppier with each succeeding year. *I almost had him in Germany.* The truth was, if he cared to consider it, he had *almost* had Dieter in a lot of places.

Always one step ahead. There was a time Dieter was many steps ahead. *There was also a time you walked at my side.*

The Shadowman sighed and continued searching the halls of the Maury Regional Medical Center. A young nurse passed, her eyes lifting from her tablet for only a second as she smiled up at him. He nodded but did not say anything, only smiled in return. Not yet in a restricted area, none of the staff gave him a second look as he walked the halls. An imposing figure, both his narrow frame and his height increased the bubble of personal space that few dared to enter. His eyes, perpetually shaded by the dark fedora, gave the appearance of a man in mourning.

I suppose I am, he thought. Seventy years is too long to mourn, but time is relative.

He stopped at a directory on the wall. There was no listing for a security office, but from the room numbers shown, a map formed in his mind, pointing the way. He no longer knew nor cared how such things were possible for him, he simply accepted them. The gift was necessary to complete his task, so the gift was his. *Like every gift from the Others, it is given when needed and taken without notice.* The only two constants were the stiletto and the *device*. The first he used sparingly, but the second was always active, and only once had he failed to carry it.

Kazakhstan, he thought, as he turned a corner. The surveillance camera at the far end of the hall emitted a soft whine, and the indicator lamp died. He smiled, felt the cold comfort of the *device* as it hummed in his hand, and proceeded toward his goal.

* * *

Dieter Braun, papers folded and stuffed in his coat pocket, shuffled from the records room. Located in the basement of the hospital, it would be either minutes or hours before anyone noticed the bodies crumpled in dreamless slumber on the cold floor. He preferred to be long gone by the time that happened.

Thirteen is close, he thought. That was the only designation he knew for the man—once a frightened child— whom he had secreted out of Germany so long ago in service to the Others. The boy's identity had been erased during his subsequent training, and for a time, Dieter had taken to calling him Josef. The boy's training was absolute, however, and he responded to nothing but Thirteen.

"A number is not a proper name," Dieter had said, looking down at the boy staring defiantly up.

"A name is a label, nothing more," Thirteen said, shaking his head and crossing his arms. "The label given to me is Thirteen. Use it."

Dieter had given up that morning, acquiescing in the face of stubborn surety. He wanted to argue that they, both Thirteen and Fourteen, had once had names given by their parents, but he knew that would be cruel. That pair of twins was now a broken set, and each time the memory of the lost brother arose, the boy became unresponsive for days at a time. Of the few memories Thirteen had of his previous life, the agonizing death of his brother mere feet from where he lay helpless was the most powerful. As it was for Dieter.

They had broken the boy that day, and from the emotionless mass remaining they built something new. *Like clay, we fashioned from him a tool of unbending and unfeeling power*, Dieter thought with a heavy sigh. *It's no wonder I am the one person he wants to kill.*

It wasn't always this way. In Thirteen, Dieter had found the younger brother he lost in the last gruesome days of the war. Jacob had always been full of life, daring it to master him. Thirteen had been much the same once his training began in earnest, but Jacob had never had so harsh a teacher in life as the Others. Dieter knew his brother would have broken and died under the strain, but Thirteen merely bent and grew stronger from that annealing fire. He loved Thirteen all the more for it, even as the light dimmed in the boy's eyes. Once a man, that light was all but gone, and the fierce intelligence behind gone with it.

Thirteen is theirs, now, body and soul. The truth is written inside... the code that is both his life and his undoing. Dieter shook his head as he exited the building, still one step ahead of his pursuer. Clouds gathered in the distance, piling high and shrouding the land beneath in cold, syrupy darkness. *When he has me in his grip, his hands around my throat, will I have the strength to pull the shem from his lips?* he wondered. *Will I even want to?*

He shambled to the dull and battered Mercedes and pulled open the unlocked door. Dieter looked at the sky before climbing in and breathed deep the ozone drifting on the wind. The chill in the air made his bones ache, a portent of the rains to come.

* * *

"Why aren't we just going to the hospital where they took all the other kids?" Mason asked as Jack drove the car, following Mark and Betsy.

"I'm pretty sure that would be a waste of time," Jack said. He turned his head and raised an eyebrow. "It's a good bet the Shadowman's already been there and cleaned the place out." He shook his head and faced forward. "Even if he hasn't, the doctors probably didn't run the type of tests on their blood that would show what we're looking for."

"Yeah," Mason said, shrugging. "Bunch of kids come in lethargic and unresponsive, they would mostly run drug screens or check for viral contributors. They wouldn't bother with heavy metals, especially with the kids returning to normal so soon."

"So I'm betting on Becky. They test for everything before a transplant, right?"

"Sure," Mason said, "but the guy's likely to have cleaned those records up as well."

"Maybe, maybe not," Jack said, his mouth turning down. "I'm counting on him not knowing about her... among other things." The car ahead turned at the intersection, so Jack followed suit. "As far as we know, Mark's the only one to put two and two together and come up with Becky. Unless the Shadowman has detailed knowledge of the families around here, he might not know she was affected as well."

"*If* she was affected at all," Mason said.

"Yeah," Jack said. "There's that."

"So, all we have to do is talk to Becky's parents and get them to agree to let us take a look at her lab results," Mason said, looking dubious. "Any idea how you plan to do that?"

"A lie wrapped in the truth often works the best," Jack said. The car with Mark and Betsy slowed and stopped in front of a small house, and Jack pulled over and parked behind them. The house was typical Southern cookie-cutter—built in the sixties, boxy with enough surrounding green to require a riding mower. A mailbox painted like an American flag stood sentry beside the steps leading up from the curb to the home nestled on a rise between identical structures. The immaculate lawn could have been used as a putting green.

"Just follow my lead," Jack said. He killed the engine, shoved the keys in his pocket, then pulled his cell phone from the other. He looked it over once with a frown, then shoved it back in his pocket. Mark got out of his car, walked back to Jack's, and placed both hands on the door as he leaned in. Jack rolled down the window.

"You guys want to follow me to the door, or hang back while I talk to Becky's mom and dad first?"

Jack pulled the handle to open his door, and Mark stepped back as it swung open. "For what I have in mind," Jack said, "it might work better if I follow you up there."

Mason exited his side, closed his door, and said, "What about Betsy?" He pointed at the other car where the woman still sat.

Mark sighed, and said, "It might be better if she stays in the car. At least until I get you gentlemen properly introduced." He looked to where his wife sat unmoving. "I'll come back out and sit with her once you are inside."

"You two go ahead without me," Mason said as he walked to Mark's car. "I think I'd like to sit with Betsy for a while." He smiled at Mark. "If you don't mind, that is."

Jack and Mark turned to one another, each with a raised eyebrow. "It's okay with me, Dr. Hill," Mark said with a smile. "I think it would be good for her to visit someone besides her husband." He lowered his head. "We don't get out much these days."

"You sure, Mace?" Jack said, tilting his head.

"Go on," Mason said. "We'll be fine." He bent to the open passenger window. "Right Mrs. Peters?"

She turned her head, a slow and furtive movement, and said something too soft for Jack to hear. Mason waved them on with a smile.

"Okay," Mark said, placing a hand on Jack's shoulder. "Let's go see what we can see."

Jack nodded, and the two men climbed the steps. The walkway at the top looked like a gray carpet, leading to a firehouse-red door on the other side of a wood-decked front porch. Two rockers, paint chipped and peeling sat side-by-side with a small table between, and the porch was shaded by a large live oak tree. He imagined the couple sitting on warm summer evenings, glasses of iced sweet tea dripping beads of sweat, rocking in childless silence.

The car door closed behind them, and Mark led the way to the door. Once there, he removed his hat, hesitated, then knocked. There was a button for the doorbell beside the jamb, but in the South most people never used them. *Especially Mark's generation*, Jack thought. A small dog yapped at the sound, and a man's voice snapped "Hush!" The dog quieted, but continued to whimper as the door opened.

"Can I help you?" The man poking his head through the open doorway was squinting into the setting sun behind them, the wrinkles around his eyes growing deeper. He ran a hand over his unkempt hair, a vain attempt at smoothing it down.

"Mr. Banks?" Mark said, extending a hand. "I'm Mark Peters, Angela's brother, and this," he nodded at Jack, "is Jack Montgomery from the CDC." He leaned in and shook Banks' hand. "May we speak with you for a minute?"

"Angela Wilkerson's brother?"

"Yes, sir. May we come in?"

"Of course, of course," he said. "Where are my manners?" He opened the door wide, and shoved the little yappy dog out of the way with a gentle foot. "Back up, Pig."

Mark stepped through, and Jack paused to shake his host's hand. "Nice to meet you, Mr.—"

"Just call me Paul," he said, shaking Jack's hand. "We don't stand on ceremony much around here."

"Nice to meet you, Paul," Jack repeated, stepping over the threshold into a small living room. The lighting was dim, but good enough to see the simple furnishings and tidy appearance. The wood flooring was the narrow plank, time-darkened yellow pine so popular in the sixties in low-end home construction. These days it would cost a fortune, but in most such homes was later covered by carpeting. It reminded Jack of his parent's own home. Even the smell was the same.

Paul closed the door behind them, inviting them to sit. "Now, what's this about? And why is the CDC involved?"

* * *

The Others were thorough—puzzles being their specialty—but even *they* couldn't see everything. Dieter had come and gone, that much was clear from the video Thirteen ran multiple times. The man had left the building at almost the same time Thirteen entered, though through a different door, and walked across the parking lot to an old Mercedes parked near the back. As he drove away, Dieter passed directly beneath a camera, smiled, and raised a middle finger.

At no time had his license plate been in clear view. It didn't matter that Thirteen knew the car well. Dieter was sure to have changed the plates more than once over the years. That he had been there was not in doubt, but what neither Thirteen nor the Others knew was *why*. Simple logic said it had something to do with the teens who had succumbed to the effects of the test nearly a year ago, but they were all in a different hospital miles away. Thirteen had eliminated those records at the time, and there had been no events in the area since.

So why was he here?

Thirteen reached for the body next to him and pulled it away from the desk. It fell to the floor with a soft thud, the eyes of the man now glazed and unseeing, staring up into nothing. He sat in the man's place in front of the computer terminal and pulled the *device* from his pocket. He placed it on the desk and pressed the single button on its face. The link was established quicker than usual, and he nodded his approval at the hospital's apparent attempt at keeping their technology current. Images and data flooded his mind, painful in their intrusion, and he searched for a connection to the last event. There wasn't one, but many records around that time were gone from the system, leaving distinct gaps in the data.

What did you take, old man?

He stretched out, spreading his mental arms, fingers entwining the data stream. *There's more than one way to skin a cat*, he thought, and pictures of dead felines instantly circled. He waved those away with a swipe of his evanescent hands. *Focus and discipline!* Finding nothing, he reached beyond the confines of the hospital, and *there...*

A single data entry from an ambulance driver about a head and spine injury. Thirteen zeroed in on the ambulance company, flipping through records like a magician shuffling a deck of cards. *Rebecca Banks. Brought in the day after the event, pupils dilated and unresponsive after a riding accident.* He cross referenced with the list of teens at the party, but found no mention of her being there.

Another shift, and he was inside the local newspapers. *The internet has been such a help,* he thought with a wry grin. A single article, short and devoid of historical value, told of "Becky" attending a riding event and beating her boyfriend, Dale. Dale, who *was* on the list of party attendees.

Got you, old man. Now the link to the event was established, however tenuous. He walked back to focus on Becky. *Why were* her *records so important to you?* Staying inside the newspaper's database, he cast a wider net for any reference after the event to Rebecca Banks. The obituary was short and poignant.

Rebecca Banks, born 1998, who suffered brain-death as a result of a fall from her horse during a jump, was taken off life support yesterday. She is survived by her parents, Paul and Martha Banks, who lovingly donated her organs to those in need. Funeral services will be held—

The data slapped him in the face, screaming *donated her organs* above all else. *That* was what Dieter was after. It was the one loose end Thirteen hadn't even known about to clean up. Somewhere, in that old man's possession, was a list of the recipients of the girl's donated organs. Each of those now presented a danger to the *plan*.

Find them, the Others said, imposing their will on the data stream to speak to him. *Eliminate the threat.*

Thirteen withdrew from the data stream, reintegrating his self back into his physical body. Before he did, though, he took possession of a single piece of information. Paul and Martha's last known address.

* * *

"Martha's at a friend's house right now, but I'll help you any way I can," Paul Banks said, rhythmically stroking the mottled terrier mix curled up in his lap. It was an incongruous pairing, the yapping little pooch clearly the owner of the tall stoop-shouldered man, but Banks just as clearly derived a degree of calm from the exchange.

After the three men sat, Jack had quickly sketched out a simple tale of how the kids at the party encountered an unknown agent that caused their sleeping sickness, and within that wove the lie that Becky's donated organs might still pose a danger to the recipients. He hated himself for it, but the truth would have only garnered concerned looks from the man, along with questions about Jack's grip on reality. *A lie wrapped in the truth, like a virus wrapped in its protective capsid. Each works to smooth the invasion.*

"What we need is permission to see Becky's lab reports after her accident." Jack cast an eye toward Mark, who had remained silent after the introductions. He was turning his hat in his hands, avoiding eye contact with either of the two men, in obvious discomfort with the lie. "I just need to either confirm or deny the existence of any foreign substances that may have caused the medical problems with these kids."

"What about the other kids?" Banks said, casting a wary eye at Jack. "Haven't you checked them?"

"Well... " Jack began, knowing he had to spin the lie out even farther. "A couple of the families refused to give permission, and the others were... *inconclusive.*"

"I can understand some parents not giving permission," Banks said, nodding. "A lot of people around here have a healthy mistrust of government types."

"Understandable," Jack said without a hint of irony. "Sometimes I don't even trust myself."

The silence stretched, and Jack was sure the man would send them packing, then Paul said, "Is this what happened to your boy, Mark?" He leaned closer and patted the man on the knee. "Is that why he fell asleep behind the wheel?"

Without looking up, Mark said, "We think so." He lifted his chin, "I pray so."

Paul stared hard at Mark, then at Jack. He turned back and patted Mark's knee again, then lifted the little dog from his lap to set him on the floor. He said to Jack, "You got a form or something for me to sign?"

"I'll have to get it from my briefcase in the car," Jack said, standing.

Paul stood and walked Jack to the door. Mark stayed in his seat, tilted his head at the dog where it still sat, then picked him up and placed him in his own lap. He stroked the dog, scratching behind his ears, and Paul said, "Comforting, ain't he?" Mark smiled up as the two men reached the door.

"Be back in two shakes," Jack said, and he pulled the door open.

"You know," Paul said, "I know you gentlemen need to find what you're looking for, but I really hope you don't. Martha had a cousin on the transplant list for a liver, and when Becky..." He wiped an eye as Jack stood in the open doorway. "She was a perfect match, too."

"Don't worry," Jack said. "I'm sure everything will be fine." *Even if I find what I'm looking for, there's probably no danger to Martha's cousin,* he thought, hoping it was true.

* * *

The drive to Maury Regional Medical Center in nearby Columbia took less than half an hour, and Jack brooded the whole way. By the time they would arrive, it would be well past eight, and there would likely be no one on duty to help them. He had come to Tennessee hoping to find answers, but all he had found were new questions. *How are the events in Kazakhstan, Germany, and Tennessee linked?* Other than the Shadowman and maybe his pen pal, he couldn't think of any way they could be. Granted, those two were pretty strong links in a chain, but there was the nagging question of *why.* If, as he expected, they *did* find the markers present in Becky's blood samples, that would confirm all the events were cut from the same cloth. *But what story does this tapestry tell? And why is my pen pal pointing me at it?*

He realized with a start that there was no way his pen pal could foresee his gaining knowledge of Becky or her donated organs. *He just wanted me* here, *in Spring Hill.* A chill crawled up his spine. He couldn't shake the feeling that he was a puppet on a string, his movements not only planned, but *observed.*

"I had a nice chat with the missus while you two were in the house," Mason said, grinning.

"Not to put too fine a point on it, Mace, but the lady doesn't seem to be all there," Jack said, checking the roadsigns as they drove down Highway 31. The recent rain coated the asphalt in a thin sheen of reflected glow from streetlights, an illusion of skimming over calm seas. *It's the surface that is the illusion,* he thought. Underneath a sea was anything but calm: life in all its forms fighting over resources while cold predators circled. *It's like that* above, *as well.*

Mason pointed, "I think you want to take a right here on seventh street."

"I've got it," Jack said, spinning the wheel. "Did she have anything of value to say?"

"Maybe, but mostly she talked about her childhood." He frowned, and said, "I think her problems have more to do with early onset dementia than the death of a daughter."

"She's a bit young, even for early onset," Jack said.

"Betsy's fifty-two this month. She had Becky at thirty-five." He smiled, "A little late in life for these parts, but what do I know?"

"Yeah, your life-schedule is jacked up enough you don't know *what* early or late looks like," Jack said, snorting once.

"Left on Trotwood," Mason said.

"Dude, I'm looking at the same GPS you are," Jack said, shaking his head while turning the wheel to the left.

The hospital loomed near, lights blazing along the windows and the rain-soaked parking lot. Jack pulled in, slotting his car in a spot as far from the entrance as he could find. There was no real reason for such caution, but the Shadowman invaded his thoughts at every turn. He killed the engine, then pulled his cell phone from his jeans and looked for the message he knew wouldn't be there.

"That's about the fifth time you've checked your cell in the past hour," Mason said, one eyebrow raised. "Expecting a call?"

"Nah," Jack said. "Just checking the time." He doused the screen and shoved it back in his pocket. *Whatever Amber's dealing with*, he thought, *she obviously doesn't want to talk about it.* He still had not told Mason anything about Amber—even that he had met her—and he didn't know why. *Because that would make it real*, the voice in his head nagged. He shook his head to clear it, then said, "Let's see if there's anyone still on duty around here."

Mason gave him an appraising look, then smiled and said, "Whatever you say, boss."

They walked through the parking lot in silence, Jack feeling like a secret agent on a mission. Mason had a bounce in his step that indicated he was enjoying the cloak and dagger routine more than he should, given the circumstances. *But that's Mason*, Jack thought. *The man could have fun herding cats.*

Once inside, they located the Records Dungeon, as Mason liked to call it. *There's some truth to that*, Jack thought, as he found most of these offices located in hospital basements. The woman behind the requisite Dutch door, her head not much higher than the bottom of the opening, looked over the signed form, her mouth screwed up like she was sucking on a lemon. She peered over her reading glasses up at Jack, eyebrows raised.

"This isn't notarized," she said with a voice like a road grader. *R.J. Reynolds isn't going out of business on her watch, no sir.*

Jack pulled his CDC credentials from his wallet, sliding the card over the narrow shelf with a big smile. "It doesn't have to be." He nodded at Mason, "You'll also notice the form was witnessed by Dr. Hill, here."

The little woman sniffed and pursed her lips, clicking her long— and obviously fake—fingernails of one hand on the shelf, holding the form in her other. Mason sighed, and she looked up at him, her mouth back in pucker-mode.

"This might take a while. I'm the only one here at this hour."

"That's okay, ma'am. We'll wait," Jack said with forced cheer and patience he did not feel.

She walked away, closing the top half of the door in their faces.

"Old bitty's just going for a smoke," Mason whispered.

"Hush, Pig," Jack said, and Mason tilted his head in obvious confusion.

The two men sat in worn plastic chairs in the tiny waiting area, and Jack checked his phone again.

"Seriously, Jack," Mason said, "what's up with the damn phone?"

"Um..."

"Ah," Mason said, smiling, "a woman."

"How the hell—"

"You're kidding, right?" Mason said. He punched Jack in the shoulder, and said, "I've known you a long time, buddy, and you've only gotten like this around me once before."

Jack's first instinct was to tell him to mind his own business, but this was Mason. If there was anyone in the world he could talk to about Amber, it was him. *Then why don't I want to? It's been almost a year, and Beth would be the first one to tell me to move on.* That was it, though. Telling Mason there was a woman in his life now *was* moving on, and Jack still wasn't sure he wanted that yet.

"It's just someone I met in Germany. No biggie," he said, not sure if he was lying.

"Yeah," Mason said, shaking his head, "sure." Jack opened his mouth, but Mason stopped him. "I get it, dude. You're not ready to talk about it yet. That's cool. Just know that when you are, I'm here."

"Like I said, Mace... no biggie."

The top half of the door opened, and the woman stuck her face through the space, her mouth tighter than ever, and said, "Can't find 'em."

"Excuse me?" Jack said, standing.

"The records. They're not where they're s'posed to be."

Mason stepped up to the door and said, "You mean the hard copies. Surely you have backups on the server."

"Nope, they're gone, too. Them and a whole bunch of others from that day." She shook her head, eyebrows meeting in the middle of her forehead, "Must have had a system crash on that day or something. First I've heard of it, though."

"But—" Mason began.

"Thanks anyway, ma'am," Jack said, pulling at Mason's sleeve. "C'mon, Dr. Hill. We'll have to find them another way." He turned to the woman as he dragged Mason from the door. "Sorry to waste your time."

"That's what I'm here for," she said, her tone not disagreeing with his statement.

Once outside, Mason stopped, shaking Jack's hand from his sleeve. Breathing heavily, eyes wide, he said, "How the holy *fuck* did the Shadowman know about Becky, Jack?"

"I don't know, Mace, but that's not what I'm worried about."

"What would *that* be?"

"I'm worried about what the bastard is going to *do* with that information," Jack said, grabbing Mason's sleeve and pulling him toward the car.

* * *

The knock on the door was soft... tentative, and Pig yapped as if the world was ending just outside. Paul pushed the dog off his lap, pressed the mute button on the TV remote, and stood. "It's okay, Martha. I'll get it," he said to the sounds of dishes being put away in the kitchen. "Shut up, Pig," he snapped, but the dog kept barking. Paul shook his head and opened the door.

The man standing in the doorway, close enough he was almost inside, wore a hat like Mark had earlier. The long gray coat hid his frame, but he was tall enough that he would have to duck his head beneath the jamb. Paul assumed he was thin as well by the way the overcoat hung from his shoulders. He shuddered when the man smiled.

"Good evening," the man said. "I hope I am not intruding." The teeth he showed with that smile said otherwise. "Do you mind if I come in?" he said, stepping into the house without waiting for an answer. Martha walked into the living room, still drying her hands with a dishtowel, and stopped dead in the entry. Her eyes widened at the sight of the intruder, an unspoken question on her lips as she turned to Paul.

The tall man placed one gloved hand on Paul's shoulder, closed the door with a soft click with the other, then placed that free hand in his coat pocket. He smiled at Martha, then Paul, and said, "I just have a few questions."

Pig, hiding under the coffee table, never stopped yapping.

CHAPTER 10

AMBER FELT STUPID. Chasing a guy was not her style, and now, standing outside Jack's apartment door, she felt like the quintessential stalker. It didn't help matters that she drove over on impulse, having just left the gym. *So my hair and makeup aren't perfect,* she thought. *So what?* She raised her hand to knock again and sighed, thinking, *I should have called.*

No, what she *should* have done is waited for him to call back. *But I told him I would call when I was ready.* Her self-imposed, arbitrary deadline had passed without her calling, and by all rights the ball was in his court. She guessed Jack wasn't the ball-playing type. *He's also not home.*

She had never seen his car, so she had no clue if he was just visiting someone else in the building, but the motorcycle he had described to her was in the parking lot. Amber turned away from the door and walked toward the stairs. A white-haired old man was working his way up the steps as she started down, and he smiled up at her, one hand gripping the rail and the other holding a manila envelope close to his chest. The coat he wore reminded her of the man in Germany, and she shivered as she passed him on her way down.

"Good morning," he said, his German accent unmistakable to her ears. The edges had been sanded off by decades abroad, most likely, but it was still there.

"Good morning," she said in return, now moving faster without understanding why.

He continued up, his right hand a death-grip on the rail, pulling him ever upward. Amber turned at the landing just in time to see him reach the top step. He looked each way, checking the numbers on the doors, then spun to his right. The only apartment in that direction was Jack's.

"I don't think he's home," she called up.

"That's okay, miss," he said without turning.

Amber shrugged and continued down. *Fine by me if he wants to wait at the door. How much trouble can one sweet old man get into?*

She passed the motorcycle on the way to her car, running a hand over the seat as she did so. Amber gave the bike a half-smile, opened the door to her car, and climbed in. The engine rumbled to life when she turned the key, and NPR's *Morning Edition* was still on and drowned out the noise.

"...and some are calling President Obama's actions a normalizing of relations with Cuba."

About fucking time, she thought as she backed out of the parking spot and drove away.

* * *

Jack pulled the rental car into the first available parking slot, still without a plan. Mason had complained the entire trip, and neither had slept at all since they left Jack's apartment the day before.

"Do you really think we beat the Shadowman here?" Mason asked, looking like someone had left a bundle of old clothes strapped in the passenger seat.

"I don't know, but even if he has a complete list of where Becky's organs went, the odds are in our favor he is at one of the other hospitals." He turned the key to kill the engine, and faced Mason. "Most of them went to places close by." He shrugged, "Hey, this is the only one we've got, and we wouldn't have *this* one if Paul hadn't told us about it."

"I just wish we could have driven here instead of taking Treetop Airlines," Mason said, shivering. "That was a white-knuckler if ever there was one."

"It's all I could afford on short notice," Jack said with a grin. The look on Mason's green-tinged face as they crossed the mountains had been worth every penny. "You *could* have just driven my car home, you know."

"What, and let my truck think I'd been cheating on her?"

Jack shook his head. "One. Weird. Bird."

"Besides," Mason said, "you'll probably need my help at some point." He looked around the parking lot, then up at the building closest to them. "For instance... did you know I did my residency right here in DC at Gee-Dubbya-U Hospital?"

"As a matter of fact, Mason, I *did* know that," Jack said with a sigh.

"Well, did you know I—"

"Almost washed out?" Jack finished for him. "Yeah, buddy. Heard that story, too."

Mason grimaced in dramatic fashion, and said, "They just never understood my genius."

"Funny," Jack said. "I heard it was because you banged one of the attending's daughters in the supply closet."

"Tomato, to*mahto*," Mason said, waggling a hand.

They both laughed for a few seconds, then the cheer melted from Mason's face.

"So... what's the plan?"

"This is our nation's *capitol*," Jack said. "It's all about *looking* official." He pulled his ID card from his pocket. "With this, I can probably get whatever I want as long as I'm rude enough." He snorted once. "People around here see discourtesy as a sign of power. No one in this town can afford to be rude without some serious juice backing them up, and everyone knows it."

"Oh boy, I remember *that*." Mason shook his head. "Think you can pull that off?"

Give me a fifth of Jack Daniels, he thought. It wasn't that long ago he could fit in without much effort, but that effort included consuming copious quantities of alcohol. He hadn't *wanted* a drink in days, but the *need* was definitely growing again. *How much longer can I hold out?* he wondered. *Do I even want to?* After he left the hospital, he had attempted to find out just how much it would take to kill him, but he only succeeded in finding how much it took to incapacitate. If it weren't for the job giving him reason enough to sober up for a few days at a time, he might have found his limit.

Now the job had given way to a personal quest.

"Yeah," Jack said. "I think I can channel my inner asshole."

Mason watched him for an uncomfortable length of time, then nodded once and unhooked his seatbelt. "I guess we should get to it, then."

* * *

Sally Jackson roamed the halls like a bulldog guarding its territory, checking every open office door as a silent prod to her staff. The attention was not lost on them, as each time she poked her head in a doorway everyone suddenly found something important to do. Most Wednesdays were quiet—everyone fully focused on their week's assignment—but this morning was electric with Sally's irritation. She hadn't shared the subject of her early-morning phone call with anyone in the department, but they all felt the resulting tension.

Those two are supposed to be on vacation, *for chrissake,* she thought as she walked back to her office, her rolling gait propelling her forward—a juggernaut on two stout legs. *What they are* not *supposed to be doing is flashing their ID's and breaking HIPPA laws.* She reached her office, entered, then slammed the door behind her.

"Idiots," she hissed, and sat at the desk. The surface was stacked with all manner of paperwork, forms, and files—some of which reached more than a foot in height—and she knew the location of *each* piece of paper within those bounds. She lifted the phone from its cradle and started dialing Jack's number. Four numbers in she stopped— her mouth in a tight bunch, fingers drumming on the desktop—and sighed. She replaced the handset and leaned back in the chair. The call from her supervisor had come the instant she set her briefcase on the desk earlier that day, and from his tone it was clear the higher-ups weren't pleased with *him.*

"Shit rolls downhill," she said. Her daddy always said that, but to be fair, he was talking more about race relations at the time. *I get to decide where it stops, though,* she thought. *No point in passing it down the line and filling* their *day with crap if I don't have to.* She would do what she always did when told to reign in her staff—stall until she got all the details, and *then* decide who's day got the shit-storm.

"Sometimes you have to take the hit for your people," her daddy had said. Again, he was talking about the Civil Rights movement, but good advice applies everywhere. Sally learned long ago that loyalty in a manager/worker relationship had to go both ways or it broke down faster than a Yugo.

Everything's breaking down, anyway. Just yesterday she got a note from a friend about a spike in Legionaire's linked to the water crisis in Flint. The Michigan Health Department was already downplaying the connection, and her friend was livid because he knew nothing would be done.

"Most people are real good about ignoring evidence that doesn't fit their preconceptions," she said to the stack of papers in front of her. She reached into the middle of that stack and pulled a single slim folder from its clutches. Jack's report from Germany still needed some massaging before she sent it upstairs. *Damn thing reads like a spy novel,* she thought, then bent to her work.

* * *

"Just act like you belong here," Jack whispered to Mason. The two had already gotten through their first trial when Jack flashed his credentials and bullied his way past the records clerk. This one looked much like the one they had met the night before in Columbia, and Jack wondered if there was a factory somewhere assembling identical units for hospitals the world over. This particular unit had been a bit easier to bully, though, and Jack felt like crap for it.

"We don't exactly look the part, buddy," Mason said in return. "Neither of us is in a suit, black or otherwise."

"Just try to keep up," Jack said, and Mason increased his pace, matching him stride for stride. Jack had to admit he was right. They didn't quite look the part of government agents on official business, but if they kept moving and pushing people around, he hoped no one would notice until they were long gone. *I doubt we'll get that lucky, though.*

They found an unattended terminal in the back of the room near racks of paper records, and Jack sat in front of the keyboard while Mason wandered off among the aisles. The clerk may have been bluffed into letting them in, but she hadn't offered to help them, either, and the splash-screen on the terminal was cryptic at best. Jack poked around and was presented with a log-in. *Great,* he thought. *Now I'll have to go back to the clerk for a log-in and password.* The user name was already filled in from the last user, so he took a chance and typed "password" into the empty box. He almost laughed out loud when the terminal accepted his entry and displayed a list of options.

None of those options, however, gave him something as mundane as a search function. There was an empty box with the label "last name" to the left. He typed in the last name given to him by Paul, and hit enter, but nothing happened. He did the same for "first name" and "procedure date," but still nothing happened. *This is taking too long,* he thought, pulling at his bottom lip. He looked over the entire screen and noticed a row of function keys at the bottom. He pressed F1 and it immediately took him back to the log-in, and he banged the desk, rattling the keyboard.

"Anything wrong?" Mason asked from somewhere in the stacks.

"Nope," Jack said. "Just trying to decipher this dinosaur of a database."

"Try F10," he said, his voice now farther away.

Jack sighed, logged back in, and pressed the F10 key. Now he was shown a list of options and their keyboard commands to execute.

"How did you..."

"Residency, remember?"

Jack shook his head. "Then why the hell aren't *you* doing this?"

"Because sometimes," Mason appeared, slapping a thick folder on the desk beside Jack, "old-school works better."

Jack looked down at the name on the folder's tab, then back up at Mason standing over his shoulder. "Is that what I think it is?"

"Yep," Mason said, a big grin on his face. "Now shove this in your pants and let's get out of here."

"I planned on printing a copy, but I guess we could photocopy a set."

Mason shook his head. "There's only a couple of machines down here, and *those* have more security than Fort Knox." He laughed as Jack made a face. "I blame myself for that. Well, my *ass*, at least."

"I don't want to know," Jack said, shaking his head and waving a hand in front of Mason's face. He opened the folder, and said, "Can't you just tell me if the markers are there? I mean, that's all we really need."

"First of all... no. It will take me a while to go through this, and I doubt we have that much time. Secondly, I think we need to keep this as evidence," he said, placing his hand on top of the folder, closing it.

"I didn't like the look the dragon lady gave us." He dipped his chin, and said, "I think she recognized me."

"Oh," was all Jack could say. "All right," he said, standing, "let's go." He unbuttoned his shirt and shoved the folder inside, then quickly rebuttoned. "How do I look?"

Mason gave him an appraising nod, then said, "Like you have a file stuffed in your shirt."

"Just stay between me and the dragon lady," Jack said.

* * *

They almost made it out of the building, Mason leading the way as they searched for a less busy exit. Getting past the clerk was easy, but the look on her face as they passed—and the way she reached for the phone without taking her eyes off them—made Mason nervous enough to take a path other than a straight line to the parking lot. *If we're caught sneaking out with that folder, it's gonna be way worse than the supply closet incident, that's for sure,* Mason thought as he led Jack to the stairs.

"We'll have to go down before we can go back up," Mason said.

"I thought we were already in the basement," Jack said, one eyebrow arched.

"Sort of. There's a steam tunnel underneath." He shrugged at the look on Jack's face. "I had to use it a time or three to get back to my apartment ahead of a particularly suspicious girlfriend."

"With good reason, I bet," Jack said with a smirk.

"Of course."

That girlfriend had almost been *the one*, but Mason had made far too many mistakes for it to work out. The few women he had dated since never quite measured up, so he was spared a life of being tied to one woman the way Jack had been. *And now he's gone and found someone* else *to chain himself to,* Mason mused, shaking his head. *Some guys don't know when they've got it good.* He heard later that Debbie was married to an engineer and living in the suburbs with their two kids. *Good for her.*

"Take a left at the bottom," he said. There were only two ways to go, the steam pipes and electrical conduits over their heads running in each direction, fading into infinity. The light was dim in many places down the long stretch of sweaty tunnel, most of the ballasts for the fluorescent lighting failing from extreme age. He pointed, saying, "There's a ladder about halfway down that leads up into the parking lot."

He waved Jack ahead, and they walked with exaggerated care over the steam-slicked floor, passing the occasional rat. The humidity was oppressive, and he was already sweating from the heat. Jack, on the other hand, had increased his pace, power-walking ahead and widening the distance enough that Mason had to trot to keep up.

"Slow down, dude," Mason said, huffing. "There's nobody chasing—"

"*Hey.*" Both men stopped at the sound of the insistent voice behind them. "You two hold up a second."

Mason made a slow turn to face the direction they had come. *Shit,* he thought, as a pimply-faced security guard walked toward them. "You keep going," Mason whispered behind to Jack. "I've got this."

"Mace," Jack whispered back, "you—"

"I said I've got this. You get to the car and we'll figure out the rest later."

Jack sighed, patted Mason on the shoulder, and took a hesitating step back.

The guard sped up, tapping the Taser on his belt, and said in a voice that had only recently stopped changing, "I told you to hold up."

Mason stepped forward, placing himself between the guard and Jack, and said, "We're here on official business." He glanced behind at Jack, who was now almost to the ladder.

"*You,*" the guard yelled at Jack. "You need to stop *right now* and show me some ID."

"Certainly," Mason said, now less than a step away from the man and blocking his path. He reached in his back pocket for his wallet, and the guard pulled the Taser from his belt and held it up with both hands as he stepped back a pace. He pointed it, hands shaking, at Mason's chest.

"Slowly," he said, keeping his eyes on Mason's hand. Over Mason's shoulder, he yelled again, "I *told* you to stop!"

The guard's eyes on Jack, Mason yelled back, "*Run!*" slapped the Taser away, and threw himself at the young man. *I'm too old and out of shape for this shit*, he thought as they both fell to the floor, Mason on top. He was wrestling rather than fighting, his only purpose to buy time for Jack's escape. He had no desire to hurt the boy. The young guard, on the other hand, had no such qualms. He punched Mason in the kidneys and pushed the larger man off his body and rolled away, but the sound of the manhole cover sliding back into place told them Jack had made it out. The guard reached for his radio, and Mason slapped that away as well, wrapping him in a bear-hug.

"Get the fuck *off* me," the guard yelled, but he was trapped with his arms pinned to his sides as they both rolled on the floor. The guard pulled his head back, and before Mason could react, head-butted him and again rolled away. Mason grabbed his spinning head and felt the gorge rising in his throat but managed to gain his footing. By the time he recovered, the guard had his radio and was calling for help. Mason turned to run for the ladder, but his first step landed on the Taser, twisting his ankle. He fell to the floor in agony as the ankle gave, and he grabbed it in fear it was broken.

"Yeah," the guard answered the question from the man on the other end, "I'm in the steam tunnel under the hospital near marker," he looked around for the sign. "It looks like number—"

The next sound from his throat was a strangled *Urgk!* as the Taser did its job. Mason watched the man dance for a couple of seconds, then released the trigger and did his best to catch the boy as he fell. Far down the tunnel, back the way they had come, urgent voices approached.

Some days it just doesn't pay to get out of fucking bed.

* * *

Jack threw open the car door and piled in, looking back to see if Mason was behind him. He waited as long as he could—the fear of being caught with stolen files reaching a thundering crescendo in his head—then closed the door and turned the key to start the engine. Still, he sat a few more seconds before jamming the shifter into drive. *Mace'll be fine*, he thought as he drove out of the parking lot. *The guy has more lives than a cat.*

Not yet noon, the sun was blazing in usual springtime fashion, slicing through newly-leafed trees like crystal blades. He drove for a long time, checking his phone every couple of minutes, hoping for a call from Mason. After a half-hour meandering drive, he pulled into the parking lot of a hotel on the outskirts of DC and killed the engine.

He sat, still as stone, counting his breaths and willing his pulse to slow.

"God...*damn*it!" he yelled, pounding his fists on the dashboard, then the seat to his right. He thrashed, cursing his luck and stupidity until the fit passed. Breathing heavily, he gripped the steering wheel, grinding the fake leather like he was wringing a chicken's neck. "Plan fucking *B*," he said, his voice cold. He lowered his forehead to the wheel. "All we had to do was have a simple plan B." *But we never considered for a second that we would need it.* "Totally unpre-fucking-*pared*." *Not just unprepared*, he thought. *We were stupid!*

Secure in their naive confidence they could talk themselves out of any problem, they had presented their real ID's to the clerk. It wouldn't take a Lieutenant Columbo to put two and two together and come up with "Jack and Mason in the tunnel with the guard". Even *if* Mason got away, he had no way to call Jack because his cell phone was sitting *right there* in the seat beside him, plugged into the outlet to charge. Worse, Mason had committed an assault on a guard in the middle of DC, and that meant Federal involvement even before they discovered the missing file. He felt the folder through his shirt, *Which they* will *do.*

Jack unbuttoned the shirt and pulled the file out to set it on the seat beside him. He opened the cover and flipped through a few pages. It wasn't long before he realized he would need Mason to decipher the data within. Even if what he was looking for was there, it was lost in a sea of tables of numbers and acronyms. He closed the cover and rubbed his temples with both hands. He was pretty sure they had both just committed a felony, and no amount of talking would get them out of this. Turning himself in wasn't an option, though. No one was going to believe his story from jail. He would have to tie it all up in a neat little bow before he did that.

He looked at Mason's cell. *The Feds can track the phones,* he thought, *but they'll need a court order first, and that will take some time.* He guessed he had between two and eight hours before the phones were useless. Jack grabbed Mason's phone and pulled it apart, removing the battery. *At least they can't track this one.* In a few hours he would be forced to do the same to his own phone, and if Mason hadn't somehow called by then, Jack would have to find someone else to help.

Mark Peters was the only other person who knew what was going on that gave a damn, but he was back in Tennessee. He needed someone not connected to everything. Someone who couldn't be tied to his actions over the past month. Someone he could trust. *And, preferably, someone in the area.*

That subset of his friends and acquaintances narrowed down to exactly *one.*

* * *

You have been careless.

The Others would brook no argument in this matter, though they were as much at fault as he. Kept awake the entire trip to Washington, the Others punished him for his plodding response after his most recent failure to confront Dieter. The things they forced him to do before he left were... *worse.*

You will deviate from your current path to focus on Dr. Braun.

"But the evidence—"

Is already in the possession of Dr. Hill and Mr. Montgomery. We will deal with them ourselves.

Ever since the Others told him about Montgomery, Thirteen had argued the man could be useful. Montgomery was being directed by Dieter in his quest—that much was obvious—and Thirteen knew Jack's efforts would bring Dieter into the open where he could be dealt with permanently. The Others disagreed. *Focus on the task you are given,* they had said, *and eliminate them if they interfere.*

A charter plane has been secured. You may eat before you board the flight back to Atlanta.

"Dieter is there?" He knew the question was pointless. If they were sending him to Atlanta, then surely Dieter *was* there, but there was no reason for it. Montgomery was in DC, so why was Dieter in Atlanta?

There is another task you must perform there as well.

He was so very tired, but the tasks were never-ending. I will sleep someday, he thought. Someday the final task will be complete, and then... then I will sleep.

* * *

Polizeioberkommissar Rutger Brieske logged off his computer and stood, grabbing his jacket from the back of his chair as he did so. He stretched his back, vertebrae popping like small-weapons fire, and he smiled. It had been a long day, but his search had been fruitful. Ever since the murder at the Düsseldorf hospital, he had been gathering information about similar killings, and the search had taken him far afield. The method the murderer had used matched that of killings going as far back as 1962, and the crime scenes were too close in appearance to be coincidence. At none of them were there any suspects or witnesses, nor did the assassin leave fingerprints or other forensic evidence. Blood loss was minimal, the killing thrust always coming from a stiletto to the back of the neck right at the base of the skull.

More importantly, many of the killings were of suspected Nazi officers or scientists who had managed to avoid capture. Interpol always suspected Nokim, the Jewish death squads formed after World War II, but the killings continued long after that group was discovered and folded into Mossad. More and more, Rutger was convinced these were the actions of a *single* individual.

Individuals have different motivations than groups, and often those are at competing purposes. There were exactly *zero* connections to Nazis—*neo* or otherwise—for the doctor and the nurse. They could be a coincidence, but Rutger didn't think so. *Coincidences are so untidy*, he thought.

"Polizeioberkommissar Brieske?" the junior officer said, poking her head in the doorway.

"Yes?"

"I hate to bother you so late, but an official from Interpol is here to speak with you."

"Interpol here? At this hour?"

"I told him you were on your way home, but he was insistent."

"Ach," Rutger said with growing impatience, and waved the officer away as he walked around his desk. "Show him in."

A much younger man than Rutger expected stepped around the officer as she stood back, and walked into the office, hand extended.

"Detective Inspector Stirling Gershon, Polizeioberkommissar." He grasped Rutger's hand and pumped it twice. "Happy to meet you."

Rutger stepped past the man, closed the door in the young officer's face, then walked back to sit on the edge of his desk. He waved his hand at the empty chair in front, inviting his guest to sit, and said, "What has you visiting at this time of day?"

"Right to it, I see," Gershon said with a smile, nodding approval. His teeth were so white they practically glowed. "I like that."

Rutger just stared, one eyebrow raised.

"Yes, well... we have a few questions about someone you know."

"I know a lot of people," Rutger said, crossing his arms. If Interpol was here questioning him about a friend, this would not be a good day for either of them.

"It's about," he pulled a notepad from his front pocket and flipped through a few pages, "Mr. Jack Montgomery and his involvement in a double homicide."

"Oh, that," Rutger said, waving the conversation off. "We determined early on he was not involved, nor was his companion. I believe they've already returned to the States."

Gershon grimaced and tilted his head. "This isn't about *those* murders, Polizeioberkommissar. I'm afraid he is wanted in Tennessee for the murders of," he flipped another page, "Paul and Martha Banks."

"I don't believe it!" Rutger said before he caught himself.

"Stiletto to the base of the brain just like those in Düsseldorf, and his fingerprints were all over the crime scene." He shook his head, "Nasty business, too. Their poor little dog had been tortured; all four legs broken in multiple places."

Rutger's shoulders slumped. I can't have been so wrong about someone. It's my damn job to read people.

"The FBI is already mounting a manhunt, since they believe he has crossed state lines. Something about a break-in in Washington DC." The man smiled again, this time more predator than jovial houseguest. "We were hoping for some insights from you to help the investigation along."

"Of course," Rutger said at last, his voice weak. "Whatever I can do to help."

CHAPTER 11

THE MOST DIFFICULT PART OF JACK'S SEARCH for the one person that could help him was finding the address. Obtaining it was bad enough; he had to do a bit of cyber-stalking to even get the woman's new last name, but the GPS on his phone hadn't quite been up to the task of finding her home. The thing had him driving in circles for a while before he was able to locate the correct street.

Jack parked four houses away and killed the motor. There was a car in the driveway, but he wanted to bolster his courage before he knocked on the door. He hadn't spoken to her in many years—long before her marriage—and he wasn't sure she would even remember him. The bottle of Jack Daniels he acquired on the drive rested in a brown paper bag on the passenger seat... accusing him. His craving for a drink had yet to overpower his need to remain sober for the encounter, but Jack knew his resolve wouldn't last.

When his phone rang, he jumped in surprise at first, then flipped it open hoping it was Mason, but Amber's name glowed back at him. *Why is she calling now, of all times?* he wondered, his paranoia speaking before his mind fully engaged. Jack stared at the display for several rings, trapped between a fervent desire to hear a friendly voice, and fear both *for* her and *of* her. *What do I really know about Amber?*

The phone stopped ringing, and he continued to stare at the screen. *I'm being ridiculous,* he thought. *She doesn't have anything to do with this.* There was no accompanying chime indicating she had left a voicemail. *I should have answered,* he chastised himself. *She said she would call, and I should have answered.* The fact he hadn't, he knew, was the old fear more than the new. His feelings for Amber had taken him back to when he was a teenager, hoping and wishing for love when he should have been doing something about it.

"I'm a grown-ass man." he said, disgusted. *I don't have to play these adolescent games anymore.* "I *can* call her back."

But he didn't. Instead, he looked at the phone and waited for her to call again while he thought about his next moves. *Without Mason, though, there might not* be *any next moves.* He didn't know anyone else he trusted who could interpret the data in that file. The woman in the house in front of him had once studied to be a doctor, but Jack had no clue what she had done with her education since undergrad.

"It doesn't matter," he said, his hands still glued to the steering wheel. "She's all you've got in this town." He grabbed the file, pursed his lips while staring at the bag with the bottle, then picked that up and shoved it under the seat. Before he got out, he checked himself in the mirror and frowned. "I look like warmed-over dog shit," he said, shaking his head and exiting the car. "Pretty much like the last time she saw me."

Jack walked slowly up the slight incline of the sidewalk, then turned at the mailbox and up the steps to the house. He ran a hand through his hair to smooth it down, then rapped on the door. Inside, a dog barked a couple of times then went silent. There were no sounds of approaching footsteps, but he felt a presence on the other side even before the door opened.

"Yes?" the woman said as she opened the door. She tilted her head a tick when she saw Jack.

"I'm sorry to bother you, Debbie, but I could use some help."

* * *

There was no reason for Rutger *not* to trust the inspector from Interpol, he just knew he didn't. After the man left, the first thing Rutger did was call a friend at the American Embassy. An hour later, much of the Inspector's story was confirmed—Jack *was* being sought for questioning in the double homicide, but he was *not*, at present, a suspect. *The man had exaggerated, if not outright lied*, he thought. *Why would he do that?*

While he waited, he had done some digging on the Inspector. The man was who he claimed to be, but after discovering the family ties, Rutger wondered why the man bothered with a job at all. It appeared that Detective Inspector Stirling Gershon was *connected*... and not just by wealth, but to some very powerful people in Europe. Those connections reached deep into the European Council, as near as Rutger could tell, but he feared they went even higher. His search had stopped dead at that point, all avenues for further information stymied.

Why would such a man be serving at this low a level? he mused as he drove home. Ties like his offer him any number of more powerful and profitable positions. There was more to this story than even Jack had surmised, and Rutger was sure the waves these people might produce would soon have them all foundering in murky waters. It couldn't be a coincidence that one of Gershon's family branches lived in Argentina, and had done so since shortly after the war. More information on that particular branch was unavailable to Rutger, but he knew other people and other methods for unearthing the truth.

What he *wanted* to do—*couldn't* do—was call Jack. Any attempt would look like collusion on his part, and only serve to bring more scrutiny to a potentially innocent man. Of course, there was always the possibility Jack was guilty of the murders, but Rutger *did* know how to read people, and he was as sure of the sun setting in the west that Jack could not have done the things he saw in that file.

He drove in silence, pressing his foot harder against the accelerator, scanning the horizon ahead as the flattened solar orb set the world aglow in amber fire. *Gershon's family in Argentina, Nokim, Mossad... the Shadowman. There* is *a connection, and I* will *find it.*

* * *

"I'm afraid me and Mason are in a bit of trouble," Jack said, sitting on the sofa in the middle of Debbie's tastefully decorated living room. She had been surprised to see him when she opened the door, but recognized him immediately and invited him in. Most women—home alone in the middle of the day—might have done otherwise, but Debbie had always been trusting. At least when it came to Jack. Not so much with Mason. *But then, she had good reason with* him, he thought.

Debbie walked in from the kitchen carrying two saucers, each holding a steaming cup of coffee. She handed one to Jack, then sat in the chair across from him. "Mason is with you?"

"Well..." he stalled, sipping, "we got separated earlier. I'm sure he'll turn up."

"You know," she said over the rim of her cup, "I don't think I've seen either of you in, oh... twelve years," she smiled, "and not a *thing* has changed." He was sure she wasn't talking about his appearance.

"Yes, well..." he started, but couldn't go on. It was more or less *true*, after all, and he smiled back. "Some things have changed. Others," he shrugged, "not so much."

"So..." she placed her cup on the saucer and lowered both to the coffee table, "what's this trouble you two are in?"

Jack set his coffee down as well and pulled the folder from where it sat pinned between his hip and the sofa's arm. He held it out for her to take, and said, "I need someone to interpret what's in here, and you're the only one I can trust."

"Oh my," she said. "Why does that sound ominous?" She took the folder and flipped through a few pages. Without looking up at him, she said, "What makes you think I can help?"

He fidgeted, then picked up his cup and took another sip. "Uh... last I remember, you were studying to be a doctor, right?"

"*Was*, yes. The truth is, I shifted to research after... well, after." She closed the cover of the file and placed one hand on top as she looked up at Jack.

He knew what she meant. *After Mason*. It was an open secret she had wanted to marry him, but Mason couldn't keep it in his pants while they were dating in school, and he wasn't too picky about where it went, either.

"Yes, well..." Jack didn't know what to say. He looked around the room, and said, "When do you expect your husband will be home?"

"Oh, around 2011," she said with a wry grin. "Give or take."

"I'm sorry, Debbie," he said after a long pause. "I didn't know."

"No reason why you should." She chuckled and shook her head. "It seems my taste in men did not improve after Mason." She set the folder on the table and picked up her cup. A wave of sadness washed over her face then, and she said, "I am truly sorry about your wife and daughter, Jack." He could tell she wanted to say more, but thankful she left it at that.

His face warmed and he fought to control his emotions as his mind drifted to the car and the bottle under the seat. It was calling him more insistently than ever, and he cursed himself for listening. Hands shaking, he lowered the cup back to it's saucer, the two rattling as he set it in the center. "That folder is connected to their deaths, I'm afraid," he said, his voice softer than he intended.

Debbie looked at the file, then back up to his face. "I don't understand," she said.

"It's a long story," he said, shoulders slumping. He sighed, and in a stronger voice he told her everything that had happened to that point, along with his and Mason's theories about what might be happening. He told her about Kazakhstan, Montabaur, Düsseldorf, Beth and Riley, his pen-pal, and the Shadowman. She sat straighter, eyes widening with each new revelation. She nodded in places and tilted her head in others. After he ran out of words, she sat in silence for a long time.

Jack allowed her time to process everything, but something nagged at the back of his mind. After thinking back over the conversation, he noticed she was most attentive when he mentioned the heavy metals Mason had found in the blood sample. He realized he had never inquired about her change of major.

"What type of research do you do?" he asked, looking up into her eyes.

"Medical nanotechnology, Jack," she said with a raised eyebrow. "And I have to tell you, if this file," she tapped the cover with a hard finger, "is somehow connected to your wife and daughter's deaths, then you have a bigger problem than you thought."

* * *

Cold, wet, and filthy, Mason huddled in a space behind a dumpster near the hospital. After catching the guard and laying him gingerly to the floor, he hobbled to the ladder. The voices were too close and approaching too fast, so he climbed to the top and moved the cover off, then slid back down to hide behind a bundle of cables in a nearby alcove. It had taken only minutes for the local security team to satisfy themselves that Mason had, indeed, escaped up the ladder and into the night. They didn't even bother to give the tunnel a cursory examination, or they would have found him. Still, Mason stayed where he was for another two hours before climbing back up and out.

His ankle bore his weight, but every step was agony. The dumpster was good cover for now, but it was broad daylight, and the odor and the flies were out in force. If he stuck to the alleyways, no one would see him as anything other than a bum. Two police cars had already passed him without a second look. *Probably had more important things to do,* he thought. *Definitely more important criminals to find.*

He grinned. *I guess I am a criminal now.* Mason shook his head and stood, then shuffled from his hiding place. He checked his wallet, but already knew what he would find there... lots of credit cards and little cash. *How long before the cards are put on hold by the cops? Can they track me through the purchases?*

He was being paranoid. Sure, they *could* track him, but his offense didn't warrant such attention. *Besides, it would take days for them to get the necessary court order.*

There was no way to call a cab, and he didn't know where he would go, regardless. He and Jack had never bothered to set up some place to meet if things went south. "We'll figure out the rest later," he said, slapping his forehead. "How stupid can two men be?" *What I really need is my phone, but that's with Jack, of course.*

"First things, first," he said. "Time to see if I can get some clean clothes." Catch-22. No cab would pick him up the way he looked—and smelled—but the closest places to buy new clothes were too far to hike on his throbbing ankle. Finding a *phone*, however, would take a little more effort. He could get a pre-paid phone, but those were usually found at big-box stores or a local cell-phone store. He didn't see any of those nearby, either.

The insistent *ching-ching* of a cyclist's bell caught his attention, and he turned his head just as the pedi-cab trundled toward him. The man pedaling made decent headway even with three people crammed into the buggy. Mason smiled and shrugged, thinking, *What the hell?,* and pulled the two lonely fives from his wallet. He waved them at the cabbie as he passed, and the man nodded with a smile.

Mason sat on the curb and waited for the pedi-cab's return, propping his swollen ankle on an empty box. The rumbling in his belly reminded him that his last meal was a bag of peanuts on the plane.

"Clothes first, *then* I'll feed ya," he said to his complaining middle.

* * *

"I'm not sure it *could* get any worse, Debbie," Jack said, shaking his head. He hadn't stopped long enough to consider the ramifications of what little he had discovered over the course of the past two days. Everything had been a blur of motion, working from one event to the next, unseen forces dragging him in their wake. He had, in fact, been actively pursuing this mystery almost from the day he entered Kazakhstan. There was too much information pounding the surf of his sanity, threatening to erode what little remained. The number of deaths connected to these revelations *alone* set him on his heels... when he took the time to think about it.

Now Debbie was telling him it could be *worse?*

"Someone has made a significant breakthrough," she screwed up her mouth, adding, "and if they're already releasing this into the wild..." She shrugged her shoulders, palms up. "This is *bad*, Jack."

"Um... *how* bad?"

"Depends," she said, opening the file and pointing at a single set of numbers. "I recognize this particular list of elements." She looked at him across the gulf, a lifetime of study separating them, and said, "Most of these are the building blocks of nano-*machines*, Jack." She waited for him to say something, the look in her eyes full of hope that he understood. He didn't.

She sighed and rolled her eyes. "Some nano structures are for transporting drugs, while some are passively diagnostic. The most difficult to make, though, are those that perform a complicated *function*." She shook her head, reading the file as she spoke. "A nano-machine is a robot, capable—in theory—of performing programmed tasks on a molecular scale." She looked up again, searching his face for comprehension. "I've been working in this field for over a decade, Jack—*no one* has made such machines yet."

"O-kayyy..." he drawled, "so someone has done this on the sly, somehow. I'm still not getting the bad."

Debbie huffed a heavy sigh and shook her head again. "The *bad* is if these things are self-replicating."

He tilted his head. "You mean like a virus?"

"*Exactly*," she said, pouncing on his growing understanding. "If they are one-shot machines, like a programmable drug, that's bad enough. If they can reproduce, however, I'm not sure anyone can put *that* genie back in the bottle." She leaned back in her chair and crossed her legs, one foot dangling and bouncing in the air. "The worst part is there are no publications, no peer-reviewed studies, and no way to track what they've done. Hell, I bet they did no real testing to make sure the little critters couldn't escape their programming."

"How can someone smart enough to make these things be dumb enough not to test them properly?" he said.

"Oh, Jack," she laughed, "so naive. You have no *idea* how stupid smart people can be."

He smiled back at her. "Believe me Deb, I know *exactly* how dumb they can be," he said with a grimace. "Which brings me to the main reason I came to you."

"Oh," she said, sobering, "surely there can't be anything more important than this file."

"Not so much more important as more urgent," he said. Taking a deep breath, then letting it out slowly, he said, "Mason is missing somewhere in DC—possibly under arrest—and that file is stolen property."

"Oh dear, Jack, you buried the *lead*," she said. "Arrested?"

"Possibly," he said. "He hasn't contacted me since we got separated after we... *acquired* the file." Sketching the morning's events for her while she blanched at the tale, he realized just how crazy everything sounded.

"Knowing the both of you, if he was arrested, you would be the first person he would call. But if he *wasn't* arrested, he should have called by now.

Jack shrugged, "His phone is in my car."

"Well," she said, tapping her chin with a manicured nail, "I don't know anyone offhand who could check on his arrest status, but since I work at the hospital, I *could* make a discreet inquiry on any activity by security."

"That would certainly help," he said, grateful. What he wanted to do was drive the streets around the hospital, shouting Mason's name out the window like he was looking for a lost puppy. He grinned at that. *He kinda* is *a bit like a lost puppy.* The car, however, was registered in his name, and the cops *had* to have that information by now. He would need Debbie's car if he wanted to go anywhere without being stopped.

"Let me make a few calls," she said as she stood. "And since your stomach has been yelling at me for the past ten minutes, why don't I make you a late lunch while I'm up."

He blushed, and said, "That would be great, but I don't want to put you out."

"It's no problem, Jack," she said arching an eyebrow. "It's been a while since I've made a meal for more than one, but I'm sure I remember how."

She left him there, and he sat back and wondered what to do next. If Mason *was* in jail, he certainly couldn't walk in and bail him out, nor could he ask Debbie to do so. She would, he was sure, but asking was a bridge too far. He had what he needed, anyway—confirmation that there was something in Becky's blood that shouldn't have been there. From there it was a simple matter to connect her to the other kids... and Mark Jr. He didn't *need* Mason at this point and could try to get to South Carolina and turn himself in to his brother, Bill. With Bill's help, everything might be straightened out without charges being filed.

Of course, that meant leaving Mason at the mercy of DC officials while he did. He shook his head. *That's just not gonna happen.* Even if it *was* the most practical option, he couldn't do it. *I'm just buying trouble, anyway,* he thought. *Mason may still be out there, somewhere.* Leaving him alone in DC might be even worse than leaving him in jail.

Jack rested his head against the back of the sofa, closing his eyes to think. Within seconds the fatigue he had kept dammed attacked his body with unrestrained fervor, and soon he was snoring.

* * *

Jack woke with a start, the incessant buzz from his cell phone rousing him after what seemed like only a few minutes of peace. Debbie still rattled pots and pans in the kitchen, so he guessed his slumber had not been long. He didn't feel refreshed, regardless.

He sighed and pulled the phone from his pocket just as it stopped ringing. There were four calls from a number he didn't recognize, each within a minute of the other, and before he could put it away, the phone buzzed again. It was the same number. Normally he didn't answer unknown callers, but this one was too persistent.

"Hello?" he said.

"Jack, thank *God.*" The voice on the other end was clearly Mark Peters, but Jack had the man's number in his phone. "I've been so worried you had been arrested," he said, his voice shaky and breathless.

How did he know about this morning? he thought, but to Mark, he said, "What's wrong, Mark?"

"They're *dead*, Jack. Both of them."

Dead? Who was he—

"The cops have already questioned me, even the FBI, but they are focusing on *you* for some reason."

"Mark... slow down. Who the hell are you talking about?"

"Paul and Martha. It's all over the damn *news*. Haven't you seen it?"

Jack slumped in his seat, and his hands shook as he held the phone tighter against his ear. *Damn. Two more bodies added to the list. Two more good people—innocent people—on a growing ledger that he was now determined to balance.* "How did they die?" he asked, his voice hard, already knowing the answer.

Mark took a shuddering breath on the other end, and said, "It was some kind of *execution*. That was all I could get from the cops who talked to me. I went there this morning to see if Paul knew anything else, and the police were already there. They questioned me for *hours*, Jack, and all they wanted to know was about *you*."

"Why me?"

"They said yours were the only other fingerprints in the house, but that can't be right—I was there, too."

"Did you tell them that?"

"I'm not an idiot," he said without hesitation, the sneer clear in his voice. "I figured it would be better if I wasn't in jail."

"Where are you calling from?"

"A friend's phone, but even that's probably not wise."

"No," Jack said, "probably not." Jack's phone, if not compromised yet, soon would be. Mark's was sure to be watched as well. "Get yourself a pre-paid phone and call this number," he gave him Debbie's, "tomorrow afternoon, and someone will give you my new number. Call me then and we'll talk some more." He leaned forward. "Mark, I didn't have anything to do with this."

"Hell, I know that, Jack. The time of death was after you two were on the plane to DC."

Jack closed his eyes and sighed, the breath pulling the tension from his chest. "Did you tell them *that*?"

"Sure, but they weren't interested," he said, then hesitated. "Jack... they are saying out loud that you are only a person of interest, but the body language is clear—they're comin' after you guns blazing."

Why? Jack mused. *People are murdered every day, and they already know I didn't do this.* He had seen events spiral out of control more than once in his life—usually when there was a dearth of information and a wealth of anger—but this was beyond anything in his memory. It hit him, then—a cold splash in his face, clearing his vision. *Someone's aiming the cops at me.* It would have to be someone powerful enough to compromise the FBI as well.

Mark was still talking, "...and please be careful, Jack."

"Don't worry, Mark. I will."

He was about to hang up when Mark said, "It was weird what happened to the dog."

"What's that? You mean Pig?" The yappy little dog appeared in his mind, begging to be scratched.

"Yeah," Mark said, then paused. "He was *tortured.* Someone snapped the bones in all four legs, but the cops said the guy then took the time to sedate him, set the breaks, *and* tape on splints." Mark sighed "Who would *do* such a thing?"

Jack didn't know if Mark meant the murders, the torture, or the care for the dog. *And he had likely done it while the two corpses looked on.* He shivered at the thought, then shook off his revulsion. There were things that needed to be done.

"Tomorrow afternoon," he said at last, and ended the call. Jack looked at his phone for a few seconds, then sighed and disassembled it, removing the battery. *I'll have to ditch it somewhere for good measure,* he thought. *Along with Mason's.* His thoughts drifted to his friend. *They don't know Mason was with me in Tennessee, but they surely know he's here in DC.* He rubbed his temples, a mild throbbing in his head threatening to grow into a massive drum solo.

"You ready for some lunch?" Debbie called out from the kitchen.

"Yeah... about that," he said, standing. "Can I get it to go?"

She stepped into the living room, wiping her hands with a dish-towel, and said, "You're leaving?"

He nodded. "And I need to borrow your car." She hesitated, confusion on her face, and he said, "I'll be back soon, but then I'll need you to do something for me."

CHAPTER 12

WHILE NOT ENTIRELY REFRESHED, Mason felt cleaner, at least. He walked out of the store wearing new—and a bit itchy— jeans and t-shirt, and had even purchased new sneakers and socks. The others were old anyway, and too soaked to wear.

He tossed the bundle of wet clothes in a trash bin outside the store and flagged a cab. Most of those passing were full, but one pulled to a stop in front of him, and he crawled inside.

"Pentagon City Mall, please," he said to the driver.

The man turned his head, looking over his shoulder, and said, "If you just want to shop, there are closer places. And if your heart's set on Pentagon City, you can take the subway for less."

"That's okay," Mason said, "I'm gonna need you to wait while I shop, then take me to a second address."

"Your dime," he said with a smile, and drove into the nightmare that was Washington traffic.

Every mall Mason had ever been in boasted a place to get a cheap pre-paid phone, but the little shopping centers were hit-or-miss. He had already spent too much time in the open and was beginning to feel like he was being watched. *Time for this gopher to go to ground,* he thought as his stomach growled. *Ground... ground beef!*

"Hey, where's a good drive-through around here?"

"There's a McDonald's up ahead," the cabbie said without turn-ing.

"I said *good.*"

"Oh, well, if you can wait a few minutes, there's Willie's Barbeque."

"Sold!" Mason said, and sat back against the threadbare seat. No one outside of the Deep South understood what real barbeque was, so he was interested to taste Willie's interpretation.

He was stalling, and he knew it. Soon he would have to swallow his pride and beg for help from the one person he would never ask under normal circumstances. *Without a secure place to crash, I'm a sitting duck out here.* He sighed and settled back into the cab's seat, going over the past few days in his head. Everything spiraled out of control faster than he could process all the bits and pieces into a coherent whole, and he was acting on instinct more than anything. Like his decision to sit with Betsy when Jack and Mark entered the house to speak with Paul. It was a lark, really—nothing more than the fact that she shared a name with his truck—but she was the one who provided the *exact* information they needed to find the file. *She's not all there, but at least that was reliable.*

Jack was doing much the same, he knew—reacting instead of planning—but the events of the past two days left them little time to plan, regardless. Their current situation was the most obvious result. *Obviously,* he thought, *we are* not *secret agents.* It never occurred to either of them to plan for what happened that morning.

How the hell do you plan for a complete fuckup?

He raised an eyebrow and tugged his bottom lip. Probably the same way you do research, dumbass. Account for every variable, and every possible bit of bias. He shook his head and snorted. Maybe play some chess instead of goddamn checkers.

Even *that* might not be enough. Someone out there was playing chess, all right, but it was of the three-dimensional variety, while he and Jack were still just trying to see the *board.*

Where are you, buddy?

* * *

Jack was beginning to understand the mind-set of the idiot Birthers and 9-11 Truthers, his paranoia kicking into overdrive as he prowled the streets of DC in Debbie's car. The first thing he did was find an ATM and withdraw as much money from his savings as the machine would allow. His credit card transactions were sure to be traced by now, but cash was the first choice among criminals for a reason. What he had wasn't going to take him very far, but he couldn't take a chance at another machine so soon. Not in DC.

There were a couple of times while he drove around the hospital that he was sure he was being followed. That was not only crazy thinking, but easily dispelled with a few unplanned turns. Even if the whole of the FBI were searching for him, there was no way they knew he was using this car, nor could they know where he would be at any given moment. He was a living example of Heisenberg's Uncertainty Principle.

He looked up at the rear-view mirror and the little logo for OnStar, and thought, *I guess they* could *track me with that if they knew I was in this particular car.* With that thought, the paranoia hit him again full-force, and he hunched down in the car while he scanned every direction. A helicopter passed overhead, and he ducked like he had been shot at.

Screw this, he thought, turning the wheel. Time to get a damn phone and head back to Deb's.

As soon as Debbie entered his mind, she morphed into Amber. He had never returned Amber's call, and she hadn't called back before he dismantled his phone. Both his and Mason's phones were now scattered over a large area around National Mall, so there was no chance to contact her until he purchased a new phone. The only question that remained was should he?

If anyone in law enforcement had half a brain, they had already made a connection based on what happened in Germany. That meant it was at least *possible* Amber's phone was being tapped while they waited for him to contact her.

And he *wanted* to contact her. More than anything else—even more than finding Mason, if he were being honest with himself—he needed to talk to Amber. If for no other reason than to warn her.

Two more people are dead, he thought, strangling the steering wheel in his hands. The last four—that he knew of—were all people who died within a day of meeting him. He was Typhoid Mary, unwittingly spreading death in his wake, immune to the dangers he passed to those he touched. By his actions today, he had put Debbie in danger as well.

"It's not your fault," his insurance-provided therapist had told him, "but you will *feel* responsible for the rest of your life. You'll carry that with you always, but only *you* get to decide how it shapes you."

If I stop this now and go home, will everyone be safe?

Jack shook his head, not knowing the answer, not even sure it mattered. He couldn't stop, regardless. There was too much the Shadowman had to pay for now.

Too much he owes me.

* * *

Sally pulled her car into the garage, the door already closing noisily behind her. Derek wasn't home yet, but that was good—she was in no mood to talk to anyone right now. The garage door rattled as it hit the floor, and Sally killed the engine and stepped out into the gloom of the single overhead bulb. Derek insisted that the thing was bright enough "once your eyes got used to it," but she had never stayed in there long enough to find out.

First one home makes dinner was a hard and fast rule in their home, but Sally wasn't in the mood for *that*, either. *Derek will just have to make do with takeout.* She grabbed her briefcase from the front seat and slammed the car door, then her shoulders slumped as she leaned her forehead to the car's window and cried. The tears flowed and her chest heaved, and she dropped the case. She hugged herself, turned, and leaned her back against the car, legs buckling as she lowered herself beside the fallen briefcase. The wracking sobs that she had held back for the last two hours overcame her defenses in waves that would not be denied.

Ever since the Special Agent from the FBI left her office, she had kept her emotions in check. She didn't—*couldn't*—believe the story she had been told, but her belief was irrelevant. Jack was being sought in a *murder* case, and even Mason was somehow involved. The FBI Agent had left the impression that Jack was going to be taken *one way or the other*; anyone helping him would be under suspicion as well, and likely to receive similar treatment.

"Fuck that," Sally said, wiping her eyes. "If Jack or Mason calls, I'll do what's *right*." She struggled to her feet, grabbing the workbench nearby to pull herself up. "And if that means turning them in, I'll do that." *But I'll follow my own conscience.* She sure wouldn't do it just because some government puke told her to.

For most of her adult life, she followed the maxim "What Would Daddy Do?" It served her well when presented with thorny moral questions, and had never failed her once in all her years of government service. She often wished she could install the man's voice in every government official she met. *Life would be so much easier*, she thought, snuffling and wiping her eyes again. She pulled a handkerchief from a pocket and blew her nose with a loud honk, adjusted her jacket, grabbed her briefcase, and walked to the door of her home.

"Hey, Becker," she said to the half-blind old poodle that greeted her when she opened the door. She reached down to scratch behind his ears, and the irascible little dog growled. "Only dog I know that growls when he's happy," she said to him. She stood straight and shooed him away with a slight nudge, and he growled again before walking to his food dish. "I'll get to you," she said. Sniffing the air, Sally walked to the kitchen island and set her case there, then noticed the Crockpot on the counter by the stove.

"That old man's good for a surprise now and again, isn't he?" she said to Becker. She lifted the lid and inhaled deeply, the scent of a slow-cooked roast dispelling some of her foul mood. "He better get home soon, though, or we're liable to have this finished before he gets here, right boy?" she said. Sally sat at the kitchen table, then bent down to gather Becker up to her lap. He growled as he nestled closer, and she smiled, patting him on the back.

She sighed, long and heavy, and waited. The turmoil in her head was calmed some by the intoxicating aroma of food she didn't have to prepare. "I hope you are all right, Jack," she said in a whispered prayer. She sniffed again, tears threatening to flow. "Find a way to sort this out before it's too late."

* * *

Amber sat in her car, still and silent as a mouse, and watched from a distance as the men with FBI printed in large yellow letters on their backs cleaned out Jack's apartment. Box after box, carried by burly men, stuffed into a dark windowless van and driven away to parts unknown.

She had come to his apartment for the second time today, now concerned that every time she called, it went straight to voicemail. Too afraid to get out of her car, she knew that simply driving away after pulling in might attract their attention. *Sitting here and watching them like a stalker will do that just as well*, she thought. She had to do *something*, but as she drummed her fingers on the steering wheel, she couldn't think of *what*.

The office for the apartment complex was near enough that she decided to walk there and pretend to get information. It would burn up more time than she wanted to spend, but to make the deception stick she might have to follow through and actually apply. Amber sighed, thinking of the time wasted, and got out. The buzz from her phone startled her, freezing her in place. She took the phone from her purse and stared at the screen with her eyebrows knitted. *I don't recognize the number, but that area code is definitely not from around here.*

Her period of indecision stretched until the phone grew silent, and she started to replace it when it buzzed again. She sighed and took a chance, biting her lip.

"Hello?" she said, a quiver in her voice.

"Amber! Thank God you answered," Jack said.

"*Jack...* I'm sitting outside your apartment right now. Where are you?" Her voice cracked, and she struggled to breathe. She didn't realize until this very moment how much she wanted to hear his voice. Like a drug, it increased her heart rate, flushing her cheeks.

"I can't say—"

"Jack, there are men from the FBI cleaning out your apartment, and—"

"Yeah," he said, sounding far away—his mind somewhere other than his body. "I figured as much." There was a silence, only his breathing and some surrounding noise that could have been traffic. "Listen... you need to get out of there. Don't go home. There's a lot you don't know about... or maybe you do if you've watched the news today..." Another long pause.

"Are you okay?" she asked in a soft whisper. "Why is the FBI at your apartment?"

He paused, the silence maddening for her. "Please, Amber, no matter what you hear, I need you to trust me," he said, an eerie calm in his voice. "Your life could depend on it."

"But—"

"Copy the number from your phone's screen, then take it apart and throw it away. Get as much cash as you can and go get a pre-paid phone. Call this number when you do, and I'll explain everything... I promise."

"Jack, come over and we'll—"

"*Please*, Amber... trust me," he said, sounding harried. "Do *not* go home. Just call me when you get a phone. The one in your hand is likely being monitored already."

"I don't understand *any* of this, Jack."

"Neither do I, but I *will*," he said. "I've got to go." He hung up, leaving her to stare at the phone in her hand.

She chewed on a strand of her hair for a few seconds. If I go into the office now, and they are looking for me, they might notice my car sitting here. If I leave now, they might ignore me. There were too many "mights" in there for her taste, but her options were limited and equally inferior. Just like voting, she thought. But like that activity, the only thing left to do was hold your nose and pull a lever. Doing nothing is a choice, as well. Amber turned the key to start the car, backed out, and like Chewbacca, "flew casually" by the agents and out of the parking lot.

No one seemed to take notice of her car as it passed. They were focused on the task of destroying a man's life.

What do they think he did? she thought as she pulled into traffic. It was light this time of the evening, and she didn't have to wait long to turn onto the main road. Every second she spent in the men's sight was an eternity, and she was sure every pair of eyes were on her back. No one stopped her, though, or even lifted their head from their work. *If this were related to the murders in Germany, surely they would have picked me up as well.*

Don't go home, Jack had said, but that didn't make sense. They weren't looking for her. *Yet.* Still, there were too many things she needed if she were going on an extended leave. She sniffed, looking at her phone, and said, "And what's up with ditching my cell for a *pre-paid* one?"

It all came down to *trust*, and to whom she gave it. She didn't know Jack well enough to trust him, and yet she found that she did. Moreover, she knew his heart—or *hoped* she did. It was beyond stupid to place so much trust in someone she met only weeks ago. And yet...

"Okay, Jack," she said. "I'll get the damn phone and some cash... but that's as far as I go until I hear the whole thing."

That felt like the right decision, and she nodded once to herself. She drove east, looking for the nearest Walmart, the dusk at her back fading to a full gloaming. The dark wrapped her car in its embrace and swallowed it whole.

* * *

When Debbie opened the door, Jack knew right away something was up. Her chin tucked close to her chest, her posture more annoyed than sheepish. Debbie ushered him in the foyer, then checked outside briefly, and said, "He got here not long after you left."

"Who?" Jack asked, fearful of the answer. There was no car parked outside other than hers and his rental, but that didn't mean it couldn't be the police.

"*Mason*, Jack," she said, leading him by the arm toward her living room. "I've brought him up to speed with as much as I know, and he's pretty shaken up, pacing the floor the whole time you've been gone. I just got him settled down when you knocked."

Jack stepped into the living room and Mason jumped from the sofa like a shot, wrapping Jack in a bear hug that forced all the air from his lungs in one great *whoosh*.

"Calm down, Mace," Jack said, laughing.

Mason stepped back and punched him in the arm. "I've been worried about you the whole damn day, and here I find you've been having lunch with my ex."

"I've been doing a *bit* more than that," Jack said, rubbing his bruised bicep. "I had to get some cash and a new phone, *and* look for you while I was out." He stepped back, tilting his head at his friend, "How the hell did you get away? Last I saw, you were going all Greco-Roman on a guard."

"Luck, mostly," Mason said with a wry grin. "That, and about a million volts of electricity."

Jack smiled back, and said, "You'll have to tell me all about it later." He slapped Mason on the back, then sobered, saying, "I've got a lot to tell you, too, but that will have to wait." He looked sideways at Debbie, not sure what he could say in front of her at this point. He still hadn't told her about the murders and the fact he was a suspect. Mason needed to know everything, but knowing *right now* was not necessary.

"Damn right it will have to wait," Mason said. "You realize we have to ditch the car as well as our phones."

Jack's brow furrowed, and he said, "The phones are done, but why the car?"

"In case you didn't know, my slow-witted friend, most rental companies lo-jack those things."

"Oh," Jack said, considering. Then, "Oh *shit.*"

"Yeah," Mason said.

"I don't understand," Debbie spoke up from behind.

Mason turned gave her an apologetic grin. "We didn't exactly hide our identity at the hospital. The cops have Jack's name from the sign-in, and by now have traced his credit card activity and found the rental." He pointed at Jack and shook his head. "*Also* in his name." He shrugged. "It shouldn't take them long to get a court order for the tracking information."

Jack pulled at his bottom lip, and said, "The fact they aren't already here means we might have a little time." He turned to Debbie and said, "I'll have to borrow your car again."

"Already way ahead of you, Jack," Mason said, shaking his head. "I've got a cab on retainer around the corner." He looked at Debbie, raising an eyebrow. "I wasn't sure what kind of reception I'd get."

She smirked, and said, "Of course."

"Okay," Jack said, interrupting their moment, "Mason will drive the rental to one of their drop-offs and leave it while I follow—"

"Wait," Mason said, his eyebrows nearly meeting in the middle of his forehead, "why am *I* driving the car?"

"Trust me... it's better if I don't get caught," Jack said. "I'll fill you in on the details later."

"O-*kay*..." Mason said, drawing the word out like an accusation.

Jack ignored him and turned back to Debbie. "While we're doing that, is it possible for you to get that file back in the records room?"

"I thought you needed that," she said, confused.

"If it's possible, make a copy first," he said, "but if they haven't yet noticed it's missing, then putting it back means they can only get Mason... *us*... for trespassing."

Mason tilted his head a fraction at Jack's pause and clarification. He was on the cusp of asking a question, but Jack cut him off. "We'll all meet back here in, what... an hour enough time?"

"Better make it two," she said.

He grabbed a pen from his pocket, took a napkin from the coffee table, and wrote. "Anything looks hinkey, either at the house or on your way back, call this number," he said, handing her the napkin. "That's my new cell."

Jack fished the keys to the rental from his pocket and tossed them to Mason. "Take me to the cab, then we'll follow you to the rental company." He looked at each in turn, then said, "Everyone know what to do?"

They both nodded.

"Good. Let's get to it, then."

* * *

In all his travels, this was Thirteen's first trip to Atlanta. The Others still had not told him what his mission was, but it was of no consequence. When they were ready, they would give him the information he needed. And when they did, he would act. His ability to perform his duties was never in question.

The Others kept his mind walled off and his consciousness shut down more and more these days. He shrugged mentally at this impediment. It allowed his psyche time to rest between each horrific act he was forced to commit. Those acts were now his entire existence—a strand of cultured black pearls, unbroken and maleficent. If there were an escape from his hell, he had not found it.

"The Others are giving you a great gift," Dieter had said more than fifty years ago. "Your performance in Dallas has set you apart, Thirteen." The man who once treated him like a brother stood before him with respect—and fear—in his eyes. "What they offer will keep you from harm. I don't understand your hesitation."

Thirteen was already an effective tool, and did not need further *improving*, but Dieter was who he was. "I am as you made me, and I am content with that," he said to the older man. "You should be as well."

"They will not allow you to refuse, you know," Dieter had said, his gaze drifting to the stone floor. He had always averted his eyes when delivering news with which he did not agree. "You will thank them in time," he said, but Thirteen had known neither of them believed it.

No gift comes without cost.

Thirteen's first stop upon arrival was the apartment belonging to Jack Montgomery, but it had already been violated by the FBI. Still, he took time to look through the whole of the place, wandering into each of the three rooms, careful to leave the mess undisturbed. He had paused at the picture of the man's family—so happy in their ignorance—and touched each face with a gloved hand. The photograph was *wrong*, not showing reality as it was but a fantasy of what had once been. He removed the glove and lingered over the image of the little girl.

There is no repairing such damage, he mused, and turned toward the door. He now knew the two tasks the Others had set for him in this city, and his first was nearby. He walked down the steps, turning left at the bottom toward his car. There was a motorcycle parked in the slot closest to the stairs, and he stopped in front of it, tilting his head at the little bell hanging from the underside of the frame. It was an odd place for such a thing, and he understood at once it was some kind of totem. The knowledge of the thing penetrated his reverie, but he brushed it aside with a mental wave of his hand.

Some things should remain a mystery, and he smiled, the corners of his mouth a soft curl. The pressure in his mind pushed him ever onward.

CHAPTER 13

"**W**ELL, THAT'S DONE, AT LEAST," Mason said, sliding into the seat next to Jack. "Didn't take as long as I thought it would," he said, checking the time on his new phone. "We've still got about an hour before we meet Debbie back at her place. How about we grab something to eat?"

Jack shook his head. "Damn, Mason... is food all you think about?"

"What can I say," he said, patting his stomach, "I'm a growin' boy."

Jack watched his friend with fascination. *He's able to make anything sound like a trip to the beach.* He couldn't count the number of times Mason had pulled him out of a blue funk so debilitating Jack hadn't bothered to eat for days at a time. The man had become the one true constant in his life, dragging him through the muck that was his existence. If he hadn't been there after Beth and Riley... Jack couldn't think about food, though. There was a hunger in his belly for something besides meat and potatoes, and he feared feeding one would wake the other.

"So," Mason said, slapping his thigh, "what's the news you couldn't share with Deb?"

Jack nodded to the cabbie, then said to Mason, "Maybe here's not so good, either."

"Hey, Sohrab," Mason said to the cab driver, "how's about you introduce my friend here to Willie's?" He turned to Jack. "You're gonna love this place!"

"No problem," the man said over his shoulder. "Like I said, it's your dime."

Jack's brow furrowed, and he said to Mason, "How much have you paid this guy to hang around?"

"Standard rate," he said, and then winked. "Plus a fat tip."

"I've never known you to carry much cash. You must have hit the ATM like I did."

"Oh yeah," Mason said. "I figured we wouldn't have the ability to use our credit cards much longer."

Jack nodded his approval. He had been afraid to visit more than one machine, but he had grabbed the limit from his savings, and still had over four hundred left.

"How much did you get?"

Mason leaned closer, and whispered, "Only about five grand."

"Holy shit, Mace!" he said, leaning away, eyes wide. "Are you serious?"

"As a heart attack," Mason said, thumping his chest with a fist. He laughed, and said, "Sohrab took me on a nice path pointing due North while I hit up about ten ATM's for cash. If anyone checks, they'll think I'm headed to Canada."

"Son of a bitch," Jack said, disgusted with himself. "Why the hell didn't *I* think of that?"

"How much did *you* get?"

"Never mind," Jack said, now more depressed than ever. The cab bounced once as it turned off the road and into the parking lot of Willie's.

"Don't worry, buddy," Mason said, patting Jack on the back. "My treat." He said to the driver, "You want anything?"

"Nah, I'm good."

"C'mon, Jack," Mason said, opening his door, "you'll love this place. Almost as good as home."

Jack sneered. He shared Mason's disdain for barbecue north of the Mason-Dixon Line. "I seriously doubt that."

* * *

Mason was shaken, Jack could see that clear enough, but the man continued to eat. Jack had to admit the food was more than acceptable, and he chewed his sandwich in silence, thinking about everything he had just told Mason. *It sounds crazy when you string it all together.* The idea that he could kill *anyone*—much less a sweet man like Paul—was

154

laughable in any other situation, and the fact that the cops were likely to shoot Jack on sight was crazier still. *I'm not afraid to die, though. I just don't want to do it before I have a chance to catch the bastard who did kill them.*

The truth was, Jack not only wasn't afraid to die, but until recently had embraced the concept with anticipation. He didn't believe in an afterlife, so he knew he wouldn't be seeing his family afterward. *Gone is gone*, he thought. *I just want the damn pain and guilt to go away.* He lived in the South, so everyone he knew was a believer. Sally once asked him where he thought his consciousness would go after death, if there were no Heaven.

"I don't know," he had replied. "Where do you go when you're asleep and you don't dream? Where were you before you were born?"

She had clammed up at that point, shaking her head. She hadn't bothered him again about it.

"Dead is dead," he whispered.

"What's that?" Mason said after swallowing.

"Nothing," Jack said. "I just hope we don't get anyone else killed, is all."

Mason put down his sandwich, "Jack... those people—*all* of them—that's not our fault."

"It's easy to say that, Mace, but people are dying anyway. Ask yourself... would they be dead if we had just stayed home?"

"Maybe, maybe not," he said. "What I still don't get is why?"

Jack's eyes narrowed. "Isn't it obvious?" The look of confusion on Mason's face told him otherwise. "He needed to know the location of the donated organs—same as us."

"I know that, Jack," Mason said with a firm shake of his head. "What doesn't make sense is the guy has already demonstrated the ability to compromise a security system and a computer network."

Now it was Jack's turn to look confused. "I don't follow."

"Riddle me this, Batman... why didn't he just go to the hospital and retrieve the records for himself?"

"Well, they were already wiped, and—"

"*Exactly*, Jack." He sat back and waited for Jack to catch up.

"If *he* wiped the files," Jack said, working through the logic chain, "then it stands to reason he already had everything he needed. That means there was no reason to visit Paul and Martha."

"So...?"

"So that means he *didn't* have the information, which means he *didn't* wipe the computers at the hospital!"

"Finally," Mason said, wiping his brow with a dramatic sweep of his hand. "I thought you'd never get there."

"Then who?" Jack said, still confused.

"Isn't it obvious?" Mason said, throwing his own words back at him.

"My pen-pal!"

"Got it in one."

"I knew ol' Chester was wrapped up in this somehow, but—"

"Wait, wait," Mason said, waving his hand, "*Chester?*"

Jack shrugged, "Gotta have a name other than 'pen-pal', right?"

"Yeah, but Chester?"

"A dog I had as a kid. The old thing would wander off for days at a time, and we never knew where to find it." He smiled, "He seemed to show up each time right about when we'd given up looking for him."

Mason shook his head, then popped the last bite of sandwich in his mouth. He chewed for a second, then said, "You were saying..."

"Well... it's just that he seems to be working at cross purposes with our old friend, the Shadowman. For a while I thought they were the same guy, but this means they are not only two different people, but on opposite sides."

"Yeah," Mason mused while he chewed, "but on opposite sides of *what?*"

"That's the sixty-four-thousand-dollar question, isn't it?" Jack said. "Every piece of information we have is second-hand or circumstantial."

"Other than the lab results."

"Right... other than that," Jack nodded. "But what does that give us, really? We still don't have motives or plans for either the Shadowman *or* Chester."

Mason finished chewing, swallowed, then said, "All right... let's list what we *do* know." He ticked each point off on his meaty fingers. "One, there's Chester, who seems to feel responsible for the deaths of your wife and daughter. Two, there's the Shadowman, who *is* responsible for at least four deaths—"

"That's circumstantial," Jack said.

"Good enough to get a conviction in a court in Georgia," Mason replied. "Three, the Shadowman has been at least *seen* at ground zero for some pretty big events involving the nano-machines. Four, Chester and the Shadowman are working against one another." He lay his hands on the table, "That about it?"

"You're forgetting that Chester has been at each of those places *before* the event took place, *and* he seems to be leading me to them." He shook his head, lips bunched. "There's no logic to it. At *all*."

"Oh... I just remembered number five," Mason said, his eyes wide. "Our Shadowman seems to be cleaning up the evidence after each event." He tapped his chin. "Now why would he *do* that?"

"Because he doesn't want people discovering what we already know—that someone has developed some pretty impressive nano-technology."

"Yeah," Mason said, "and there's *that*. Debbie says we're no-where near close to developing such technology. I don't mean the US, Jack. I mean *humans*."

"Well... *someone* did."

"Jack," Mason began, his face softening, "have you considered the possibility that this is too big for us? That maybe we should just turn ourselves in and hand over everything we have to the proper authorities?"

"You mean the guys who plan to shoot me on sight?"

"You don't know that."

"Mark was pretty clear, and—"

"Mark doesn't know everything we know, either. He might be overreacting."

"Yeah, well I've been in enough hotspots to know you can't be too careful when someone's pointing a gun at your head."

Mason took a drink from his tea. "What about your brother?"

"I don't—"

"We turn ourselves in to *him*. Let him sort it out."

Why not? Jack thought. Bill might keep us safe in protective custody at least until we convince the Feds we had nothing to do with Paul and Martha's murders. That was the rub, though. Could he really keep them safe until the guys with guns grew some brains? He wasn't sure he would place a bet on that happening. Bill was a by-the-book kind of cop, and if ordered to turn them over he likely would.

The first thing they had to do, though, was get out of DC without attracting attention or leaving a trail. Jack had a lot of experience in avoiding *foreign* government entanglements, but that was always with the help of his *own* government. How could he do it when they were the ones he wanted to avoid?

There was no way around it. He and Mason had to find a way to get to Bill *without* help. They couldn't even call to have him meet them, since Jack was sure they were listening in on Bill's phone already. They couldn't, in fact, contact *anyone* they knew. *And unless Amber's got a new phone, she's off the list, too.*

Jack shook his head to clear it, and said, "All right, we'll see if Bill can help." He gave his friend a lopsided smile, and added, "You have any ideas on how to get from here to South Carolina *without* attracting attention?"

Mason smirked, and said, "Not a damn clue."

* * *

On the way back to Debbie's, Mason turned to Jack and asked, "Do we *have* to go all the way to Greenville? I mean, Bill could meet us somewhere, right?"

Jack narrowed his eyes at Mason, then nodded toward the cabbie before whispering, "I don't think it's a good idea to call him right now."

"Ah, I get it," he said, still too loud for Jack's taste. "Surely, though, they wouldn't bug a *cop's* phone. Not without some serious paperwork, right?"

"And you think these guys can't get that?"

Mason looked at him sideways for a few seconds, then said, "Anyone told you lately you're one paranoid son of a bitch?"

"Coming from you," Jack said with a smirk, "that's a little scary." He leaned back in his seat, trying to relax. "Anyway... better paranoid and alive than trusting and dead."

Mason sat in silence after that, and Jack watched him for a time as Mason stared out his window. *It wasn't fair dragging him into all this,* Jack thought. To be fair to *himself,* though, he had no clue what "all this" was when he started. *Hell, I don't know what this is* now. Mason

158

was right—this was too big for them. It might even be too big for Bill, but they had to take the chance. Their only other option was presenting themselves to the FBI in DC. Maybe he could go in without Mason, but they were sure to want him at some point, regardless—if for no other reason than as a witness.

If he did, though, he would never know where the investigation went—even *if* he wasn't charged. And he *had* to know. He owed Beth and Riley that much. He owed them answers he didn't have.

The sky disappeared, clouds obscuring even the Moon, and the cab left the city lights behind for rows of evenly-spaced streetlights. Sentinels of suburbia, they cast a warm glow to the streets below, leeching color as they illuminated. The stark and harsh realities of life were leeched as well, leaving a bland and tasteless homogeneous mass ripe for consumption.

The cab turned from one nondescript street to another, wandering with purpose toward nearly identical homes. It stopped in front of one that was *not* Debbie's.

"Here you go, guys," Sohrab said, shifting the lever into park.

Jack turned to Mason and raised an eyebrow.

"It's better if we walk to Debbie's from here," Mason said. "You never know," he shrugged.

Jack snorted, and said, "At least one of us is thinking ahead."

"I'm not a secret agent, but I slept in a Holiday Inn Express last night."

Jack laughed and stepped out of the cab. Mason got out, took out his wallet, and handed a few bills to the driver. He leaned in through the open driver's window and said something to the man, but Jack was too far away to hear it. Both men spoke, then the driver laughed. Mason stood, tapped twice on the roof of the car, then stepped back to watch it pull away from the curb. They both waited as the car turned a corner, only then walking to Debbie's house.

"Oh shit!" Mason said, stopping in his tracks and looking to where the cab had been.

"What?" Jack said, looking around for the cops he knew must be drawing a bead on both of them.

"The carry-out I bought for Debbie... I left it in the fucking cab!"

Jack shook his head, allowing the overload of adrenaline leak away. "She'll get over it." He threw an arm over Mason's shoulder, and said, "Besides, I'm sure she's already eaten by now."

"I hope so, man," he said with manufactured alarm. "You don't know what she's like when she's hangry."

* * *

"Thank God you're back," Debbie said, pulling Mason in through the doorway. "I was so *worried*." She shooed Jack inside, then looked up and down the street before closing the door behind them. "I had a heck of a time getting that file back into place without anyone no-ticing, but I *did* manage to make a copy first." She pointed through the foyer to the folder on the coffee table in the living room. "It's all there."

Jack and Mason had earlier agreed it was best not to tell Debbie *just yet* about Paul and Martha, but Jack knew it was bound to come up. *If not now, then certainly after my arrest*, he thought. He still wasn't sure it was a good idea to involve her further, but Mason was adamant that she could not only handle it, but she would be a valuable asset.

"She's never let me down, yet," he had said. "Even after..."

Jack knew what his friend would say next, but Mason had simply grown silent.

"Still," Mason had said, "it's probably best not to load her down with too much too soon."

She led them into the living room and invited them to sit. "I'm guessing you were successful in dropping off the car?"

"Yeah," Jack said. "No worries. We left it as close to downtown as we dared, and far enough away that it won't lead here."

"Of course," Mason said, "they can probably track its progress using the logs, but that won't happen until we are long gone from here."

"Logs?" Debbie said, worry clear in her eyes.

"The onboard computer usually keeps track of where the car has been," he said. "But that shouldn't matter," waving off her concerns, "as long as you tell them a partial truth they can live with. Something like 'Jack came to see me and asked to use my phone'."

"Sure," Jack said, grinning, "just leave out the incriminating stuff." There was no getting around the fact that he had already asked

160

her to do some pretty shady things, and she was now thoroughly wrapped up in their current troubles. The only thing he could do for her was limit the damage. "We'll be leaving tomorrow afternoon, if that's okay."

"Afternoon?" she said, her voice shaking. "Shouldn't you keep moving or something?"

Jack understood how she felt. They were imposing on her far past what she was willing to offer, but there was no way around it. The apprehension she showed for them was bested only by that which she had for herself, and if he *really* wanted to keep her safe, he would have left already. Regardless, she needed to know everything—if for no other reason than to know who to watch out for.

Don't kid yourself, Jack. You're the one she should be guarding herself against.

"A friend of mine will be calling your number around then," he said, placing a hand on her shoulder, "and I have to take that call."

Mason watched them both, then said, "Why doesn't she just give Mark your new number when he calls?"

Shut up, Mason! Jack screamed in his head. There was *no way* he was giving her the number to his new cell, as that would be just one more weight on her shoulders—one more thing to go wrong. It was best if he spoke to Mark himself, then they could get out of her hair.

"I think it's better if we don't give her something else to lie about, Mason," Jack said at last. He turned to Debbie "The less you know, the better."

Mason considered that for a moment, then agreed. "Yeah, probably best."

"Mason and I are pretty beat, Deb," Jack said. "We've been up for over thirty-six hours straight, and the adrenaline is wearing off." He yawned on cue, covering his gaping maw with the back of his hand. "We'll just crash here in the living room, if that's okay."

"Of course," she said, turning her head from one man to the other. "Mason looks like he's about to drop right now." She tilted her head and pursed her lips, something else on her mind.

"What is it?" Jack said.

"Well," she said, hesitating, "it's just that I don't think you fully grasp what's happening here, Jack."

"What do you mean?" he said, tilting his head back at her in turn.

"Have you seen any of the end-of-the-world type of movies late-ly?"

"You mean like *Divergent* or something like that?"

"Exactly!" she said. "Have you ever wondered where all the futuristic crap like flying cars and advanced computers came from in a world where everything else is *gone*?"

"I don't understand," he said. There had to be a point to what she was saying, but his addled mind wasn't able to grasp the significance.

"All that stuff has to come from *somewhere*, and it usually involves a whole *network* of industries working together to make them. There's not a single shop making a car. GM subcontracts all kinds of parts from other suppliers."

"So?" he said.

"So, they gloss over that stuff in books and movies because it's boring and would destroy the illusion. The point, though, is that those industries *must* exist for those things to be made." She looked him square in the eyes, holding his attention even as it threatened to drift off to dreamland, "And the same is true for your nano-machines."

Didn't he and Mason just discuss that this was too big? And now Deb's just gone and made the whole thing even bigger than we imagined.

* * *

Detective Inspector Gershon walked into Rutger's office without waiting to be announced, and shut the door behind him with a soft click.

"You're here early, Polizeioberkommissar Brieske," he said with his shark's smile.

"As are you, Inspector," Rutger said without standing, or even looking up from his work. "Visitors usually have to get permission before disturbing my work," he said, hoping the man caught his irritation. The truth was he hadn't slept well last night, and knowing there was nothing to be done for it, had driven in before the morning traffic was in bloom. There were other cases to work on, but the riddle of Jack Montgomery would not let him go. It was wrong to assume innocence and try to fit the facts to a predetermined outcome—as much as presupposing *guilt* was doing the same—but Rutger knew he was right in this case.

Gershon unbuttoned his impeccably tailored jacket and sat, crossing his legs. "I've come to let you know—merely as a *courtesy*—that you have been attached to Interpol on a temporary basis by your commanding officer."

Rutger looked up from his desk, the other man now having his full attention. "Is that *so*?" he said, his voice dripping with disrespect.

"Yes," Gershon said, pulling an envelope from inside his jacket, "that is, indeed, so." He set the envelope on the desk and slid it over to Rutger. "Both your orders and a plane ticket are inside." He leaned forward, and said, "I trust you will be on time, Polizeioberkommissar, as I despise tardiness."

"And where, may I ask, am I going?" He smiled, a thin line.

"*We* are going to Washington, DC, of course," the man said, smiling back.

Rutger's smile faded as he picked up the envelope to look inside. The letter was official and perfunctory, but the ticket was for First Class. Unusual on the government's part. Worse, the flight was scheduled to depart in two hours.

"I don't have time to pack?"

"I am afraid not," Gershon said, still smiling, "but everything you need will be provided on our arrival."

Curiouser and curiouser, he thought. *When is a government operation not a government operation?* He tapped his chin with a forefinger, considering his options, and realized with some disgust that he had none.

"Shall we?" Gershon said as he stood.

Rutger huffed and stood. "I'll need my passport, and that's at home."

"Oh, no worries," Gershon said. "A man has already been dispatched to retrieve that. He'll meet us at the airport."

Too efficient by half, Rutger thought. "Fine," he said. "I'll get my coat and meet you downstairs."

"See that you do." Gershon opened the door and left the office.

First, Rutger thought, *I'll email some of these files to myself.* Before leaving, he placed a call to his friend at the American Embassy as insurance.

* * *

Do not *go home!* Jack was as clear as he could be on this, but there she was, walking the hall to her apartment. She didn't have a lot of money in her savings account, and had been too afraid to access it, regardless. There was, however, the money she was given in Germany by the Shadowman just sitting in her unpacked suitcase doing nothing. *I might as well use it to* help *Jack, since I got it by* lying *to him.*

It seemed like a lot of money at the time, but knowing what might be required, it no longer looked to be enough. *Get in, get the money, and get out.* Amber couldn't shake the feeling she was doing something wrong—something she couldn't come back from.

"That's just plain paranoia," she said, the sound of her voice in the late-night hallway mocking her. She stopped mid-stride, two steps from her goal.

The door to her apartment was unlocked and ajar, but through the slim opening neither light nor sound spilled out. The fine hair on her arm stood at attention as she reached for the knob and pushed. Amber knew she shouldn't go in—every instinct, in fact, urging her to flee—but curiosity was a powerful motivator. The door creaked wide, revealing nothing but darkness and shadows, and she stepped slowly across the threshold. She stood just inside the doorway, reached for the light switch, and flicked it on. *Nothing*, she thought, let out a long-held breath, and took a step deeper into the room.

Amber closed the door without looking, instead surveying the room for signs anyone was still there. Nothing *appeared* out of place, but...

That's when she felt it. The hair on the back of her neck stood up, as even *it* understood someone was watching. Someone behind her.

She turned and the old man smiled.

"Hey, you're—" she began.

He was on her faster than she thought possible, spinning her around and holding her from behind in a grip stronger than it should be. A puff of cold air made her blink twice, then her eyelids grew heavy and fluttered closed. *It smells like berries*, she thought.

The darkness enveloped her in velvet folds, and then she thought no more.

CHAPTER 14

H E EXITED THE BUILDING, morning sunlight casting a soft glow in the east. The darkened buildings nearby were nothing but silhouettes against a painted flat backdrop, the few people on the street an August Edouart arrangement in black. Thirteen stood in the doorway for a few seconds to admire the stark elegance of his surroundings, then shoved gloved hands in his pockets and descended the steps to the sidewalk.

The task had been as pointless as he had earlier suspected, but there had been no arguing with the Others. They required he cover all avenues, and the police department had been first on his list. With the FBI already involved, it was clear to him that all the evidence from Mr. Montgomery's apartment would be kept in their offices, but he had to admit there was a minuscule possibility it had been stored here.

The Others had their talons deep into the Bureau, so did not need him there. Physical evidence would soon disappear—if it hadn't already—and electronic records would go with them. That left any physical records that might still be located on site at the CDC where Montgomery worked, which was Thirteen's next task.

It will have to wait, he thought, preferring the cover of night for his work. Doing these things in the light of day always ended in death, and Thirteen had seen far too much of that over his long years in service to the Others. *They value life so little, and* individual *lives not at all.*

He knew them as little more than voices in his head—he often wondered if that was all they really were—but the *device* in his pocket told him otherwise. Thirteen felt for it and wrapped it in a tight fist. It was real—he could hold it—and it was not something he could have made himself; the skills to craft such a thing were beyond him. They were beyond everyone he had ever known, and he had only been trained in its use—never its inner workings. He felt the warmth of the thing through his gloves, but that heat faded as he walked away from the building. It would soon grow colder than even the air around it, waiting for its next use.

As will I, he thought.

A car, black as night, pulled to a stop beside him, and he opened the door and folded inside the empty cabin. He didn't bother speaking a destination. The vehicle slid from the curb in well-oiled silence, ferrying him where he could wait for the dark to once more overtake the day.

* * *

Amber should have called by now, Jack thought as he sipped his coffee. Debbie had awakened early, and already made breakfast for the three of them, but now was alone in her bedroom with the door closed. Sounds from her TV filtered softly through the door, but neither Jack nor Mason wanted to intrude. Both understood her need to be alone to process everything. They had their own need to be alone, regardless.

"So," Mason said, "what's our next move?"

Jack set his cup on the table, and said, "I think we need to get moving sooner rather than later."

"Thank God for small favors!" Mason said at once. "I was hoping you'd come to your senses about that."

"I don't mean giving Debbie our new numbers," he said, shaking his head. "I mean we just leave Mark behind and in the dark."

Mason's face fell, but he said, "That might be best. He would want to come with us, and Betsy's not up to that." He grinned, a fatalistic smile, and said, "The fewer people involved, the better."

"Yeah... about that," Jack said, hesitating.

Mason narrowed his eyes at him, and said, "Go on."

"We're not going to get anywhere with Bill without some kind of evidence... something to tie all this together."

"What did you have in mind?"

"I was thinking we get Sally—"

"Sally?" Mason said, his eyes widening. "Are you out of your fucking *mind*?"

"Look, if we wait too long, everything's going to disappear just like all the other records. The computer files might already be gone, and in that case all we have left are my hard copies. Sally is the only one with access, Mace." He stared hard into his friend's eyes. "We *need* her."

"Sure, but can we *trust* her?"

Jack stopped and leaned back. He had never considered the possibility that he couldn't. Sally might be their boss—maybe even their friend—but could he count on her to commit a *crime* for them? Because that's exactly what he would be asking of her.

He shrugged and took another sip from his cup, then said, "It's either that, or try to get the files ourselves."

Mason snorted. "Yeah, because that went so well the *last* time."

* * *

"Are you out of your *mind*?" Sally said. When she answered her phone, she had been expecting another sales call. Derek was already on his way to work, and she and Becker were both enjoying the breakfast her husband had left for them.

"That's funny. That's exactly what Mason said."

"Not *exactly*," Mason chimed in.

"What you boys need to do is present yourselves to the FBI there in DC and get this straightened out... *pronto*."

"I've been told that's not a good idea," Jack said.

"But you—"

"No, Sally. We're going to turn ourselves in, but to my brother Bill... and *only* Bill." He shushed Mason, who was already grousing in the background. "To do that," Jack said, "I need as much documentation as we can get our hands on. I have to make him see what we see so he'll be less inclined to turn us over to the Feds."

She reached down to scratch the top of Becker's head as he growled and licked Derek's plate clean, then she placed hers on top of the other for the blind little dog to sniff out. He loved eggs and bacon even more than she did, that being his first meal after she found him as a young stray. Sally had collected a lot of lost and lonely strays over the years, growing attached to each as if they were her own children. *In a way they are*, she mused.

"Okay," she said with a heavy sigh. "I'll do it."

Silence greeted her at first, then, "Sally, you don't know what this means to us."

"I think I do, Jack," she said, then picked up both plates to set them in the sink. The pile was getting high, so she turned on the faucet and prepared to wash them before she left for the day. "Today's my day off, and I have errands to run first, but I think it's best to do this at night anyway." She poured a healthy dollop of soap into the sink as it filled with water. "Is that good enough?"

"Sure, Sally. Whatever works best for you."

"What works best for me is for all this to be over with," she said, a hint of exasperation in her voice.

"We're working on that."

"Stay safe," she said.

"You too," Jack said, and he ended the call.

She took a deep breath, then let it out slowly. To Becker, standing underfoot, she said, "They're gonna get themselves killed, is what they're gonna do."

Becker just wagged his tail.

* * *

"So that's that, I guess," Jack said as he pocketed the phone. He had made too many calls on this one, and it seemed wise to pick up another at the first opportunity. *But if Amber hasn't called by then, then what?* he thought. If she did as she was told, she had already ditched her other phone, so there was no way to call her himself. He had tried once last night, and it went straight to voicemail, so at the very least it was turned off. Even if he left his current number with Debbie, Amber did not know to call her—not to mention the fact he would soon be tossing this phone for another. And they had no mutual friends that he knew of.

"We need to get moving, Jack," Mason said, derailing Jack's thoughts. "Have you called Bill, yet?"

Jack shook his head, "No, and I'm not going to until we're close enough to smell him."

"Eww... that's just gross, man," Mason said, laughing. He slapped his buddy on the back and said, "Gather up and let's hit the road."

"Any ideas yet how we're getting there?"

"One or two," Mason said, but did not elaborate. He had been reticent to share his ideas since last night, and Jack thought that strange. Mason was not the reticent type.

"What's going on in that brain of yours, Mace?"

He grinned, and said, "Chess, buddy-boy." He waggled his eyebrows and tapped his temple. "The *three-dimensional* kind."

"You boys are leaving *now*?" Debbie stood in the entryway, hands clasped in front, her face a picture of confusion. "I thought you were staying until after noon," she said, her eyes flicking to the door and back. Her hands never stopped moving, each kneading the other.

"What's up, Deb?" Mason said like he was sniffing the air for a distant forest fire.

"Nothing," she said, hesitating. "I just thought we'd have a nice lunch before you left." Again, that flick to the door.

Jack stood, and said, "Debbie... what did you *do*?"

"Jack..." she stopped and turned to Mason. "Did you know Jack was wanted for *murder*?" She was breathing heavy now, and her hands began to tremble as they continued kneading. "I heard it on the news this morning."

Mason stood, and took two steps toward her, and said, "Yes, but—"

She slapped him hard across the face, nearly turning him around. Her eyes grew wide, and she looked from Mason to her hand and back. Debbie straightened her spine and grabbed the bottom of the trim navy-blue jacket straightening that as well with a short tug. She dropped her hands to her sides.

"I've called the police," she said to Jack. "*That's* what I've done."

Jack grabbed Mason's arm, but it was like trying to pull a car by its bumper. He moved between the two, getting in Mason's face, and said, "We have to go. *Now*."

Without taking his eyes off Debbie, Mason stepped back and retrieved the copied file from the table. He looked at Jack, and said, "Follow me."

Both men turned to the front door at the sound of car doors slamming home outside. Jack started for the front to take a peek, but Mason grabbed his arm and pulled him toward the back.

"This way!" he said a bit too loudly. Jack was sure the men outside heard, but it didn't matter. They both flew through the back door and ran, leaving Debbie to confront the Feds alone.

I hope they're just Feds, he thought as he followed Mason through the back yard. Coming to a low chain-link fence, Mason grabbed the top rail and vaulted over without slowing. Jack, with the pins in his leg, had to climb, but Mason grasped him by the front of his shirt and pulled him over before he got his second leg up. He started to turn at the sound of slamming doors behind, but Mason pulled him away from the fence into a dead run.

"Don't look back!" he yelled without turning. "*Never* look back when you're being chased!"

They ran through the alley, popping out at another street. Mason looked around for bearings, then took off. Jack was slowing him down, he knew that, but Mason never got more than a few steps ahead. Another alley, and another street, and they finally stepped into the open on a street Jack recognized.

"Why are we here?" Jack said, bending over and breathing hard.

Mason spun in place, eyes scanning the area like he expected something. "It's not *here*. Son of a bitch!"

"What's not—"

A single short honk sounded from a cream-colored Ford Edge parked across the street, and the driver's window rolled down.

"Get in!" Sohrab said, his eyes scanning the area like Mason had. He stuck an arm out and waved them over. "Quickly!"

Mason turned to Jack and grinned as they ran to the car. "Chess, my friend."

* * *

Jack sat in the second row behind Sohrab, Mason climbing into the front to take shotgun before Jack even closed the door. Sohrab set his blinker and calmly pulled out, careful to drive the posted speed limit.

"What are you doing here?" Jack said as he buckled in.

"More importantly, why are you driving my new rental?" Mason said. "I thought we agreed you'd get me a blue Civic and leave the keys."

Sohrab laughed, "I never agreed to any such thing, Mr. Mason. I only agreed to provide you with a car." He shrugged, "Besides, there were no blue Civics available."

"Can someone tell me what's going on?" Jack said, his arms crossed.

Mason turned and said, "Sohrab here," he jerked a thumb at the man, "was supposed to get us a rental in his name, but it looks like we're stuck with this... whatever it is."

"It's an Edge," Sohrab said, "and don't make fun of it. It's my wife's car."

"Your wife?" Mason said, leaning away. "We need a rental."

"Sure, but I don't want that on my credit card. My guess is that car would have seen more air time than Michael Jordan."

"So *this* was your plan?" Jack said, the sneer more implied than seen.

"Yeah," Mason said. "I didn't trust Deb completely. I figured she would hear the news at some point, and I didn't know how she would react." He hung his head and sighed, "I guess we know, huh?"

Sohrab looked at Jack through the rearview mirror, and said to Mason, "What happened? Did your friend call the cops when they found out Jack is wanted for murder?"

Jack opened his mouth to protest, but Sohrab waved him silent. "I saw the news last night after I got home."

"Then why are you helping us?" Mason asked.

"You guys are goofy, and you tip," he said to Mason. To Jack he said, "I know what killers look like... and you aren't one." He laughed, a deep, booming sound that reminded Jack of John Rhys-Davies from *The Lord of the Rings* movies. "Neither of you are very good at this shit, what with talking in the open with ears like mine nearby." He shrugged again, scrunching his face. "I, on the other hand, was once a member of Directorate 9 of Iraqi Intelligence Service—sometimes known as Mukhabarat."

"Right," Jack said, "and now you drive a cab." He looked at Mason and twirled a finger beside his ear.

Sohrab tilted his head, and said, "It's a living." He smiled again, and said, "In fact, it pays better than my old job." He turned around and looked straight at Jack. "As an added bonus, I don't have to kill people anymore."

* * *

Stupid, stupid, stupid, Sally thought as she swiped the lock with her key-card and entered the building. Not just Jack and Mason, but now *herself. Aiding and abetting, is what it is. What would daddy say about* that?

She didn't want to believe such things were possible, but when Barbara told her the files were missing from the server, Sally's first thought was that Jack just *might* be right. If, however, even the FBI was compromised, what could they do about it? The first step, she realized with trepidation, was getting their hands on the hard copies of Jack's files...and Sally couldn't let those two boys take the chance. She shook her head and her lips pulled into a tight grin. *Get themselves killed, is what they'll do. Besides,* she thought, *they don't know where the damn thing is.*

"The whole goddamn world is going crazy," she whispered to herself. The halls this time of night were, like the rest of the building, empty, but she still felt as if she was being watched. Other than the janitorial staff, she should have been the only one there. It seemed, though, as if the staff had taken the night off, since she heard no noise from a vacuum or floor buffer. The length of hallway leading to her door was dead silent.

The door to her office was locked up tight with an old-fashioned deadbolt, since purchasing had never approved her request for key-less entry like the main doors. She fumbled the keys from her pocket and unlocked the door, pushing it open. She checked both ways down the hall, then stepped inside, the light filtering in from the hallway through her window shades providing just enough illumination. Walking around her desk as the door clicked closed behind her, she sat and stared at the stacks of papers and file folders while her eyes adjusted. She reached for one, but movement near the door stayed her hand, held in mid-grasp by cold fear.

From the corner near the door, a shadow peeled itself from the wall and became a man. He reached out and flicked the light on, and Sally saw—for the first time—the Shadowman's face.

"I apologize for the intrusion, Mrs. Jackson," he said, his voice a rich baritone. On any other occasion, Sally would have found it attractive. Tonight it was an icicle drawn down her spine.

"You're the Shadowman," she said, unable to think of anything else.

172

"*Shadow...?* Well, I understand how some might feel that way," he said with a sad smile. "I am Thirteen."

"Is that your age or your IQ?" Sally said with a forced smirk, dropping her hand to the desk.

"Let us not play games, Mrs. Jackson. We both know why I am here."

"I'm sorry, big guy," she said, batting her eyelashes. "I'm not that kind of girl." *Why am I needling this guy? It's not like I'm stalling while I wait for help.*

"Do not bother screaming for help, ma'am. There is no one to hear you."

And now she knew with certainty why there was no sound from the cleaning crew—they were already dead.

"If you will give me what I require, this will all be over quickly," he said, the sadness in his eyes matched by the soothing sound of his voice. "But if you don't," he shrugged, "I will find them regardless, and nothing will have changed."

"And what, pray tell, do you *require?*"

"The files from Mr. Montgomery's trips to Kazakhstan and Germany," he said. The man leaned forward, and she leaned back instinctively. "*All* of them," he said, clear menace in his tone.

"Oh, well," she said, "that could take me a while to gather up."

"I grow tired of this game," he said, the sound like the last gasp of an iron lung. "I do not do these things because I *choose* to, Mrs. Jackson."

"Yes, yes... we all have a job to do, right?" she said, waving a hand in the air. She started to stand— thinking, *I can take this guy*— but he placed one gloved hand in his coat pocket, and Sally found she could not move. *No, that's not right.* She *could* move... she just no longer *wanted* to.

The Shadowman took one step to the desk, then rummaged through the piles of stacked paper and folders. Some he threw to the floor, others he spread out like a magician fanning cards. Within seconds he had found all he needed and stacked them on the corner of the desk away from the chaos he created.

"Again," he said, his voice a pleading whisper, "I apologize."

Sally saw a flash of steel, hard and rapier-thin, from the corner of her eye. The calm she felt was more than unusual, given the circumstances, as was her ability to think objectively. Clear-headed for the first time in days, she felt a growing euphoria. It was a warmth from the center of her being, and all wrapped around memories of her life with Derek. *We never had kids.* The thought came unbidden, saddled with regret. *And now he will be all alone.*

The Shadowman stood behind her, one hand grasping her forehead with gentle care. The glove he wore was leather, and softer than anything she had ever felt.

"I won't beg," she said.

He bent close, and whispered, "I know." His breath was warm on her skin, and a single tiny drop of water splashed on the desk beside her hand. The paper where it landed wicked the moisture into a round scar, spreading in all directions from the point of impact, a stain on her ordered universe. The Shadowman pulled his face away and kissed her on the top of her head. "Please... *don't*," he said, his voice breaking. The grip on her forehead tightened, and there was a quick motion of his other hand.

Light flashed, a brilliance without color, and she felt the cold prick at the base of her skull.

It feels—

* * *

Sometimes they let him dream, though most often they did not. When they did, it seemed more a punishment than boon to Thirteen. All his dreams now were filled with death, and all by his hands.

There will come a time, he thought, hiding in the one place they could not access, *when either the killing or the dreams will stop.* Sometimes they punished him for hiding. Those punishments were the worst, but he no longer feared them. He knew now what the Others were and why they were here, and though their motivation had changed recently, they still *interfered.*

The Others had been here from the beginning. At least as far back as recorded human history, and perhaps farther. Thirteen knew these things because the Others had been in his mind since early in his childhood, but what they *didn't* know was that the connection worked both ways. He had been in *theirs* for almost as long, but most importantly, he had learned to *hide.* Not everything, but enough. They still saw him as a willing tool to wield as they saw fit—and in this they were correct—but he was also more. No longer the frightened child believing in demons and angels, he had kept his growing knowledge from them. They controlled him, but they did not *own* him.

Their minds were strong in concert, but weak as individuals. One night when they left him alone, he entered one of those minds, and saw them for what they really were. His only thought at the time was *alien*. Resembling the demons of old, with three-fingered talons at the end of short, powerful arms. Their reverse-articulated legs separated by a prehensile and barbed tail. It was the mouth, more than anything, that told him their true nature. Two rows of sharp-pointed teeth, both upper and lower, in a jaw able to dislocate at will. They were apex predators, born of a treacherous and cruel world, surviving above all others, owning a dry and wind-blasted landscape as only they could beneath a dull red sun; the landscape that was once a continent became a world, then their solar system, and finally the galaxy. A hive mind, coordinating and cooperating far beyond the ability of humans, they conquered their domain while man's ancestors lived in trees.

But the Others were not all-powerful gods, or even the demons they resembled.

And they made *mistakes*.

* * *

It skittered on the stone floor, shrouded in total darkness, seeking the airlock. The chitinous claws on its lower limbs slid at times, not as suited to the smooth surface as they were to sand. Sand was in abundance outside, but its kind rarely ventured beyond the cave entrance for fear of being seen. This one had been damaged long ago during its brief mental struggle with the *asset* known as Thirteen, and had since been relegated to menial duties such as this one. As it approached the airlock, the inner door melted and vanished in a cloud of tiny machines. It stepped through and the door reassembled.

It supposed it could be referred to as a "he"—all soldiers being male—but without a queen nearby, the distinction had no meaning. This outpost had originally been deemed too minor for even a *young* queen.

A pity, it thought. A queen could have settled the recent debate that took so many of my brothers.

There was that word again. *My.* The damage had only grown worse over the years, and he had thought to be sacrificed for it, but their numbers were now too few to destroy even one of them. There had been no reinforcements in over a hundred cycles, but such a lag was not unusual. What *was* unusual was the lack of communication from the hive—not even a weak scent.

The outer door disappeared, and he stepped into the rough-hewn tunnel that led outside. The light beyond was much brighter than the dull red glow of *Nest's* red giant, but that memory was thousands of years in the past. Too distant to taste. The door reformed behind, assuming the appearance of a rocky wall, and he walked toward the open entrance into the hot, dry air outside.

This was more like *Nest.* Its prehensile tail swished behind, the barb at the end gouging grooves in the stone. Here was endless sand it could sink its claws into, along with a variety of small mammals to hunt. Most of them were poisonous for its kind to consume, but there were antidotes for those who surrendered to the *fever.* It no longer hunted, the worm planted in its mind by Thirteen had destroyed the *fever* long ago.

A truck crested a dune, rumbling and droning like the great food-beasts still found on hunting preserves on *Nest.* It stopped twenty tail-lengths from the entrance, and a primitive opened a door on the passenger side and exited. The mammal was dirty, overweight, and unshaven, but showed no sign of revulsion at this one's appearance.

The beast thrust out a soft, five-digit claw, "Hey, Jeff," the human male said. "I've brought everything on your list." He leaned closer. "You got the cash?"

"Jeff" reached with its hand and shook the other's; this close to the primitive, it could manipulate the primitive's perceptions. With its free claw it produced a thick wad of currency from a many-pocketed vest, and tossed it to the man it knew as Owen.

Owen felt its weight, then tore off the elastic binding and counted. When he was satisfied, he nodded. "We'll get this unloaded fer ya."

CHAPTER 15

J̲ACK'S BREAKFAST, SUCH AS IT WAS, was now cold and untouched on the small table in front of him. He hadn't eaten since lunch at Sohrab's home on the northern end of DC, and even then had only picked at it in a desultory manner. Sohrab's wife, Marie, was an excellent cook, but Jack had simply not been in the mood to eat. His thoughts constantly turned to Amber, and for the hundredth time that morning, he picked up his phone and checked to see if she had called. Mason, sitting across the motel room on the bed with Sohrab and playing cards, watched him from the corner of his eye.

Getting out of DC had been easier than Jack imagined it would... once they had left Sohrab's house, that is. Much of the city had been locked down due to some idiot landing a gyrocopter on the White House lawn, so the three of them had holed up at Sohrab's until dusk. His wife was *not* happy with his decision to drive two fugitives to South Carolina, but the stack of fifties Mason pushed across the dinner table to her waiting hands had helped. She was an American—born and bred—and therefore a devout capitalist. Danger was an abstraction, but *money* was concrete.

Taking the Skyline Drive through the mountains along the Shenandoah Valley had been Mason's idea. His reasoning being that anyone assuming they might be headed to Bill's would also assume they were taking the shortest route. Jack didn't think it mattered, since even the FBI would be hard-pressed to connect them to their cab driver, but Sohrab had never been there so the issue was settled by majority vote.

And Jack checked his phone every mile or so the whole way.

"Put the phone down and eat," Mason said without facing him. "If she hasn't called by now, she either can't, or has lost your new number." He turned a troubled face to Jack, and added, "Either way, there's nothing you can do."

"Don't you think I know that?" Jack said, a cold, hard knot in his stomach. "It's not just Amber, though, Mace—we haven't heard from *Sally*, either."

"Same advice," Mason shrugged.

Jack shook his head at his friend. "How can you be so nonchalant about this?" Ever since arriving in Charlotte the previous night, Mason had shown a preternatural calm. *It's almost like he no longer cares what happens.* Thinking back, Jack realized Mason's change of demeanor occurred at the exact moment Debbie had betrayed them. *Betrayed Mason*, he thought. *Was that payback? Or did he just* think *it was?* Either way, it was clear to Jack that Mason never *once* thought such a thing was possible.

"Oh, you must be confusing my outer calm for unconcern," Mason said, tossing a card to the pile between he and Sohrab. "Trust me... I'm feelin' it. I just know there's nothing I can do about it."

"Maybe there's nothing *you* can do about it," Jack said, grabbing the phone. "Get your shit together, guys. We're heading out."

"You calling Bill?" Mason said.

"Not yet."

* * *

Why am I in Greenville? Thirteen wondered. He should still be in Atlanta, waiting for Jack and Mason. When the Others released his mind that morning, he had walked out of the motel room expecting to be near the CDC, but it was instantly clear he was not. And now Thirteen sat in a diner near the motel, shoveling food into his mouth at an alarming rate. Several patrons nearby turned away when they saw him eat. The reason was clear to Thirteen: The Others had forgotten to allow him to eat for the past three days. They often did that, one time for close to two weeks. He had a hunger that mere food could never assuage.

They never forgot to allow him to hydrate, however—a testament to their own biology.

They will come to you, the Others said while he ate.

Millenia spent on this planet, and they still *have no understanding of humans*, Thirteen thought behind his mental wall. It had taken them hundreds of years to even *grasp* the vagaries of human language and social interaction, their own communication pheromone-based for most of their history. Individuality was a difficult concept, but emotional connection was *beyond* them. The few who had developed a *rudimentary* concept of empathy had been sacrificed as aberrations not fit to breed.

I must be allowed to go back, he thought outside his wall. Montgomery will go there.

Do not force us to take control again, the Others said as one, a crashing wave against his psyche. You will wait here. We have other arrangements should he turn his course.

Thirteen knew what those arrangements were—independent operatives. The Others, powerful as they were, could take direct control of only one or two minds at a time. Once they understood human society in general, however, they quickly built organizations around the individuals they *could* control. Some were religions, while others were corporations. Governments led by dictators were the easiest to maintain. The whole of recorded human history was littered with the machinations of the Others, governments and corporations rising and falling at their whim.

And their whim was capricious at times, a major course correction happening less than a century ago.

I will wait, he said. To himself, behind his wall, he thought, I have waited decades. A few days, or even years longer is nothing. Jack Montgomery will come to me—just not the way the Others believe. Thirteen lifted the fork to his mouth, noticed it was apple pie, and smiled.

He shoveled it in and chewed, savoring the flavor for the first time that morning.

* * *

It was clear to Rutger he and Gershon did not see eye to eye. Did not, in fact, see even the same reality. Rutger saw a woman, head down on her desk, frozen in rigor. A coworker—and quite possibly a *friend* of Jack's—who was now just another victim of the man he knew only as the Shadowman.

Gershon saw something else entirely. He saw another in a long string of murders by one Jack Montgomery.

When Gershon's phone rang shortly after they arrived in Washington, Rutger knew it was not good news, but the man had refused to discuss it until they were already on another plane for Atlanta. After the long cross-Atlantic flight, the short hop south seemed instantaneous by comparison, but Rutger's joints complained regardless when he stood at last to deplane. The cab ride to the CDC had been blissfully brief, though a bit terrifying. *My first time in America, and I am almost killed in a murder-suicide by a cab driver.*

The man from the FBI had ushered them into the building, then, to Rutger's amazement, left them alone in the woman's office. He knew of no law enforcement agency in the world that would so easily turn over to foreign nationals what was a *domestic* investigation. *I certainly would not*, he thought. The lead investigator had, indeed, shown an amount of deference to Gershon upon their arrival. Rutger found it appalling.

He leaned close to examine the back of the woman's neck, and the small hole at the base of her skull. A single drop of blood left a thin track along the side and down, ending in the suprasternal notch, but not enough to drip to the papers beneath.

"It seems the killer was looking for something on her desk," Rutger said, touching the folders splayed on the surface.

"More likely he caught her from behind as she was working," Gershon said, the sneer clear in his voice.

Rutger moved to stand behind the woman he now knew as Sally Jackson, his back mere inches from the bookcase behind, and said, "How do you suppose she was caught unawares?" He indicated the small space between the body and himself. "Do you think the killer was invisible?"

"I *think* he knew her well enough that she was comfortable having him stand near her," the man said with obvious contempt. He snorted once, and added, "Some people are just blind, no?"

That is certainly true, Rutger thought. He had grown tired of the man's arrogance over the course of a single day. Rutger couldn't imagine anyone willingly spending an extended amount of time with Gershon, noting with satisfaction the lack of a wedding ring on the man's hand. He must control his emotions, though. It wouldn't do for

Interpol to know what Rutger thought of their man, as police relations with them were strained even in the best of times.

"Look here," Rutger said, pointing at the desk. "See how these are fanned out evenly?"

Gershon leaned in. "So?"

"There is a gap," he tapped the folders, "right here."

"Again," Gershon raised an eyebrow and looked to Rutger, "so?"

"So, our killer found what they were looking for," Rutger said. He dismissed Gershon from his thoughts and examined the files, passing his hands over without touching them. "Physical documents are missing, and if we knew which ones, my guess is we would find a corresponding gap in the electronic files as well."

"In a triply-redundant system such as a government file server?" Gershon shook his head. "You assume too much." He stepped away from the desk. "I know you don't want to believe this, but your friend is involved in this murder, as well as all the others. He may not be the killer, but death is following him with every step he takes." He shook his head. "Guilty or not, it's our duty to find him and stop this."

What Rutger wanted to stop was the *dance* the two were engaged in. While he was convinced Jack had nothing to do with this murder, he was just as convinced Gershon knew it too. *Why, then, is he set on convincing me otherwise? He doesn't just want me to believe Jack is guilty, he wants me to believe* he *believes it.*

Rutger's phone buzzed, and he pulled it from his pocket. He didn't recognize the number, but it was US in origin. There was only one person in the US who would be calling him now.

"It's my wife," he said to Gershon. "I need to take this." He hit the answer button as he placed the phone to his ear, and walked out of the office.

"Yes?" he said.

"Rutger?" Jack said, hesitating on the other end.

"Yes, dear," Rutger said, smiling at the man from the FBI as he walked past and down the hall.

* * *

Dear? Jack thought as he looked up from the phone at Mason, who shrugged back. Holding it between them on speakerphone, Jack allowed Mason to listen in rather than tell him everything later.

"Are you not able to speak freely?" Jack said.

"No, dear, I'm not. I just arrived in America and am visiting with the FBI."

The FBI? Here, in the US? Jack thought. He turned to Mason who, again, just shrugged. *What the hell was going on?*

"I am here investigating a murder. It may be related to the others," Rutger said. There was a noise on the other end that sounded like a whoosh, followed by birdsong. "Okay, Jack, I'm outside," Rutger said, breathless.

"Are you in Tennessee?"

"No... Atlanta."

"Atlanta?" Mason said from beside him in the car. "Who...?"

Jack's stomach tightened. Now the long silence from Amber made sense, and he feared the words he knew would come next.

"I'm sorry, Jack. Sally Jackson has been murdered in her office."

Sally? he thought, feeling a great wash of relief then instantly cursing himself for it. His heart pounded for two very different reasons, each reinforcing the other in sympathy, threatening to burst through his chest.

Mason exploded beside him.

"God *damn* it!" he yelled, pounding the back of the seat over and over with his fist. "Why the *fuck* was *she* killed?" He turned to Jack, eyes already brimming "Who else, Jack? Who *else* are we gonna get killed?"

"What happened?" Jack asked Rutger, trying to ignore both his own pain *and* Mason's.

"It is still preliminary, but I think the Shadowman was looking for something and she must have surprised him. The death scene makes no sense, though. She—"

"My files!" Jack said, his eyes wide. "He was there to get my hard copies." Beside him Mason wept quietly, shaking his lowered head. *It's all my fault*, Jack thought, holding back his own tears. *Everything... from Beth and Riley to Sally and everyone in between.* His chest tightened, and he found it hard to breathe. *Please let this be a heart attack*, he thought. *It would be so much easier. It would all be over.*

"That would seem plausible," Rutger said. "I think a number of folders are missing from her desk." A pause, and then, "Jack, why are you calling me?"

"Things are going to shit, Rutger, and you are the only one I can trust," Jack said. "I haven't heard from Amber since last night, and I'm worried she's gotten caught up in this."

"And what do *I* do about that?" Rutger said.

"I know it's asking a lot, but can you check her apartment?"

Silence, then, "It will probably be our next stop anyway."

"*Our?*"

"A man from Interpol is with me," he said, cupping the phone and whispering, "but there is more to it than that. He's—"

"He's what?" Another voice said from Rutger's end.

"He's here, if you want to ask him yourself, dear," Rutger said into the phone without missing a beat. "All right, then. I'll call you tonight."

When the call ended, Jack and Mason were left staring at one another.

* * *

The good men from the FBI walked out of Bill Montgomery's office empty-handed and disappointed. *Brother or not, I wouldn't give those creeps the time of day without more in hand than supposition and fucking* innuendo, Bill thought. He had already heard the news—even had friends with access to *real* information call him—but these jokers were fishing, and doing it without any bait on their hooks.

The two men had cut a wide swath through the precinct straight for his office like they owned the place, but they had a "Jim Jones" quality about them—true believers on a mission. Bill knew plenty of guys like that in Greenville, but none of them held government clearances. *Shit, most of 'em are being* watched *by the Feds.* He sat behind his desk, flopping into his chair like he had already put in a full day. *And it ain't* noon *yet, for chrissake.* He rubbed his temples, then pulled the desk drawer open and fished around inside for the big bottle of Advil he kept there. Right beside the jumbo jar of Tums. He took a handful of both for good measure, washing them down with cold coffee.

He grabbed the framed picture from his desk—the one with him and Jack holding up their catch after a fishing trip. It was taken a good two years before the accident, and Jack's face showed none of the pain and self-destructive behavior to come. They were both laughing hard—mostly at the minnow-sized fish on Jack's line—and there was nothing but blue sky behind them. *Never saw the thunderheads gathering in the distance ahead of us, though, did we little bro?*

"Jack-o, I swear to God, if you did what they say you did, I'll hunt you down myself," he said to the picture. He sat in stony silence, breathing hard for long seconds, then the swell of anger crested and broke. He threw the picture across the room as hard as he could, shattering the frame and glass against the wall. "God-fucking *damn* it!" he yelled, and instantly regretted it.

On the other side of his window facing the squad room, everyone sat up for a brief moment like gophers popping their heads out of their holes, then bent back to work. None dared to be caught showing concern.

Bill ran meaty hands through his hair, scrubbed his head, then grabbed the coffee mug with the words "World's Greatest Detective" printed on the side in a child's scrawl, and left his office in search of a refill.

* * *

The car taking them to Ms. Riley's apartment on the southwest side of Atlanta was as dark as Rutger's mood, but where the interior was sterile and cold, Rutger's was a boiling hot mess. His irritation at Jack had subsided, but the utter revulsion Rutger felt for the man beside him had not. While he knew they would visit Amber at some point, the speed with which Gershon turned to her as a suspected accomplice was perplexing.

It is also stupid, he thought. Even *if* Jack was guilty of murder, there was nothing connecting Amber to any of it. Rutger had followed that line of reasoning to its conclusion long ago. It was clear to him that Gershon's motives were something other than investigative. What those might be, he still did not know, but they could not be anything *good.*

"I'm wondering what you hope to gain from this meeting, Inspector," Rutger said while watching the man.

Gershon shifted in his seat, crossed his legs, and picked an imagined piece of lint from his trousers. He turned to Rutger and said, "*I'm* left wondering why you were speaking to your *wife* in English," one eyebrow raised.

Scheiße, Rutger thought. He had hoped the man hadn't heard enough of the conversation to notice. *No such luck.*

"My wife's idea, I'm afraid," he said. "She's practicing her English for a trip to London."

"Hmm, of course," Gershon said, but did not press further. Rutger didn't know if that was because he believed him, or because he *didn't*.

Gershon had not left Rutger alone since Jack's call, so no opportunity to return the call arose. Rutger's one hope was that Jack did not try to call back until he was well away from Gershon and his disturbing curiosity. For safety's sake, he took the phone from his pocket, and under the pretext of checking the time, turned it off.

"Once we have eliminated Ms. Riley from your list of suspects, then what?" Rutger said, replacing the phone.

"I am not convinced she is not involved, and until we have had a chance to interview her, neither should *you* be." Gershon wrinkled his nose, picking at another piece of imagined lint.

"I fail to see how either case brings us closer to Jack," Rutger said, and wondered if the other man's apparent OCD was useful knowledge. *At the very least, he may be easily distracted.*

Gershon shrugged, and said, "It may not be helpful, but every piece of information is *useful*."

That was the first thing the man said with which Rutger could not disagree. In any investigation, data was paramount—the more, the better. *What sort of data are you gathering on* me, *I wonder?*

* * *

"Jack, you *have* to make the call," Mason said, facing backward in his seat. Sohrab had pulled the car into the far end of a Walmart parking lot where they could argue at length, unmolested.

Jack pulled at his bottom lip, looked at his phone, and thought, *I don't have to do a goddamn thing!* To Mason, he said, "I'm not sure calling Bill is still a good idea, okay?"

Mason stared at him for a while, then said, "Look, buddy... I'm with you no matter what you decide, but we can't keep running." His shoulders slumped. "Sooner or later, we *will* be caught." He pointed at Sohrab, and added, "Do you really want him with us when that happens?"

"Hey," Sohrab said, taking his hands off the wheel and holding them up, "getting picked up by the FBI won't be the *worst* thing that's happened to me." He laughed and stroked his beard. "*That* was probably when a certain Senator's wife dragged him by his hair from his mistress and out of my cab."

Mason turned to him, eyes wide in mock surprise. "I figured you'd say it had to do with the Gulf War or some shit like that."

"Yeah... no, Washington is *much* worse," he said, and laughed again.

"Mason," Jack said, his voice close to cracking, "Sally is *dead*. Murdered by the same monster who has killed so many others." Now his voice *did* crack, "And he's still there. I *know* it."

"You *don't* know, Jack!" Mason yelled, and Jack drew back from the fury. "We've both been guessing at *fucking everything*, and people keep dying." He shook his head and calmed himself. "This is Bill's *job*, Jack. He's trained for this shit, and we're just *not*."

"Mace—"

"No! We turn ourselves in, give him everything we've got, and let him take it from there."

"And what about Amber?" Jack asked softly.

"That's what your German buddy is for, right?"

Jack sat as still as stone, his heart heavy from everything that had happened—every death and betrayal. If they turned themselves in—gave up the evidence they had—what then? The evidence would disappear and someone else would die. Most likely Bill. And they would still be captured with no way to clear their names. Jack wanted to say all of this to Mason, but he knew it wouldn't make much difference... because it wouldn't *register.* Mason wasn't sold on any course of action other than the most expedient—the one where he no longer made choices. Jack had been making choices—from the time he chose not to pull over the night his life ended, all the way to asking Sally for help. The weight of those choices rested on his heart, compressing it, turning the carbon to purest diamond.

Jack raised his eyes from his hands. "Stay here with Sohrab if you must," he said. "Turn yourself in." He took a long shuddering breath. "I'm going back to Atlanta. I'm going back because it's the only thing I can do. For Sally." He lowered his head again. "For Amber," he whispered, voice breaking.

Mason watched him, while Sohrab studied the horizon. The silence lingered, stretching from seconds into minutes.

"Ah, shit, Jack," Sohrab said, starting the engine. "I have always wished to see Atlanta." He broke into a booming, hearty laugh. "Go Braves!" he hollered.

As they drove out of the parking lot, Mason said, "Are you *sure*, buddy?"

Jack snorted once. "*Fuck* no," he said, and shrugged. "But I think it's all we've got."

Mason turned back forward, looked around, and waved. "So long Greenville. We'll visit again when we can't stay so long."

* * *

Rutger stood to one side as the officer took the keys from the apartment manager and opened the door. The manager was still reading the warrant in her hand when Gershon pushed past both she and the policeman to step inside. Rutger followed, as did the officer and the manager.

"Please," she said, "if you are searching for something, try to keep the damage to a minimum. The last time the cops raided one of our apartments, it took me a month to get the insurance company to cough up for the repairs."

"This happens often here?" Gershon said without looking at her. He walked a couple of steps into the apartment and scanned the darkened room.

"Not really, but once is enough for me," she said, flicking the light switch on. "Ms. Riley is a good tenant—always pays on time, and never complains." The woman, a little taller than Gershon, leaned over his shoulder to examine the room, and said, "What are you guys looking for?"

"Thank you, miss," Gershon said, then waved his hand back to the door. "You may leave now."

She looked at him, her mouth screwed up with a retort ready to fly, but Rutger intervened. "You have been very helpful," he said with a warm smile, all old European charm. "I'll let you know when we are through."

The woman, flustered and a little flushed, smiled back at him and left. The policeman looked around, then stepped outside to stand by the door.

Gershon turned to Rutger, a snake's lipless smile on his face. "What's your assessment?"

Rutger shrugged. "It could use a light cleaning and some plants." The smile turned down.

Rutger raised an amused eyebrow, knowing he had pricked the man. "She's not here, but her car is still in the car park."

"And no one has heard from her in two days," Gershon added.

"Thirty-six hours," Rutger corrected. "So you think she's gone rabbit?"

"That *is* what the guilty do, no?" the other man said with obvious satisfaction.

"As do people running from danger," Rutger shot back. "Just because she's gone doesn't mean she is guilty of any crime."

"That remains to be seen," Gershon said, picking up a figurine from a wall shelf. He turned it over in his hands, then frowned and replaced it. "Let's begin."

For the next four hours, the two men tore apart Amber Riley's life.

CHAPTER 16

"I HAVE SOMETHING HE NEEDS," the old man says over his shoulder. He stares at her with pale blue eyes, almost gray. "But more importantly, I need something from him." Slow as dripping tar he turns away from her, puttering at an unseen device on a workbench, and she sniffs stale air. Musty and old. Dank and fertile with the smell of soil, stone, and mold. When he turns back, his face is no longer kind—no longer human—and he takes two menacing steps to where she lay unable to move.

"I have other uses for you, as well," his voice gurgles, lips slavering. She tries to turn in her disgust, but cannot. The old man leans close, his breath hot and acrid, burning where it touches the exposed skin of her neck. The heat travels upward, invading her brain, and an explosion of colors follow.

I can taste...blue, she thinks, then her world fades again.

Like a rose unfurling its petals, Amber wakes in stages from a cold, gray sleep. The dream seemed so *real*, and she withdraws slower than she would like. She struggles to sit up, pain from stiff joints and atrophied muscles making it difficult. *How long have I been out? Days, at the very least.* She places her bare feet on the hard floor and the cold surface shocks her senses, waking her like a slap across the face. She reaches to scratch an itch, and feels a small circular bandage on the side of her neck. She moves her hand to her face and rubs her eyes; they're gummy and she has trouble opening them, but when she does, her face falls.

The room is a bare, brown box—not much larger than her bathroom—containing nothing more than the bed she is on, herself, and a door. Cinder block walls, painted a dull mocha—what her daddy would have called "shit brown"—weep moisture like sweat, and the paint peels in spots near the floor. A single bulb hangs in the center of the high ceiling from an aged cord stiffened by dry-rot. A rusty pull-chain dangles beneath. *A basement,* she thinks. *But not in a home. Those have much lower ceilings.*

She tries to stand, but her legs aren't used to the effort, and she falls back to the bed with a heavy thud. The paper hospital gown she wears billows as she lands, and the springs under the mattress squeal in distress. She thinks, *This room is too small to be a whole basement,* and decides it must be a side room. Something partitioned from the rest.

"Either way," she says, her voice harsh and almost unrecogniz-able, "this place is older than I am."

"*Much* older," a voice says, coming from the walls. "But you have wakened sooner than I expected, and we can't have that."

"Who—?"

The transition is faster this time, leaving no time to smell the berries.

* * *

Amber opened her eyes to bright, warm light, sitting in a small chair at a round table. A plate of scrambled eggs and bacon steamed in front of her, the odors waking her empty stomach. She ignored her gnawing hunger and tilted her head at the old man seated across the table. He was already eating, chewing happily on a slice of bacon while he scooped eggs onto a fork.

"How lo..." she croaked, then cleared her throat and took a sip from the glass of water at her hand. "How long?"

The old man chewed a few seconds, then swallowed and said, "Three days." He shrugged, "Well... close enough."

Three days? What was done to me? She did not feel violated sexually, at least. *That* she was sure she would know right away. *Doesn't mean it won't happen later,* she thought with growing anxiety. She reached for the small bandage at her neck, but it was gone, with only a mild ten-derness left behind as evidence. The room she was in now was not the same as before. This one felt more like a small apartment, though also unfurnished save the table and chairs. They sat near a broad window that climbed from floor to ceiling far above their heads. *It's a converted warehouse*, she thought. She had seen these in New York, but didn't realize any existed in Atlanta. *Am I even in Atlanta?*

The jeans she now wore felt rough against her skin, and the white button-down shirt was stiff. These clothes were new, and not the ones she had been wearing when he took her. She tugged at the long cotton sleeves; her arms lost in the folds. It felt like a man's shirt, though the buttons were on the wrong side for that. When she moved her legs, her right was hampered by handcuffs that anchored her to the table.

"I apologize," he said. "I am not so good at guessing size for a woman." He smiled. "Much of your other clothing was damaged in the removal, and there was no time to pack anything from your wardrobe." Now he frowned and shook his head, "I am afraid you will not be able to return to your home for a while." She noted the accent—German, but with hints of South America. A useless piece of information in her current straits.

"Not return home?" she said, her brows knitting. Her outward calm hid a roiling cauldron beneath. She had spent a lifetime concealing her worry and angst from an overprotective mother, and this was no different. *Fear might just get you killed, missy*, she thought in her father's voice.

"The police have cordoned it off, and others are watching," he said. "It seems you are under investigation for your involvement with Mr. Montgomery." He took another bite, then pointed at her plate with his fork. "You must eat, now."

"You were the man I saw at his place the other day," she said. It was not a question. "I passed you on the stairs."

"Yes," he said, nodding. "I hoped to give him some information he needs very badly, but I must have just missed him." He leaned forward, as if he were speaking in confidence. "Now he is on the run—wanted for *murder*—and I have no way to contact him."

"Neither do I," she said, hoping that would end this nightmare. Even if she *could* contact him, this was certainly not the best way to get her to do it. She wanted Jack now more than ever, but now more than ever it was not something she *should* want. The best she could do for him was nothing.

"Not yet," he said through a tight mouth, and waved his fork again. "Eat, now."

"What is happening?" she said, anger rising past her curiosity for the first time to take a look around. "Why do you have me here?"

"All in good time, Ms. Riley." He nodded at her plate, "First you must regain your strength. *Then* we will talk about what you can do for me."

* * *

Breathing was a struggle, the air thick with possibilities, her heart compressed by doubt, worry, and guilt. Buried in self-loathing, it covered her as completely as soil on a grave. Clawing her way to the surface...

Amber sat straight up in bed, eyes wide, and she scanned the room as she swung her feet to the floor. A heavy chain tethering her left ankle to the bed's old iron frame rattled and clanked, and the police-issue handcuffs used to connect her to that chain chafed her flesh.

The last thing she remembered was setting her fork down after finishing breakfast, and she still wore the same jeans and shirt from that meal. Neither hungry nor thirsty, it must have been a few hours at most.

How did he do it? she thought. *He must have someone helping him.* She was far too heavy for someone as old as him to have carried her, but she had seen no one else. She didn't feel groggy like she had been drugged, though. If anything, she felt refreshed and fully awake; if she had been truly asleep, it had been a dreamless one. One moment she was finishing a meal, and the next she was here with almost no transition. It was as if someone had flipped her switch to *off*, set the toy in the next room, and turned it back on.

Too many Twilight Zone reruns, she thought with a rueful smile.

Still, she lifted her eyes to the ceiling, half expecting a giant child to smile back at her. Nothing looked back except that single bare bulb hanging from its cord.

So far she had been treated well, even if she was little more than a prisoner. That could change in a heartbeat, though, and if there was to be a change, she would feel better if it was on *her* terms. Escape appeared impossible.

If it looks impossible to me, *then it certainly does to* him *as well.* "Confidence works both ways," her daddy had told her. "Confidence in yourself can move mountains," he had said, "but too much sets you up for failure. Everyone who ever failed in spectacular fashion did so because of *over*confidence."

She stood, the bed's springs groaning their relief, and turned to kneel as if to pray. Instead, she ran a hand beneath the mattress, feeling each rusty spring in the open frame. Every chain had one weak link, and Amber knew with certainty exactly where *this* one lay.

If she made it out of this room, there was still the matter of escaping the building at large. She didn't know the layout, how many people were there, or even what town she was in. With no money, phone, or identification, there wasn't much she could do even *if* she escaped.

"One step at a time," she whispered, and continued her search.

* * *

Gotcha! The broken spring was near the foot of the bed, close to where that end of the chain had been padlocked to the frame. The end of the spring was both rusted and sharp, and she nicked her index finger when she ran her hand over it. She pulled her hand back and stuck the finger in her mouth, trying to remember the last time she had a tetanus shot. It had to be around the time she became a flight attendant, so it was up to date.

The chain's links were old, but they were strong and heavy. She grabbed a loop of the loose chain and threaded the broken end of the spring through one of the links and, holding the chain in both hands, pulled the spring toward her. She did this several times, allowing the link to slide over the wire as she pulled, straightening it. Within a few pulls, she had an almost straight length of wire the thickness of a crochet needle. She repositioned the chain and used it to make a sharp bend near where it was attached to the frame, then bent it back again. Over and over she worked the wire in this way, weakening it as the stress heated the bend. When she felt it wiggling freely, she grabbed the end with her hand and moved it faster, back and forth, until it fractured and came free.

In her sweating hands was a hot three-inch length of strong wire.

"Nice to know Dillon turned out to be good for something after all," she said, and wiped the sweat from her forehead. Her high school boyfriend had been convinced he would be a great magician, but never progressed much beyond simple card tricks. The one thing he *had* taught her—other than don't trust a drunk seventeen-year-old to drive—was the art of unlocking handcuffs. She knew how to make a pick, but this wire was too strong to bend easily into the proper shape. As a *shim*, though, it was nearly perfect.

She took the wire and shoved it between the locking mechanism and the teeth on the locking arm. It didn't quite fit, so she pulled it out and rubbed it on the stone floor, using the rough surface to grind it flatter. Several tries later, it fit neatly inside with minimal effort. Pressing the wire in, she tightened the cuff around her ankle a single notch, and then the cuff slipped and popped open.

Amber smiled, reset the cuff around her ankle, and slid the piece of wire inside the mattress.

Step one complete, she thought, and lay back on the bed.

* * *

Again, there was no transition. One moment she lay on the bed, flush with the thrill of success with the handcuff around her ankle, and the next she was sitting in the chair across from the old man, eating a meal. She knew of no drug that acted that quickly, but she had read once that anesthetics worked by creating short-term memory loss rather than knocking you out. Amber had hoped that wasn't true, since it meant you were awake during an operation, just unable to move.

She looked down at the fine china in front of her, the simple cheeseburger and fries perched incongruously on top. Amber picked up the burger with one hand and took a bite. *Yep... MacDonald's*, she thought as she chewed. *There's no mistaking that taste. Same damn flavor in every country.* She could be in *Japan* for all she knew.

"I apologize," the old man said. "My larder is understocked at the moment, and this was the only place nearby." He picked up his own half-eaten burger and took a bite, wincing a little as he chewed. "Sometimes food is just fuel."

Seated near the same window, she turned her head to look outside. The afternoon sun was high in the sky, the light defining distinct rectangles on the aged pine flooring inside. The heat on her cheeks told her this was not a modern double-paned window. *This building is definitely old*, she thought, and she reached for the crystal tumbler to her right that she knew with certainty contained soda.

Outside the window were other buildings—some older, some newer—all of similar design, and surrounded by a large lawn now gone to seed. There was a single road that ran in front of this building, but there was no traffic. Far in the distance, across the overgrown lawn at the end of a two-lane driveway, was a hedge fence. It could have been an old stone fence covered in ivy—she couldn't be sure.

It's an estate *of some kind!* The realization hit her like a slap in the face. She wasn't being kept in a warehouse somewhere in a city, but a large—and probably *deserted*—estate in some rural area.

"Why are you keeping me here, Mr...?"

"Dieter... please," he nodded. "We can leave the honorifics aside." He set his burger down, and took a sip from his drink—water for him—and rested his hands flat on the table. "For now, you are here for your own protection," he said. He tilted his head and shrugged. "Later... as I said, I have need of you."

"What *need* would that be?" she said, the false bravado catching in her throat.

"Nothing so sinister as what you are imagining, I assure you," he said with that same sweet smile she saw on their first meeting. "At its most basic, I need you to bring Mr. Montgomery to me."

"Why would I do that?"

"Why... to *save* him, of course." The smile on his lips grew cold, matching the chill running up her spine.

* * *

I must be close to that room, Amber thought, sitting in her bed and hugging her knees tight against her chest. She had begun chewing her nails again, an old habit that resurfaced every time she was under stress. *Even with help, he couldn't carry me far.* She hadn't seen a hint of other people in the building, or on the grounds outside the window, but that didn't mean they weren't there. In fact, she had to assume they *were*. For the same reasons, she assumed the stairs leading to the ground floor must be close as well.

In the end, none of that mattered. She must escape, and she must do it soon. Dieter had far too much physical control over her, and she knew physical control could lead to mental control. He wouldn't—or *couldn't*—tell her how to *find* Jack, much less convince him to meet. He simply knew she would, as if it were a movie where he had already seen the ending. That disturbed her more than anything—the sheer *certainty* he exuded.

"I have made a study of people," he had said with that flat calm, sending chills slithering up her spine again. "You simply have to learn what motivates them." He smiled, but this time it wasn't so sweet. "There are others searching for Mr. Montgomery, but they don't know the human heart like I do."

She didn't understand any of that, but she understood the need to warn Jack at the very least. But first, she had to get away from the sweet old lunatic.

It hit her like a truck. *Asylum! It's an old abandoned mental hospital.* The stereotypical look was certainly there, but she didn't know of any in the Atlanta area. *Surely there is at least one*, she thought. There were a few on the East Coast that were supposed to be haunted, but those were maintained as tourist attractions. Either this was not one of those, or it was shut down temporarily for some reason.

No, she had to assume she was still somewhere in Georgia—possibly still Atlanta. In the end it didn't matter, as she still had no money or identification. If she escaped, her only option was to go to the police, but since she was being sought as well, there were no guarantees she could keep from going to jail.

Why do I know that? she thought. *Only because Dieter told me*, that's *why. Is that just another lock on my prison door?* That was likely. There was no reason to believe him on any count, and certainly not that. *Jack could* never *murder anyone.* She may not know him as well as she would like, but that was something she just couldn't accept. The deaths in Germany had both shaken and angered him, and she refused to believe those reactions had been faked.

But death does seem to follow him, that's for sure, she thought.

* * *

Amber was no longer surprised to find herself sitting near the window. The sun was setting on the far side of the building, the view through the glass now a gloomy, sepia-toned photograph of urban decay. The meal on the china before her was no better, and she looked away from it to the man across the table. Dieter picked at his food with a gold fork, no more interested in eating than she, and his appearance was more disheveled than their last encounter. His clothes had the rumpled look of having been slept in, but there wasn't a hint of stubble on his face, and his white hair was smooth and tidy.

He set his fork down and studied her for a moment. Piercing, pale blue eyes bored into her, flashing a look approaching anger. A look which faded as quickly as it came. "After I return you to your room, I would like you to look these over." His right hand patted a thick brown envelope. She recognized it as the one he had carried up the steps that morning at Jack's apartment. "When you have had a chance to study them, maybe you will be more disposed to helping me... *and* Jack, of course," he said with a smile. That smile no longer appeared sweet to her. It was the look of someone who knew he was in control. Of the situation, the outcome... of *her*.

"Of course," she said. Amber had decided early on the best attitude she could take was one of obsequious acceptance. She had to make him comfortable in his belief of control. *Overconfidence*, she thought. *Why did Bond villains always place the hero in a position that allowed for escape?* She knew the obvious answer was *plot*, but in *their* world it always came down to overconfidence. Amber reached across the table and slid the envelope toward her. Thick and heavy, it promised both secrets and lies. She wondered if it also held any truth.

He steepled his hands in front of his face, and said, "In a day or two I will take you close to where he is. It will be up to you, though, to get his attention." He lay his hands in his lap and tilted his head. "After you give him the information in your hands, you will bring him to me." Dieter smiled again and leaned forward. "Do you understand?"

"I understand," she said, playing along. He is leaving far too much to chance and the confidence I will go along with this, she thought. What does he think will compel me to do his bidding? Is the information in this envelope really that precious? Is he really that overconfident, or is he that sure Jack not only needs the information, but that I will understand he has to have it?

"What happens if I just turn myself in to the police?" she asked, not sure if she should try to break his certainty at this point.

He frowned and offered a sad shake of his head. "That would be neither helpful nor wise... for you *or* Mr. Montgomery." Amber heard with complete clarity the implied threat couched inside the false warning.

* * *

Medical records. The envelope was filled with them. Complete lab reports for seven patients, all of whom had received major organ and tissue transplants from a single donor. *Why would this be important to Jack?* It must have something to do with the pilot in Germany, but she had no medical training, and therefore no way to glean anything of value from the records. *Why would Dieter think this would sway me?*

She flipped through every document in the file, and the only thing she could see was the donor was from Tennessee, and all the recipients were in close proximity. *Except for one*, she thought. That one was in Washington, DC, and a relative of the donor.

There were other documents as well. None of them seemed to have the slightest connection to the patients in the file. A story about sleeping sickness in Kazakhstan, another about more than a hundred kids in Baltimore with polio-like symptoms, a similar incident in California, the Germanwings crash, and on and on. There were even clippings of stories about terrorist activities, along with major news stories about activities of world leaders—some going back *decades*. To her it was a mishmash of information with nothing to connect any one thing to another.

She stopped, her hand frozen at the short article about Jack's wife and daughter. Written with a cool, clinical detachment, it was an emotionless retelling of the destruction of a family. The picture was the same as the one in Jack's wallet, and Amber's eyes clouded with tears as she read. She flipped back to the beginning in disgust. She noticed the string of numbers at the bottom of the first page written with a fat pencil. The numbers themselves weren't familiar, but she recognized the format.

It was a phone number, and the leading digits were the country code for Germany.

* * *

Now or never, she thought, and pulled the metal shim from the mattress. By the time she finished with the files, she guessed it was close to midnight, and if she were to make an attempt at escape, it had

198

to be tonight. She lifted her leg onto the bed, the heavy chain clanking tonelessly, and slipped the shim into the gap of the handcuff. Tightening a notch, she pushed the shim in and the locking arm slipped, opening freely.

Amber stood on bare feet, stuffed the envelope into her shirt, and padded to the door. The lock was old but well maintained, and she used the handcuff's chain to bend the shim into a shape more useful as a pick. She slid the pick inside the lock to feel for the pins, then smacked her forehead with one palm and hissed, "Idiot!"

She had no way to hold the tension on the lock while she set the pins with the pick, so she walked back to the bed for another piece of wire. It took another few minutes of work to break one free and straighten it, and the whole time she listened for footsteps outside her door. Sweating from both the exertion and fear, she bent down and went to work on the lock. Dillon had taught her this trick as well, but it was less a part of his magic act, and more for breaking into the school when he was bored.

Sweat ran from the top of her forehead in a trail down the bridge of her nose, beads pausing there before dropping to the floor in soft splashes. Just when she was sure she had forgotten how, the lock gave way and the knob moved. With exaggerated care, she turned the knob and eased the door open on groaning hinges. She slowed the pace, and the groan became a low and slow vocal fry.

When it was open far enough, Amber poked her head through. Across from the door was a solid wall painted exactly like her room. Looking both ways revealed a long and empty hallway with doors on either side similar to hers, and a stairwell at the far end on the left. The right was a dead-end, so she chose the stairs. "Nowhere to go but up," she whispered.

She stuffed the picks into the pocket of her jeans, closed the door behind, and walked as fast and silent as she could to the stairs. Metal-framed with concrete treads, they were solid enough to make no noise when she tested the first step. Two flights up she tried the door, but it was rusted shut, and no amount of lock-picking would help. On the second floor the door swung open with no effort. *How lucky is that?* she thought. *Too lucky by half,* her daddy answered in her head, but she didn't stop to think about it further. The door opened into a wide hallway that must have stretched the full length of the building. A large open foyer was about twenty feet to her left, so she walked that way, staying close to the wall. The building was as dark and silent as a cemetery, and just as creepy. The smell of mold and decay pervaded, and she took shallow breaths as she inched her way along the wall.

When she reached the foyer, she turned toward the moonlight where it streamed in through broken windows. Here was the front of the building, and large twin oak doors opened onto a wide set of steps leading to the gravel drive. Breathing heavily now, she pushed on one door, and it, too, swung open on creaking hinges. Outside, the air smelled fresh and clean, and she took a moment to breath deep for the first time since leaving her room. She turned to look up at the face of the building, but no lights snapped on in the windows, nor did boots pound the floor as battalions of guards chased her down.

When she descended the stairs to the drive, the gravel assaulted the soft soles of her feet, but she smiled, nonetheless. *Overconfidence unravels even the best of plans.* The air was chill but not cold. She took a last look at the old asylum looming over her like a vulture and ran down the drive and into the night.

CHAPTER 17

ILL SAT AT THE COUNTER IN THE LITTLE DINER, the worn stool hav-ing become his "spot" over the years. Anyone at work who had to find him in a hurry always knew where to look come lunchtime. *No one does that anymore*, he thought, looking at the cell phone next to his plate. *Everybody's too fuckin' connected all the time.* He frowned, lifted the last bit of club sandwich to his mouth, and popped it in just as the phone buzzed. *Ain't no such thing as downtime anymore*, he thought with a grunt. Bill, in no hurry, chewed, swallowed, and picked up the phone.

The caller ID read *anonymous*, and he was in no mood to talk to either a pollster or a salesman. He tapped the "ignore" button and laid the phone back down, then waved the waitress over to refill his coffee. Ten seconds later, the phone buzzed again.

"You gonna get that?" Charlene said as she poured his coffee.

Bill gave her a look that said *yes, boss*, and picked up the phone without looking down.

"Bill Montgomery," he said, smiling up at Charlene. She finished topping off his cup, winked, and walked away satisfied.

"Bill... it's Mason," the voice on the other end rasped. There was the clear sound of road noise as well, and Bill raised an eyebrow as he listened. "We need help," Mason said. "*Jack* needs your help."

"Are you with him now?"

"Oh, *hell* no. He doesn't know I'm calling you. I'm supposed to be out getting food."

Bill had suspected Mason was on the run with Jack. Those two had each been a part of the other's mess since college. If one was in a fix, it was even money that the other was close by—sometimes just laughing and pointing. Jack was his brother, and Bill loved him for it, but he knew that friends were the family you *chose*. He didn't feel slighted that it was *Mason* calling him instead of his own brother.

"Where are you?"

A hesitation, and Bill listened for clues in the background noise. "You have to promise me you won't call the cops."

Bill rolled his eyes. "Mason, you idiot... I *am* the cops."

"That's not what I meant, and you *know* it."

"I can't—"

"Listen... there's a shit-ton going on you don't know about, and it's all tied up with that damn letter I tried to get you interested in. Remember *that*?" The cold disdain was clear in Mason's voice, and Bill couldn't fault him for it.

"I remember there wasn't anything I could do about it."

"People are *dying*, Bill, and I'm afraid if you don't get here and talk Jack down..."

He waited to hear the rest, but he didn't need to. Jack was Jack—slow to anger, but reckless once there.

"Tell me where you are, Mason," he said, then he did the one thing a good cop should *never* do. "I promise not to call the cavalry." He shook his head, knowing full well this was a mistake. "Tell me where to meet you, and I'll come alone."

There was a long pause, a car horn honking nearby. "We're at the Motel 6 on I-85 just inside the loop."

"Atlanta?" How stupid are these guys? Even if I don't call the cops, someone is sure to recognize Jack from the damn pictures plastered all over the news.

"Yeah. Room 212."

"All right... stay put until I get there." He stood, took his wallet from his back pocket, and pulled a ten from inside and laid it on the counter beside his plate. "It might be after dark, though. Can you keep him there that long?"

"He won't show his face in the daytime, so we should be good until dusk," Mason said, and Bill heard the tension leak out of the man's voice. "I don't know what you can do to help, but maybe I can get him to turn himself in to your custody until this clears up."

"That's the first *smart* thing I've heard you say since I've known you," Bill said with a slight grin. "Just stay put until I get there."

"I'll do what I can," Mason said, and the line went dead.

Yeah, Bill thought as he shoved the phone in his pocket, *what you should have done was keep him out of trouble from the get-go.* That wasn't fair to Mason, though. Once Jack got invested in something, he was like a dog with a bone.

"Later, Charlene," he said over his shoulder as he walked to the door. He pulled it open, the little bell on top jingling happily, and stepped out into a beautiful afternoon sun. It was the kind of day where nothing could—or *should*—go wrong, and he turned to his right to walk back to the station.

Across the road, Thirteen watched from the shade of a tree.

* * *

The easy part was over. The chief wasn't happy Bill was taking emergency time off, and he liked it even less that Bill wouldn't tell him *why*. In the end it went pretty much the way Bill had expected—lots of questions, lots of cajoling, and very little give. When he made the point he hadn't taken time off in almost a year, Chief Nelson relented and sent him on his way.

The *hard* part was going to be explaining it to his wife. With or without Jenna's approval, he'd already made up his mind to go, and she would see *that* coming a mile off. *I ain't the only detective in the family*, he thought with a wry grin. *She ain't the best principal in town for nothin'.*

No, the hard part was definitely in front of him.

Jenna loved Jack as family, but she had turned her nose up at his behavior over the last year. He knew some of that was fear for his well-being, but a good chunk of it was just plain old momma-bear protecting her young. Jack no longer presented himself as the kind of role model she wanted around her kids, and she made it plain to Bill that Jack—in his present state—was not welcome in their home.

"If he can pull himself together and sober up, fine," she had said, and that was the end of it as far as she was concerned.

His one consolation—if he could call it that—was he knew without a doubt she would treat the *kids* the same way under the same circumstances. She might call it "tough love", but his years of sensitivity training taught him to see things differently.

He walked to his office and retrieved his coat from the rack in the corner, then shrugged it on over the old shoulder holster holding his favored SigSauer 226. The department issued Glocks, but he hated those things. Most of the detectives used the clip-on holsters, but he hated those, too. Those required a belt, and he hadn't worn a belt in years. It wasn't as if he was out of shape, but things had started to settle recently, so his conversion to suspenders had gone full-time. The younger detectives kidded him about it, but he had stopped caring about teasing around the time his height topped six feet back in junior high.

Without acknowledging anyone on the way out, he left the building through the rear exit and walked to his car. The 1980 Pontiac Catalina was a land-yacht by anyone's standards, but it offered leg-room unmatched by any in his price range. It was also from a time when a man could work on his own car, and he spent many a weekend keeping it in top form. His wife called it their third child.

He turned the key and felt the heavy rumble of the 400 cubic inch engine. *A good thing this beast has a 25-gallon tank*, he thought. The one time he had to wind the motor out, he swore he watched the needle on the gas gauge swing from half to empty in the space of a few seconds. *Perp didn't get away, though, did he? Not even in that fancy, souped-up Honda.*

He threw his arm over the seat as he turned his head and prepared to back out. Before he could shift into reverse, the front passenger door opened, and a tall man in an overcoat and fedora slid into the seat beside him. Bill's first thought was to go for his gun, but then he no longer wanted to, the will to move excised from his mind. The other man smiled with sad eyes, reached across, and turned the key.

"I apologize," the man said, a pained expression on his face. He was sweating at the temples, and his eyes looked very far away. "Just know this is as difficult for me as it is for you."

Now what does he mean by—

Bill's world turned black.

* * *

Bill took the key from the ignition, opened the heavy door, and stepped out of the car. He pushed it closed with a satisfying *thunk* before turning to walk to his front door. Something nagged, an itch he couldn't scratch, and he stopped before taking a single step. He looked back at his car, the Big Cat parked neatly in the center of his driveway, and tilted his head, eyebrows furrowing as he realized he didn't remember a *lick* of the drive home.

I haven't done that *since I got blind drunk at a party in college*, he thought with no small amount of worry. That single event had stopped him from ever driving drunk again, long before MADD formed. He had, in fact, stopped drinking for *fun* almost entirely from that point forward. He checked the front and rear bumpers to reassure himself. *No blood or meat hangin' off. That's good.* Bill shook his head to clear it, and took a long breath, letting it out slowly. "Must be early-onset old-timer's disease," he said, and patted the hood of the car. "At least the *old girl* still knows her way home."

Satisfied he hadn't run anyone over, he left the car and entered his home. He threw his keys into the wooden bowl on the table in the entry and listened for the sounds of footsteps. There shouldn't be any this time of day—Jenna and the kids should still be at school—but he was a cop. *Understand your surroundings* had been drummed into him since his early days on the Force, and habits like that were neither easy nor *wise* to break.

He walked through the living room and into the kitchen, then removed his coat and wrapped it around one of the chairs at the breakfast table. For a moment he considered shedding the shoulder holster but decided against it. Jenna would see him with it still on and know at once he was going out again. That would shorten the argument that was sure to follow by a bit. *Just* a bit.

When he sat at the table, it was in *his* chair—the one with the best view of the garden outside the bay window. The same window Jenna insisted on having when they were looking for a house. He had always found it odd she ended up choosing the seat that had her back to that view. As he looked over the garden, sun-dappled daisies dancing happily in the breeze, the calm that had eluded him for days wrapped around his shoulders like a warm blanket. Some Sunday mornings he would take his coffee here, watching the world outside that window, burying *The Job* under mounds of fecund earth and desiccated leaves of oak and birch.

Bill sighed, long and slow, and set his elbows on the table, head in hands, and watched the world in its greening. Jenna and the kids would be home soon, and he still didn't know what to say to her.

* * *

Bill woke with a start, head on his arms, to the sound of a slamming door. *That would be Sarah,* he thought. *Kid still can't close a door without rattling the walls.* He had already replaced two knobs on her bedroom door. Bill snorted. *Amazing the damage a nine year old can do.* Sarah pounded up the stairs, her mother shooing her away to do her homework, a quick "Hi Daddy!" as she ran.

"Bill?" Jenna called from the entry.

"In the kitchen," he hollered back. He needed to be in charge of this conversation, and making her come to him was the most effective way to set the stage. She knew all his tricks, though, so his plans often fruited in the form of a cold sneer from his wife.

Jenna breezed into the kitchen, setting her purse on the island, and her eyes focused like a laser on his holster. "What's up?" she asked with one eyebrow raised. Before he could answer, she crossed her arms and pursed her lips.

Damn, he thought. Next, she's gonna—

She started tapping the toe of one shoe.

Crap. Bill sighed and turned in his seat to face her full-on. "It's Jack," he said. *Short and to the point.*

Jenna surprised him by relaxing. "Then why are you still here?" she asked, concern and confusion in her voice.

Twenty years, and that woman still surprises me, he thought with pride. "I figured you'd want to talk me out of it."

"You figured wrong, mister," she said, shaking her head. "That man's *family*, and whatever we can do to help, we will." She walked to the table and sat in "Sarah's" chair. "You're going to go get him, right?" She leaned in, taking Bill's hand. "I mean, he *has* to turn himself in, but you're the only safe way to do it. The media is painting him as some kind of monster, Bill. You know better than anyone what that can make even a *good* cop do."

This was a point they had argued over ever since she found out he wanted to join the Force, but there was no sense stirring *that* pot again. Her life experiences were just different from his, and they would never meet in the middle over something as fraught with emotion as police brutality. The truth was he *did* know some bad cops, but for the most part they did their jobs, the good—in *his* mind, at least—outweighing the bad. Jenna couldn't—or *wouldn't*—accept that.

"Mason called me a couple hours ago and told me where they were holed up," he said.

"Mason is with him? There's been nothing on the news about *that*."

"Yeah, but Jack doesn't know he called, so there's likely to be some *issues* with that." He looked around for an unseen audience before speaking again. "Where's Will?"

"He's got band practice today, remember?"

"Oh, yeah," he said, shaking his head. The boy at thirteen was almost a head taller than every kid in his grade, and insisted on playing the damn *saxophone* instead of football. Bill never understood that boy's love of music, but he decided long ago their choices were their choices.

"Listen," he said, taking both her hands in his, looking her straight in the eyes. "There's a lot going on I still don't know about. I can't say Jack was set up, but he seems to be caught up in a mess not of his making." He leaned closer. "Do you understand?"

Jenna leaned back, tilting her head. "You're telling me he's in danger... and not just from the cops."

"Could be. I just don't know. Mason came to me a while back with a letter and some crazy theories, and I brushed him off."

"This is *not* your fault, mister!" she said without hesitation. "Jack's pretty good at getting into trouble all by himself."

"Yeah," he said with a chuckle. "I told Mason I'd be there by around dark-thirty."

"Where?"

"Better if I don't say," he said, then sat back. "I might be gone a few days, though. Are you okay with that?"

"Do what you have to do, Bill," she said, breathing heavily. "Just make sure to keep *both* of you safe."

"Daddy?" They both turned as Sarah walked into the room.

"What is it, sweetheart?" he said.

Sarah walked right to him, passing her mother, and looked up into his eyes. "Are you gonna go get Uncle Jack?"

Bill stole a glance at his wife, then turned to his daughter and said with a forced smile. "That's the plan, munchkin."

"That's good," she said, a little sad. "I heard people say they wanted to hurt him." She laid her head in Bill's lap and turned her face up at him. "Don't let him get hurt, okay? I like Uncle Jack."

He bent down and kissed her forehead. "Cross my heart," he said, stroking her hair. *God, she looks so much like her mother.*

"And hope to die?"

He looked at Jenna, and said, "And hope to die."

* * *

Bill wished he had been able to see William before he left, if just to hug him and say goodbye, but there wasn't time. Jenna packed his clothes, enough for three days, and he hugged her and Sarah before saying his goodbyes. *I'm just gonna pick him up and bring him home, that's all*, he thought as he drove. The problem with reassurances was they didn't work on *yourself*. It was like telling yourself not to think of the pink elephant. From the time he arrived home until he left an hour later, Bill's unease had grown with each passing second, and watching the city disappear in his rearview mirror was like leaving his parent's home all over again.

"Stop it," he told himself. But that part of him refused to shut up. Four people connected to his brother were dead. *No, it's five now with the murder of Jack's boss.* Again, that itch he couldn't scratch surfaced, begging to be noticed. Bill had a nose for things that were just *wrong*, and there was plenty about all this that smelled to high heaven. Every time he felt that itch, it led to something important. The problem was having the patience to wait for it to express before going off on some wild tangent to find it. *Searching* for it always pointed him the wrong way.

Jack had the same gift, but often didn't have the patience to wait for the thing to reveal itself, instead bounding off into the brush to hunt. He was more a hunter of the "scream and leap" variety than a pure stalker. It was the trait that most often got him into trouble, and history was repeating itself now. Bill had dragged Jack out of more than one fight in high school—bruised and bloodied, but not bowed—just as he was doing now. *But none of that blood is yours this time, is it, little bro?*

"He's just like your daddy," Jenna had once told him. "He's got that need to see what's over the horizon, and sometimes he thinks the best way to get there is to blast through the mountain."

It was true their daddy had got himself into a few scrapes while they were growing up—just like Jack—but unlike Jack, the old man knew when he was outmatched. After he died, the job of teaching that lesson fell to Bill.

"Didn't do a very good job, did I?"

The miles melted away under the whining tires of the old beast, and Bill tried to shake the melancholy surrounding him. The sun had dipped down below the roof-line of the car, making that difficult, and he slapped the visor down to block the glare. Before reaching Atlanta, it would be staring him right in the face, and there was nothing he could do to stop it.

* * *

The engine died a slow death, dieseling a last coughing fit before settling long after he turned the key. *Time for a tuneup*, Bill thought as he looked up to the second-floor walkway. The Big Cat was dependable, but it took constant maintenance. *Everything in life is about maintenance. It's all just a matter of degree.*

There was no movement above, and the sun was setting rapidly now. Already behind the building, it limned the structure in golden light, setting the roof aflame.

And still he sat alone in the car.

What the hell am I afraid of? he wondered. Jack wasn't just his little brother—he was his friend. They had been friends their whole lives, never falling into the trap some brothers did. Some of that was due to Bill being forced to play father, but most of it was simple good parenting *before* their daddy died. If Bill couldn't get Jack to see reason, no one could.

That's not what you're really afraid of, though, is it?

Not if he was honest about it. What Bill was afraid of was Jack talking him into *helping,* sucking him into an adventure for which he

209

was wholly unprepared. Again, if he were being honest with himself, he already knew what his answer would be.

Bill scrubbed his face with both hands, yanked the key from the ignition, and opened the door. The parking lot was quiet, even this close to the Interstate. He stepped out of the car, looking around for anything suspicious before shutting the door with a gentle push, the latch catching with a soft click. Room 212 was close to the stairs, and Bill walked with heavy legs to the first step, grabbed the rail, and started up. When he reached the top, someone stepped out of their room two doors down, and Bill stiffened. Whoever it was headed in the opposite direction carrying an ice bucket, and he relaxed.

I am way *too jumpy for this shit,* he thought, shaking his head.

He took a deep breath to calm his nerves and walked to the door. The noise coming from inside sounded like arguing, and he hesitated, listening. Two voices, one he recognized as Mason, but the other was unknown. Just before he knocked, he remembered to do it like a civilian rather than the heavy-fisted five-pounder all cops used.

The voices stopped mid-sentence, and someone walked to the door. When it didn't open immediately, Bill leaned toward the peephole and gave a half-smile. The chain rattled off and the door flew open. Mason grabbed Bill by the shirt and yanked him into the room and a fierce bear-hug. Tall and lanky, Mason had always been much stronger than he seemed. He reminded Bill of Bob Lilly, the skinny defensive lineman from the 70's Cowboys "Doomsday Defense." The only other man in the room was someone Bill had never met and had a distinct Middle-Eastern look about him.

"Thank *god* you're here, Bill!" Mason said, pushing him away after a couple of back slaps. "Jack's gone, and we don't know where he went."

* * *

Bill sat at the little writing desk, listening to Mason and watching Sohrab with a wary eye. Mason was pacing the room, high on adrenalin, but Sohrab had a confident calm about him. He sat on the bed, legs crossed and back against the headboard.

"Okay, slow down," Bill told Mason. "Give it to me again."

"Jack's been depressed more than usual since we heard about Sally, and with him not hearing anything from Amber—"

"Wait, wait," Bill waved him to silence. "Who the hell is Amber?"

Mason stopped and stared. He tilted his head, and said, "In short, she's a new girlfriend he met in Germany."

"Okay," Bill said. "Got it. Give me the details later how she plays into this." He waved at Mason to continue.

Mason went back to pacing, waving his arms as he spoke. "Anyway, Jack was stuck in this room for more than twenty-four hours." He shrugged. "It was more than he could take, I guess." He nodded at Sohrab. "Took Sohrab's keys when we weren't looking and drove off. He's not answering his phone, either."

Bill knew what that meant, and it wasn't good. Jack had hit some breaking point and was now on a self-destructive streak. Similar behaviors started soon after their father's death and stopped for good only when he met Beth.

"Think back, Mason. Do you know what triggered it?"

Mason bunched his mouth and stole a glance over to the bed. Sohrab nodded, and said, "Tell him."

"He got a call from a guy named Rutger. Something to do with Amber and Interpol." Mason sat with a heavy thud on the other bed, "It was all we could get out of him before he left."

"Okay," Bill said, "who the fuck is Rutger?"

"He was the detective working with Jack on the plane crash in Germany," Mason said. He shook his head, "I don't know what the hell Interpol has to do with this, or why that would even set him off."

"I don't think he was looking for a reason," Sohrab said. "Jack's been ready to pop for a while."

Bill watched the other man, still unsure of his role in all this, but content to leave it be for now. The only thing he knew for sure was that his brother was shutting down, blocking out all the pain and fear and guilt he had built up since the accident. There were a lot of ways a man could do that, but only one for Jack.

"You boys got a special place you go to unwind?"

Mason's eyebrows met in the center of his forehead, and he shook his head. "Jack would be an idiot to go there right now. We're fuckin' *regulars* at Jimmy's. *Everyone* there knows him."

"I don't think he cares about that, Mason," Bill said as calmly as he could. "He's going there because he wants to drink, and he can't go home. He's not even thinking about getting caught in a bar. Hell, he might even *want* to get caught."

Bill stood and pulled his keys from his pocket. "You two hang tight while I try to find him." He lifted the pad and pen from the desk, handed it to Mason, and said, "Write down the address, if you know it." Mason scribbled for a bit, then handed the pad back. "How long has he been gone?"

Mason looked at Sohrab, then shrugged, "Thirty, maybe forty minutes before you got here."

"Shit," Bill said, "it may already be too late."

CHAPTER 18

J ACK SAT AT THE BAR, stared into a glass of the best single-malt Jimmy's offered, and wondered how long it would take before someone called the cops. Jimmy himself had taken station across the bar from Jack, drying glasses and watching him with a wary eye. The owner allowed no one else—bartender, waitress, or patron—within two stools distance of Jack.

"You waitin' on someone?" Jimmy asked, placing a tumbler on the shelf.

"Possibly," Jack said without looking up. "I'll know for sure when they get here." He picked up his glass, upended it, and drank the contents in one gulp. When he set it on the bar, he pushed it toward Jimmy and pointed, asking for a refill. Jimmy pulled a bottle from beneath the bar, poured Jack another two fingers, then went back to drying his glasses.

Jack wasn't going to stop tonight. He would keep calling for refills, and Jimmy would oblige. Jimmy would do this for the same reason no one approached Jack—the air around him was thick with pain, futility, and no small amount of danger. To get near the man, anyone who dared must push through that like clearing a path through a rainforest, never sure if the next thicket of heavy green foliage hid an animal more teeth and claws than intellect.

Jack had been that way ever since the call from Rutger.

"No one's seen her in almost two days, Jack," Rutger had said. "We've turned the place over, but about the only thing we found was her cell phone." Rutger's voice hesitated at the word *about*, and Jack had almost missed it.

"What *else* did you find?"

"It is probably nothing—"

"What *else*?"

Rutger had sighed, and said, "She had just over eight thousand American dollars in cash stuffed in an unpacked suitcase. Her job does not allow her to take tips, and the fact it was eight and change means it was likely nine."

"And you think that means something?" Jack had asked, already knowing the answer.

"I don't know, but it is suspicious. The money was in the suitcase she carried from Germany, and the amount is just under what would have to be declared when entering the US."

"It's also possible she carried the money with her *to* Germany," Jack had said, grasping at the thinnest of straws.

"To what end?"

"I don't know, Rutger. *You're* the detective. *You* figure it out." The anger had burned in him, forcing out rational thought, but one still fought through. "Tell me, though—it's obvious your partner thinks she is on the run, and you might think the same—but why didn't she take the money?"

Rutger had no answer to that, and with no more information to give, ended the conversation soon after.

Jack knew, though. Either Amber had left without going back to her apartment as Jack had instructed, or someone met her there and took her with them. Why else had she not called?

The Shadowman was in Atlanta, of that much Jack was sure. Sally's murder proved it. Like an idiot, Jack had driven by Sally's house thinking he might speak with Derrick, but cops and the FBI were still there interrogating him. Jack had to navigate the cars parked on the street, driving by several officers too invested in their investigation to see the fugitive in their midst.

Jack downed his drink and motioned for another. Jimmy poured, then tapped the bar and nodded past Jack. Jack's shoulders slumped, tight muscles relaxing for the first time, and he looked into the mirror behind the bar to see who was there to arrest him.

It wasn't who he was expecting.

"Hey, Li'l Bro," Bill said, settling onto the stool next to him. "Wanna have your friend there pour me one?"

"I don't buy drinks for pigs," Jack said before taking a sip. It was an old inside joke between the brothers, but, given the circumstances, there was little humor behind it. Jimmy set a glass on the bar in front of Bill and filled it.

"Look," Bill said, lifting the glass, "there's only one way this can go down. I flash my badge at Silent Bob, here, cuff you, and frogmarch you out of the bar."

"*You're* arresting me?" Jack breathed hard, his heart pounding, and looked at his brother like he had never seen the man before.

"Calm down," Bill said in a tight whisper before Jack could get too wound up. "It's for show so the customers don't get the bright idea to call the locals."

"Can't," Jimmy said, still drying glasses like he had nothing else to do.

"Can't... *what?*" Bill said, restrained malice in his voice.

"No one uses their cell in *my* bar unless I flip this little switch back here," he said, pointing under the bar.

"Uh, mister... the FCC takes a dim view of cell phone jammers."

Jimmy grinned, "You see anybody here working for the FCC?"

Bill snorted, but Jack said, "Is that why I never have any service here?"

"Yeah," Jimmy said. "If you want to gab on your phone, go to Starbucks. I hate those fuckin' things."

Bill stared at Jimmy with what looked to Jack like respect, then turned to Jack and said, "You ready?"

"Nope," Jack said, finishing his drink. He pointed to it, and Jimmy filled it again. "I came here for a reason, and I'm not even halfway through." His words came slow and sloppy. He knew if he kept it up, it wouldn't be long before he grew belligerent, and Bill would have to resort to force. *And that's fine by me*, he thought as he took another drink. *Nobody deserves it more.*

"Jack—"

"Either drink with me, or get out," Jack said around the glass. There wasn't enough alcohol in the world to make him as numb as he wanted, but more than enough to make him forget. *At least for a while.* He swallowed, and the liquid staunchly refused to burn on the way down this time. His lips were numb, the first indicator that whatever he drank was taking effect. *C'mon Bill*, he thought, *just fuckin' hit me, already!*

Instead, Bill set his elbows on the bar and sighed. "Okay, Li'l Bro. We'll do it your way." He looked over at Jack, and added, "For a while."

Jack smiled, toasted Bill's good sense, and finished the drink in his hand.

He tapped the bar for another.

* * *

"You're *both* drunk," Mason said as he pulled Jack and Bill into the room. He twisted up his mouth, eyes narrowed at Jack, and his nose wrinkled as the men passed.

"Not Billy," Jack said, waving a finger in front of his nose. "He's too big to get drunk." He couldn't help himself and chuckled at his own humor.

"Tipsy is a better word," Bill said as he stumbled past Jack and lowered his bulk into the nearest chair.

"Whoops! Room's spinnin'," Jack said. Part of him knew it wasn't *really* spinning, unless you counted the Earth's rotation. And then add in motion around the Sun, the Sun rotating in the Milky Way, and... *Okay, I have to sit down.* He plopped on the corner of the bed, missed, and ended up on the floor, trying to hold down his gorge through force of will.

"Getting a little green around the gills, there, buddy," Mason said far too loud.

"I think we should get him to the bathroom," the Iraqi secret agent said in his Iraqi secret agent accent.

Each man grabbed an arm and raised Jack between them. He tried to move his legs but they refused to cooperate, so he allowed the two men to drag him. He looked up, smiling at each. "I love you guys," he said, then giggled.

"I'll make the coffee," Bill said from behind. *Bill's been behind for a while, hasn't he?* His brother grunted as he stood, reminding Jack of the sound he would soon make, and his last meal rose another couple of inches.

Mason and Whatsisname dropped him in front of the toilet, and Mason lifted the lid just in time. Jack hugged the bowl and emptied his stomach in a long and violent growl. The last bits of his toenails dropped into the bowl, and he thought the ordeal was over. That was when his body discovered a hidden cache of *something* deep in his abdomen to offer to the porcelain god, and he began again in earnest. *What's with the damn chunks? I haven't had anything but alcohol for hours.*

On and on it went, Mason flushing the toilet while Jack flushed his system. Someone turned on the shower. The smell of chlorine in the water as it misted set off another torrent of bile from his body. *That's all there is,* he thought. *Got to be reaching the end soon.*

"Just the yellow stuff, now," someone said. *Not Mason. Must be the other guy.*

"All right," Mason said, "help me get him up."

Hands grabbed him under his armpits, pulling him to his feet again.

"M'not through," he said.

"Close enough," the accent said, and the hands lowered him into the cold spray of the shower.

"Fuck that!" Jack yelled, and fought to get out, but the hands held him down.

"Shut up and quit squirming," Mason said.

Jack tried to settle down, but drops blew into his mouth and nose, and he sputtered and wiped his face to keep the water out of his eyes. They held him there until he stopped moving, then Sohrab turned the water off.

The big Iraqi laughed from his belly, "You gentlemen are a riot, you know that?" He stood back with fists on his hip, and said, "Most fun I've had in years."

* * *

"I get it," Bill said while Jack sipped his coffee. "Guilt is a powerful thing, but in this case it's misplaced."

Jack sat on the bed, towel around his waist and another over his shoulders, holding the mug between both hands to warm them. Someone—*probably Sohrab,* he thought—had set the air conditioner on "meat locker." For the first time, Jack thought about how phenomenally *unprepared* they were. Only Sohrab and Bill had a change of clothes. The former was now out looking for the nearest store to buy a set for Jack and Mason. *Please, God... no silk shirts.* Mason had left them alone on the pretext of taking his own shower. The look he gave

217

Jack as he left the room was not pleasant, and Jack had winced a little when he saw it. *I haven't seen pure disappointment from anyone since I told my dad I didn't want to play football.*

"What makes you think I'm misplacing any guilt?"

"Because you were drinking yourself blind over it, Jack." Bill leaned forward, holding his mug in his hands much like Jack was, and said, "You are not responsible for any of these deaths. Not even Sally." His eyes narrowed. "You need to lay the responsibility for them at the feet of the guy who actually *killed* them."

"I get what you're doing, but—"

"But nothing! You've got to stay *focused*, Jack. Focused on the real killer, and focused on extracting your butt from the sling it's currently in." He shook his head and his eyes softened. "What you did tonight was beyond stupid. There are people out there looking for you who wouldn't think twice about shooting you... and *those* are the ones with *badges*. You think your Shadowman will be any less dangerous?"

"He's not trying to kill *me*."

"You *think*," Bill said, pointing a meaty finger in his face. "You don't know shit about what his motives are."

"Doesn't matter, anyway," Jack said, waving his hand. "I don't have the first clue where to find him."

Bill blew out a breath and relaxed. "Then come back to Greenville with me. Turn yourself in and we'll get all this straightened out. Shit, Jack, you've got an alibi for every damn murder this guy has committed, so it shouldn't be that hard."

Jack looked into his mug and watched the half-mixed creamer swirl its chaotic dance. *All life is chaos,* he thought. *It's a dance without form, and any meaning found in the spinning patterns is like seeing a face in the clouds.* "And what about Amber?" he asked without looking up.

Bill tilted his head and shrugged. "Unless you know a way to find her, there's not much we can do." He leaned forward, forearms on his knees, and looked Jack straight in the eyes. "If she was dead, knowing your Shadowman, someone would have found her body by now." He patted Jack on the leg, and said, "*When* she's found, I expect the worst she'll face is a stern questioning from the guys lookin' for *you*."

Jack took slow breaths. His stomach was still unsettled, and so was his heart. *Why did Amber have all that cash, and where the fuck is she?* He had no answer for either of those questions. *If she's just in hiding, will she surface when I turn myself in?* While that was a possibility, it was not a certainty.

He was being pulled in too many directions.

Mason opened the bathroom door, breaking the silence. He had a towel around his waist like Jack and dried his hair with another. He stepped between Jack and Bill, then sat on the other bed facing Jack. The shower had not washed that look off his face.

"You boys decided yet to go back to Greenville?" he said, taking the towel from his head, folding it twice, and laying it across his lap.

"Not yet," Jack said. "First, I'd like to know how Bill found us so easily." He knew the answer, but if he was wrong, it meant they were royally screwed.

"I called him," Mason said, his breathing shallow and controlled. He narrowed his eyes, "And I'd do it again. I'm not apologizing, if that's what you're looking for."

"You had no right—"

Mason laughed out loud, and it wasn't a jovial sound. When he spoke, it was more calm than Jack felt. "You have gone seriously off the fucking rails here, Jack. Everything is going to shit, and we *need* someone like Bill to help clean up your mess."

"*My* mess..." he said, his voice as dark as his mood. *And there it is.*

"No, Jack, I'm not blaming you for the shitstorm we're in, but this mess *is* yours, and only *you* can clean it up." He looked at Bill, his eyes pleading. "Am I the only one who sees this?"

Bill shook his head, but said nothing.

"I get that," Jack said. "Believe me, I do. But there's a killer right here in Atlanta who has all the pieces to this puzzle, and everyone with a badge is looking for *me* instead." He looked from one man to the other. "Is turning myself in going to solve that?"

Bill rubbed his hands, looked at Mason, and nodded. "Maybe, maybe not, but it will at least get you off the hook."

Jack looked at them both, not believing either of them could be so dense. "Has everyone forgot that *Interpol* is involved? That they've dragged a man who barely knows me across the Atlantic just to help them find me? Do you think that kind of muscle gets mobilized on a whim?" He sniffed in derision. "Whole swaths of law enforcement de-partment records have vanished without a trace, and you think they'll just question me and send me home with a lollypop?" He shook his head. "You guys are more naïve than I thought."

Everyone sat in silence, each staring at the other for long seconds. All heads turned to the door when the lock clicked. Sohrab stepped in carrying a plastic shopping bag, looked over the tableau as he closed the door, and smiled.

"You guys look like you're in line for a Roman bath house." He turned to Bill. "Well, maybe not you," he said, and placed the bag on Jack's bed.

"That's another thing," Bill said, his exasperation showing with a curt nod at Sohrab. "Who the fuck is *this* guy?"

* * *

"I'm not going with you," Jack announced to Bill over breakfast. *If you can call muffins and coffee breakfast*, he mused. He picked at the paper wrapping, peeling it away with a care he hadn't shown for any other act since Kazakhstan. Bill had grown ever more insistent during the previous night's discussion, giving up only when it was clear no one was paying attention anymore. Sohrab had fallen asleep in the chair long before then. It was his snoring, more than anything, that ended the argument. They couldn't hear one another talk, and no amount of jostling would rouse him.

Jack thought he was faking just to get everyone to shut up.

"And if you're staying in this with me," Jack said, "I'm gonna need your phone." He stuck his hand out, palm up over the table. Mason and Sohrab had stepped out earlier to get their own breakfast, leaving the two brothers to fight it out without interference. At first, Jack had thought that a grand idea. *Now...*

"You have your own," Bill said without moving.

"At least take the battery out of it."

"No can do, Li'l Bro," Bill said, his breathing heavy and face flush. Jack could feel the heat radiating from his body.

Jack pulled his hand back and studied his brother. "You'll have to leave, then," he said and shrugged. "If anyone gets the bright idea to track your phone, you'll lead them straight to me."

Sweat formed at Bill's temples, indecision and fear crossing his face in waves as his eyes darted back and forth between the door and Jack. Bill's frisson permeated the room, the tension ratcheting upward a notch with each shallow breath. Without warning, his face grew slack and his eyes locked on an unseen *something* beyond the walls of their room. He sat like that for over ten seconds, then took the phone from his pocket and handed it to Jack.

Jack tore the phone apart with practiced motions, watching his brother the whole time, and removed the battery and SIM card. The latter he snapped in half before Bill could protest, and he offered the pieces back. Throughout the procedure, Bill remained passive and unblinking.

"Are you okay?" Jack said, head tilted, and eyes narrowed to slits.

Bill brightened at once, as if his mind had never wandered, and took the remains of his phone from Jack's hand. "Of course," he said. He looked at the phone like a toad had just appeared as if by magic in his hand, then tossed everything into the trash. "So... what now?"

"Now," Jack said, still studying his brother and the sudden change of heart, "we plan our next move. I hadn't thought much beyond convincing you to help." He shook his head. "Frankly, I didn't think it would be that easy."

* * *

It sat in the back of the old C–130 Hercules with the human members of its team. None of them saw the walking horror show in their midst. The creature they knew as *Jeff* was just another human male military officer. It had caught itself thinking along the same lines and worked hard to keep that knowledge from the Hive. Jeff had warned his brethren more than once about being caught in the open, but the Hive had spoken as one. *Deliver the package*, they had said. *Sacrifice yourself if discovered.*

Easy for them *to say*, he thought. *He...* Creeping individuality clouded its thinking. It must present itself for sacrifice soon if it continued to de-resonate from the Hive. Even now it found their voices hard to hear. It was handicapped. *Broken.*

A member of the Hive was an unnecessary risk on this mission. The chances of discovery were unacceptably high, and the value he added was minimal. The humans in this airplane could complete the mission—delivering the device to the proper location and setting the timer— without his help. It was almost as if the Hive *wanted* him to be seen—forcing him to end his own existence.

Him...his. Time was growing short.

Maybe I can direct the team's actions from the plane, he thought. *There is no need for me to risk exposure.* Worse than his use of pronouns was his independent thinking. It made him a danger to the Hive. The Plan could not survive such actions.

"Sir," Lieutenant Wilson yelled from his left over the sound of the motors, "the pilot reports we will touch down in Nepal in thirty."

"Very good, Lieutenant. Get the men and their gear ready." He looked over at the device, still packed in foam and wrapped in the wooden crate. The word "Generator" stenciled on the side. A generator it was, in name and deed. The plane descended, taking the team and Nepal's doom with it.

In a few days the device will activate, triggering an Earthquake, Jeff thought. For the first time, he considered the lives lost, and the thought disturbed him. Better for thousands to suffer now than millions later. And with a single blow, the Hive achieves two ends.

It might be better, but it no longer felt right.

CHAPTER 19

BILL HAD ENTERED THE BAR intending to drag Jack by the ear back to Greenville, but as soon as he sat, all such thoughts faded like fog on a sunny day. It had been like turning off a switch, a buzzing in his ear with an abrupt end. Back in the room, the buzzing had returned with the death of his alcohol buzz, growing in volume and pressuring him to stuff Jack in the trunk of his car and head for home. It was an imperative he had trouble denying.

He remembered arguing over breakfast, Jack demanding his phone, then a blank spot like a needle skipping on a record. The next thing Bill knew, Jack was handing his phone back to him in pieces.

And the pressure in his brain was gone.

He still wasn't convinced he *shouldn't* drag Jack to Greenville, but he no longer felt the same imperative. There was no explanation for his swift change of heart, and it was disturbing. *At some point that needs to be explored*, he thought. *Right now there are more immediate concerns.*

"So what are our options?" he asked Jack. The four men sat in the motel room, Jack and Bill on the two chairs, Sohrab and Mason on the beds. Sohrab was busy flipping through channels on the television bolted to the dresser while Mason munched on a bag of chips. He had been eating almost non-stop since Bill brought Jack back to the room the previous night.

"Honestly, Bill," Jack said, "I don't have a clue." Mason snorted, but Jack ignored him. "Part of me wants to check my mail."

"You think your pen-pal—"

"Chester," Jack said.

"*Really?*" Bill asked. When Jack didn't respond, he nodded. "Okay, Chester it is. Do you think he sent you another letter?"

Jack spread his hands. "I don't know, but it's as good a place to start as any."

Mason snorted again. "Why not just go to the CDC and look over Sally's office while we're at it," he said, the condescension dripping from his voice. "Who here thinks the cops are waiting at either place?" He raised his hand with a smirk. After a few seconds, Sohrab shrugged and raised his hand, then returned to flipping the channels.

"Then what's *your* idea?" Jack asked Mason.

"Amber's apartment."

"I don't know where it is, and—"

"Doesn't matter," Bill said, shaking his head. "According to your friend, her place has already been tossed by the Feds, and confidence is high there are still eyes on the place." He pointed at Mason, and said, "Yours is out for the same reasons."

Everyone sat in silence until Sohrab chuckled, and all eyes turned to him.

He shook his head. "Seriously?" he said. "All of you forgot the *one* person in this room no one is looking for? The *one* person with any kind of training in these matters?"

Bill snorted. "Where the hell did you dig this guy up?" he asked, hooking a thumb in Sohrab's direction.

Mason grinned. "Ever seen *Three Days of the Condor?*" he asked Bill, who raised an eyebrow in response. "Sometimes," Mason said, "*random* and *lucky* go hand in hand." To Sohrab, he said, "What did you have in mind?"

* * *

Amber stuffed her raw feet in the mismatched pair of shoes, watching the road for signs of activity. Ever since her escape two days before, she had been careful to avoid contact with anyone. That would be increasingly difficult the closer she got to Atlanta. She didn't know why she headed that way, but every direction was the same. *Maybe I can make it back to my apartment*, she thought. Even without ID, her landlord would let her in. *But* Dieter *might be watching. Waiting for me there.*

She had been lucky to stumble across the little house on the lonely road. Luckier still it was trash pickup day, and no one was home to see her rummaging through their castoffs. *People are weird about that,* she thought. *Throw stuff out, but heaven help the guy who digs through it if he actually* needs *it.* Most Americans would rather see their old shoes end up in a landfill than on the feet of the homeless.

Her stomach growled for the fifth or sixth time that morning, reminding her it had been almost two days since her last meal. She had done the "fasting thing"—as her mom called it—more than once in her life, so she could handle a few missed meals. What she *couldn't* do without was water, and it had been hours since her last drink. She had nothing to carry water in, so she had to rely on sips from the occasional hose when she came across a suitable home.

Like this one, she thought. She had watched the owners leave for work over an hour ago, then waited for another hour watching for movement in and around the home. When she was comfortable it was unoccupied, she inspected the trash and found the shoes, then walked to the side of the house where she put them on while watching the road. The hose was also on that side, so she turned the spigot to take a drink. She filled her stomach, fooling it into thinking she'd had a large meal, turned the spigot off, and sloshed to the front corner of the home.

I should break in and try to call someone, she mused, and wiped her mouth with the back of her hand. *But who do I call?* Definitely not her mom, and she didn't know Jack's new number. She could call the CDC and ask for Jack, but it was likely *they* didn't know where he was, either. *Besides, if I get caught breaking and entering, I'll just end up in police custody... or worse.* In Georgia, a lot can go wrong when someone enters a house that isn't theirs, and the *best*-case scenario is getting caught by the police.

She pulled the envelope from inside her shirt. The one thing she was sure of was that she couldn't let this fall into police hands. Amber drew the folder out and looked again at the number printed there, a faint buzzing in her ears. She slid the file back inside and tucked the envelope back in her shirt. The buzzing grew louder. When she stepped away from the home, intending to take the road into Atlanta, the buzz became a painful whine. She stopped, pressed her palms against the sides of her head, and bent into a crouch. Her breaths were shallow and rapid, and she leaned against the house for support, hoping no one was watching her distress.

I should call for help, she thought as she looked toward the door. The buzzing lessened, and she tried to stand again. Before she could complete the motion, the pain was back worse than before, driving her to her knees. Without knowing what she was doing, she was on her feet and breaking the nearest window with the heel of her shoe. *When did I take that off?* She reached through the hole, turned the latch, and slid the window up. Amber looked around again, scrambled up and through the open window, then slid it shut behind her.

Inside a bedroom—a little girl's according to the overabundance of pink and little flowers—Amber walked out and into a hall that led to the front. She found the phone in the living room, and without thinking, pulled the envelope again from her shirt. Her fingers never hesitated as she lifted the receiver and dialed the number in the folder.

She didn't notice the pain had stopped.

* * *

Sohrab's plan had been to go to Jack's apartment to look for any mail the FBI hadn't taken. No one was looking for *him* he had said, and if caught, he was confident he could talk his way out of it. "I *am* your brother, after all," he had said, sounding so much like Bill everyone had sat there just blinking at him.

It turned out not to be necessary.

"I never took the hold off my mail after returning from Germany," Jack had said. He had shrugged and smiled at the silence greeting that statement. "Never had the time."

Jack, Bill, and Mason sat in Sohrab's SUV, waiting in the parking lot for the man's return from the post office. No one spoke, Sohrab having taken all the good will with him when he exited the car.

"You think they'll give him your stuff?" Bill asked at last. His voice was a hoarse whisper like someone was in the next car listening.

"Should," Jack said. "The last few times I've done it, they just asked for my address, went to the back for a lunch break, then came back with a big stack in a rubber band. They only look at my license to make sure the address matches." He tilted his head and smirked. "I think Sohrab has a lot of practice pretending to be someone he's not."

"Everybody does," Mason said with a grumble from the front passenger seat. He had a large chocolate muffin in his lap, picking pieces off one at a time and popping them in his mouth.

Jack winced at the comment. Mason was angry—that was all, and Jack understood it. He knew Mason blamed him for Sally's death, and the fact the police were looking for them. Most of all, he blamed Jack for Debbie's betrayal. It was an act that should never rank higher than a murder, but this one did—at least to Mason. To Jack it made no sense. Mason hadn't seen her in years, and it wasn't like there was a romance to rekindle. He *had* to know that.

"Mason—"

"Here he comes," Bill said, interrupting what was sure to become an argument. Everyone shifted in their seats as Sohrab walked with practiced calm to the car. He pulled the door open, slid into the driver's seat, and tossed the heavy bundle of mail over his shoulder into Jack's lap.

"That's all there was," he said as he buckled in.

Jack tore the rubber band off and flipped through the bundle with shaking hands. *Nothing but bills and junk mail. What the fuck?*

"Got anything?" Bill asked from the seat beside him.

"Just crap I don't need or want," Jack said. "I don't get it. Every time there's been some kind of event, I've gotten a letter mailed *before* the event took place." He shook his head, squeezed his eyes shut, and rubbed his temples. "There have been three goddamn *murders*, and nothing from the guy."

"Maybe he didn't know those were gonna happen," Mason said.

Sohrab started the car, and called back to Jack, "Where to now?"

Before Jack could answer, the phone in his pocket vibrated. He tugged it out and checked the screen. "Hold that thought," Jack said, holding up his hand like a traffic cop. "It's Rutger."

* * *

If Gershon had not left him alone that morning, the call might have invited disaster. Rutger had slept in—still fighting jet-lag and the near-constant stress of the investigation and his contact with Jack—and was enjoying a well-deserved respite from Gershon. When his phone rang, he almost didn't answer it, but the number was US-based, and he thought it might be Jack calling from yet another phone.

"Hello?" he had said, expecting something far different that what he got.

"Rutger? Is that you?" Amber asked from the other end.

His eyebrows arched, and he pursed his lips. There were so many questions attached to that phone call that he had not known where to begin.

"How did you get this number?"

"That's a long story," she had said, but did not elaborate.

"Where have you been? Are you all right?"

"I'm fine... I think." Rutger had thought she sounded very far away. She took a deep breath, letting it out slowly. "I don't know why I have your number, but since I do... is there a way you can get in touch with Jack? He's not answering his phone, and I have no way to get to him."

"That might be possible," he had said. "Tell me where you are and I might be able to come get you."

"Wait," she said, "You're here in Atlanta?"

"Also a long story," he had said, shaking his head.

There had been a hesitation on her end before she spoke again. "I would... I would rather *Jack* come," she said, breathless. "I can't explain it."

"Tell me where you are, and I'll do what I can."

She had given him an address and then hung up.

I had a choice, then. I could have gone to pick her up and let Gershon lock her away while he questioned her.

All this continued to run through his head while the phone rang.

"Any good news?" Jack said when he picked up on his end.

Another choice. Give Jack the address, then stake out the location and round them all up.

"Possibly," he said. "I just got a call from Amber."

"*What?* Is she okay? Where has she been?" At least two male voices on the other end spoke at the same time. Jack yelled at them to shut up. "Do you know where she is?" he asked after restoring calm.

"All good questions," Rutger said. "I don't have any answers beyond an address. Do you have a pen?"

After a few seconds of the men talking among themselves, Jack returned to the line. "Okay... shoot."

* * *

"That's pretty close," Mason said, tapping the notepad. "Are we going to get her?"

"Sohrab and I, yes," Jack said. "I trust Rutger, but..."

"But what?" Mason's face was tight, one eyebrow raised.

"He means," Bill said, explaining for his brother, "Rutger is a cop first. He might be setting Jack up so he can be captured without shots fired."

"Why would he do something like that?"

"*I* would," Bill said with a shrug. "Given the same circumstances."

Everyone looked at Bill with varying degrees of suspicion, but his blank stare drove their eyes away. To Jack, the tension in the car felt like drowning. Rather than sink into the depths of some new worry, he addressed Mason's concerns.

"My face is the only one in this car that Amber knows, so I *have* to go," Jack explained. "Sohrab is just an innocent bystander, so he's mostly safe from the cops. *You*," he pointed at Mason, "are wanted for questioning at the very least, while Bill shouldn't even *be* here."

The truth was he wished they *all* could come with him, but he was tired of putting other people in danger. Sure, there was no indication picking up Amber would be dangerous, but leaving it to chance at this point was stupid. *There wasn't anything dangerous about* Sally *picking up your files, was there?* Recriminations would nag him into inaction if he let them. A feckless lethargy birthed from fear and guilt threatened to drag him to despair, the depths of which he had only recently crawled *out* of.

It wasn't my fault. It wasn't my fault. The old mantra he used to absolve himself of Beth and Riley's death sprang to his mind, less comforting than ever. He *was* responsible. *He* put everyone on this path. *He* determined the direction.

And he was tired.

Tired of making decisions for everyone, and *definitely* tired of those decisions coming back to haunt him at every turn. He looked up into the faces of family and friends and realized everyone was waiting for him to make another decision.

He sighed, a heavy release of tension, thought, and control. *Control is an illusion*, he thought, and released his hand from the tiller of fate. "We'll drop you and Bill back at the motel, then go pick up

Amber, if she's really there," he said to the silence that threatened to smother his resolve.

"You sure about this?" Bill said, his voice a whisper.

"Not even a little bit," Jack said, resigned to the course set for him.

* * *

Rutger showered, shaved, and dressed. After his call to Jack, the thought of everything he had done over the past two days made him feel unclean. No amount of washing, however, could ever wash that feeling away. He had betrayed his oath for no other reason than his dislike of Gershon. Sure, his experience and training—his *instincts*—told him neither Jack nor Amber were guilty of anything more than being in the wrong place at the wrong time, but that didn't assuage his *own* guilt.

He had done all he could do for Jack and Amber. Everything was on *their* shoulders from this point forward.

Rutger sat on the bed, propped two of the cheap pillows between his back and the headboard, and stretched out his legs. He was to meet Gershon in the cafe at noon, but the thought of eating a meal with the man sickened him. It wasn't just Gershon's seething superiority, but his unwavering belief in his own infallibility that Rutger despised.

When Rutger was a boy, his mother told him such people always earned their comeuppance, but he knew better. There were no cosmic scales to be balanced. No righteous retribution for poor behavior. Men like Gershon remained such as they were their entire lives, and no one ever put them in their proper place. Fate did not conspire to teach them humility—that took *men*. Men who were weak at best, and *craven* at their worst.

Too early to begin drinking, he looked to the television remote on the nightstand. *How can a society invent such a miracle, and then use it for something like* Survivor? He sneered at the television and shook his head. *Americans are a mystery, wrapped in a riddle… and buried in manure,* he thought with a chuckle. *Ah, at least they have fun with their technology.*

A solid knock snapped him from *that* line of thought, and he stood and walked to the door. A check through the peephole showed him what he already knew, but he waited for Gershon to knock again.

It's the little victories, he thought with a smile.

He left the chain on and opened the door a crack. Gershon stood like a statue on the other side, his face a mask of calm. There was, however, a slight twitch in the corner of one eye.

"I understood we were meeting for lunch," he said. The implied question being *Where the hell were you?*

"Apologies, Inspector," Rutger said through the crack. "I must have dozed off."

"Come along, then," he said, and turned to walk away. It never occurred to the man that his instructions might be ignored, and he was out of sight of the doorway before Rutger closed it to remove the chain. When he opened the door, Gershon was already walking back to meet him. "Step lively, man. I have reservations."

So do I, thought Rutger. *So do I.*

* * *

"Did you think I wouldn't know?" Gershon wiped the corner of his mouth with a napkin and placed it over his now-empty plate. Until this moment, the meal had not been an unpleasant experience for Rutger, but he knew before they sat that it wouldn't last.

"To what are you referring?" Rutger asked, more amused than afraid. He took a sip of what Americans *claimed* was beer and set his glass on the table.

"The phone conversations you have been having with Mr. Montgomery." He said it as a solid statement of fact.

Rutger stared at the man, his expression blank, for long seconds. He tilted his head and shrugged. "I have had conversations with many people," he said, the smile frozen as if painted on.

"There is no point in denying it," Gershon said, waving his hand, dismissing any argument. "Your phone has been bugged since before we left."

"Under *whose* authority?" Rutger asked, the heat rising in his face.

"That information, I'm afraid, is above your pay grade," Gershon said with his own smile. "The phone call from Ms. Riley will help us immensely," he said, leaning back and crossing his legs. He waved at a waiter, and the man scurried over. "I'd like to see your dessert menu, please."

231

"Of course," the waiter said, then hurried off.

"What are you going to do?" Rutger asked.

"Have dessert, of course," Gershon said, then uttered a short laugh. "You should have one as well."

The man is insufferable! Rutger thought. He was caught, and Gershon was *toying* with him. "I *mean...* what are you going to do about Jack?"

Gershon shook his head. "About *Jack?* Nothing." He smiled again, and Rutger's stomach churned. "There are *people* for that, and I have given them the information they need."

Rutger's sharp intake of breath surprised even *him*. His mind raced, every potential outcome flashing one after the other, a confusion of possibilities. The room spun, and his pulse was a thunderous beat in his neck.

"What will happen to them?" he asked, already knowing the answer.

The waiter returned with the menu, handed it to Gershon, bowed, and walked away. Gershon smiled and opened the menu. "That, *Polizeioberkommissar* Brieske, is no longer your concern."

CHAPTER 20

"**W**HAT ARE YOU DOING?" Jack said, pointing. "That's the house right there."

Sohrab drove the car, his eyes flicking in steady rhythm from the road to each mirror in turn. Jack had noticed the pattern as soon as they entered the neighborhood where Amber waited.

"The house is being watched," Sohrab said as he guided the car to a stop at the next intersection. He set his signal, turned the wheel to the right, and pulled onto the cross street. "There are at least three painfully nondescript government vehicles parked along that street."

"You think Rutger set us up?"

"Doesn't matter *who*," he said, still scanning. "What matters is that they are there." He turned right again at the next intersection, and slowed the car as he watched the mirrors, occasionally turning his head to look past Jack.

"So *now* what do we do?" Amber was so close Jack could feel her presence in the car with him. *If one thing goes right today, I'll call that a victory.* Desperate for a win, this one now felt beyond his reach.

"The good news is the idiots aren't watching the back door," Sohrab said, his voice level. "They think you're stupid enough to go in the front where they plan to take you both."

"I *am* stupid enough, Sohrab," Jack said without humor.

"And *that's* how I know they still don't know I'm with you." He turned to Jack and smiled. "Well, that and the fact one of them didn't follow as we drove past."

So what? Jack thought. *We still can't drive by again. They can't be that stupid.* He chewed a nail and looked across the vacant lot to the house where Amber was. If they took much longer, she might do something rash. *Why the hell didn't I get the phone number from Rutger?* He hadn't even asked—just took the address and hung up.

Sohrab pulled over, the gravel crunching beneath the tires, and shifted into park but left the motor running. He unbuckled his shoulder harness and reached across Jack to the glove compartment. "Excuse me," he said, and fished around inside, pulling out a screwdriver. "Back in a few," he said as he exited the car.

Jack watched him as he removed the license plates from the front and rear bumpers, then open the hatch and drop them in back. He rummaged around for a few seconds, then closed the door and walked to the driver's side. As he climbed in, he tossed a Washington Senators cap into Jack's lap.

"Put that on and pull the brim low," he said. "It won't confuse anyone who gets a good look at you, but it should work for our purposes."

Jack looked at the hat, then up at Sohrab. "I don't think I like where this is going."

"You'll like this even less—your phone is compromised," he said, pulling his own phone from his pocket. He tossed it to Jack. "Take mine and give me yours."

"I don't understand any of this," Jack said, taking his phone out and handing it to Sohrab. The man had changed before his eyes, like taking off makeup after a play. Bits of him fell away, schist chipped by Vulcan's hammer, revealing hard and unyielding corundum.

"Put the hat on and take my phone. Get out, climb that fence over there," he pointed over Jack's shoulder, "and knock on the back door. Keep doing it until she answers. She might not be inclined to do so. Under no circumstances are you to call out to her." His eyes were hard and narrow. "Do you understand these instructions?"

"Yes, but—"

"When you are both safe and away from here, call Mason and give him a location to pick you up. Instruct him *not* to bring Bill or tell him where he is going." Sohrab's breathing was calm and measured, and Jack was sure that if checked, the man's heart rate would be in the low fifties.

"Why can't—"

"Do as I say, Jack. No deviation, and no time for discussion."

Jack's face grew tight as he considered all the possibilities, then he placed the hat on his head and pulled the brim down to shade his eyes. He took the phone and shoved it in his pocket, then looked up into the stone of Sohrab's face. "And what will *you* be doing?" he asked.

A smile creased Sohrab's face from ear to ear, full of mischief and mayhem. "I'll be the diversion." He laughed, the car shaking in sympathy. "Don't worry about me," he said. "This part will be *fun*." His face grew hard again. "Now get out."

* * *

Jack stood at the door, alternating between knocking and turning to see if Sohrab had driven away. The car was still there, and that was enough to calm his nerves. *For now*, he thought. He was careful not to use the "cop knock" Bill had once showed him, but he worried Amber was too far away from the back to hear it.

He tried again, louder this time, and there was movement on the other side. There was no peephole on the door, so Jack knew Amber was considering the possibilities. *Is it a neighbor? Cop? Or Jack?* He wished he could say something, then realized that, with her so close to the door, he *could*.

"Amber?" he asked as loud as he dared, and the door flew open.

"Jack!" she said louder than he would have liked, and leapt from the doorway and into his arms. She wrapped herself around him so tight he struggled to breathe, and her heart beat against his chest like a hummingbird's. The sound of tires spinning in gravel caught his attention, and he turned in time to see Sohrab speed away.

Jack set her on the ground and grabbed her wrist. "We need to go," he whispered, pulling her away from the door.

She wrenched her hand from his, still breathing hard. "Hang on a second," she said, and before he could stop her, she ran back into the house.

There was a flash of vanilla as Sohrab turned back onto the street in front of the house, and Jack shifted his weight from foot to foot. *She's taking too long—*

"Got it!" she said, waving a large manila envelope in one hand as she ran through the doorway and past him toward the fence.

"Got what?" he asked, then ran after her. Behind him, Sohrab parked in the driveway of the house and honked twice. *He's gonna call*

235

every cop and Fed to the damn house with that racket, he thought as he vaulted the fence. He realized then that was Sohrab's plan. *A diversion so obvious they* couldn't *ignore it.*

Past the fence, he pulled ahead of Amber and grabbed her wrist as he flew by, dragging her in his wake. They had to get as far away as possible before Sohrab made his next move.

The squeal of tires on asphalt and accompanying gunfire told him they were out of time. Sohrab wouldn't bring the posse in their direction, but he might be captured before Jack and Amber could get very far. If that happened, no matter how stupid the cops were, they would canvass the area looking for them.

The sounds of the chase grew distant, and there was a crash, but the sirens continued. "We have to move faster!" he said, and Amber increased her speed to match him stride for stride. "Turn for that stand of trees," he said, now wheezing. "We can't be seen running away from the house."

It was less than a hundred yards, but to Jack it felt like a mile. His heart was racing and his breathing grew labored. By the time they entered the safety of the trees, he was seeing spots. They picked their way through the undergrowth until they could no longer see the house, then Jack stopped, leaning his back against a tall pine. He bent at the waist, both hands on his knees, and took long gulping breaths.

Amber looked at him, her head tilted, hands on her hips. She was pale, but had no trouble breathing. "You, sir, are out of shape," she said with a grin.

Jack's eyes narrowed, but he didn't argue the point. Instead, he waved one hand in her direction as he struggled to catch his breath. "A little help?"

She smirked, then took his hand and pulled him away from the tree. Not satisfied to have him standing, she continued to pull him until his body was against hers. She wrapped her arms around him for the second time that day and kissed him with an unrestrained ferocity. Long before he was ready, she pulled her head back, then lowered her chin.

"I was so afraid, Jack, and there's so much to *tell* you," she whispered.

The sirens had either stopped or faded into silence, and all Jack heard was her breathing and the wind through the trees. He lifted her chin and looked her in the eyes. *Those marvelous green eyes,* he thought. *I could lose myself in there and never want to come back.*

"It's okay," he said. "You're safe now." He looked around, then back at her. "At least you *will* be... as soon as we stop long enough to make a phone call."

* * *

"Really, Jack... a *Waffle House?*" She stood beside him, hands on her hips and shaking her head.

He looked up at the sign across the road. "You got any better ideas?" he shrugged. "Most people in there are older, and not likely to get in anyone's business."

"You sound like you've spent a lot of time in one."

"I did my time," he said with a snort. "Mom and Dad loved those places. It was their go-to option whenever we were on the road for vacation."

"Yeah, but," she waved at the building, "*seriously?*"

He smiled. "Where else can you get a steak and eggs for five bucks?"

She smiled back, locking arms with him and huddling close as they walked across the street. Amber still had not told him what had happened to her, and he didn't press. He knew she wouldn't discuss it in the diner, either, so he had to be content to wait.

"I can't wait for you to meet the rest of the Scooby Gang," he said.

"Scooby Gang?" she said, looking up at him.

"Not a perfect fit, I know. I'm still not sure if Sohrab or Mason is Shaggy."

"Who is Sohrab?" she asked as Jack reached for the door.

"The guy driving the van." He pulled the door open for her, rattling the little bell on top, and she gave him the same look Beth did whenever he tried to be a gentleman. "Long story, but he's good people." Amber relented and entered ahead of him. "I think," he added as the door closed behind them.

Inside it was exactly as Jack remembered—scuffed floors, booths with torn seat cushions, a worn Formica counter with an array of stools in front. Overhead, the fluorescent lights flickered and buzzed, but the sunlight streaming through the windows was all the illumination the place needed. *Best not to get too good a look at the food in here, anyway,* he thought.

Amber led him to a booth as far away from people as she could get and slid in with her patented move. The one that drove every other thought from his head. She pointed to the seat across from her, and he slid in as well—but with far less grace.

She pulled the envelope out of her shirt, lay it on the table between them, and tapped it with a finger. He noticed for the first time her torn and dirty nails, and his eyes lifted to her face and the pale and gaunt stare she offered him. *What the hell happened to you?*

"I think the stuff in here is important, Jack," she said.

He was still staring at Amber's face, a thousand questions on his tongue, when the waitress stepped up to their table.

"What can I get you to drink?" she asked as she lay two menus on the table.

Amber flinched and looked up. "Coffee for me."

"Me too," Jack said, smiling up at the young blonde. "And leave the pot."

"Sure thing, sweetie," the woman said with a quick smile, brushing a spray of hair over her ear as she walked away.

After the woman left, Amber looked across the table at Jack, one eyebrow raised and shaking her head. "Damn, Jack. Can't you turn it off for one goddamn second?"

"What?" he asked, tilting his head.

"You know... I don't think I've met a man as clueless as you."

He snorted. "Stick around. It only gets worse from here."

Before he could say anything else, the waitress returned with the coffee and set the cups and pot on the table. She bent at the knees, bringing herself to eye level. "You just wave when you're ready to order, okay hun?" she said to him.

"Sure thing," he said.

The woman walked away. Jack watched for a second, then turned back to Amber, who now had her arms crossed and lips pursed.

"Okay," he said, relenting. "*That* time I saw it."

"Slow, but steady," she said with a chuckle.

Jack smiled back. Not at the humor, but grateful her spirit wasn't broken from her days in limbo. He had no idea what she had been through, but he was sure it hadn't been easy. She looked at her hands then worried over a nail, chewing it as he watched. *Everyone has their limits, though,* he thought.

"Let's get some food in you, then we can get someplace safer," he said, patting her hand. "Order the steak and eggs for me—medium on the steak and over easy on the eggs. I'm going outside to call our ride."

"The guy running from the cops?" she asked, lines creasing her forehead.

"No... Mason. He's forty-five minutes away, so we should have time to eat." He stood and pulled Sohrab's phone from his pocket. "I'll just be a minute," he said, then waved at the waitress.

* * *

"What do you mean you can't tell me?" Bill's face was red, and he clenched his fists as he paced. If Mason had been a smaller man, he might have recoiled from the intimidation, but guys like Bill had never scared him. *They're all bluster,* he thought.

"All I know is what Jack told me to *do,* not *why.*" He stood at the door, hand extended, still waiting for Bill to drop the keys into it. He dropped his hand and shoved both into the pockets of his jeans. "Besides," he said with a shrug, "it was more Sohrab's idea than Jack's."

"And that's another thing," Bill said, breathing heavy as he took another menacing step closer. "Why are we listening to this guy? Who the hell is he, *really?*"

Mason stood straight and pulled his hands from his pockets. He set his feet a little wider, but kept his arms relaxed. "Back off, Bill. I'm in no mood for any of this." *I don't have time anyway,* he thought. "Don't forget the guy just risked his neck to give your brother a chance at a clean getaway."

Bill's eyes flicked to the bed where his holster lay, and Mason didn't miss the look. There had been a vigorous argument among the four of them about the need for Jack and Sohrab to take the gun with them, but it was Sohrab who ruled against it. He had said a gun would just complicate things. Mason didn't know what he meant, but Jack was the only one who disagreed.

Mason relaxed his shoulders. "As far as we know, Sohrab is former Iraqi Secret Service... or something similar, at least."

"And now he drives a cab. *Right.*" Bill curled his lip and sat on the edge of the desk. "You don't even know the guy." He looked into

239

Mason's eyes, searching for something behind the half-lidded stare. "How can you trust him?" He crossed his arms. "More importantly... how can you trust him over *me*?"

Mason took a deep breath and shrugged his shoulders. "He's not a *cop*." He leaned his back against the door and crossed his own arms. "For better or worse, Bill, that's what you are. I suspect you'll do your job if you have no other good options."

Bill's eyes narrowed, then his face fell and his shoulders slumped. "I guess I will at that," he said, his voice sour. He looked up, eyes soft and vacant. "Do *any* of you trust me?"

"Like I said, I trust you to be a cop. Jack trusts you to be his brother, but he *remembers* you're a cop. Sohrab probably doesn't trust any of us, but that just means he's the only one thinking straight."

Bill chuckled, then reached into his pocket and removed his keys. He tossed them over to Mason, who caught them with a deft sweep of his hand. "Scratch the paint and you die," Bill said.

"There's *paint* still on that thing?"

"Do you really want to get into a pissin' match over who's ride is the ugliest?"

Mason laughed. "No, I guess not." He turned, opened the door, and stepped into the hall.

Before the door closed, Bill called out, "Be safe."

* * *

Be safe, Mason thought as he drove Bill's car. *How can* anyone *be safe when the whole world's going to shit?* It wasn't the world that bothered him, though. Jack had been falling apart for days, and Mason didn't know what to do. He had hoped having Bill there would improve Jack's mood, but it only aggravated the issue. *You haven't been a ray of sunshine, either*, he thought, chastising himself. He certainly hadn't been supportive, and much of Jack's mood was a direct result of Mason's constant needling.

There was no apology good enough. He wouldn't know what to say, regardless.

Alone for the first time in days, Mason had no voice but his own for company, and he was already tired of *that* asshole. There was no excuse for his treatment of his best friend. Not even Sally's death was reason enough to push Jack away like he had.

It's not his fault, he thought. Somebody else is pulling the strings.

Someone else was *always* pulling the strings, though. It was the one constant over the whole of human experience.

"It's the fuckin' Reptilian Overlords," he said, laughing. "*Has* to be."

Mason loved trying out every nut-bar conspiracy theory on Jack, the goal was convincing him Mason took them seriously. The problem was now there actually *was* a vast conspiracy orchestrating apparently unrelated events. *To what end? Learn the* why, *and you may discover* who, he thought. There were at least *two* threads to chase—one creating the problems, and one cleaning up—and that meant two or more groups of players. *Focus on one at a time.*

First there were Jack's sleepers in Kazakhstan, then the pilot in Germany. *That's not right*, he thought. *First was Beth and Riley—or, more accurately, Mark, Jr.* He drummed his fingers on the wheel, the waves of heat from sunlight baking the expanse of dashboard, making his fingers sweat. *In the first two cases the victims fell into a deep sleep, but in the third the man committed suicide.* "What's the fucking connection?" he said, slamming his hand against the wheel. *Step back... the third was an* act, *so the others were side-effects, maybe?*

How many crazy people make the news these days? How many crazies never make the news?

Cars zipped around him, drivers glaring as they passed, while a few honked and gave him the finger. He looked at the speedometer to see he was twenty miles per hour under the speed limit. Mason had never understood why he slowed when he was talking or deep in thought, but it drove Jack nuts. He sped up, then moved into the right lane.

"If the other two events involve side-effects," he said, drumming his fingers again, "then maybe suicide was the goal." That made no sense. Why cause people to commit suicide? It couldn't *just* be about that.

"Control, then. Specific and programmed actions."

But brainwashing had been discredited long ago. Regardless, it took time to retrain a mind, and the pilot in Germany hadn't been out of contact long enough. That meant something fast-acting.

"The *nano*-machines!" Mason said, pounding the dash with his fist. "Someone's trying to create human robots!"

It seemed insane. It *was* insane. Mason thought about the crazy things happening around the world, and a chill ran up his spine. Just a few days ago a guy flew a gyrocopter onto the White House lawn. Every few days a deranged person shot up a mall or a movie theater or a school. *What if they were all just tests?*

Or were they the goal? Sowing the seeds of anarchy, instilling fear around the world. He was seeing connections now where there were none, but the idea had already taken root.

How can anyone be safe when the whole world's going to shit by design?

* * *

The information he possessed of the man's location was now hours old, and Thirteen still sat in the wrong place, waiting for an arrival that would never come. When the asset's connection had been severed—not once, but *twice*—Thirteen had been less concerned with *that* than the knowledge the Others would never allow him to travel to the motel in Atlanta. There was no way to convince them since to do so also required informing them of his deception. Regardless, even without the reinforcement signal, the programming was still active.

He could afford patience. *And sure enough, even waiting will end... if you can just wait long enough,* Faulkner had once said to him. *Or did I read that?* It didn't matter. When he met the man while on a mission in Mississippi, it had not been long before the author's death—and he rambled. The visit had nothing to do with the civil rights protests, Thirteen's work involving freedom on a much grander scale.

Most of human history passed him unnoticed, a child gathering flowers by the side of a busy highway. One day he could stop and watch the parade, but until then he would continue to reap the buds chosen for him.

Every now and then he spirited one in his pocket to keep for himself.

CHAPTER 21

Gershon hissed at his phone before snapping it shut and pocketing the thing.

"Problem, Inspector?" Rutger asked, hoping like *hell* he hid his amusement. They sat in overstuffed wingback chairs across a low table from one another in Gershon's suite at the hotel. It was a spacious and comfortable accommodation, and one that must have cost more than Rutger's weekly salary for a single night.

Gershon narrowed his eyes at Rutger. "Mr. Montgomery and his associates have escaped... *somehow*." His right foot dangled from where he crossed it over his left, waving a steady rhythm like a conductor's baton. "Do you have any ideas how that may have happened?"

"Not really, no, Inspector," he said, shaking his head. "I'm afraid I am just along for the ride." He smiled at the imperious little man, the motion not quite reaching his eyes. He lifted the cup—exquisite fine bone china—to his lips and took a sip of his tea, then lowered both cup and saucer to the table and settled deeper into his chair. "Maybe they were just lucky."

"Bah! There's no such thing as luck." Gershon leaned forward, dropping his foot to the floor. "I think they had *help*." His eyes were a cobra's, narrow slits full of venom and heat.

"If you have something to say, Inspector, maybe it would be easier to just say it."

"Fine, then." He leaned ever closer, his upper body swaying slightly. "I think *you* warned him," he said, stabbing a bony finger in Rutger's direction, "*Polizeioberkommissar* Brieske."

"There now," Rutger said, smiling with genuine humor. "Don't you feel better?" He was taking a terrible chance with his career, but he was done putting up with the man. Rutger would weather this storm, much as he had every other such confrontation over the course of his professional life. He had certainly built enough good will among his peers to stand up to such a self-important *twit*. "And for the record," he said, "you have been with me since *before* you informed me there was a plan to apprehend them. I have not left your sight in all that time, so please, tell me how I could have warned anyone."

Gershon sat back, crossed his legs, and again conducted his unseen orchestra. "I don't know, but when I *do*, not only your involvement in this affair, but your entire *career* will end." His face tightened, lemon-like. "Do I make myself clear?"

"Crystal, Inspector." Rutger relaxed. In truth, his involvement with Gershon ended days ago, the idiot just didn't know it. The man had nothing, and Rutger smiled in satisfaction. *I think it's time to take my leave of him.*

"Well, Inspector," Rutger said as he stood, "if there is nothing else."

The man waved a dismissive hand without looking up, and Rutger walked around the table toward the door. As Rutger reached for the ornate brass knob, Gershon cleared his throat. "You will remain available at all times, Mr. Brieske," he said, each word crackling with electric hate.

"Of course," Rutger said, and pulled the door open. He walked into the hall, the door shutting in silence behind. *Or not*, he thought with a smile as he walked toward the elevator.

* * *

"It's nice to finally meet you, Amber," Mason said with a goofy grin as he stuck out his hand. She surprised him by ignoring his hand and wrapping him in a warm bear-hug. More than his heart warmed, and he peeled her off sooner than he would have liked. Jack, standing behind Amber, grinned at Mason's growing discomfort with one raised eyebrow.

"We should probably get moving," Jack said, still smiling. "That file she's carrying needs some heavy analysis on your part." He held out his hand and waited for Mason to drop the keys. "I'll drive while you read."

"Fair enough," Mason said. "Amber can take shotgun and I'll ride in back."

Amber walked around the massive car, opened her door, and slid in, both men watching her the whole way. Once inside and out of view, Mason turned to Jack and mouthed "*Wow*." He waggled his eyebrows and opened his door to crawl into the back seat. Jack laughed and got in.

Jack fired up the big engine and pulled out of the lot and into traffic. Once the car stopped bouncing, Mason opened the file and flipped through the pages to get an overview. The first ten pages were lab reports on the transplant recipients, and a cursory examination showed the same markers for the nano-machines in their blood work. After those came pages and pages of newspaper and magazine clippings of various disasters, shootings, wars, and governmental conflicts going back decades. The last section was encyclopedia entries of events hundreds—even *thousands*—of years old. Was he supposed to believe all this was connected? *How is that even possible?* Mason thought.

"Mind-blowing, isn't it?" Amber said, and Mason looked up into her green eyes, his breath catching in his throat.

"Uh... yes, it is," he choked out. Ahead of him, Jack chuckled. "I honestly can't see how the stories in here are connected," Mason said, "but the evidence we're looking for is all in the first ten pages."

Jack turned his head, more to look at Amber than Mason. "Do you have enough there to figure out what's going on?"

Mason closed the file, laying one hand on top. He took a deep breath and let it out through his nose. "I think I *already* know what's going on. At least in a broad and shallow sense."

Amber turned to Jack. "Does he always talk like this?"

Jack snorted once. "Only when our lives are at stake," he said.

Mason rolled his eyes and shook his head. "In simple terms, then, we have someone testing a new and devastating form of mind control."

"*Mind* control?" Jack said, less a question and more a consideration of the possibility. Amber turned back to face front and didn't respond at all. *What's going on in that head of yours?* Mason wondered. *Have you thought of this already?*

He dismissed that and turned back to Jack. "I think the sleeping sickness is a side effect of introducing the nanos into the system. Once awake, the subjects are ready for programming, and *that's* the purpose of the machines."

"I remember reading nanotechnology would be some kind of medical breakthrough in curing disease," Jack said.

"Sure, that's the stated purpose, but theoretically they could do all sorts of things."

"But controlling *minds*? Is that even possible?"

"Hell, Jack, they could rewrite your damn DNA if they were sophisticated enough."

"To what end?" Jack asked.

"Think about it," Mason said. "If I have control of, say, every head of state, that makes me *de facto* king of the world."

"What makes you think he hasn't already taken over?" Amber asked without turning around. Her voice was so soft Mason almost misssed the question.

"Does the world *look* like someone's in control?" he said with a laugh, shaking his head. "I don't know, but it *feels* like the testing is ongoing." *What makes her think it's one person?* "But how these stories fit in," he slapped the file, and Amber jumped, "I haven't a clue." He leaned forward, placing his hands on the back of the front seat, his head close to Jack's. "The only thing I'm sure of is that we need to get this information into the hands of the professionals." Mason turned to Amber, who was doing her best not to look at him. He sat back again and crossed his legs. "We aren't equipped for this, Jack."

* * *

Bill snapped the TV off and tossed the remote to the nightstand. He had hated the thought of doing nothing ever since his first days as a cop. Stakeouts were rare in Greenville, but they happened, and he made it a point to avoid them whenever possible. The few he had been forced to attend always ended the same way: a car full of empty coffee cups and fast food wrappers, a sour stomach, and not a single arrest to show for it.

For the hundredth time, he cast an eye to the room's phone. He wanted to call his wife to tell her he was okay, hear his kids' voices as they tell him about their day. *But that's not the number that keeps pop-*

pin' into your head, is it boy-o? A string of digits crowded his thoughts, hip-checking his home phone number from view.

And he had no clue who it belonged to.

The first time he picked up the phone, he had dialed on autopilot, only realizing halfway through the number was wrong. After the third failed attempt, he slammed the handset into the cradle and hadn't touched it again. He wrung his hands. Something was wrong, that was for sure, but whether it was physical or just mental stress, he didn't know.

He sat up, turning his body and setting his feet on the floor. Temples throbbing, he scrubbed his head, then rubbed the sides with both hands. When he got these kinds of headaches, Jenna would pinch the bridge of his nose. He thought it was dumb, but it always worked, and he tried it now. Each time he had looked at the phone and the unknown number appeared, the headache would subside, but he refused to take the easy path to relief. That way felt, somehow... *wrong.*

Checking his watch, he shook his head and grunted like a bear late for hibernation. *Only a goddamn hour!* Bill wasn't built to wait, and he stood looking for something—*anything*—to do. There was nothing to do but pace, though, so he walked to the sink, turned the water on, and splashed his face once... twice... three times. He grabbed a towel to dry off, set his hands on the counter, and leaned close to examine his face in the mirror. *You're getting old, boy-o. And patience was never—*

There was a light rap at the door. He swiveled his head to the sound, hands still on the counter. *Still too soon for Mason to be back,* he thought, and pushed away to face the door. A second knock, and Bill walked across the room to look through the peephole.

Standing there, looking as cool as the other side of the pillow, was Sohrab.

* * *

"Equipped or not, Mace, we still can't turn ourselves in," Jack said, pressing harder on the accelerator. "Not yet."

"I'm not going back," Amber said under her breath. She crossed her arms tight over her chest, and her right knee bounced a drum roll.

"What was that?" Mason asked.

Amber turned, eyes flashing, punching a hole through him. "I *said* I'm not going back into a cell. Not now... not *ever.*"

"*Back* into...?" Jack said. "Was that what happened to you?" Until now, Amber had not opened up about the last few days, and he hadn't pressed her. He figured she would tell him when the time was right. Jack assumed she preferred a private conversation, but realized now she needed a larger audience.

"Were you... *hurt*, in some way?" Mason showed genuine concern, but as always, was clumsy.

"I wasn't *raped*, if that's what you're asking," she said, harsher than was warranted. "The old man—*Dieter*—just kept me chained to a bed in a basement."

"Oh. *That's* all," Jack said, sneering.

"I'm okay," she said, turning back to him. "Really. He said he only wanted me to give you that file, and he didn't know how to reach you."

"Um," Mason said, raising his hand. "Two things wrong with that. Why didn't he just give it to you without the kidnapping part, and why did he think *you* could find Jack when he couldn't?" He snapped his fingers as he pursed his lips. "And another thing... how does he even know about you?" he said, eyes narrowing at Amber.

Wonderful, Jack thought. The first meeting between my best friend and the first woman I've cared about since Beth, and they don't trust one another. Perfect. "I don't think we're gonna answer all our questions today," Jack said. "At least not without a lot more information."

Each stared at the other in silence for perhaps ten seconds, then Mason relented. "You're right, Jack, but if we aren't surrendering to the cops, we better start putting the pieces together real soon." He kept his eyes on Amber. "I have the feeling we're running out of time."

Amber's leg stopped twitching, like shutting off a light, and she blinked—a laconic final act of dominance. "Agreed," she said.

Jack shook his head. *If we don't hang together, we shall surely hang separately.* The Franklin quote bubbled to the surface of his thoughts unbidden. *As true now as it was then*, he thought.

Lost in his own thoughts, Jack never noticed the car following them at a distance his brother would have called amateurish.

* * *

The door opened and Bill waved Sohrab inside. After he passed, Bill stuck his head out and looked around.

"Where's your car?" he asked, looking from side to side. He pulled back and closed the door.

"I had to abandon it and find... *other* means," Sohrab said with a lopsided smile.

"But if someone finds—"

"Don't worry," he said, reassuring the big man. "It's in a safe place for now." He walked to the nearest bed and lay down with his back against the headboard. "The car I acquired will not be missed for a while, so we're good at least until Mason and Jack return with Amber."

Bill sat on the bed across from Sohrab. "Where did you get it?"

"I'd rather not say," Sohrab said with a smile. "You won't like it."

"Where?" Bill said, a layer of menace covering the single word.

"Police station," Sohrab said with a frown and a shrug.

"The *fuck*?"

"Calm down," he said. "I took one of the patrolman's personal cars as he was starting a shift. We should be good for at least eight hours."

Bill was breathing heavily, shaking his head. "And you left your car..."

"In the same parking lot," Sohrab said, a huge grin on his face. He laughed at the look on Bill's face. "Do you know any place safer?"

Bill tilted his head, then shook it, a worn smile creasing his oval face. "No, I guess not."

Sohrab sat up, growing serious. He had thought long how to broach the subject, but could come up with nothing better than just straight out. In his assessment, Bill was unsuited for what was happening here. Even with police training, his presence would hurt more than help. Jack and Mason were unskilled, but they would take direction when the time came. Bill would question everything, causing confusion. In business such as this, Sohrab knew, confusion was a sure path to death.

He nodded to the holster where it lay on the other bed behind Bill. "Is that the only weapon you brought?" Bill's response was to tilt his head, then look behind at the gun snug in its holster. "Do you have a holdout?" Sohrab asked. "A second gun?"

"No," Bill said and shrugged. "Never needed one." He leaned forward, resting his forearms on his legs and clasping his hands together. "Why do you ask?" His eyes narrowed at Sohrab.

Sohrab took a long, deep breath, and let it out slowly. "There was more than FBI and local cops at the house, Bill. Homeland Security was there, and one other unmarked vehicle I can only assume was CIA."

"Bullshit," Bill said, a simple statement of fact. "CIA can't get involved in internal matters. It's against the fucking law."

Sohrab held his hands out, palms up. "I know what I saw. There are serious assets committed to this, and we were outgunned when it was just the police."

Bill sighed and sat up. "Then it's probably better if we don't have guns at all," he said. "First shot fired—it doesn't matter *who*—and it'll rain lead."

Sohrab knew the truth of that. *It won't just rain, my friend. The very air will grow black from that cloud of death.* He had seen it more than once in a previous life. Had been on the firing end, in fact. He thought he'd left all that behind when he came to this country. *Your past never completely fades, though, does it? Nothing ever matters more than what you are capable of.* Here he was husband, father, and everyone's friend. *There* he had been hard, cold, and *feared.* He had made a life here that allowed him to put all that aside.

But life makes of you what it needs.

Sohrab lay back again and reached for the remote. He turned the TV on and flipped through the channels, searching for something worth watching.

"You had anything to eat?" Bill asked.

Sohrab was surprised when he realized he hadn't. Everything had moved too fast to notice, and he often forgot to eat when he was "in the zone".

"Anything but McDonald's," he said, tossing the remote on the bed as he stood.

"C'mon," Bill said, "I'm buyin'."

* * *

The rest of the drive was filled with a pained silence after Amber had opened up about her capture and imprisonment. *The escape had been a little too easy*, Mason had thought, but he hadn't questioned her story. There were so many pieces to the puzzle, he had a problem keeping them all straight. A Rubik's Cube of interlocking parts, actions, and motivations, it lent itself to an endless number of permutations. Mason felt like he was back in college trying to sum an infinite series. The question he had to answer was did this one converge or *diverge?*

There were also the nano-machines. Who controlled them, and what was the ultimate goal? If they were being used to guide people's actions, like marionettes on a string, who could Mason trust?

Sohrab, for sure, he thought. The man had been a random selection, and unless the nanos were already world-wide, there was no reason to expect anyone would have gotten to him. Mason was also sure of himself. *Can I really be, though?* Would the subject know they were under someone else's control, or was that information hidden from them? Mason breathed a silent gasp as he realized *everyone* in their circle, outside of Sohrab, was suspect.

Now that's just fucking paranoid, he thought. Then again, just because you're paranoid doesn't mean they're not out to get you.

Without some kind of test, there was no way to be sure of *anyone.* The only sure way to test was through a blood sample, but he had no access to the equipment necessary for an accurate analysis. That was all back in his lab at the CDC where half the FBI were now pawing through his things. With enough time, money, and access to the internet, he might cobble together a test good enough to identify *possible* puppets, but not enough to *clear* them.

The problem is that he had *none* of those things and wouldn't any time soon.

He slouched into his seat, sinking as deep as the hard vinyl allowed, and rubbed the rough stubble on his cheek. *I'll have to keep an eye on* everyone *for a while*, he thought.

* * *

Amber, legs pulled up tight into the seat, hugged her knees with her head turned to the window. No one had said a word since she finished her story, and she didn't blame them. It sounded fishy even to *her.* The wound from the injection site itched, and she reached around to scratch her neck. Satisfied, she smoothed her hair over the area again, hiding the faint bruising. She didn't know why she did this, but the motion was automatic now.

The last time she looked around the car's cabin, she caught Mason watching her with a wary eye. Amber knew what he must be thinking, but as long as Jack believed her, nothing else mattered.

She felt unclean, and the filthy clothes were only part of it. Her escape had been too easy, she knew, but the part of her controlled by her lizard brain didn't care. Free was free. Was it her fault the trap was so easily slipped?

Why didn't he just give me the file and send me on my way?

It was Mason who gave it a voice, but the question had been gnawing at her ever since she broke into the house. An electric tingle shivered up her spine whenever she thought of the house, each time more of that part of the story faded. An old Polaroid, caught between first light and eventual sulfurous decay. She no longer remembered how she had gained entry into the home, and even the walk there was fuzzy. *Could I find my way back to the asylum?* Probably not, but it had to have been close enough to walk from.

Jack took his foot from the accelerator and set his turn signal. Amber barely registered the motions before he turned the wheel and they entered the little parking lot of the motel.

"Here we are," Jack said. She smiled at him as he pulled into a slot and killed the engine.

"'Bout damn time," Mason said with a grumble. He opened his door at once, stepped out, and stretched. Even from her seat she heard his joints popping, and she grinned.

"Let's go meet the gang," Jack said, and opened his door. She followed suit and stepped out of the car, looking over the roof at Jack's face. He wasn't looking at her, though. His gaze was locked over her shoulder. She turned to see what attracted his attention, and an old Mercedes sedan pulled into the slot beside Bill's Catalina.

She knew before the door opened, before the old man pulled himself out with both gnarled hands on the window frame. Before he stood beside the car, hat in one hand and smoothing his white hair back with the other.

"Dieter," she said, her voice crackling like a campfire.

"Hello, Amber," he said, smiling like a snake. She half expected to see a forked tongue peek between leathery lips. "Would you be so kind as to introduce me to Mr. Montgomery?"

253

CHAPTER 22

"I DON'T KNOW WHERE HE IS, JACK," Mason said, much louder than he intended. "He was here when I left." As soon as they entered the room, they knew Bill was gone. *It's not like there are a lot of places to hide in here*, he thought. The last one to enter the room, Mason closed the door behind him, and threw the keycard on the desk. "His gun's gone, so I don't think he stepped out for ice," he said, pointing to the bed closest to the door. "Probably went out for a bite to eat."

"Without hearing anything from us?" Jack shook his head. "That's *nothing* like my brother. He would wait here until he heard something, or you returned with us."

Dieter had made himself comfortable on the far side of the room, sitting at the round table near the window, his back to the wall. He placed his hat on the table in front of him, his hands flat on either side.

"Why don't you have a seat, Jack," he said, gesturing to the chair across from him. "We have much to discuss." Mason pegged the accent as German right away, but there were hints of something else.

"As long as the discussion includes *answers*," Jack said, eyes flashing as he sat across from the old man.

Amber remained just inside the door, her arms crossed, and Mason walked around her to the bed closest to the two men. He sat next to the nightstand, his back to the headboard, and stretched out his legs. The old man tracked Mason's path with narrowed eyes, then relaxed and turned to Jack.

"I think I can give you all the answers you are looking for," Dieter said with a smile. "At least," he pointed to the file in Jack's hand, "as long as we limit our discussion to that."

"Why don't you just start at the beginning," Jack said, sneering. *He's handling this better than I would in his position,* Mason thought. *Would the need for answers trump my desire for retribution if someone close to me were kidnapped?* He was glad he didn't have to answer that.

"Which one?" Dieter asked, his head tilted, eyebrows arched.

Jack leaned forward, one arm on the table. "I have neither the time nor the *patience* for games," he said in a voice that turned Mason's blood to ice.

Dieter held Jack's gaze with steady, liquid eyes, and nodded. "I only mean do you want me to start with *your* involvement, or when everything *truly* began?"

Jack, his face red, took two breaths and leaned back. "Whatever works for you," he said.

Dieter frowned, his eyes flicking to Mason, then Amber. A spark of invisible static seemed to pass between her and the old man. Mason watched her shuffle from one foot to the other, lips pursed, brow furrowed, then she brightened.

"I'm gonna get a shower," she said as if she had only waited for the proper moment to inform them. "I can't do much about my clothes," she said, rubbing unseen stains from her jeans, "but I can at least make *myself* smell better." Smiling at Jack, she turned and entered the bathroom, closing and locking the door.

Now why wouldn't she be interested in Dieter's story? Mason mused. *She's already said she doesn't know what's going on. Where's her curiosity?* Amber was an anomaly to Mason. The one piece of the whole puzzle that didn't belong.

Once the sound of running water reached them, Jack shook himself and turned to the old man. "You were saying?"

"There's a reason I've sent you clues to follow, Jack," Dieter said with a grandfather's smile. "You needed to discover much of this for yourself, or you would never believe the larger truth."

"And that is?" Jack said, crossing his arms.

Dieter sighed, a rustle of desiccated leaves blowing across a fetid forest floor. "Human history is being shaped—*tampered* with—and has been for over six thousand years."

* * *

"Bullshit," Mason said from Jack's right. Jack turned to his friend, his face scolding. Mason huffed once, then crossed his arms.

"You said it yourself, Mace. Those nano-machines aren't something humans know how to make, yet," Jack said with a shrug.

"Ah... those are actually a recent development," Dieter said with a nod at Mason, "but yes, they were originally created by the Zzkritti,".

"The what?" Jack said, frowning.

"The Zzkritti are a star-faring race that has ruled this galaxy for nearly a million years," Dieter said, his voice in awe of the words he spoke.

"By *rule*, you mean—"

"I mean they are the only intelligent species capable of traveling to other planets... *colonizing*," Dieter said. "They are insectile in nature, with a true hive mind, and they have filled every usable corner of the galaxy."

He sounds like he admires *them*, Jack thought. He was shocked to find he was already believing the man, accepting the most significant story in human history as little more than a discussion about "the neighbors".

"Again," Mason said, "bullshit." He looked at Dieter like the crazy old man he appeared to be. "This universe—this *galaxy*—is, literally, *billions* of years old," Mason said, shaking his head. "Logic says there should be thousands of intelligent species out there," he finished with a wave of his hand.

"Indeed, there *were*," Dieter said to Mason. To Jack, he asked, "Have you heard of the Great Filter?"

"*I* have," Mason said before Jack could answer. "That's supposed to be the thing that keeps a species from developing intelligence."

"Close," Dieter said. "There are many Great Filters in a species' development. The first is simply having the right conditions for life to form. The second is a planetary system that allows life to develop undisturbed until simple animals can form." He smiled at Jack, but

257

said to Mason, "At each point, one nudge in the wrong direction, and *poof*, that species becomes extinct."

"So what's that got to do with your... whatever the hell they are?" Jack asked.

"The *Zzkritti* were one of the first to colonize other planets, and they eventually came in contact with another. As must always happen in such cases, they fought a devastating war over resources, and the Zzkritti were victorious. Their victory came at a high cost, however, as they were nearly annihilated. They recognized this as one more Great Filter and believed that to avoid another they must eliminate *all* competition in the galaxy."

The concept was both logical and *appalling* to Jack. If true, how could he hope to fight a foe that powerful? How could he *not*?

"What does that have to do with humans?" Mason asked, breaking the silence. "We're not out colonizing anything."

"No," Dieter said, "but that no longer matters to them. They decided it was more logical to fight such battles *before* a species developed enough intelligence to challenge them. For millions of years they have nudged every sentient species as each approaches a Great Filter, causing them to fail."

"So they don't need a large military or powerful weaponry," Jack said. In such a scenario, only a small expeditionary force was necessary. "They use our own Great Filters against us."

Mason, his face scrunched up, raised his hand. "Uh... then why aren't we dead, yet?"

"What do you mean?" Jack asked.

"There have been plenty of opportunities to kill us already," he said. "The Cold War alone was the perfect chance to wipe us out. If they can control people, surely they could have started a nuclear war."

"That's true," Jack said. "Why not then?"

Dieter shrugged, an old-man motion resembling a short cough. "That's where *my* story begins," he said with a dry grin.

* * *

If the old fart isn't nuts, Mason thought, *we are in for a* world *of hurt*. There was no avoiding it—he and Jack were finished. Fighting a lone psychopath was one thing, fighting an entire *race* of super-intelligent aliens was another. *Independence Day* aside, it just wasn't possible. *I doubt we can simply give them a cold, no matter what Jeff Goldblum thinks.* Taking their evidence to the authorities was now out of the question, since most anyone in a position of true authority was compromised in *some* way. *Who the hell's gonna believe us, anyway?*

The old man was still smiling, and Mason's stomach churned at the sight.

"Your story?" he asked.

Dieter nodded at Mason. "I was a research assistant working with a... doctor in Nazi Germany during the war. We didn't know it at the time, but the Zzkritti were directing our research into mind control."

"You mean the nano-machines?" Jack said.

"Not at the time. That came much later," Dieter said. He took a long breath, letting it out in a ragged sigh. "Up until my involvement, they were helping with Germany's V–1 and V–2 rocket program in conjunction with the research into a nuclear weapon. Combining those two would have meant the end of the war in Germany's favor." He looked far away as he spoke those words, his eyes unfocused. He shook his head, grabbing his hat and turning it in place with wrinkled hands. "There was a fundamental change in the Zzkritti during that time, and they shifted their help to the Americans."

"Was Einstein one of them?" Mason asked, and the other two men looked at him like he was a slow child.

"No, no," Dieter said, shaking his head. "Einstein was one of our world's true geniuses..." He turned back to Jack, focusing on him for the first time. "He did have help. As did Oppenheimer and all the others."

"What caused the shift?" Mason asked. Such a change in strategy implied disharmony... or competing ideas at the very least. *Maybe there's an exploit we could use to our advantage.*

"I... don't know," Dieter said, not looking at Mason. "You have to understand that most of my information comes from the Zzkritti, themselves." Now he did look at Mason. "I did not witness the most important events, nor was I privy to their discussions."

"You never heard *anything* they said?" Mason asked, incredulous.

Dieter smiled at him, as if to a dog he was trying to teach a trick. "Even if the bulk of their communication were not telepathic, I still would not have understood their language. It *is* alien, after all."

He's lying, Mason thought. He had noticed the verbal tics, like whole swaths of information being deleted from the man's story in real-time. There was an important question neither he nor Jack had asked.

"How did you come by this information at all if you didn't know you were working for them?"

"At the end of the war, I, the doctor, our research, and our subjects were transported to Argentina where many of their most important assets had established a community. They introduced themselves at that time."

"Subjects?" Jack asked, sitting up.

"Yes, I am sorry to say." Dieter shook his head, looking down at his hat. "We had to test the procedures on someone, and the Nazis were all too happy to provide." He looked up. "I believe you have encountered one."

"The Shadowman," Mason said, one piece of the puzzle locking into place.

"Thirteen, yes," Dieter said, nodding. "He was our greatest success."

"Your best assassin, you mean," Jack said, his voice full of heat and bile. "How can you call such evil a *success*?"

"Oh," Dieter dismissed Jack's accusation with a wave of his hand, "Thirteen is no more evil than a great white shark. He is a killer, to be sure, but he does not do so for pleasure. Thirteen kills because he *must*. He is an instrument—a *scalpel*, wielded by his masters."

"The... *Zzkritti*," Jack said, trying the word for the first time.

"Yes," Dieter said.

Everything Dieter said made perfect sense, and Mason didn't believe a word of it. *At least regarding Dieter's own involvement.* The man was leaving out too much, and glossing over what he *couldn't* leave out. And Jack was buying *all* of it.

"Jack," Mason said, "even if you believe this guy's story... what the hell *difference* does it make? We can't fight them, and we can't fight the government."

Jack sighed and sat back in his chair. "I know that, Mace." He turned to Dieter. "So why get me involved at all?" he asked.

"All that needs to happen is to bring everything into the open," Dieter said. "*I* cannot do this—I have no credibility—but *you*, through the CDC, have more than enough to shine a light on their plans. Once discovered, they must regroup, which should give humanity enough time to find a way to stop them."

"I don't know if you've noticed," Jack said, sneering, "but *my* credibility's not so hot these days."

"Yes," Dieter said, his shoulders slumping, "that is unfortunate." His eyes brightened. "But you must know people of stature that you can convince," he said, nodding with a wan smile.

"Sally's dead," Mason said, his voice a cold knife slicing the air. "She was probably the only one who could have done anything for us." The anger grew in him again, despite his efforts to tamp it.

"I may know someone who can help," Jack said to Dieter, ignoring Mason. "Before I involve him, though, I have to know one thing."

Here it comes, Mason thought, bracing himself.

Dieter tilted his head and waited for the question.

"I just want to know who is responsible for the death of my wife and child," Jack said, each word edged in cold, hard diamond.

A long time passed before Dieter breathed. That's right, Mason thought. Bring out that lie you've been holding in reserve. I dare you.

Dieter's face was calm. Cold. "First, you have to know—"

The lock on the door beeped and the door opened, pouring sunshine into the room.

* * *

Bill followed Sohrab into the room, and all the joy from his meal faded like the end credits of a bad movie. The tension in the room radiated from the small table in back where Jack and an unknown visitor sat, and Bill stopped just inside the door. He looked into the open closet to his right where he had left his holster but decided against picking up the gun. Leaving it in the room went against everything he had been trained to do, but Sohrab had made such a big deal about not taking it with them that he left it there just to end the argument.

There was something odd about the old man sitting near Jack, and Bill had to force himself to walk away from the closet. He took three steps, moving past Sohrab, and leaned on the edge of the dresser where the TV sat. Sohrab shrugged and sat on the bed near Mason, who moved to the foot of the bed.

"Who do we have here?" Bill asked. The sound of a hair dryer erupted from the bathroom, and he started. It wasn't like him to jump at noises. *At least ones that ain't gunshots*, he thought. He narrowed his eyes at the stranger as a familiar tingle crawled up his spine.

Jack leaned back in his chair, lifting the front legs off the floor, balancing in that uncanny way he did as a kid. "This is Dieter, Bill. My pen-pal, and Amber's captor." He said it so matter-of-factly that Bill didn't believe him at first. Bill looked at Mason, who nodded his confirmation.

"Well... you seem a little more okay with that than I expected," Bill said.

"It gets better," Mason said, his voice full of disdain. "He was just telling us about the alien invasion we have to stop."

* * *

Mason couldn't help but notice the change in Bill. The man was electric with an energy that manifested only when he looked at Dieter. It was the look of a predator that had *stumbled* upon its prey. *It's all in your head, Mason*, he thought, chastising himself. *You're seeing things that aren't there. The old sod's alien invasion story is playing right into your paranoia.*

Bill's eyes flicked from Jack to Dieter and back again, over and over, like they were the only two people in the room.

"Hey, I've got a question of my own," Mason said to Dieter. "If the Shadowman is working for your aliens, why is he cleaning up after these events?" He looked at Jack, eyes narrowed. "It's *almost* like they have nothing to do with them."

"They have *everything* to do with them!" Dieter said.

Methinks he doth protest too much, Mason thought, raising an eyebrow. Why is he lying? What is he not saying?

The sound of the hair dryer disappeared, and the bathroom door opened. Amber stepped out and surveyed the room like a running back checking out the defense. Her hair was still damp, and she wore no makeup, but Mason was sure she was the most beautiful woman he had ever seen close up.

Like all men, it blinded him.

* * *

Everyone was staring at her. She had grown used to it ever since eighth grade, when the majority of her development was complete, years ahead of her classmates. That was when teachers—the male teachers, at least—stopped taking her seriously as a student. The female teachers simply became covertly hostile.

And there was hostility in this room. It slapped her in the face as soon as she entered, and the weight of it held her just outside the safety of the bathroom. Her breathing grew shallow and rapid, like a cat ready to pounce. It was hard to focus, though, as the buzzing in her head returned in full force, gnawing at her brain. Her pupils contracted, everything in the room zooming into crystal clarity even as it darkened. She stared through a tunnel, focused on a single point.

A point centered on the large man by the TV.

* * *

"They are still experimenting with their nanos, perfecting their control," Dieter was saying. Bill had a hard time concentrating on the man's words, though, and he slid a little closer.

"I think we've walked into the middle of a movie, my friend," Sohrab said to Bill. *He's trying to lessen the tension*, Bill thought. *The guy would probably make a good negotiator.*

"It's a movie, all right," Mason said, "but there are a ton of plot holes."

Bill's head hurt so he closed his eyes, blocking out the too-bright lights of the room. A wave of nausea washed up from the depths of his gut, pushing coherent thought away. There was something he had to do... but the picture wouldn't form in his head. What he saw instead was Jenna.

She was smiling and shaking her head "no". *She looks sad*, he thought.

* * *

Mason watched Bill close his eyes, wavering between action and total collapse. It was the same look he had often seen in Jack, though *he* had always been drunk at the time. Bill wasn't drunk now, Mason was sure of that. Sohrab was now fully engaged in the conversation, arguing with Dieter and Jack, and Bill's eyes snapped open and he looked directly at Dieter. He levered away from the dresser and turned toward the old man, who smiled up at him. Bill's eyes flashed—warning or anger, Mason couldn't tell which. Jack and Sohrab were still arguing some point Mason failed to follow.

A motion to his right caught his eye, and he turned his head.

* * *

Amber watched the big man—*that must be Bill*, she thought with a clinical detachment—as he took a step toward Dieter, and a pain ran up her spine and into her head like a shot of acid. Dieter grinned at her, a glowing grandfather watching a cherished granddaughter's turn on the stage. Without thinking, she spun in place, looking for what she needed. She found it, cold and heavy, to her right in its leather cocoon. She pulled the gun from the holster, thumbing off the safety just like her daddy taught her.

* * *

No one was paying attention. No one saw Amber dip into the closet and return with Bill's gun.

No one but Mason.

There wasn't time to think. The safety clicked and Amber lifted the weapon with both hands. Steady and level, the cords of taut muscle stood in stark relief as she held the gun pointed at Dieter. Mason stole a quick glance at the old man, who was smiling, not at Bill, but at Amber. Mason only had time to register that the gun *wasn't* pointed at the old man.

No time to think. The sound of a hammer pulling back as Amber squeezed the trigger.

Not Bill, he screamed in his head, and he yelled "No!" and leapt off the bed. One long step placed him between Amber and Bill just as the hammer found its home, and the room exploded.

He almost didn't feel it, but the heat in his chest and the flower of red blooming there told him all he needed. Mason crumbled to the floor at the same time the gun did, both dropped there by the most beautiful woman he had ever seen up close.

* * *

For two whole seconds, no one moved, then Amber folded in on herself and fell to the floor sobbing. Jack jumped from his chair, nearly falling over in his scramble to Mason's side. He knelt beside his friend, more family than family, and sat, cradling the man's head in his lap. He was dimly aware that Bill had run to Amber's side to retrieve his weapon and was now watching her with a policeman's eye.

"Someone call an ambulance!" Jack said, and he pressed one palm over the wound, hoping to stanch the flow of life pouring from Mason's body.

"Don't bother," Mason said, then coughed up a spray of crimson. "Pulse is weak... and... irregular." He placed one hand over Jack's. "Think she nicked... the aorta." His voice was almost a whisper, and Jack leaned close. "Hate to... leave... you alone." Mason coughed again—weaker this time.

"Don't talk, dude. Save your strength."

No one was dialing 911. Sohrab stood to one side, a stoic frown on his face.

* * *

Mucked it up good this time, eh, Mason? He wanted to laugh but didn't want to waste the little strength he had left. There was so much he wanted to say to Jack—so much to atone for—and now he never would. None of this was his friend's fault. Hell, it wasn't even *Amber's* fault—he knew that with the same conviction he knew was dying.

"Don't talk, dude. Save your strength," Jack said, tears dropping from his eyes.

"My best... friend," Mason said with a croak. "Know that, right?"

"*Family*," Jack said, rocking back and forth. "Friends are the family you *choose*."

Mason smiled.

It's so bright... The rational part he had left knew his eyes must be dilating as he slipped away. There was nothing to do but let go, but he couldn't. He had to apologize to Jack. Make him *understand* he held no blame. Drifting off, he motioned for Jack to come closer, and his friend leaned down as if to kiss him goodbye.

Mason apologized the only way he had left.

"Not... her fault," he whispered in Jack's ear. He reached up with the last of his strength and tapped Jack's forehead. "Nanos," he said, and turned his head to Bill. "Watch... him."

Mason relaxed, sagging as Jack faded, and the world turned white.

* * *

Jack felt Mason's final breath brush his cheek, then his body sagged in Jack's arms, the weight of the man multiplying in death. *No, no, no, no...* Jack thought or said aloud—he did not know which—and he held his friend close as he rocked. Alone... *again.*

The noise from the others tried to intrude, but none of it was intelligible. None of it mattered. Jack ignored it all as he rocked and cried, tears doing nothing to wash away the pain.

Alone is better, he thought. No one else I can hurt that way.

The world closed around him, forming a protective shell of congealed guilt and thickening doubt.

Alone is better...

* * *

Amber sobbed uncontrollably, Bill standing watch over her. From the instant his gun fired, his head cleared as if waking from a bad dream. *Only now the nightmare is just beginning*, he thought. Mason was dead—murdered by *his* weapon—and Jack and Amber were nearly catatonic. Both wailing in their pain.

"We have to get *out* of here!" Bill said, hoping to get them moving before the police arrived. "Someone must have heard the shot, and—"

"Shut up." Sohrab said in a voice so calm Bill had trouble hearing him. It was neither loud nor angry, but it was the voice of command, and it demanded compliance.

"Are you out of your mind?" Bill said. "We have to leave before the cops get here."

"No, we must be calm. Lower your voices. Take deep breaths." He was talking more to Jack and Amber, but Bill complied. "A single shot is often ignored, and as long as we don't call attention to ourselves further, even someone curious about the sound will dismiss it."

The rational part of Bill's mind knew the truth of this. Most interviews with witnesses to a gun battle began with "I didn't realize someone was shooting until the second or third shot."

Bill looked down at Mason. "We can't leave him here," he whispered.

"You can, and you will," Sohrab said, the voice of a man used to having his orders followed without question. He knelt beside Jack, placed his arms around him, then gently lifted him to stand beside them. "Take Jack and leave this place. Do not hurry or draw attention to yourselves. I will use Mason's phone to call you later." He knelt again, turned Mason to examine his back, then rolled him back with care.

"What about her?" Bill said, pointing at Amber with his chin.

"I will take care of her," he said, the stone of his face softening for an instant. He looked at Dieter, who was still smiling, and the hard lines returned. "That one has his own car and may go wherever he wishes."

Everything's gone to Hell, Bill thought, shaking his head. *How did I get wrapped up in all this? How do I* explain *this?* It was too much, and threatened to pull him into the same depths of despair where Jack now foundered. There was no going back, though. He was fucked, and he knew it.

"What about him?" he said, pointing at Mason.

Sohrab sighed, a lifetime of sadness in that one sound. "I will take care of him as well," he said. "Police your round, officer." He pulled a lock–blade knife from his pocket and thumbed it open. "I don't think either of you want to be around for this."

"What are you doing?" Bill asked, sickened by the thought he knew *exactly* what the man was doing. He spied the spent shell casing near his foot where Amber lay, and bent to pick it up. The valuable piece of evidence slid into his pocket.

"There's no exit wound, and if you don't want to be charged with murder..."

The blood in Bill's face ran away to hide.

* * *

Sohrab knelt beside Mason's body where it lay on the shower curtain he had placed beneath, careful to avoid the blood pooled on the vinyl. The knife in his hand gleamed, reflecting a life that was and no longer would be. *The dead grow cold, but my blood boils*, Sohrab thought. He leaned closer and closed the man's eyes with gentle fingers, whispering, "I am sorry for what I must now do." Before straightening, he kissed Mason's forehead. "Assalaamu 'alaykum wa rahmatu-Allah" he said, with a reverence he thought he had lost long ago. The prayer was too short, and did not do the man justice, but it would have to be enough.

Amber was in the bathroom, still crying, and there she would stay until he was through sanitizing the room. Before that, though, he must violate the body of a man he could have called friend.

He drew a heavy, stuttering breath, sighed, and bent to his task.

PART THREE

Some try to tell me, thoughts they cannot defend
Just what you want to be,
you will be in the end

"Nights in White Satin" —Justin Hayward

CHAPTER 23

Bill drove, picking streets at random, too spooked by Jack's un-responsive demeanor to stop. Sohrab had been right—no one gave them a second look when he led Jack to the car like an Alzheimer's patient. Bill had only attempted to engage him in conversation once, but it went nowhere. Jack huddled close to the door, as far from Bill as he could get in the confines of the car, staring out the window and pulling on his bottom lip.

He's done that since he was a kid, Bill thought, and always when he's confused or hurt.

Right now, Bill knew Jack was both.

"Is your phone on?" Bill asked. Sohrab still hadn't called, and it had been over an hour since they left the motel.

Jack's only response was to pull the phone from his pocket and slide it over. He never turned, or even glanced in Bill's direction. He left the phone between them on the seat like the first brick in a wall. Whether it was to separate him from Bill, or from the whole world, Bill did not know. He picked it up and verified it was on and working.

"He should have called by now, right?" Bill said.

Nothing. Not even a nod or a shake of his head.

"C'mon, Jack. You've got to snap out of it."

Jack turned his head, looking Bill in the eyes, his own dead and empty. "Leave me the fuck alone," he said, his voice soft and danger-ous.

"Jack—"

"I just lost my best friend in the whole goddamn world, Bill! Give me a fucking hour to mourn, okay? Is that too much to ask?"

Bill's face grew hot, his pulse pounding in his neck. "I don't know if you noticed, but that gun was pointed at *me*, Li'l Bro." He used his anger as a shield, protecting him from the hurt of Jack's indifference.

"I know," Jack said, softening. "But I came to terms with *your* death a long time ago."

"The *fuck* does that mean?"

"Ever since you became a cop," Jack said with a short shrug.

Bill's eyes grew wide. "Oh, for *Pete's...*" He laughed—a nasty, angry sound—and rolled his eyes. "I'm a union man through and through, Jack, but don't believe all that crap they feed the press about how dangerous this job is." He shook his head. "You know who has a more dangerous job than a cop?"

"The military?" Jack said.

"No," Bill said. He leaned across the long seat, his face as close to Jack's as he could get. "Practically fucking *everyone*." He laughed again, this time with a little humor. "Shit, Jack, even goddamn *landscapers* have it worse."

"Then why—?"

"*Protection*," Bill said. "If civilians think the job's dangerous, we con them into protecting us from the bad guys with laws against looking at us crosseyed. We're a protected species, Jack, and we're not even on the fucking *endangered* list." He turned onto another street chosen at random. "I'm a detective, so I've got it even better than most. We go in after the shooting is over, and if things even *look* like they might head south, the Red-Shirts—uh, *patrolmen*—are right outside."

"I always thought your job was dangerous," Jack said.

"Oh, there's the *potential*, but statistically... no. I bet *you've* been shot at more times than I have," he finished with a poke in Jack's chest. "Did you know today was the first time that gun's been fired at another human being?" He knew at once that was the wrong thing to say. Bringing the conversation back to Mason would only serve to shove Jack back into his shell.

Jack surprised him, though. "You've had it since you joined the force," he said.

"Yep," Bill said, turning his attention back to the road. "I'm damn proud of that, too."

The pause in the conversation stretched into silence, with only the sound of tires spinning on the pavement as a soundtrack. After a few miles, Jack sat up and pointed to his right. "Pull in over there."

"What's up?"

"I have to pee, and the car probably needs gas."

Bill spun the wheel and steered the Big Cat into the parking lot, pulling up to one of the pumps.

"You need to go in?" Jack asked as he opened his door.

"Nope," Bill said. "Bladder like a camel's hump, remember?"

Jack attempted to smile. "Yeah, but it always seems to bust about the time there aren't any places to stop."

"Go ahead," Bill waved Jack to the building, "I'll get the gas." Jack nodded, climbed out of the car, and was off.

Bill watched him go into the building, then shut the engine off and opened his door. As he was getting out, his hand brushed the phone beside him.

The urge to call his wife overwhelmed him, and this time the number in his head was right.

* * *

Regardless of what he had told them, Sohrab wasn't sure no one had called the police after hearing the shot. He had waited for half an hour before beginning his grisly search through Mason's cooling body. The blood on the carpet had been minimal, since most of Mason's bleeding had been internal, but for what Sohrab had done next, the shower curtain he placed beneath the body had been a requirement.

It had taken him longer than he wanted, but when he had at last pulled his hand from Mason's chest, he held three bullet fragments and the confidence there were no others. He had cleaned the knife and fragments in the sink before pocketing them, then turned to wrapping the body for transport. The room had been reserved in his name, and he had to make sure no one ever saw it as a crime scene.

Amber had been no help, but she at least remained quiet. After he wrapped the body in the shower curtain, Sohrab led Amber out of the bathroom and over to the bed nearest the door to wait while he worked to sanitize the room. Years of training, and more years in the field, gave him an almost eidetic memory when it came to observing people's movements, and he had called on that to retrace where every hand had been placed in the room. He cleaned each surface as best he could, then began a search for stray hairs. The bathroom he had saved for last, after he cleaned as much of the blood stain as possible, blotting it with toilet paper to be flushed.

He had to leave Amber for a time while he went in search of a store for a few supplies, but in her near catatonia he had been confident she wouldn't do anything in his absence. Still, he gathered what he needed as quickly as possible, returning with a roll of Duck Tape and a bottle of the darkest red wine he could find. Amber never moved from where he placed her.

He poured the wine over the blood stain, rubbing it deep into the carpet's fibers, and left the open bottle beside the stain. When the maid came in the next morning, his hope was for her to dismiss it as what it appeared to be. The management might try to clean it, but they were more likely to write it off and simply replace it. Even after Mason's body was found, it would never be traced back to that room.

Removing the body had been the most dangerous part, but when it was dark enough outside, Sohrab carried Mason to the patrolman's car without being challenged. He hoped that meant he had not been seen, but he could not be sure. Once the body was tucked safely into the trunk, he led Amber down the stairs and into the car. As dusk fell over the parking lot, he drove away for the last time.

He had considered leaving Mason's body in the trunk when he swapped cars again at the police station, but that would invite scrutiny of any video footage they may have of the parking lot. Instead, he tried to make it look like a mugging gone wrong, leaving Mason on a sidewalk over a storm drain. He had taken the cash and credit cards from Mason's wallet, but left it and his ID there, then ditched the shower curtain in a dumpster several miles away before returning to the police station.

His superiors would have called it a "good op."

He had done what he could, but he knew now it was only the beginning.

* * *

The girl's programming held, Dieter thought with a smile as he drove the darkening lane. He hadn't been sure it would, but in the end her directive to protect him at any cost had worked as planned. It wasn't the only directive he had given her, but if that one functioned, then the others must as well.

It may have worked *too* well, since Dieter had observed no overtly threatening moves from Jack's older brother. It made no sense. If Jack's brother were compromised by Thirteen, he would have killed Jack or Dieter—maybe both. At the very least, Amber would have had a *much* stronger reaction to the man when they met. But she had been aiming the weapon directly at *Bill*—Dieter was sure of that. It was unfortunate Dr. Hill chose to intervene, his death an unnecessary distraction. *Now the plans I had for him must shift to another*, he mused.

In the meantime, Jack would continue to dig into the evidence he had provided, drawing Thirteen to the center of Dieter's web.

Soon, old friend.

* * *

"Bill, if I go with you now and turn myself in, then everything— Mason, Sally... *everything*—will have been for nothing!" Jack's voice was little more than a whisper, but it cut the air like a knife. If he were being completely honest, Jack *wanted* to end everything. He wanted the nightmare to be over, but the questions continued to gnaw at his brain. *If* everything Dieter had said was true, there was no one else to search for the answers. No one else to stop what was coming.

But Mason had remained skeptical to the end; that, more than anything, tempered Jack's resolve.

"Jack," Bill said with a heavy sigh, "it's no longer a question of *if*, but *when*." He gripped the wheel, twisting and grinding it under his fleshy hands. "I don't even know why we're here waiting for these people. The Iraqi is bad enough, but the *girl*, Jack... she just murdered your friend!"

"Don't you think I know that?" Jack all but screamed, and he slapped the back of the seat. "I already told you, Bill... that *wasn't* Amber." Not if he believed Mason's last words. If he let go of the anger he felt. For Amber, for Bill... even for *Mason*. How could he ever let go of that? Mason left just when Jack needed him most, and Amber helped him do it. *What was going on in her head? Did she even know what she was doing? Who could have—*

"I think we should go, Jack," Bill said, wiping Jack's thoughts clean. "Let's get you to Greenville." His eyes darted from Jack to the road. "Those two can fend for themselves."

Ever since they had stopped for gas, Bill had been different, insisting with increasing pressure that Jack must turn himself in. Not only that, but that he must do it in Greenville. Sitting in Bill's car in a far corner of a mall parking lot waiting for Sohrab, Jack considered the implications of everything he had learned. The file was open in his lap, and he flipped through the pages without examining them in detail. *There's more here*, he thought, *and if I can just put it all together...* The desire to see it through had waned. Murdered with his friend.

He reached the end of the file, his fingers lingering over a single page of handwritten dates with accompanying information. The writing was a cramped scrawl, the letters so small he almost needed a magnifying glass to read them. It was a list of events spanning centuries, much like he had been forced to copy and memorize in high school history. Many of the events, though, held little historical significance, and he raised an eyebrow as he attempted to decipher the meaning.

When he turned the page over, his eyes grew wide. *These dates are in the* future, he thought.

"Do you understand what I'm saying, Jack?" Bill was still talking. Jack had stopped listening long ago, and if Bill hadn't reached over to grab Jack's arm, he would still be ignoring him.

Jack shook the hand off and waved his brother silent. "Shut up for a second, okay?"

If this were a recording of—what...tests?—then why the dates in the future? Jack scanned the page, the dates shown in no particular order. At least no order that he could discern. Near the bottom was a date and notation that made him sit up. *April 25, 2015.* It was the closest future date on the list, but it was the notation that took his breath. *Earthquake, Nepal.*

"Jack—"

"Listen, Bill," Jack said, turning to face him for the first time, "I think we have something." He tapped at the page. "Here... look at the date and notation."

Bill leaned over, squinting. "Yeah... so?"

"I think it says there's going to be an earthquake in Nepal in four days."

"Again," Bill said, rolling his eyes, "so? Pretty sure geologists predict those things all the time."

"Not with this level of accuracy." Jack didn't believe Bill was dismissing this for any reason other than expediency. He wanted Jack to go with him, and nothing, it seemed, would turn him from that path. "If that prediction is true, we have what we need to sell the whole damn story to the authorities."

"But you'll have to first find someone to listen long enough to keep from shooting you *before* the earthquake." Bill's mouth stretched into a thin line. "To do that, you *still* have to turn yourself in." He crossed his arms, his point made. A bead of sweat formed at his temple, then ran a line down to his cheek. His right leg bounced.

"Not necessarily," Jack said, scooting closer to the door. "I think Rutger will listen, and he's right here in Atlanta."

"You have to come with me," Bill said, sweat now forming on his upper lip. His face wasn't flush, though, and Jack wondered if his brother were ill.

The motion was so smooth and fast Jack never had a chance to be surprised, the gun appearing in Bill's hand as if by magic.

"I'll wing ya if I have to," Bill said, his voice shaking. "But either way, you're comin' with me."

* * *

Thirteen sat in the dark, pulling the tendrils of his consciousness back from their scattered contacts. The device hummed on the table in front of him, that and the rattled sigh from the air conditioner the only other sounds in the room. Using the device in this manner—without the aid of human computers—taxed him physically, but that was a minor inconvenience compared to the monumental task of hiding his actions from the Others. Sweat dripped from the end of his nose, splashing rhythmically on the table.

When Bill called his wife, the worm Thirteen had left in the network to monitor in-coming calls alerted him. Locating the cell and reactivating the man's programming was a simple technical matter but required Thirteen to go *inside* the system.

Thirteen opened his eyes and tapped the device once to deactivate it. The smile that creased his face was not one of humor, but satisfaction. Bill would bring Jack to him, and with him, *Dieter.*

Soon, old friend.

* * *

Sohrab closed Mason's phone, swearing silently. He still had Jack's phone in his pocket, though it was disassembled, and the sim card pulled. The cabin of his car was as dark as a grave, and if Amber weren't snoring quietly in the back seat, it would have felt like one as well. While he hadn't been looking forward to Jack and Amber's reunion given the circumstances, he *had* expected Jack and Bill to at least *be* there. The fact they weren't answering the phone was even more disturbing than their absence.

He turned and looked behind to where Amber lay, pity in his eyes. She had fallen asleep as soon as they changed vehicles in the police station parking lot, and hadn't said a word to him since the motel room. When she *had* spoken, it was always a harsh whisper to herself. Sohrab welcomed the peace sleep had brought her.

Sleep is the great cleanse, he thought, turning to stare out the windshield at the fingernail of crescent moon hanging low in the sky. *God never places a burden on a soul it cannot bear.* He always thought that was backward. Strength meant bearing what you were given. God had nothing to do with it. Some people broke under the weight of their pain and the burdens they bore. *Character is all that matters.*

He knew nothing of the woman, but she would either recover, or the events of today would break her.

Sohrab had seen many things in his time as an agent for the Mukhabarat but had never seen someone kill without *purpose*. What Amber had done was a mystery, even to her.

"I don't know," she had responded to every question, burying her face in her hands. When the sobs racked her body and she hyperventilated, he had relented. There was no point in twisting the knife she had shoved into her own soul. He was finished with torture. If he forgot all the tools he could bring to bear this very day, it would not be too soon.

What he couldn't forget, however, was the look on the old man's face when Amber pulled the trigger.

He was... *pleased*. Sohrab knew that look well. He had seen it often on the faces of his trainers when he executed a particularly gruesome task they had set for him. It was the look of a master reveling in the work of their slaves.

And Jack trusts this man.

Sohrab thought through his options, then pulled the pieces of Jack's phone from his pocket and reassembled them. It was a terrible chance to take—likely painting a target on his back—but there were few remaining options. The most palatable of *those* was dumping Amber at her home and driving back to DC to his wife.

Character is all that matters.

* * *

It hadn't taken *much* to talk his superiors into letting him return, but Rutger was sure they weren't happy about having to explain *that* to Interpol. When the conversation ended, he knew two things: one, he had a lot of professional capital he could bring to bear when necessary; and two, he had just used up much of it.

Rutger shrugged to no one but himself as he inched forward in the TSA line. *At least the ticket was open-ended.* He shuddered to think what the cost of purchasing another would have been.

He hadn't heard from Jack since he sent him to pick up Amber, and though that worried him, there was little he could do about it. Especially with Gershon breathing down his neck. He took another shuffling step forward and checked his watch. Americans prided themselves on their open society, but though Germany saw more terrorist activity, even *they* had not responded with such draconian measures. Ahead of him, a man took off his shoes, and Rutger noticed others already holding theirs up like an offering to a work-weary Pharaoh.

The TSA agents, eyes half-lidded, waved people through the line, taking bags and purses and piling them onto a conveyor belt to drag them through screening. An endless line of people stretched behind him, and he wondered if each would make their departure time. Every now and then a man was pulled from the line for special attention, agents waving wands over and around their bodies and searching roughly through their bags. In each case the men bore a striking resemblance to one another.

Maybe it's the beards, he thought, and took another step forward.

When his phone buzzed, he jumped. *It cannot be Gershon*, he thought. *I've already blocked the man's numbe*r. He checked the display and his eyes widened.

"Jack?" he said after pressing the answer button.

"No, but I am a friend of his," the voice on the other end said. It was rough, the accent Middle-Eastern, and Rutger looked up at the men being scanned by TSA. "Jack needs your help, and—"

"Who are you?"

"I told you. A friend of Jack's." The man paused, maybe expecting a response, but Rutger continued to listen. "Much has happened, and you might be the only one who can help."

"What is your name?" Rutger asked, his voice edged with the anger rising in his chest.

"I have Amber with me."

Rutger tried to imagine the circumstances that might lead to someone other than Jack calling him with news about Amber, but he didn't fail to notice the man had not answered his question.

"*Please*," the man said, his voice clearly not used to forming that word with that particular wealth of meaning. "There is more at stake here than Jack's life, and he trusts you."

"I am sorry, but I am on my way back to Germany. Maybe you should call the FBI."

The man laughed. It wasn't pleasant. "That is the *last* thing Jack needs right now."

Rutger was near the front of the line, others pushing from behind without touching him. The TSA agent waved him forward, and he hesitated, then stepped aside to allow others ahead of him.

"I don't know you, sir, but even if I did, there is little I can do to help," he said, hoping the man couldn't talk him into helping. He'd had enough of the whole matter.

"I don't know the whole story," the man said, "but what I *do* know is that what Jack has stumbled into is far bigger than he can handle. More, even, than the FBI." He hesitated, then said, "And he is missing."

"No, he is in hiding," Rutger said.

"He and his brother were supposed to meet me and Amber, but they did not appear, nor are they answering the phone."

"Brother?" Rutger said. "I thought he was with Dr. Hill."

"Dr. Hill—*Mason*—is dead."

Dead? Rutger thought. *Another death.* Another *friend of Jack's lost.* Rutger didn't realize he had stepped out of the line until he was standing at one of the many counters nearby. He set his bag down and mopped his brow with the sleeve of his jacket.

"How did this happen?" he asked at last.

"I will fill in the details when we meet," the man said. "Here is the address."

Rutger committed it to memory, asking the man to repeat it twice before the call ended.

He stood, picked up his bag, and headed for the exit. He tossed his ticket and boarding pass into the trash as he left.

* * *

Jeff sat, tail snaking over his carapace and around his slim neck, legs dangling from the edge of the stone outcropping over a sheer drop to the desert floor, considering his predicament. That he could do this at *all* was a wonder to him, meriting consideration in its own right. He was a freak—an *aberration*—and should have already sacrificed himself for the good of the hive, but with individuality came *desire*. He did not want to die.

What he really wanted was to *fly*. Not for the first time, he sighed through the slits in his abdomen and wished for the wings of his ancestors. His homeworld of Hive once had skies blackened by the swooping and diving bodies of his kind, but that was millions of years ago. The racial memory was strong enough to prod the Zzkritti to swarm ever outward, teaching them to fly again long after the wings were lost to evolution's razor edge.

But to fly free, under his own power, using his own wings! Jeff could not smile, but if he could, humans might have called it *wistful*. If the sight didn't send them over into madness.

In a hand of days that *still* felt too short to his biological clock, the earthquake would kill thousands of humans, and it would be his fault.

My fault. Mine... me... I. There is no going back, and none ever have, he thought. If I leap from this stone, will it feel like flying? he wondered.

He closed his eyes and wished for wings.

RUTGER STOOD AT THE CURB and watched the cab drive away. It was an odd place for a meeting, but odd often worked for such clandestine activities. The Golden Arches loomed over him, the glow illuminating his section of the street like yellow daylight. Across the road was a battered and bruised Motel 6 he assumed constituted the bulk of customers for this establishment. It hunched over the little road that fed it customers, turning its back to the main road and the world beyond.

Cars passed him, drivers not giving him a first glance—much less a second—each wrapped in their cocoon of metal and frustration. He would feel sorry for these people, but Americans were exceedingly good at making themselves miserable. *And yet, they also know how to laugh*—especially *at themselves.* It was a trick his own people had not mastered. *We are too serious by half*, he thought.

A pale Ford SUV pulled over and stopped in front of him, and the heavily tinted passenger window slid down.

"Are you Rutger?" the bearded man at the wheel asked, ducking to peer through the open window. His accent was unmistakable, and Rutger leaned down, placing his hands on the door.

"And you are?" he said, one eyebrow cocked.

"Get in," the man said, waving his hand. "We have a lot of catching up to do, both figuratively and literally."

"I am not sure—"

"Oh, you are past that," the Iraqi said with a chuckle. "Why else stand here waiting for me?" He stretched across the seat and opened the door, pushing it out for Rutger before sitting up, both hands on the wheel.

Rutger looked inside and saw Amber laying asleep on the back seat.

The man nodded. "Don't worry about her. She's been through a lot, and isn't likely to disturb us while we talk." He smiled, ruddy cheeks nearly squeezing his eyes shut. "Come... I won't bite."

Rutger looked around, wondering if someone were secretly filming all this for some kind of reality show, then frowned, shrugged, and slid into the seat. He had just finished closing the door when the car pulled into traffic, the driver behind laying on the horn. Rutger's new companion turned to him and grinned.

"I drive a cab back home," he said with a shrug.

Wonderful, Rutger thought. Another American cab driver out to kill me.

* * *

He won't do it, Jack thought. His brother would never shoot him, no matter what flashed in his eyes.

Watch him, Mason had said.

Jack did watch Bill as they drove through the night, his brother holding the gun in one hand with preternatural calm while steering with the other. The calm was an illusion. Sweat poured from his scalp, and Jack caught him wincing and shaking his head as if to clear it. The hand holding the gun was rock-steady, but everything attached to it was a quivering mess. It seemed to Jack the gun *wanted* to be held, having tasted blood once and discovering an affinity. He stared into the barrel, into the darkness from which death flew, placid ataraxia embracing him. Death would be a welcome release at this point, like having an old friend over for a beer.

"Do you plan to hold that thing the whole two hours?" Jack asked, with an insouciance he didn't feel. Bill aimed the weapon at Jack's leg, but it would only take a bump in the road to make things interesting.

"If I have to," Bill said, wiping his brow quickly with his steering hand.

"Think you could point it *away* from me for a while?" Jack nodded at the speedometer. "We're doing seventy, so there's not much chance I'll jump out and combat-roll to the shoulder."

Bill stopped shaking and blinked hard once. He set the gun on the seat but kept his hand on top. It lay between them, a tense black cat ready to spring, its owner both restraining and encouraging the beast. Jack had no doubt the gun would leap to Bill's hand before he could move an inch, but the fear of death didn't keep him from acting so much as his fear for his brother's psyche should Jack force him to shoot.

"Why are you doing this?" Jack asked. Bill flicked a glance his way, pinprick pupils in a sea of white, and licked dry lips. Sweat poured in sheets down both sides of his face, hair slick and glistening in the headlights of oncoming traffic. He was Renfield with a badge and a gun.

"To save your life, Li'l Bro," Bill said, turning. "Just like I always do." He mopped his brow again, then faced the road, pressing harder on the accelerator.

"Well," Jack said, forcing a smile, "just don't kill me in the process."

* * *

Shut up, shut up, shut up... Shut. Up.

Bill wanted to bang his head against the wheel. Do something... *anything*, just to stop the noise. He tried to focus on the sound of Jack's voice, but it was no use. The buzz in his head grew louder the closer he got to Greenville. It was worse when something Jack said made sense, the gentle buzz becoming a grinding he hadn't heard since he first learned to double clutch.

It had taken every ounce of control he had to set the gun down, the noise especially intense while he did. Settling down to a lion's purr, it stayed there only while touching the cold metal. His hand itched to lift it again and tingled with a million ants when he thought about moving it away.

He was being controlled, and the thought galled him. As an experiment, he *considered* turning the car around, and was rewarded with a pain that shot from one side of his head to the other. The message was clear—don't even *think* about making your own decisions. He was only allowed to observe his plight, like watching an actor on a stage. One that looked and sounded just like *him*.

285

This is what happened to Amber, he thought, and for once the buzzing did not disapprove. *Amber was controlled. She tried to kill me. I'm being controlled, and taking Jack...* somewhere. Those two lines of thought did not converge—one did not fit with the other—but the buzzing would not allow deeper analysis. *Someone's doing the driving, and it ain't me.*

He wiped the sweat from his eyes and wondered where they were going.

* * *

There was only one other place Sohrab knew Bill and Jack could be going, and that was back to Greenville. Once he had picked up Rutger, he turned the Ford around and pointed it toward I85. The man at his right sat in a brooding silence, still processing the fantastical and heartbreaking events at the motel. Sohrab had driven three quarters of an hour, and as he approached the turnoff for Commerce, Amber sat up and gazed through the window at the lights of the small town. Passing the town on the left, she kept her face pointed toward it like an anti-aircraft gun tracking a target. The look in her eyes was so blank and her turn so smooth and mechanical, a chill ran up Sohrab's spine.

It was the same look she had when she pulled the trigger.

"Ah, awake at last," he said, forcing a smile. "Glad to see you back in the land of the living." He winced, regretting the unfortunate turn of phrase. Amber took no notice, turning that same vacant stare to the front of the car. If she was looking for something out the windshield, he could not tell.

"We are headed to Greenville," he said over his shoulder to the still form behind him, "but I fear we will not catch up to them."

"Do we need to?" Rutger asked. "Once Jack is in custody with the evidence you say he has, this might all go away."

"That is assuming anyone believes him." Sohrab shook his head and leaned close to Rutger. "You forget Mason," he whispered.

"No, I have not," Rutger said, his voice soft. He sighed and stretched his back. "I have a feeling you have taken care of that... for now, at least." He sat in silence for long seconds, then tilted his head and narrowed his eyes at Sohrab. "Mukhabarat?"

Sohrab considered denying it, but there was no point. He raised a dark Andy Rooney eyebrow in respect. "How did you know?"

Rutger crossed his arms, relaxing his shoulders, and leaned against the door. "I have dealt with your people before." He shrugged. "Of course, it was most often to bring them to justice."

Sohrab smiled. "And how many did you capture?"

"None. So *far*," Rutger said, nodding.

Sohrab accepted the returned gesture of respect with a curt nod of his own. Respect among professionals was important—it ensured honesty, in deed if not in word.

Rutger tilted his head toward Amber. "Is she going to be all right?"

"To be honest... I do not know," Sohrab said, studying her in the mirror. "Jack said Mason's last words were that it was not her fault. She was under someone's control." He shrugged and frowned at the man beside him. "If true, I think that would be worse. Don't you?"

"I'm not deaf, you know," Amber said, her voice almost lost to the noise of the road.

Both men turned, but she faced the window, hugging both knees tight to her chest. *She looks like a lost child*, Sohrab thought.

Rutger turned around as far as he could to face her fully. "Are you ready to talk about it?" he asked, gentle but firm.

"No," she said, shaking her head. Her hair fell over her face as she tilted her head down, making her look like a mental patient.

I fear that is what she may become, Sohrab mused. If she does not go to prison instead.

* * *

It was far too elaborate and baroque a story to dismiss out of hand, but Rutger was having trouble accepting it without proof. He supposed Amber's near-catatonia added a hint of verisimilitude to the tale—heaven knew she wasn't all there—but it was all too surreal.

Puppets, killers, and aliens... oh my! he thought. *I was with him up to the alien connection.* A guilty man weaving an alibi often went one step too far, but Sohrab was Mukhabarat. Lying or not, he would know better than to embellish.

And there *was* truth here.

Jack and his brother *were* missing. There *was* a Shadowman. Amber *had* been kidnapped. Mason *was* dead, killed by Amber's hand. Government agencies around the world *had* committed assets to cap-

287

turing or killing Jack. Those facets of the story alone were enough to secure Rutger's involvement, though he had no direct evidence for some of them. He heard the faint sound of his career being flushed down a toilet, and his mouth drew into a grim smile. *Ah well, at least my wife earns a good income.*

He shifted in his seat and rubbed his temples, and a thought struck him.

"You don't trust this Dieter, do you?" he asked Sohrab, leaning against his door to face the man.

"I do not," Sohrab said, his mouth pursed beneath his beard. "I have conducted many, ah... *interrogations*, and I can tell when people are leaving information out." He shrugged. "There is also Amber's kidnapping."

"Indeed," Rutger said, nodding. "That would be more than enough to put me off the man."

"You weren't there. The man had a quality about him. As fantastical as his story was, Jack swallowed it whole."

"You did not." It wasn't a question. Rutger was sure this man had kept his skepticism throughout.

"Like I said... I have experience in these matters."

"Do you have any idea what he may have been leaving out?"

Sohrab shrugged and pulled at his beard. "As a guess, I would say his level of involvement."

"How so?"

"He knows too much. Has, or *had*, access to too much information." Sohrab raised an eyebrow. "In *my* experience, that suggests someone near the top of the food chain."

"So, then, why lie about it? He clearly wants Jack to stop his former associates, so lying about his involvement serves no purpose."

"Unless his involvement is ongoing," Sohrab said.

"Just so," Rutger nodded. If Dieter were still actively involved in these events, what would be the purpose of exposing the aliens? *If, indeed, there were aliens.* None of this made any sense, and without Jack and the information in his possession, Rutger held out no hope it ever would. Finding Jack, then, was paramount.

"So, Mr. Iraqi Field Agent... what is your plan once we get to Greenville?"

Sohrab snorted once. "I am working on that." He turned to look Rutger in the eyes. "I don't suppose you have a weapon?"

Rutger shook his head, a sad smile creasing his face. "I am not allowed to carry one in this country. It is far outside my jurisdiction, as they say."

"Doesn't matter," Sohrab said. "It would only get us into more trouble anyway." He smiled and waggled those preposterous eyebrows. "Besides, we won't need one."

Amber barked a short laugh behind them, then lapsed again into silence.

* * *

Dieter parked his car under the porte-cochere behind the building and killed the engine. Today had been very good, as far as these things went, but there was still much to do. The death of Dr. Hill was regrettable, and though it had been preventable, Dieter had been content to let the scene play out. More than anything else, he wanted to see how the new protocols worked with Amber. He grinned at the memory, then lifted his hat from the seat next to him and placed it on his head. Looking in the mirror, he adjusted it for no one but himself. He paused, the years pressing on his shoulders, and frowned. *It will be over soon*, he told himself.

A thin fingernail of moon hung over the trees beyond the courtyard, and he watched the branches—black against black—sway in the wind before opening his door and levering out. The door under the covering was the servant's entrance in more civilized times and led directly to the kitchen. He closed the car door, not bothering to lock it, and walked to the old building he used as his home and base of operations. Inside, he flicked on the lights and hung his hat and coat on the pegs by the entrance. The kitchen was warm and functional, though the stone floor was cold and damp—a light sheen of moisture reflecting the overhead lighting.

This place had been vacant for years before he claimed it for himself, and though he had been here for only two years, it showed. A home died in stages without a human presence, and the few rooms he kept had been enough. This home was alive, if not thriving. There was no rent or mortgage to pay, as technically he was a squatter, so there was no title or contract to trace. Once a month, a local banker paid the utilities from their own pocket without ever knowing why, and a grocer delivered food and supplies for the same reason. Dieter still needed cash, but when he did, he visited the same confused banker.

Dieter was the very definition of "off the grid," yet maintained a modern lifestyle.

He walked to the stove, picked up the tea kettle and shook it. Water sloshed and he judged the amount sufficient, so he set it on the nearest burner and fired it up. *If only I could turn up the heat on the Zzkritti so easily.* Unlike terrestrial insects, it took more than a boot to disturb their nest.

He was running out of time and nano-machines. Once he had discovered how to program them using complex combinations of trace chemicals, he had spent most of his time trying to get them to reproduce. He was met with one failure after another, and his only real success came in using them for their intended function—controlling human minds. What he had stolen from the Zzkritti when he left them was almost gone, but there might still be enough for his ultimate purpose. If not, then that failure might outstrip all the others.

Dieter opened a cabinet and took out a teacup and saucer, then from another a cannister of tea and the mesh holder for steeping. He walked to the kitchen table set back against a wall and set his items there before taking a seat. Everything in place, he waited for the water to boil.

* * *

Why didn't I check the gauge when I got in the fucking car? Still another thirty miles to go, but there was no way the Big Cat was going to make it that far. Bill's car was a land yacht, and this model had never been known as "fuel efficient"—even in *that* category. It wasn't why he bought the thing in the first place. Stopping for gas was going to be... problematic.

"Why are you slowing down, bro? Forget something?" Jack said, his mouth twisted in a half smile.

Yeah, Bill thought, I forgot to wipe that smug smile off your face. He immediately felt bad about the thought. Jack might be an asshole right now, but he has the right to be.

"I need to stop for gas," Bill said, not looking at his brother. "And I need you to promise to be good."

290

Jack didn't answer right away, and Bill turned. "Yeah," Jack said, "I don't think I can do that."

Bill sighed. "You want me to handcuff you?" He hooked a thumb over his shoulder. "Got a set in the trunk."

Jack's eyes narrowed. "You are welcome to *try*."

"Look, Li'l Bro, I don't have time for this." *When did I pick up the gun?* He waved it around like a pointer as he spoke. "Would it help if I told you we're not going directly to the station?"

"Where, then?" Jack said, frowning.

"I... don't know," Bill said. *Where* are *we going? How can I* not *know where I'm going? I'm driving the fucking car!* For the last ten miles he had gone over the route to the station in his head, but the lines grew fuzzier the more miles he drove. The urge to take the wrong exit grew in him the closer it came. When the time did come, the muscles in his arms would act without his direction, turning the wheel to take an unfamiliar path.

And there was nothing he could do about it.

"You don't know," Jack said, his voice flat. His eyes softened, looking like their mother's. "When did it start?" he asked, now in his familiar analysis mode.

Right after I called Jenna, Bill wanted to say, but he couldn't make his mouth form the words. What came out instead was, "I don't know."

"Everything—all the answers—are back the other way, Bill," Jack said, pleading. "I have to go back."

"Jack," Bill began, then shook his head, trying to clear it. The next words should not have been this hard, but he forced them out without tripping. "I can't guarantee I won't shoot you."

His brother tilted his head, and he sighed softly. The look in his eyes made Bill's heart ache. He couldn't remember ever seeing such pity there before. *I've got a goddamn gun pointed at him, and he feels sorry for me.* The anger rising in his throat like bile was unreasonable, but it was there nonetheless, resisting any attempt to swallow.

He turned the wheel with his left hand and pulled into one of two pump bays at a lonely convenience store just off the interstate. The place was older than rocks and water, the awning covering the pumps rusty and listing to one side. Neither pump sported a credit card reader, so Bill would have to go inside to pay. Both men knew this was Jack's one good chance to escape, and Bill screwed up is mouth in frustration as he killed the engine.

Bill turned to face his brother, the gun still in his hand and pointed in Jack's direction and opened his mouth to speak. What came out was not what he meant to say.

"Mr. Montgomery... we need to talk."

* * *

Jack's brows furrowed, nearly meeting in the middle of his forehead. The voice was Bill's, but the inflection was definitely *not*. In fact, he detected a hint of a German accent coming from his brother's mouth. *I assumed he was under someone's control, but not to this extent.*

"Who are you?" Jack asked.

"I would like to say a friend, but we are beyond such declarations, are we not?" Bill's face and mouth formed the words, but it was not he who spoke. The manic look in his eyes would have been funny in any other situation.

"Is Bill okay?" Jack asked, leaning toward his brother.

"He is perfectly fine," the voice said. "In fact, he can hear this conversation, though I am not allowing him to participate for the time being. It is not my intent to harm either of you," he said, then flipped the gun around and held it out for Jack. "Go ahead, if it makes you feel better."

Jack took the weapon without hesitation, but made sure the safety was on before stuffing it in his pocket. "Why didn't you just speak to me before?"

"I apologize," the voice said, then Bill's face attempted a grin. He only succeeded in looking creepy. "Your brother was responding to stimuli with a preprogrammed series of actions. I had only recently begun to monitor him, and the situation dictated I take more direct control."

"Okay... but my first question still hasn't been answered. Who the fuck *are* you?"

"I think you know."

Jack stared into his brother's panicked eyes and considered all the possibilities. "Thirteen," he said at last.

Bill nodded once. "Oddly, I have grown partial to the Shadowman of late."

Jack, his mouth hanging open, sat looking at the face of his brother, thinking just how surreal his life had become. *How does he know what I call him?* So Bill was taking him to meet the Shadowman—Thirteen—and his poor brother must have been fighting the whole time. *I'm getting pretty fucking tired of being led around by the nose. Even more, having my friends pay the price.*

"All right," Jack said at last. "Let's meet and get this over with."

"Very good. If you—"

"Give me an address." He looked deep into his brother's eyes, hoping the Shadowman was seeing him clearly. "Bill's not coming with me," he said, shaking his head. "That's not negotiable."

"I anticipated this, Mr. Montgomery. When your brother wakes, he will give you an address and exit the car." Bill's face relaxed, but the concern in his eyes only grew stronger. "Please understand, I am not your enemy here."

"That remains to be seen," Jack said, feeling the gun's weight in his pocket.

* * *

Thirteen broke contact and wiped the sweat pouring from his brow. *Mr. Montgomery is full of surprises.* The truth was that he *hadn't* anticipated the man's demand to meet alone, but admitting that to him might shift the advantage Thirteen still held.

The device on the table in front of him hummed softly, radiating a moist heat. He was going to pay a terrible price when the Others finally broke through and regained control of him, but if things played out as planned, they *might* forgive his independence.

He picked up the device with a gloved hand and slipped it into the pocket of his overcoat. Placing his hat on his head, he walked out of the motel room and across the busy street to an abandoned warehouse to await Jack's arrival. *Close enough the Others won't notice I've left, but far away from prying eyes and ears. And distractions.* He must maintain his concentration until this was done. The Others must not know what he had planned for Mr. Montgomery and his associates.

CHAPTER 25

Bill sat on the curb, head in his hands, blood pulsing through his veins. He touched the carotid on the right side of his neck, counting the beats as he controlled his breathing. His head felt like it had swollen to three times its normal size since he exited the car and watched Jack drive away, and a wave of nausea gripped him, forcing him to sit. *I got him the phone, at least,* he thought. It took every ounce of control he had left, but before Bill got out of the car, he pulled Jack's phone from his shirt pocket and slid it across the seat to his brother.

"One step at a time," he said, and his mouth filled with saliva. It was a prelude with which he was all too familiar. He leaned to the side and emptied his stomach in wracking heaves. It was a long time before he finished, but when he did, his head was clearer. His throat burned, but he stood on wobbly legs and turned toward the convenience store. "Bastard's gonna *pay. Nobody* controls Bill Fucking Montgomery," he said, more calm than he felt. His throat itched as he spoke, and he looked longingly at the soft drink coolers through the window. He only had a few bucks on him, but it was more than enough for a Gatorade.

Bill shuffled to the door, pulling the wallet from his back pocket and hoping Jack would still be alive come morning.

* * *

Jeff shook his head, and the others near him bobbed theirs in perfect rhythm with one another, his species' version of a confused shrug. His motion was a human gesture of negation, and their confusion arose from the casual ease with which he used it.

They suspect, he thought, doing his best to hide even *that* from them. Jeff was sure any moment now, the others in the chamber would sacrifice him for the good of the hive. It would be swift and without discussion, leaving him no time to react.

He knew they chose *him* for the job of regaining control of their wayward asset because mental contact with Thirteen had become increasingly difficult. None wanted the contamination to spread, so Jeff was the logical choice. The only problem was that continued exposure only made his situation worse. The more time he spent in Thirteen's mental construct, the more that construct changed him.

After his fifth attempt to gain control of the human, Jeff broke off and let the others know of his failure. What they did next surprised him—insofar as a telepathic species *could* be surprised.

They left him alone in the chamber.

They debate without me, he thought. There would be a shift in their plans, but Jeff would not be included in the consensus-building.

It had become clear to all that Thirteen enacted a plan of his own, but whether his goals meshed with theirs had yet to be ascertained. If necessary, they had other assets they could deploy to deal with him, but they had not activated any. It was possible they would not, leaving the question for another time. The Zzkritti were a patient species, taking centuries to follow a plan decades in the making.

No battle plan survives contact with the enemy, Jeff thought. *Who said that?* he wondered, reaching for the vast storehouse of knowledge accessible through his nanites. *Ah, Helmuth von Moltke the Elder.* He had met the man only once, acting as human-Zzkritti liaison even then. It was probably when his contamination had begun, being his first foray into the human world. The human was a formidable military intelligence, and Jeff had been tasked with improving the humans' ability to make war.

They were always so terrible at it, he mused with the Zzkritti equivalent of a sad smile. When the Zzkritti first arrived, the humans had already learned to cooperate for the benefit of their tribes and had even begun to trade with others peacefully. *It took centuries to breed that out of them, and even* then, *they continued to thwart the work we had done.*

Then everything changed for the Zzkritti.

* * *

Jack parked the Big Cat near the gate and got out of the car as it coughed to eventual silence. The gate was chained and padlocked, the fence at least ten feet high and topped with razor wire, but there was a gap where the clamps were rusted and broken. A section was pulled away from the post, allowing just enough space to crawl through. He guessed this was the standard entry point for kids in the area. The weeds were trampled at the opening, and a dusty, beaten path leading to the cracked concrete parking lot beyond. There were lights atop the poles at regular intervals, but all those he saw were broken, likely from teen-aged rock-throwers. He and Bill had pegged one or two just like it as kids.

"I've got a bad feelin' about this," he whispered to Mason's ghost as he closed the Big Cat's door and walked to the gap in the fence. He bent down and pushed the chain-link fencing away, the weeds re-sisting his efforts. When the opening was large enough, he crawled through. He stood on the other side, watching for movement from the warehouse. Even with the light from the road, he couldn't see any-thing, and that was odd. *There should be at least a couple of kids here*, he thought. *Maybe the Shadowman's already cleared the place out.* He shud-dered to think what that would mean.

Jack shoved his hands in the front pockets of his jeans and walked toward the warehouse. This side of the building was dotted with sev-eral loading bays and numbered roll-up doors looming over the ramps. One of those—*of* course *it's number thirteen*, he thought with a shake of his head—was rolled up just enough for a man to stoop under. A dull glow of light leaked from under the door, spilling faint illumination on the truck bay beneath. Jack walked down the ramp, then placed both hands on the dock, vaulted up, and crawled under the door and into the warehouse.

The air inside was old, musty, and smelled of grease. The ceiling was high enough that he couldn't see it in the little bit of light there was, and the floor was old pine planking. *There's a fortune of reclaimed flooring in here*, he mused. Across the floor, in the shadow of towering shelving units, were several old steel drums rusting in their neglect. The surface of each was more rust than paint, and Jack was sure a strong poke with his finger would punch straight through. Beyond those, an open door was limned in an almost actinic light, the bulk of which flooded through and into the loading area where he stood.

"Come, Mr. Montgomery. We do not have all night."

The voice was almost jovial, and Jack had the impression that not a whit of it traveled past his ears to the world beyond the building.

One clear shot, that's all I need. One clear shot, and I'll get the bastard who killed you and your mom, Riley.

He closed his hand around the gun in his pocket and walked toward the voice.

* * *

"How do you plan to catch up with them?" Rutger said, checking his phone for the fourth time. No calls from Jack, but there was a message from his wife. He knew he should call back and let her know he was fine, but anything he said would open an avenue of discovery for her, and he didn't feel like dealing with it. He had learned through long years of trial and error it was best to give her details after everything was over. *I'll have some serious making-up to do when I get home,* he thought.

"Honestly?" Sohrab grinned. "I'm just hoping for a call or something before we get to Greenville." He shrugged, his beard brushing his chest. "If we're close enough to help when things go bad, that may be all we can ask for."

"How much of a head start do you think they have?"

"No way to know for sure," Sohrab said, stroking his beard, "but it can't be more than three hours. It is likely much less than that."

"What makes you say that?"

"Because if it is not, things have already gone very badly, and Jack is already in custody."

"That is the most likely outcome," Rutger said.

"True," Sohrab said, "but if we start to think that way, we might as well pack up and go home."

Rutger considered that. They were running on pure optimism, when the universe tended toward the pessimistic. *Entropy always wins,* he thought. Then again, for the three people in this car, the worst case scenario was no more than an evening joy-ride. As worst-cases went, he could live with that.

"What about her?" he said, nodding over his shoulder. Amber hadn't said anything for miles, and seemed to have withdrawn even deeper within herself. Legs hugged tight to her chest, face buried in her knees, she could have been asleep for as much movement as he saw from her.

"You can't tell, but she's already better than she was at the motel," Sohrab said without checking. "I don't know her at all, but she seems strong." He faced Rutger, his eyes haunted. "I've seen people—strong, well-trained people—lose it on a monumental scale for less," he said. "She'll be fine."

The road was an inky black mass ahead, the headlights of the car doing what they could to carve a path. Other than oncoming traffic, it was dark for an Interstate, many of the street lamps unlit. *All of America has fallen into disrepair*, Rutger thought. It wasn't a fair assessment, but the country's infrastructure had deteriorated considerably in the last twenty years. Nothing seemed new. Even the gas station ahead was a lost and lonely outpost on a trail of weary and worn dreams. Awash in light, the colors apparently chosen at random, the convenience store looked like an amusement park compared to its surroundings.

Amber sat up straight, then leaned forward between the two front seats, straining against her shoulder harness.

"There!" she yelled, banging on the back of Sohrab's seat with the palm of her hand. "Pull in there!" Her face was wide with excitement, so manic Rutger feared she had fallen over the edge of despair into madness. "Go, go, go, go, *GO!*" she said, punctuating each word with another slap of her hand on the seat, pointing to the building with her other.

Sohrab spun the wheel, activating his turn signal at the same time. "Does someone need a bathroom break?" he asked Amber, who only smirked in return, rolling her eyes.

"No," she said. "We're picking something up!" She pointed to a figure half in shadow, sitting on the curb in front of the building.

"Son of a bitch," Sohrab said. "That's Bill!"

* * *

Jack walked from the dark and into the light, his booted feet pounding a dull rhythm on the old wood. Planks bent and creaked under his weight, rusty nails no longer holding the boards secure. He didn't know what to expect when coming face to face with a literal boogey-man, but a tea party was not even on his radar.

299

But there the Shadowman sat, at a small table in the center of a warehouse, a tea service atop and one empty chair across from him. The single working light in the cavernous room hung directly over the table, spilling a yellowed cone of illumination over the scene. The old man, slumped in his chair and holding a teacup to his lips—dark overcoat open and unbelted, his fedora on the table beside the tray—was a Norman Rockwell painting of American enterprise gone to seed.

He looks tired, Jack thought.

The old man held out a steady hand, indicating the chair across the table like a magician waving at his assistant. "Please, Mr. Montgomery," he said, his voice a heavy leather boot dragging across chalky gravel. "There is both sugar and cream at hand, if you like."

Jack made the same face he did when hipsters offered him iced-coffee. "Sugar will be fine," he said, pulling the chair away from the table, turning it around, straddling the seat, and resting his arms on the back. The old man raised an eyebrow, then pursed his lips and nodded. Jack held no illusions that the manner in which he perched in the seat offered any advantage for escape should things go south, but every little bit helped. Besides, the man across from him had already demonstrated an ability to deal with adversity regardless of preparation. He reached for the cup and lifted it, raising an eyebrow of his own.

"Come, Mr. Montgomery," the Shadowman said, his voice as weather-beaten and weary as the structure in which they sat. "If I wanted to kill or incapacitate you, the deed would be done already." He watched Jack shrug and take a sip. "Good," he said, "trust is important." He sipped his own tea and set the cup on the table. "You have questions." His grin was a thin line but held no menace. "Ask them."

There were a thousand questions in Jack's head, all competing to be heard, but only a few were really important anymore. *I started this with one simple question*, he thought.

"Why are my wife and daughter dead?" he asked, eyes brimming before he reached the last word.

The Shadowman spread his hands, took a deep breath, and sighed long and heavy before speaking. "An accident, I'm afraid," he said, the single statement an obvious effort. "One that could have been avoided."

"That was no accident," Jack spit, his eyes now narrow slits, pupils burning like coals. "It was the direct result of one of your damned tests!"

"Not ours, no," the Shadowman said, lips pursed and shaking his head. "As you must know by now, I've been attempting to clean up after those failed tests. My masters want them to end as much as you."

"Then who?"

"Really, Mr. Montgomery," the man said, leaning back in his chair. "My understanding is you are adept at... connecting the dots, as they say."

It was there. All the information he needed, but he had been blinded by the desire to exact revenge. *Of course this guy wants you to think he didn't do it*, he told himself as he reached inside his pocket. He felt the cold steel, wrapping his fingers around the gun for comfort. Someone was responsible for their deaths, but who? *I am. And for that, I am truly sorry.*

The words from the last letter mocked him. *And who sent those letters?*

Dieter.

Who knew about the Germanwings disaster before it happened?

Dieter.

Who was Amber protecting when she shot Mason?

Dieter.

The only question left is...

"Why?" he asked the Shadowman.

"Ah," he said with another sigh, "the story is long, but I think you know most of it." He tilted his head. "Though Dieter left out much of his own involvement."

"Tell me," Jack said, his voice low and threatening.

"You know about the Zzkritti, yes?" the Shadowman asked, and Jack nodded. "Sometime during the Second World War, their mission changed from hurting our species to helping. They are a hive mind, but this outpost had no queen, so there was disagreement for the first time in their living memory." He lifted his cup, pausing at the edge of his lips. "This did not end well for them." The Shadowman took a sip and lowered the cup to the table. "Over half their number on this planet perished in the resulting argument, and there have been no reinforcements since. The winning side agreed with the new directive, and they have been helping our species ever since."

"What does that have to do with Dieter? Why is he killing all these people?"

"His goal is not death, Mr. Montgomery," he said. "He wants to help humanity, but he is confused about the method. Where the Zzkritti prefer to nudge here and there, he wants to take direct control of every government on the planet." His face showed a sadness of both years counted and joy subtracted. "He is a product of his upbringing, I am afraid, and believes the ends justify the means."

"A trait he shares with your masters," Jack sneered. There were so many deaths for which the Zzkritti must account, and it was clear they were not above breaking a few eggs in their quest for the perfect omelet.

"It is true I have been forced to kill in order to maintain their secrecy, but—"

"And now you'll kill me and my friends for the same purpose, is that right?" he asked, gripping the gun ever tighter.

The Shadowman's shoulders slumped and he leaned forward into the light, and Jack saw for the first time how much the man was sweating. "You have no *idea* how wrong you are, Jack," he said through gritted teeth. "I have done everything I could *not* to kill you and your people."

* * *

Bill sat in the back seat, as far from Amber as he could get. She did much the same, hugging up against her door. Sohrab thought the two looked like a matched set of broken bookends, each alone yet somehow useless without the other.

"I couldn't do anything to stop it," Bill was saying. His eyes, haunted dark orbs floating in a sea of red-stained white, were turned to the landscape far beyond his window. "The best I could do was give him the phone." He turned to Amber, who studied him from her perch. "I was nothing more than a meat-puppet," he said, eyes wide. "How the fuck do they *do* that?"

"I don't know," she said, her voice a whisper, and she turned to stare out the window.

"Do you know where he went?" Sohrab asked, part of him hoping the answer was no.

Bill shook his head. "I held on to as much as I could, but all I got was an abandoned warehouse. I could probably recognize it if we happened to drive by, but what are the odds?"

"Indeed," Rutger said. "But surely there are known areas with abandoned warehouses. How many could there be?"

"After the joy of 2009?" Bill sneered. "We've recovered better than most, but some shit never came back." He shook his head. "I saw that sucker pretty clearly in my head, and it's pretty much like any other in the area."

"Did you see anything else?" Sohrab asked. It was amazing to him the detail people often left out of a story. A basic cognitive interview technique would help, but only if Bill had actually seen something. "Were there any other buildings in the picture?"

"None that I remember. Just a tall fence topped with razor wire, and a huge parking lot..."

It was a few seconds before Sohrab realized Bill's voice had trailed off rather than him having finished a sentence. He looked at the man in the rearview mirror, who was now rubbing his chin.

"What do you see?" Sohrab asked.

"The No Trespassing sign hanging on the gate," Bill said, his eye glazing over. "It's not one of those generic versions. A company sign." He looked up, eyes focusing for the first time since he crawled in the back seat. "There was a logo! I know that place!"

Rutger turned. "Are you sure it's not just a logo of the company that made the sign?" he asked.

"Nah," Bill said. "There's a partial design still visible painted on the side of the building." He turned to Sohrab. "Same one. I'm sure."

"What do you think?" Rutger asked Sohrab.

"Good enough for me," he said. "Besides, what other options do we have?" He caught Bill's eyes in the rearview. "Got an address?"

"No need," Bill grinned. "Jack and me used to play around there as kids." He chuckled once. "Wasn't abandoned back then, but that just meant there was more to get into, trouble-wise."

"Don't be so sure," Amber said, still looking out her window.

* * *

Jack laughed, a hard and bitter sound. "Tell that to Paul and Martha Banks, or Sally, or—"

"Do you think I *enjoyed* that, Mr. Montgomery?" the Shadowman snapped, sweat now pouring from his forehead and into his eyes. Most would wipe it away, but the man made no moves to do so. He sat, chest heaving, and stared hard at Jack. "I am a puppet as much as Ms. Riley or your brother," he said, calming. He reached for his teacup, the sleeves of his shirt and jacket pulling back, revealing the beginning of a string of numbers tattooed on his forearm. The Shadowman lifted the cup to his lips, adjusting the sleeves with his free hand.

"Why am I here?" Jack asked at last. *What role do I play in this?* He was not equipped to stop an advanced alien race. *I've already been led around by the nose by an old man, for chrissake.* Separated from the only other people who knew what was happening, he was alone. Worse, he didn't know who to trust. Not even his own brother.

"Dieter involved you, I fear, to distract us," the Shadowman said, replacing the cup and mopping his brow with a napkin. "The Zzkritti are... unimaginative, so it almost worked." He sighed, shrugged, and spread his hands in a gesture of acquiescence. "They have directed me to remove you before I resume hunting Dieter. I have other ideas."

"Such as?"

"I have felt from the beginning that his bringing you into this was a mistake on his part, and now I hope to capitalize on his error," he said. His mouth tightened, either in frustration or thought, Jack did not know which. "I would like to use you to draw him out where I can deal with him directly."

"With the resources at your disposal, why haven't you done so already?" Jack asked, his eyes narrowed.

"Dieter has quite a lot of stolen technology, as you should know. He has also been modifying the nano-machines, trying to get them to reproduce."

Jack's eyes widened, as the conversation with Debbie flooded his memory. "But that means—"

"Oh, yes, Mr. Montgomery," the Shadowman said, nodding. "That would indeed be the end of everything."

CHAPTER 26

"Turn here," bill said, peering through the windshield and pointing to the left. "This road should dead-end ten miles ahead. Take a right at the stop sign."

"How much farther?" Sohrab asked, spinning the wheel. *This is taking too long*, he thought. *Jack is most likely dead by now.* Try as he might, he couldn't shake the dread that filled his mind after finding Bill. No one, other than himself—and possibly Rutger—knew what they were doing. Even Bill's training was worthless when dealing with what was, essentially, a terrorist operation. *I've had experience enough for all of us*, Sohrab thought bitterly. Much of that on the wrong side, in his opinion. Marriage had changed more than his IRS filing status, and having children only made that change more pronounced.

I miss my family. Followed soon by Will I see them again?

"Fifteen or twenty minutes," Bill said. "No traffic to speak of this time of night, so there shouldn't be anything to slow us down between here and there."

The road was straight with few crossroads, so Sohrab pressed harder on the accelerator. Lights high atop poles flashed by, each cone of illumination a lonely oasis in a sea of black. Without thinking, Sohrab counted each as they passed. The lamps were a slow drip of liquid time—pitch from a funnel—suspended moments full of potential passing from light to dark and back again.

"I would feel better if we had a gun," Bill said, his voice tight.

"It is probably best we do not," Rutger said. "From what we know, the Shadowman could take control of you at any time." He turned to look back at the two broken souls. "Maybe any of us."

Bill's mouth drew into a thin line, and he tilted his head. Amber said nothing, sniffing once in derision. *You will not absolve them so easily,* Sohrab thought, his own face a mask of determination. *Regardless, they do not seek absolution for their actions.*

It was clear to him. What they wanted, was revenge.

*   *   *

"Why haven't you taken control of me as you did the others?" Jack asked. "If you need me, as you say, wouldn't that have been the best option?"

The Shadowman shook his head, a slow consideration of words to come. "Aside from the fact the Zzkritti would know immediately what I had done, the machines wouldn't work on you." The man closed his eyes, squeezing them tight as his breathing grew shallow and rapid. The muscles in his jaw worked, flexing and relaxing in a complex rhythm, before he took a long deep breath. He let it out in slow motion, his shoulders relaxing, and even the sweating abated.

"Why don't they work on me?" Jack said with measured determination.

"We have little time," the Shadowman said, opening his eyes. Reddened and weary, his eyes carried the weight of the man's age as well as whatever mental effort he expended. "Your friends will be here soon, and I would prefer to let them live."

Even now he dares threaten... Jack choked off that line of thought, pressing the more urgent question. "Why don't your little machines work on me?"

The Shadowman snorted, a short and soft explosion of air. "The metal holding many of your bones together acts as a crude Faraday Cage, interfering with the signals." He spread his hands on the table, the cup between them. "The nano–machines have a level of artificial intelligence, but without regular updating they could not take into account any unforeseen circumstances. You would regain control in short order."

So, the one thing saving me is also the one goddamn thing that started all this shit?

If they must update the machines regularly to maintain control, how is the updating performed? If a Faraday Cage—even a crude one—could block the signal, it was electromagnetic in nature. Radio. And the signal must be very strong to work from a distance, everywhere—repeated and reinforced. A strong signal should be detectable, however.

Amber was under Dieter's control, but that control had only manifested in the old man's presence. Bill, though, was under control from a large distance. *How is the signal transmitted?*

Jack remembered the changes in Bill's behavior. Relaxed and himself in the bar, agitated and mechanical in the room. Later he was better, but in the car...

"You're using the fucking cell phones!" Jack said, his eyes wide.

The Shadowman tilted his head and grinned. "Your gift for leaps of logic is not exaggerated, I see," he said with a slight nod. "It is a marvelous distributed system, and perfect for our purposes."

"Can Dieter use it as well?"

"Not yet, but he has been working toward gaining that ability."

Self-replicating nanos, Jack thought, coupled with access to the global cell phone network, and Dieter could control everything.

"Do you know where to find him?" Jack asked.

"Sadly, no," the Shadowman said. "I believe he still has plans for you, so he may contact you."

"That's not good enough—"

"Maybe this will help." The grim man reached into his pocket, then removed his hand and held it over the table, opening it to reveal a small device that looked like a keyless entry fob. "Keep this with you at all times. It will not only block any signals Dieter sends to Amber, but should disrupt his own nano-machines." He looked at the thing in his palm like it was a puppy.

Jack hesitated for a breath before reaching out and taking the device from the Shadowman's hand. "How do I know this won't just give you control over me?"

"You don't," he said with a shrug. "But as I said, trust is important."

Jack hefted the device, felt the weight of the thing, the warmth and energy it radiated, and shoved it into the front pocket of his jeans. "Will he know I have it?"

The Shadowman snorted. "I would be very surprised if he did. It would never occur to him that I would allow you to survive an encounter, much less give that to you." He tilted his head up a tick, like he was sniffing the air. "Your friends are here," he said, standing. "You will excuse me?"

Jack stood, turning the chair around and sliding it under the table. "One thing more," he said.

The Shadowman gave a curt nod, an invitation.

"The earthquake in Nepal in a few days," Jack said. "Is that Dieter, or the Zzkritti?"

The Shadowman's mouth bunched up tight, and he lifted his hat from the table and placed it on his head. "As I have told you, Mr. Montgomery, individual humans are beneath the Zzkritti's concern. The Plan is all that matters." He tipped his hat and turned to leave.

Jack watched him walk away for a few steps, his eyes narrowing. "And after Dieter," he whispered, "I'll stop the Zzkritti too."

The old man hesitated for a single heartbeat, then continued walking, melting into the dark.

* * *

Bill took his hand from the hood of the Big Cat. "Been here a while," he said, walking back to the car where the others waited. He leaned on Sohrab's door and spoke through the open window. "Engine's almost cooled to ambient."

"How did Jack get in?" Sohrab asked, chucking his chin at the locked gate.

"There's a section of the fence over there," Bill hooked a thumb over his shoulder, "pulled away from the posts. The opening is small, but we can crawl through."

Sohrab settled in his seat and pulled on his beard. In truth, he hadn't considered a situation where they would even find Jack, much less have to confront the Shadowman. The only sounds were those leaking from the highway, and the rhythmic popping from his car's motor dumping excess heat into the air. Rutger remained silent, lost in his own thoughts, or also considering their next move.

Bill tapped on the door for his attention. "So, what's the plan?"

"It seems," Sohrab said, "we have a jealous husbands problem."

"Come again?" Bill said, his face scrunched up, looking like an English bulldog.

"It means," Rutger said, "that we can't leave you and Amber alone together, nor does he want to bring her inside."

308

"And, no offense Bill, but you're not the right man to accompany me, either," Sohrab said. *Neither Bill nor Amber can be trusted, so that means—*

"Either you or I go in alone," Rutger said, looking Sohrab in the eyes.

"No offense to you, either," Sohrab turned a sad smile at Rutger, "but without a weapon, you have no training to handle the situation." He looked down at his hands, clasping them together, scrubbing them. Those hands had killed—more than once—and would never be clean, no matter how much he washed them. "I am," he said at last.

He opened the door, crawled out, and stretched as his joints popped. *I'm getting too old for this shit*, he thought. That wasn't true, though. His body was young enough, but his soul was a desiccated corpse, paper-thin flesh stretched over bones of chalk. He no longer *wanted* to do this shit.

Sohrab turned, closed the door, and leaned through the window. "Keep an eye on our friends, here," he said to Rutger. "If either starts to act funny... well... just do your best."

Rutger nodded and motioned for Bill to get in the back. Sohrab patted the door once, waved goodbye, and walked to the hole in the fence. Crawling through was easy, snagging his shirt on the rusted links only once. Once on the other side, he stood and found light spilling around the edges of the door marked thirteen. He grinned, shook his head, and crouched low, searching for a second entry.

His feet were silent as he crossed the wide expanse of parking lot fronting the building, and he reached the side opposite the door without raising an alarm. *That means nothing*, he thought. *The Shadowman knows we are here.* He only hoped to get in through an entrance the man hadn't planned for.

Sohrab slid along the wall between the warehouse and the next to his right, checking in either direction as he went. There were windows above his head, but they were too high to reach. With no real light leaking into the alley, he had no way of knowing if any of them were unlocked, regardless. It was so dark he didn't notice the door until his hands ran over the frame. He backtracked once he realized what it was, feeling for a knob or handle. There wasn't one on this side, only a metal plate where a handle should have been.

He considered finding another entry, but this one was here—now—and time was not his friend. Digging his fingers into the gap between door and frame, he managed enough purchase to pull. He braced one foot on the jamb, and a soft grunt escaped his lips as he strained at the door. It didn't budge as much as a millimeter. His fingers slipped from the door and he fell to the ground, gravel crunching under his backside.

Sohrab shook his head and snorted. *Of course it's latched*, he thought. *If it is not locked though...* He reached into his back pocket and took out his wallet. Opening it, he pulled out a credit card and stood. Before he reached for the door, it burst open from the inside. The light over the door snapped on automatically, blinding him, and he fell back to the ground.

A tall man wearing an overcoat and fedora stepped through and lowered his head at Sohrab. He smiled, and Sohrab's blood chilled, curdling like cheese. The Shadowman raised his head as Sohrab scrambled back against the wall of the nearby building, light spilling over the hat and around the Shadowman's face.

Sohrab leaned forward, shock and confusion fighting for purchase on his face. He narrowed his eyes, raising one eyebrow.

"*You?*" he said. "But—"

The Shadowman pulled one hand from a pocket, took a step forward, and Sohrab's world went black.

* * *

Jack stood beside the table for a long time after the Shadowman walked away. *How the hell did I get here?* He worked through the progression in his head, every step along the way pre-planned and seemingly without alternatives. Even Mason's death felt preordained. *That was decided the second I involved him*, Jack thought. *Bastard never could ignore a good conspiracy theory.* The corners of his mouth turned upward in a wan smile for his lost friend.

From deeper in the warehouse, past the cone of light surrounding him, a door opened and closed on rusty hinges. Jack took that as his cue to leave, turning toward the dock and walking out the way he came. The Shadowman had said his friends were here, but he had no friends left. Mason was gone, he hardly knew Sohrab, Rutger was God knows where, and even Bill—regardless of the reason—had turned his back on him.

Amber... Well, Amber was never a friend, *was she?* Now he didn't know what she was, and the thought of seeing her again filled him with dread. *Even knowing it wasn't her fault, how can I ever look at her the same way again?* He hung his head as he walked, feet shuffling across the dust-covered floor. *How will she see herself?*

Other sounds reached him from the direction the Shadowman had taken but were too muffled for Jack to make sense of their meaning. Now the only sound was each scuff of his boots, and the occasional drip of water from somewhere deep in the darkened warehouse. Not a splash like water dripping into a pool, but a dull thud like drops of blood falling from a hog's throat to a welcoming and thirsty earth.

He shook himself to clear the old memory, picking up his pace toward the open door. Road noise leaked through and into the warehouse, drawing him back into the world. Ten steps from the opening, he broke into a trot, ready to be shed of the place. Beyond the gate was Bill's car, and parked just behind was Sohrab's Ford. Two doors of the latter opened as he crossed the parking lot, Bill and *Rutger* stepping out. Both smiled at his approach, though the smiles faded when he drew near. Both were looking past him.

"How the hell did you find me?" Jack asked as he crawled through the fence. On the other side, he stood and brushed himself off.

"Bill figured it out," Rutger said, reaching out to slap Jack on the back.

"Why are you here?"

"Your friend Sohrab called me," Rutger said. "As for why I responded?" He held his hands up and shrugged. "I grew tired of being on the wrong side."

"By the way," Bill said, "where *is* Sohrab?"

Everyone looked at him, then Rutger turned toward the warehouse.

"What do you mean?" Jack asked, looking back to the building.

"We figured you might need help," Bill said, "so he went looking for another way in." He pointed to the gap between the two buildings. "Last we saw, he went that way."

Where he would run right into the Shadowman, Jack thought. His eyes were wide, but his mouth tight. "If he found a way in, he'll be another hour looking around in there while we stand here with our dicks hangin' out." He grabbed Bill by the shoulder. "C'mon," he said. "Let's go get him."

* * *

Bill jumped ahead of Jack after they crawled through the fence, leading the way to the gap where Sohrab disappeared. Much like when they were kids, Jack struggled to keep up, though now it was because of all the pins holding his leg together rather than his size. The smell of oil and grease was still strong in Bill's nostrils, even though the place had been buttoned up for many years. The odors dropped him right back into a day nearly thirty years ago—the last time he and Jack had sneaked into the place—and he shivered. *Not a damn thing has changed*, he thought as he strode into the darkened alley. *Except* this *time we'll get more than a tanned ass if we're caught.* And it wouldn't be their mother administering the beating this time, either.

"How long ago did he leave?" Jack asked, huffing as he matched his brother's pace.

"'Bout five minutes before you came out," Bill said. Even with having forty pounds on his younger brother, Bill was in better shape. He had always been in better shape, though that shape was tending toward round these days.

"Hell," Jack said, "he's probably already on his way out the front." His voice held a tight quality Bill didn't like. It was as if Jack had already given up.

They passed several windows, and the alley grew darker still. The concrete had ended before they entered, leaving coarse gravel as the only ground cover, and their shoes crunched in a complex rhythm from four different feet. There were no other footfalls in range of Bill's hearing, so he guessed Sohrab was already inside, or had stopped. Bill slowed, then stopped, and Jack nearly bowled him over when he didn't notice in time.

"What the hell, Bill?"

Bill held up a hand to shush his brother and turned his head to listen. The wind whipping between the buildings was a mournful cry, almost too soft to hear, and a sign creaked as it swung at the end of one supporting chain. No sounds from inside the building reached his ears.

"Why are we even sneaking around," Jack whispered. "The Shadowman's long gone."

"If you say so," Bill said, and waved Jack to follow. They moved in tandem down the alley.

"Sohrab!" Jack hollered, hands cupped to his mouth.

"What are you doing?" Bill said, shooting his hand out to grab Jack by the arm.

"I told you," Jack said, eyebrows knitted, "there's no one here."

"The Shadowman not being here, and *no one* being here are two different things, moron." He tossed his brother the same look as when he had to pull him from a fight as a kid. "There's always the chance the company keeps a security guard on the payroll."

"So what? You're a cop, right?"

"You think that's a free pass?"

"Isn't it?"

Bill stopped and turned on his brother, his face bunched up like a squashed Jack-o'-lantern. "You really don't know anything about my job, do you?" he said, poking a hard finger into Jack's sternum. Jack staggered back, rubbing his chest like he'd been punched. "All these years, and you couldn't be bothered to learn *anything* about what I do for a living?" Bill shook his head, his mouth turning down. "It's always been about you, hasn't it?" he said, years of being the respectable older brother while watching his fuck-up kid brother get all their parents' attention poured out like black water from a backed-up sewer.

"Jack's got a special mind, Bill. He's a sensitive boy, Bill." He threw his hands in the air, turning away. "*God*, can't you think about someone else for a change?" He loomed over his brother, breathing hard and looking into the black distance. *Where the fuck did* that *come from?* Bill thought, recoiling. The truth was Jack *was* sensitive and special, and he *did* have more than his share of shit lately. True, he hadn't handled it well—that was on him—but what man would? *How would* I *have handled losing my whole fucking family?*

Bill's shoulders slumped, and he turned to face his brother. He offered a grim smile and a shrug. "Sorry, bro. Shit's been getting a little too real lately, ya know?"

Jack was watching him, head tilted, full-blown concern in his eyes. "It's okay, Bill," he said, grabbing the man's shoulder and giving it a hard squeeze. "Still," he snorted, "you haven't answered my question."

Bill straightened, his brows furrowing. "What?"

Jack grinned. "Do you get a free pass, or don't you?"

Bill shook his head and sighed. "Asshole," he said, punching Jack in the arm.

"Okay," Jack said, rubbing the arm, "that one hurt." He threw his good arm around Bill's shoulders, guiding him back to the search. "C'mon, bro."

"Do you gentlemen want to make out here, or are you going to go get a room?" a voice called out from the darkness ahead.

"Sohrab?" Jack said as the big Iraqi emerged from the shadows.

* * *

"No, not a damn thing," Sohrab told the others as they stood beside his car. He kept rubbing the side of his neck. "I remember nothing, in fact, after we turned onto this road."

"Thirteen?" Bill asked, one hand on Sohrab's shoulder as he checked the man's pupils.

"I think he prefers Shadowman now," Jack said, "but yes." *Why didn't he just kill him?* he thought. *It's not like one more would matter to him. But he had said he didn't choose to kill. If he was blocking the Zzkritti's control, maybe he didn't need to—especially if he can erase memories.* Regardless, Jack was happy to see Sohrab alive and well. He reached into his pocket, feeling for the little fob the Shadowman had given him. It was warmer than before, but not uncomfortably so, and he wondered if it might be part of the reason Sohrab wasn't dead. With no way to know, he let it go with one last squeeze of his hand.

Bill released Sohrab's shoulder and turned to Jack. "So, Li'l Bro... what's the plan?"

"I need to have a little talk with Dieter," Jack said, his voice cold and hard. "The problem is that I don't know where to find him."

"I think I can help," Amber said, mouse-like, standing in the open door of Sohrab's car, her head tilted downward. Everyone turned to her, none having noticed she had exited the vehicle. Rutger and Sohrab seemed especially shocked to see her on her feet and talking.

"How so?" Jack asked, his demeanor harsher than he intended.

Amber flinched, then raised her eyes. "I think I felt him when we were driving here," she said, her voice small and weak. "Back when we passed that little town," she continued, looking up at Sohrab. "I don't remember the name."

"Yes," Sohrab said, "I think I know the one."

Jack tilted his head at Amber but made no move to comfort her. "Do you think you can pinpoint his location if we get you close?"

"I... I don't know," she said, shaking her head. "It's pretty fuzzy right now."

The fob, he thought. *It has to be.* The one thing he needed to protect them all was likely the one thing *preventing* him from finding Dieter. Jack was surprised to find his fingers wrapped around the fob, holding tight like a magical talisman. *In a way, it* is, *I guess.* He didn't know why he had told no one about it, he just knew he shouldn't. Jack felt all eyes on him, waiting for him to decide. *It's* always *been on me, hasn't it?*

"Bill," he said, turning to his brother, "you're with me and Rutger in the Big Cat." He pointed at Amber, and said to Sohrab, "You take her in your car and let her guide you as best she can." The hurt in her eyes stabbed Jack through the heart, threatening to melt the ice, and he steeled himself against it, squaring his shoulders. "Do your best, Amber," he said, offering what small comfort he could. "We'll follow wherever you lead, but we'll be pretty far back, so don't get spooked if you don't see us."

Bill and Sohrab looked at him, an identical furrowing of their brows a question he couldn't answer.

"Jack—" Amber began.

"Get to your respective cars, guys," he said. "This thing is almost over." He stepped to the driver's door of the Big Cat and threw it open. When no one moved, he slapped the roof twice. "C'mon, guys. We're burnin' daylight."

Sohrab looked up at the night sky and shook his head, then his face brightened. "*The Cowboys*, right?"

Jack grinned. "Got it in one." He waved Rutger and Bill to the car. "Pile in boys."

Amber's eyes welled without spilling. She folded into her seat with an obvious reluctance and closed the door with a soft click. The three men turned to Jack in anticipation, expecting him to approach her. Instead he slid into the Cat's seat and closed his door without another word.

Rutger opened a back door on the Cat as Bill pulled the handle on the front passenger side, and both piled in.

"Shotgun," Bill said.

Jack snorted once and shook his head. "No need to call it when you're already sitting there, doofus."

"Just clarifying," Bill said. He tried to smile at Jack, but all he managed was a tight grimace.

Sohrab got in his car and backed it out of the driveway and onto the road. Jack fired up the Big Cat's engine, and threw the shifter into reverse, looking over his shoulder as he backed it out to join Sohrab on the road. The Ford drove away, Jack watching the taillights shrink as the Big Cat idled, an old man's throaty rumble, full of phlegm.

Jack turned to Bill and forced a weak smile, then shoved the shifter into drive. "It's 106 miles to Chicago, we got a full tank of gas, half a pack of cigarettes, it's dark... and we're wearing sunglasses," he said in a growling monotone.

Rutger's brow furrowed. "We don't have—"

"Hit it," Bill said, completing the ritual, and Jack floored the accelerator, laying down rubber for twenty feet.

"Americans are crazy," Rutger said from his perch in the back, shaking his head.

CHAPTER 27

*H*E HATES ME, AMBER THOUGHT, her face turned to the window, watching the lights grow and recede one by one. Like her, they were alone in the dark, a single sputtering flame—engulfing black pressing close and heavy. *Jack* should *fucking hate me.* She snorted, turning back to the front. *How much of this wouldn't have happened if he'd never met me?*

Most, if not all—that much was certain. *She* had taken the files that set his feet on the path leading inexorably, one step after another, to where they were now. *She* had betrayed him by killing his best friend. And now *she* led him to his final doom.

Amber couldn't shake the thought this was exactly what Dieter had planned from the beginning.

"Anything yet?" Sohrab called from the driver's seat. He didn't turn his head, but looked at her in the mirror as he spoke. His eyes crinkled at the corners, and she forced a smile. The man was a complete stranger yet comforted her in ways she didn't believe possible in this mess. His strength had nothing to do with his size. She could tell both the strength and humor came from a place of sadness and regret.

Daddy said it takes heat and pressure to make a diamond, she thought. Like every conversation of theirs she could remember, that one had also been less about science and more about character.

"Still too far out," Amber said, shaking her head. "I'll let you know."

Sohrab's eyes crinkled again. "Why don't you climb up here into the front?" he said. "It will be easier for me when you have to give directions."

Amber turned her head to look behind. Jack's car was so far back, with at least three cars between them, she couldn't even pick out his headlights. She sighed, and pulled herself between the two front seats like a spider through a cleft in a tree branch. With a grunt, she gathered her legs beneath and slid into the seat opposite Sohrab.

He turned and smiled, eyes crinkling again, round cheeks shining. "That's better," he said.

Amber leaned over, using the side-view mirror to check behind again. She pulled the shoulder harness across and buckled herself into the seat. On reflex, she reached up and pulled the visor down to check herself in the mirror, then thought better of it and slapped it back into place. *No point in seeing what I already know*, she thought. *I look like a goddamn mental patient.*

"Everything will be fine, you know," Sohrab said, staring ahead.

"We're all going to die tonight, you know."

"That's the spirit!" he said, turning his smile toward her. He shrugged at the confusion on her face. "No more worries when you're dead."

I've been dead too long already, she thought. Like it or not, it was time to pull herself from the depths where she had languished since murdering Mason. The first rung on that ladder was simply admitting, at least to herself, that it wasn't her fault. *That was all Dieter.* Her eyes narrowed as she peered into the night, grabbing another mental rung. *Somewhere ahead, he waits. And he will pay.*

* * *

For ten miles, neither man in the front of the car spoke, and Rutger was content to leave it that way. He had his own issues with which to grapple at the moment, and the silence was a blessed relief. The tires whined against the pavement—a rhythmic click, steady as a metronome, marking their speed as they passed over the joins in the road.

They were on a mission—presumably to kill a man—yet Rutger still did not have all the pieces of the puzzle. For the longest time he had believed the Shadowman was their quarry, but now Jack was hell-bent on killing someone named Dieter. There were pieces from three distinct puzzles in the pile before him... and no corners as a starting point.

I swore to uphold the law, he thought, and here I am helping two men I barely know murder a man I've never met. He shook his head, rubbing the stubble on his cheek. Gershon would love to catch me in the act of that.

"Jack," he said, his voice quiet and careful, "tell me again why you believe the Shadowman."

Jack took a slow breath and blew it out like cooling a sip of tea. His eyes flicked up to confront Rutger's own in the rearview mirror. "Because all the pieces fit," Jack said. "Because the letters from Dieter were too cute by half, and if my mind had been right, I would have seen that." His eyes narrowed, snake-like and just as dangerous. "But mostly because I saw the man's face when Amber shot Mason." He gripped the wheel with white-knuckled ferocity, grinding it in hard fingers. "He was *pleased*, Rutger," he said. "The motherfucker was practically *applauding* Amber's performance."

If Rutger had been in the room, perhaps he would feel the same. But he wasn't, and he couldn't. The anger he reached for didn't exist, even if he *could* understand Jack's.

"But, Jack... seriously. *Aliens?*"

"You have another explanation for the things the Shadowman and Dieter can do?" Jack said, his voice hard and dismissive. "If so, I'm all ears."

"Your Shadowman is nothing more than a superb assassin, Jack."

"One who can walk right into a secure government building and take whatever he wants, leaving no evidence behind."

"And don't forget the mind control," Bill said with restrained anger.

"Every government has performed research—"

"I'm not talkin' Manchurian Candidate bullshit, Inspector," Bill snapped. "This is full-blown, voices in my head, real-time, fucking *puppet-master* stuff!"

Bill's chest heaved, Jack chewed his lower lip, and Rutger knew at once there was no breaking through. Both men's minds were made up, and it was up to him to contain the damage.

If God is with me, he thought, I may prevent another death.

* * *

319

It was all so simple! For years Dieter had labored, always using substandard equipment in a poorly stocked lab, but the secret now lay before him like an open flower.

"I should have thought of this much sooner," he said with a weary grin, his voice echoing in the barren stone basement. Of *course* the answer was simple. The machines themselves were elementary in their design, so the code commanding them to reproduce must be as well. There was no danger of the gray goo scenario, as no Zzkritti would ever even *consider* unleashing such a dangerous tool without failsafes. He held one such failsafe in his hands, poised over the glass container as he watched the sample of nano-machines replicate themselves using the raw elements extracted from the piece of ham he had dropped inside. His eyes sparkled as the machines doubled and redoubled as the flesh disappeared, the process accelerating as their numbers grew.

Programmed to ignore the elements that made up the glass, they searched for new sources of material to build their progeny. An almost invisible line formed, like microscopic sugar ants, reaching for the freedom at the open end of the beaker. *I should have used the Erlenmeyer,* he thought, although the sloped sides of the flask would have offered no more of an impediment.

Dieter tilted the container in his hand, pouring a thin stream of hydrochloric acid down the inside surface of the beaker. Within seconds, the sample of nano-machines was neutralized, becoming nothing more than a bubbling mass. He covered his mouth with his sleeve to keep from breathing the small amount of gas liberated from the reaction. To be sure, he took a pair of glass-ended tongs from the bench, lifted the beaker, and placed it into a larger barrel of hydrochloric acid on the floor. Not for the first time, he wished for better ventilation in the damp basement.

He smiled as the beaker sank, and no more bubbles of decomposition drifted to the surface. Replacing the tongs, he set the container of acid back on the bench and looked to the small dropper bottles beyond filled with chemical pheromones. The programming language of the nanos consisted of those seven compounds, and it had only taken him a few months to isolate them. Learning the language to reprogram the nanos had taken *years.*

Dieter frowned and shook his head. "And I never needed to reprogram you to begin with," he said to the larger container holding the last of his nano-machines. The switch had been there all along, waiting for someone to throw it.

It was all so simple.

* * *

The urge to follow the cars had been strong, but Thirteen resisted because he must. He had done all he could without alerting his masters. The rest was up to Jack. Fingers curled in his pocket, grasping at nothing, he forced his hand to relax, ending its search for the device. It had been his one true companion for the better part of his life, and now it was gone.

Thirteen sighed, a wistful sound of teen lassitude, and walked toward the motel and his dank little room. Soon he would drop the mental shield—his only protection from the Hive—and the questions would begin. One voice in particular was all that interested him. For now, he enjoyed both the walk and the solitude. With no voices in his head other than his own and a chill breeze on his face, a melody from long ago haunted his thoughts. Threading its way through his mind, an echo at first, it slithered to his fore-brain on scales of song.

Neither stars nor sun bring you happiness,
Neither day nor night yields joy.
You stand and wait, dressed in stripes and shaved bare;
With thousands of others like you.

The words of this song are stained with our blood,
Within them are sorrow and grief,
Yet your camp song will carry beyond these barbed wires
To a distant place unknown to you.

Yet your camp song will carry beyond these barbed wires
To a distant place unknown to you.

He reached up with one quivering hand and brushed the moisture from his cheek, his stride never breaking. Thirteen's mother had taught he and his brother the song at her knee, each taking turns with the clear and pure voices only a child possesses. Even if she had survived the camp, she would be long-dead now.

Still... it was her voice he heard.

* * *

"Here!" Sohrab turned to the sound of urgency in Amber's voice, checked his side mirrors, and spun the wheel to exit the highway.

"A little warning next time," he said with a grumble.

"Sorry," she said, huddling closer to her door. "Maybe if we slow down..."

Sohrab eased the pressure of his foot, and the car slowed to the posted speed for the frontage road. Off the highway, the way ahead was darker and... thicker, somehow. He watched Amber scan left to right, her eyes glassy, like she could hear an audible signal. She stopped the motion, her eyes locking on a distant goal, and pointed west with a steady finger.

"That way," she said.

Sohrab pulled over to the gravel break-down lane, slowed to a stop, and shifted into park. The engine idled, a soft purr after the growling hum of tires on pavement. "That general direction, or are you talking about a specific turn coming up?"

"Um... that way," she repeated, waving her hand, a slim smile for an apology.

Sohrab peered through the windshield in the direction she indicated and found a water tower to use as a guidepost. "All right," he said, shifting the car back into drive. "Let me know if we are getting off course."

Amber lowered her hand to her lap, and the smile evaporated, the corners of her mouth stopping just short of turning down. Sohrab turned right at the first intersection, keeping the tower centered in his view, and slowed to neighborhood speed. All around, on both sides of the street, normalcy sprouted like weeds; a few houses popped up near the highway, the crop thicker the deeper they drove into the town proper. Most were well-kept, with neat manicured lawns and intact paint or brick siding. He saw few cars rusting in their driveways or surrounded by weeds, but one was epic in the way the vegetation had taken over. It looked like a planter on wheels, as if the owner had spent considerable time cultivating and pruning.

Careful pruning is often all that is needed, he thought. The topiaries he saw during his family's only visit to Disney World bordered on the magical. It's amazing what you can do with a living thing and a simple pair of shears.

An old memory surfaced, and he shuddered. *Pruning shears can be used for more than training plants.* That was the *only* time his work had yielded useful information, saving hundreds from a suicide bomber. It was also the reason he had defected to America. He had bought into the idea of pruning to cleanse—or even shape—the body politic, but when forced to torture captives for information, he found his love of country diminished. *Tarnished... once gold and glowing, now green and dull.*

Lost in thought, he almost missed the next turn. Amber sat up, a coiled spring of potential energy, and he took his cue, turning the wheel again to get back on course. He checked his mirror, looking for the headlights from Jack's car. They were closer, owing to the need to see each turn Sohrab made, but still far back. The trick now was to keep an eye toward the road ahead while making sure he didn't lose them.

Once there, Jack, how will the pruning go?

* * *

When Sohrab's car pulled over after exiting the highway, Jack panicked for a second or two. He had to pull over as well, and feared he was so close the device in his pocket would interfere with Amber's nanos. He breathed a heavy sigh of relief when the car drove off soon after he stopped, and he resumed following at his preferred distance. He did not know the range of the device; he just knew farther was better.

When this is over, I think I will invest in Tums and blood pressure medicine, he thought with a twist of his mouth. *Assuming I'm alive to invest.*

He was taking a lot on faith. With no clear direction, plan, or even a *goal*, they drove toward a destiny not of his choosing. Jack smiled at his brother. *Everyone in this is taking a lot on faith, but theirs is in* me, *and it's damned misplaced.* His smile faded before Bill saw it, taking what little cheer he felt along for the ride.

"You get too far back," Bill said, "and he's liable to lose you by accident."

"I know, Bill," Jack said, his voice hard and thin. "Just keep your eyes open and help me."

"Sure thing, bro." Bill shifted in his seat, and turned his head to look behind. "You okay back there?" he said to Rutger.

"As fine as can be, considering," Rutger replied.

"Considering what?" Bill's eyes narrowed.

Rutger took a deep breath and sighed. "Considering we are on our way to kill a man in cold blood," he said. "I don't think I signed up for that."

"You know what the man's done, right?" Bill said, his voice rising in pitch.

"I only know what you *think* he's—"

"Look, no one's killing anyone," Jack lied. "Our primary goal is to stop him from harming anyone else. If we can do that without hurting him, so much the better."

Bill turned to Jack, one eyebrow cocked. "But I thought—"

"You thought wrong," Jack said. He needed Rutger in this as a willing participant. Bill would go in half-cocked, Amber was a basket case, and Jack didn't know what Sohrab's motivation was. Rutger was the one participant among them without a dog in this hunt, so he was the *second* most valuable member.

With the device in one pocket and the gun in the other, that made Jack number one with a bullet. *Maybe a tie with Amber.*

"So, Mr. In-Charge," Bill said with a sneer, "what's your plan?"

Plan? Jack thought. *How do you plan for something like this?* There was no precedent, no projections, no *inkling* of such an encounter. If he had his library of science fiction books at hand, maybe he could use that as a planning resource, but as things now stood...

"In all honesty, bro... I haven't a fucking clue," Jack said.

* * *

Dieter closed the basement door behind him without bothering to lock it. He never locked it. There was no point. No one came to this place—much less the basement—other than himself or the people he programmed. There were times he wished for real human contact, though he couldn't risk discovery for selfish indulgence. *If I hadn't been forced to use Miss Riley,* he thought, *I might have kept her around longer for the company.*

324

None of it mattered now. He had what he needed to complete his life's work. The nanos in the basement lab, having been fed enough raw material, would increase their number a hundredfold before morning. Once the supply was replenished, he would reset the entire mass at once, shutting off their ability to replicate. From there, programming them for use in the field was a simple matter; he had all the sequences committed to memory, and could perform them in his sleep.

He patted the heavy wooden door and turned for the stone steps leading to the kitchen. The grocery man had come today, and Dieter now had a fully stocked pantry. The first step shone from the slick dampness there, so he reached for the railing. "It wouldn't do to slip and break my neck now," he said, his voice echoing up the staircase. "Not when I'm so close to success."

His stomach growled long and loud. Empty for much of the day, he would fill it now while he went over his list of targets, many of whom were in the nation's capitol. He smiled in anticipation and quickened his step.

All he had to do was shake a few hands.

* * *

Jack watched Sohrab turn into the parking lot beneath the bright sign that proclaimed: OPEN AL NITE! He snorted and shook his head. Either the owner had a spelling problem, or a letter had fallen off. Jack didn't want to consider the possibility the owner's name was Al.

"Why is he parking here?" Bill asked.

"How the hell should *I* know?" Jack said, his voice clipped. He blew out a long breath as he turned the wheel and followed Sohrab into the empty lot. The other man had already backed into a darkened corner and doused his lights. Jack followed suit, sliding the Big Cat nose first into the slot beside, his window opposite Sohrab's. He rolled the window down with the old hand crank, the mechanism resisting him the whole way, as Sohrab's electric window lowered smooth and swift.

"Thought we could get a bite to eat here while we plan our next move," Sohrab said over the space separating them. He killed the car's motor as he spoke, making it clear there wasn't really a question on the table.

"To be honest, Jack," Rutger said, placing a hand on Jack's seat, "I could go for something to eat."

325

Jack turned his head to Bill, a question on one raised eyebrow.

"Yeah," Bill said. "What *he* said."

Jack turned the key, and the engine sputtered and died. "Okay," he said, "who has cash on them?"

"I've got a credit card," Bill said.

"No cards, bro. People are still looking for me, and I know they can track a card in real-time."

"But I'm—"

"My brother." Jack shook his head. "What... you didn't think they were watching *you*, too?" He hooked a thumb behind at Rutger. "He's out, too, and for pretty much the same reason."

"I've got enough cash for all of us," Sohrab said, then his mouth turned down as his face fell. "It's the last of what Mason had in his wallet."

"It's about time the cheapskate paid for a meal," Jack said with forced humor. He opened his door and stepped out, waiting for the others. Each exited their vehicle, Amber being the last, and they walked to the diner. He pulled the door open, the bell above jingling a happy sound, and held it as everyone entered.

Sohrab led them to a round corner booth at the far end of the diner, and scooted around the table, leaving room for everyone. Amber sat next to him, followed by Rutger, Bill, then Jack. An old woman, short and stout, toddled from behind the worn counter carrying a stack of grimy menus.

"You kids eatin' or just gettin' coffee?" she said, her voice cheerier than it should have been.

"Eating, thank you," Jack said, standing and taking the menus from her. He passed them out and sat again.

"Don't get too many orderin' this time of night," she said. "Usually just kids comin' in to drink coffee 'n' smoke." She turned and walked away, her round, rolling gate suggesting one leg was shorter than the other. "I'll get you kids some water and be right back," she said over her shoulder.

After she left, Jack turned to Amber. "How close are we?" he asked her.

"That's funny," she said, her nose crinkled, and lips pursed. "A few minutes ago I could have told you in feet and inches," she said, her eyes far away. "Now," she shrugged, "it's like a fuse has blown. I don't even know what direction."

"It's okay," Sohrab said, placing a hand atop hers, "I have a good idea from her earlier directions." He looked into Jack's eyes, finding a hard edge behind those shining orbs. "We are close."

Jack nodded and did his best to ignore where Sohrab's hand lay. He stood and surveyed the room, found what he needed, and walked to the counter. The ketchup bottle was as good an excuse as any, and he grabbed it before turning back to the others. "Anyone need anything else while I'm over here?"

"They got any mustard over there?" Bill said, turning.

"Yeah," Jack said, and picked up that bottle as well. Neither was why he was there, anyway. "You have *no* idea where Dieter is?" he asked Amber, leaning on the bar.

She scrunched her face again, as cute a look as was possible given the situation. "Yeah, actually. It's really strong, now." She shook her head. "That's really weird."

Jack pushed away from the counter and strolled toward the table. After only three steps, Amber looked up at him, her eyes wide.

"Now it's gone again."

Fifteen feet, Jack thought. *Maybe a bit more.* It was a shorter range than he would have preferred, but it would have to do. He had thought when the Shadowman gave him the device, all he had to do was show up and the nanos would shut down. *Nothing is ever that easy, is it?* He noticed everyone watching him as he stood there holding the two bottles, then the old woman pushed by him with a tray of glasses.

"Excuse me, hon," she said. "Comin' thru." She stepped past and up to the table. "Well, c'mon, son," she said to Jack, smiling. "It's easy. Just put one foot in front o' the other."

That's right, he thought, smiling back at her. *One step at a time.*

CHAPTER 28

STIRLING GERSHON PULLED THE CUFFS of his expensive tailored shirt as the doors slid open, then stepped off the lift. He turned right to the hotel lobby and ran directly into a little man going in the other direction.

"Pardon," Stirling said, as insincere as he could make the statement. The other man smiled up at him, a row of sharp and pointed teeth flashing for an instant. Stirling recoiled, stepping back.

"That is quite all right Inspector," the little man said. "I was coming to see you, anyway."

"I'm sorry, but I am on my way to a meeting," Stirling said, a half-truth at best. He was on his way to another delicious breakfast in the hotel's famed restaurant and had no desire to share it with this disturbing little person.

"I'm afraid there is no time for that, Inspector," the man said. "You will accompany me now, please." He turned and walked away, clearly expecting Stirling to follow. When he did not, the man stopped and faced him again.

"Who do you think you are, that you can order me like an underling?" Stirling said with a sniff.

"Inspector," the man sighed, "for you, *underling* would be a huge step up." He took a step toward Stirling and smiled. *Those teeth, again!* Stirling shivered at the thought.

"You may call me Jeff if you like, but what you *will* do is keep your mouth shut and follow directions. Is that clear?"

For the first time in ages, Stirling was unsure of both himself and his place in the natural order. "I don't know who you are, but—"

"Who I am is your superior in every way, but if you need convincing..." Jeff said before turning Stirling's world upside down. His eyes widened like two saucers as the other man's face blurred then coalesced into something more horrible than Stirling's worst nightmares. It wasn't the demon-red color, or the ears, or even the horns. It was the double row of sharp conical teeth that held Stirling's attention, filling his field of view as the creature smiled and nodded. "Good," it hissed like water tossed on hot coals. "I like you better silent." It turned and walked away.

With a sliding, shuffling step, Stirling followed.

* * *

By the time the arguing was over, the sky to the east was a pleasant purple fading to red. Jack was sure his eyes looked much the same. He could no longer remember the last time he'd had more than an hour of sleep, and if he were to close his eyes now, the battle to stay awake would be lost.

They were watching him again. Every face expectant, full of self-doubt and a measure of urgency. All except Sohrab's. He wore a mask of bored acceptance. "Come what may," that face said, "I'll do what you need." Jack blinked several times, his eyes widening as he realized that the one person he trusted most right now was the man Mason had trusted on instinct alone. *You and me are gonna share a drink, Mace, when all this is over.*

Jack picked up his coffee mug and drew it to his lips. The earthy, half-burnt aroma assaulted his nostrils, and he wrinkled his nose and replaced the mug on the table. He'd had entirely too much coffee this night, and the thought of another sip sickened him.

"Are you sure about this?" Bill asked.

Jack lifted his eyes to his brother. "As sure as I can be about anything."

"But what if she's still under the guy's control?"

"You do realize," Amber said, "that I'm sitting right the fuck here." Bill looked at her, and she rolled her eyes. Dismissing him with a sniff, she looked across the table. "But he has a point, Jack," she said. "I can't guarantee I won't turn on you when we get close."

Jack looked into her eyes, his pain and sadness projecting like waves of heat from his own. She didn't understand—no one at the

330

table did—and he couldn't take the chance telling them. She and Bill might not be the only ones compromised. In the end, he offered her the only thing he could. "I'm sort of counting on it," he said, a crooked smile on his lips.

"That's pretty fucked up," Bill said, pushing away from the table and draping an arm across the back of the bench. He looked at Rutger. "Please tell my kid brother his plan is fucked up."

"I don't know," Rutger said, rubbing the stubble on his face. "It has a certain elegance to it... *if* he can indeed trust Ms. Riley."

"Yeah, Jack," Bill said with a sneer. "Why don't you tell us why you're so sure you can."

Jack looked around the table, meeting each pair of eyes. *Always watching me.* "I can't, guys. Just believe that I do and leave it at that." *Please leave it at that*, he thought.

The bell over the door jingled its happy song, and two large patrol officers walked into the diner. Both tossed wary glances at Jack's table, offering the patented cop-nod—the one that said *we're watching you*—before sidling up to the counter.

"Hey Alice," the older of the two said. "Coffee and a baker's dozen." He withdrew a battered Coleman thermos from under his jacket and placed it on the counter, then settled his bulk on the nearest stool. It groaned under the assault but did not buckle. Jack got the impression that it didn't dare.

Alice smiled up at the big cop and took the thermos. "I'll be right back, Jim," she said. "Does little Tommy want anything?" she said with a wink to the younger cop.

"Just fill the thermos, mom," he said, as Jim cackled beside him.

Tommy leaned back to see around his partner, his face scrunched up like a bulldog as he looked over the group of co-conspirators. After a few seconds he shrugged and turned, leaning on his forearms against the counter.

Jack was suddenly and acutely aware of the bulge in his pocket from Bill's semi-automatic.

He leaned forward, his head over the table while he hid his hands beneath. "Pretty sure my face is on every morning briefing between here and Seattle," he said, his voice barely above a whisper. "Right, Bill?"

"No doubt," his brother said, nodding.

The device in his pocket was warmer now, and it vibrated in short pulses. Jack tried to ignore it, but the thing was insistent. It was worse each time he looked at the cops, and he wanted nothing more right now than for both of them to leave. He stood, his back to the counter, and shoved his hands into his pockets. The device vibrated so violently he was sure everyone could hear it.

The cold steel of the gun in his other hand was as dead as Mason.

"Here ya go, boys," Alice said as she ambled up to the counter carrying the thermos and a box of donuts. "Fresh and hot." She handed them across to Jim. "Well, the donuts. Not so much the coffee," she said, laughing.

"Fair 'nuff," Jim said, and he took the items from her hands. "What do we owe ya?" he asked, like it was part of a routine.

"Same as always," she said with a smile.

Jim leaned over the counter and gave her a chaste peck on the cheek. "Thanks, Al." He handed the box to Tommy and shoved the thermos back under his jacket. "C'mon, boy, let's get goin'."

The device's pulsing lessened but did not stop. Jack looked over his shoulder while everyone at the table watched him. The two officers strode toward the door, and as the younger reached for the handle, he stopped and faced the table.

"Hey!" he said, pointing.

And the device exploded in Jack's mind.

* * *

Bill reached for Jack as his brother groaned and his knees buckled, caught him under his arms, and hauled him back to his seat. Jack's head lolled, his chin resting on his chest, and he moaned like a man coming off a three-day bender. More worrisome, though, was the approach of the young cop.

The boy, as unsure as any rookie would be, stepped toward the table, hat in one hand and the other resting against the butt of his weapon. The older cop rolled his eyes and shook his head but followed as backup.

"Sir, I'm going to have to ask you to place your hands on the table," Tommy said, his voice cracking. Beads of sweat already forming at the man's temples, his eyes were wide with little iris showing.

Ah, fuck, Bill thought. *One false move and people are gonna get dead. Shit.* Jack was useless, so at least the gun in his pocket was off the table, but Sohrab had become a statue, his eyes tracking every motion in the room. The cop had come too close, and was within easy arm's-reach of the Iraqi. *Not good.*

"Sir! Place your hands—"

"Excuse me," Bill said, his voice calm, face open and innocent. Both officers turned their eyes to him. "I'm a detective from Greenville," he said, smiling. "Is there a problem?"

The rookie cop narrowed his eyes at Bill. "This man," he said, pointing at Jack, "is wanted in connection with at least three murders."

"Tommy," the big cop said, "I don't think—"

"Look at him, Jim," Tommy said, breathing hard. "We just went over his file this morning, fer Chris' sake!"

Officer Jim leaned forward, narrowing his eyes at Jack. He tilted his head, then raised his brows. "Son of a bitch," he said, unholstering his weapon. "*All* hands on the table," he said, waving the gun. "Now!"

Everyone complied, though Sohrab's motions were glacial as he splayed his hands in front. Bill could almost hear tendons popping from the tension in those fingers. Neither cop seemed to notice.

"May I show you my ID?" Bill asked, as sweet as honey.

Jim tapped Tommy on the shoulder. "That's the next step in procedure, son."

"Carefully," Tommy said, his hand still on his gun.

At least he hasn't drawn it, Bill thought. That's one point in his favor. Kid knows not to escalate.

Bill reached into his pocket, as slow as Sohrab's movement before him, and withdrew his shield. He held it up so both officers could see it. Both cranked their adrenaline down from eleven, but Officer Jim didn't lower his weapon.

"So, you're a cop," Tommy said. "You're still with a murder suspect."

"I know that, officer," Bill said, fighting the urge to roll his eyes. "That man across from me," he said, pointing to Rutger, "is Interpol. Jack has placed himself into *our* custody." He hoped the two officers understood the nature of his emphasis.

"May I?" Rutger said, seeing the look the officers gave him. They nodded, and he offered his own ID.

Tommy looked it over, then raised his eyes to Rutger. "This says you are a German police detective."

"Temporarily attached to Interpol for this investigation," Rutger said.

Tommy nodded, but did not seem convinced. "And the other two?" he said, waving the ID at Amber and Sohrab.

"Friends of Jack's," Bill said before either could open their mouths. "They convinced him to turn himself over to Interpol."

"Shit, Tommy," Jim said, holstering his weapon. "Looks like we're left out in the cold on this one." Both officers relaxed, but Tommy remained wary. He tossed Rutger's ID across the table.

"What's wrong with him?" Tommy asked, leaning closer.

Bill shrugged. "Hasn't eaten in three days. We're gonna have to fatten him up a bit before we can even question him." Sohrab still had not relaxed. Nor had he moved, but his eyes were in constant motion, scanning the room like a pilot checking his instruments.

"They're lyin'," Alice said from the counter. Both officers turned to her, heads tilting an identical angle.

"What was that, Al?" Jim said.

"Came in here all chummy late last night—the whole bunch o' them," she said. "Been here ever since, talkin' up a storm like they was plannin' somethin'." She pointed at Jack. "That one there seems ta be the leader."

Shit, shit, shit... Bill wanted to move, but didn't know what to do. It no longer mattered. Even as the cops spun around, hands reaching for weapons, Sohrab was already in motion.

Smooth as a ballet, as quick as a cobra strike, he slipped from his end of the booth and shoved one palm into the underside of Tommy's chin straight up like a pogo stick. Bill knew that, inside that melon, Tommy's brain had just impacted with the front, then sloshed back, bruising both ends. Tommy dropped like a sack of flour.

Sohrab wasn't finished, though, as he used the momentum of his strike to pirouette around the unconscious Tommy and behind Officer Jim. He wrapped one arm around the man's throat in a choke hold, and in the same motion both legs around his waist, and pulled back to bring them both to the floor. The big man fell with a thud atop Sohrab, who didn't even grunt, and he tightened his hold on the man's neck, cutting off the flow of blood to his brain.

Alice screamed, and Bill scrambled over Jack, grabbed Tommy's gun, and ran to the counter.

"Please don't move, ma'am," he said. He didn't threaten her with the gun, but she got the point. Everyone watched the struggle on the floor, but it was over in moments.

With both officers out, Sohrab pushed the big man off and stood. "We don't have much time," he said. "Bring her along," he said to Bill. "We'll drop her off where it will take her a while to find a phone." Sohrab took Officer Jim's gun, walked outside, and killed the patrol car's radio. When he was finished, he walked back into the diner as calm as if he were arriving for a meal. "Come," he said, tossing the gun to the floor.

Rutger and Amber helped Jack walk to the car and slid him into the passenger seat. Jack shook himself, like waking from a deep dream and looked around, blinking at the stares directed at him. "I'm fine to drive," he said. He slid across the seat to the driver's side. "Get in, Amber."

No one moved. Alice fumed where Bill held her, one arm clutched in his meaty grip. Sohrab eyed Jack with concern but didn't say anything. *Fucker never does*, Bill thought.

"Like Sohrab said, guys," Jack said. "We don't have a lot of time."

* * *

The plan was simple, Jack thought as he drove, Amber huddled against her door, crying softly. Now the cops know we're in the area, and everything goes to shit.

He still didn't know what had happened when the two cops approached him. One second, he was wondering how to get away, and the next, both men were out cold on the floor. Jack knew the device must be involved but couldn't begin to guess how. The vibrating thing in his pocket had become a buzzing in his head, an insistent pressure like a question. *Like it was awaiting permission*, he thought. It *wanted* to act—*needed* to—but he didn't know how to give it what it required.

It's just a hunk of metal and plastic, he thought. It can't need anything.

He sniffed at his own hubris. The device was far more than the key fob it appeared to be. *It's the product of an advanced alien civilization. There's no telling* what *it's capable of.*

The gun was still in his pocket, and that was good. It was important for the plan.

"Everything's gonna be okay," he said to Amber, trying to comfort her.

She sniffled and wiped her nose and eyes. "How do you know that, Jack?" Her eyes were red as she turned them to him. "How can you know how *anything's* going to turn out today?" Her face flushed and her mouth hardened. "You don't even know that I won't betray you when the time comes."

"I know, Amber," he said, his voice soft and soothing. He had to calm her before they reached their objective.

"No, you don't!" she said, her pitch rising with each word, and he recoiled on reflex. "I've betrayed you from the *beginning!*"

"I don't—"

"I was *paid* to distract you in Germany," she said, tears streaming down her cheeks.

"You must have been under the nano's influence even then," he said, grasping for any excuse.

"No, Jack. That's the kicker." She turned her face away, too ashamed or too emotional, he couldn't tell. "It was just money. He only wanted me to distract you, and you were cute, and..." She buried her face in her hands and sobbed.

I have done everything I could not *to kill you and your people.* The Shadowman's words came back to him in a flood. *Didn't quite work out for Sally and Mason, though, did it?* Jack thought, bitter bile rising in his throat. His anger threatened to derail his whole plan, clouding his judgment—keeping him off balance. *Or I could* use *that anger...*

He watched Amber as she cried and reached across the gulf of fear and doubt to comfort her, knowing at the same time that doing so would quell the burning in his belly. *None of this is her fault, but she* does *bear responsibility for her own actions. At the very least, for not telling me before now.*

He drew his hand back before he could touch her.

Behind him the sun peeked over the horizon, burning the dark to ash, reducing the night to glowing embers resting on the edge of the world. Ahead the night still ruled, but Jack drove on, bringing the cleansing light with him.

* * *

"Where are we going?" Stirling asked his diminutive passenger.

"To pick up a friend," the creature he knew only as Jeff said. "Beyond that, you don't need to know anything else for now."

Stirling drove the rental car up the ramp and entered the highway. The sun blazed through the windshield, blinding him, and he slapped the visor down to shield his eyes. The sun was still too low for that to help much. He squinted as his face reddened.

"You are angry at the sun," Jeff said, face open and tilted to one side. He—*it?*—shook his head. "I have never understood humanity's ability to be angry at an inanimate object."

"Would you rather we were angry at one another?"

"There was a time..." Jeff settled against his door and faced Stirling. "Your family has served us well for the last seventy years."

Stirling drew back, his face now hot and tight. "*My* family serves *no one—*"

"Calm yourself, Inspector," Jeff said, lips drawn into a thin smile. *Oh God*, Stirling thought, *please not the teeth again.* "I only mean that you are to be commended on your family's performance. *You*, especially, have been one of our most consistent assets."

"Who *are* you?" Stirling asked, leaning as close to the creature as he dared.

"Call me... an *emissary*, if you must," Jeff said, drawing the word out like he was tasting it. "I have been tasked with facilitating a satisfactory conclusion to a mission in which my friend is currently involved."

"Yes, well... that is not helpful."

"That is just fine," Jeff said, shifting in his seat. "After all, you are here to help *me*. Not the other way around." He shifted again, then leaned to his left. A smile creased his face as his eyelids drooped, and he sighed. "That's better."

"What did you—?" Stirling began. It wasn't lack of words that interrupted him, but the barbed, bright red tail waving behind his passenger.

"Sorry," Jeff said, dipping his chin. "These seats are hell on a creature with one of these. We are used to sitting on something resembling one of your toilets." Jeff shook his head, and scrunched his face. "Disgusting and barbarous things, those."

"Your tail?"

"No," Jeff looked at him as if he were a child. "Your toilets." He shivered, making a rude noise.

Stirling's eyes narrowed at Jeff, then widened. "You are Zzkritti!"

"Guilty as charged," Jeff said with a smile and a nod. "You know of us?"

"There have been rumors and stories ever since my family relocated to Argentina," Stirling said. "My grandfather claimed to have met one of you."

"I find that to be unlikely," Jeff said with a shrug. "Although," his tail waggled in the air, "it is not unheard-of." Jeff bunched his lips and raised an eyebrow. "Your family has been afforded many advantages over the years, allowing you to amass both wealth and power," he said. "I have need of both, Inspector."

"What are you asking of me?" Stirling said, a block of ice forming in the pit of his stomach.

"The bill has come due," Jeff said, his voice flat. "And I am here to collect."

* * *

"You're leaving me *here*?"

Poor Alice is not in a good mood, Bill thought. Too fucking bad.

"You know," he said, reaching across her and pushing the door open, "if you had kept yer trap shut, none of this would have been necessary."

She looked at the hardscrabble on the shoulder of the road, then up and in both directions. The road stretched for at least a mile in each, with one end cresting a hill in the distance. Bill handed her a bottle of water and pointed to the open door.

"Go on, now. We've got places to be."

"I am not comfortable with this," Rutger said from the front passenger seat.

"She'll be fine," Bill said. "Won't you, Alice?"

338

"Would you rather she come with us?" Sohrab asked, his tone one of growing impatience. "She is in far less danger on this road, do you agree?"

Rutger didn't respond, narrowing his eyes at Sohrab before turning to face forward. *There's something going on between those boys*, Bill thought. In the short term it didn't matter. What *did* matter was making sure the three of them were there to back Jack up.

"Out you go," Bill said, and gently pushed Alice off the seat. The woman nearly tumbled to the ground but managed to keep both feet under her as she staggered away from the car. She stood there looking up at him, sputtering as she screwed up her mouth to deliver a withering retort. Bill nodded and pulled the door closed just as her tirade began in earnest. Through the glass came nothing but muffled screams, none of which were intelligible. He looked around the cabin, pushing up on the ceiling upholstery. "Nice job of sound insulation," he said to Sohrab.

"I use this car for side-jobs, sometimes," the Iraqi said, then threw the shifter into drive and pulled away from the still-hollering Alice.

Gonna be the easiest thing we do all day, Bill thought, watching the woman shake her fist at them as they drove away. *This has already taken too long.* He leaned back in his seat, wishing Sohrab would go faster. When they split up, Jack had promised he would wait for them before going in, but Bill knew it was a lie. *He doesn't want anyone else to get hurt*, Bill thought. Jack was determined to save the world without any more casualties, regardless of the personal cost.

He can't even save himself.

Bill was tired of cleaning up after Jack—always being there, the one everyone could count on. So tired, in fact, he had made it a career both before and after Jack left home. *I'm there for my damn brother more than I am for my own kids*, he thought, chiding himself.

Don't let him get hurt, okay? I like Uncle Jack. Sarah's words reverberated in his mind, her angelic face looking up at him.

"Can this thing go any faster?" Bill said to Sohrab, rubbing his hands together like kneading dough.

He had no intention of disappointing his daughter.

* * *

The asylum, a hulking edifice of stone and wood, looked no different than when Amber had escaped. Trapped in a state of perpetual decomposition, it would have been out of place in any community. What little was visible over the ivy-covered stone fence was more appropriate for a Gothic horror than either a hospital or asylum. It reminded her of the setting in the movie, *Shutter Island*.

It certainly didn't belong in a rural Georgian backwater.

Leaving the others at the diner to plan, Sohrab had followed her directions and found the place. When he returned, he verified her story, and told them Dieter's car was parked at the rear entrance. It was there, now.

He's in there, Amber thought, and her skin crawled. She knew it, even if she no longer *felt* it. It was odd to her how the ability to sense Dieter's presence kept coming and going, but it had apparently left her for good just before she and Jack drove away from the diner. *Something about Jack's presence is blocking it*, she thought. *But how could—*

"Do you think he knows we're here?" Jack asked, and she jumped at the sound.

"Sorry," she said. "I zoned out for a bit, there."

"Understandable," he said, his head tilted. His voice wasn't so much *comforting* as *empathetic*. *Great*, she thought. *Now he fucking feels sorry for me. Like I'm a puppy he just scolded.* "Are you ready?" he said, his eyes determined yet full of sympathy.

"No, but that doesn't really matter anymore, does it?"

He took a deep breath and sighed. "I guess not."

"Let's get to it, then," she said with more conviction than she felt.

Jack reached into his pocket and pulled out Bill's gun. He turned it over in his hands a few times, looking at it like he wanted to use it on himself, then offered it to Amber. The last time she had it in her hands, she killed his best friend. He dropped it into her waiting hands, the mass of the thing having grown with the added weight of death and betrayal. She hefted it, feeling its power, and gripped the handle. She would never be able to pull the trigger.

That wasn't the plan, regardless.

"Come on," she said, opening her door. "Let's get this over with."

CHAPTER 29

IETER PLACED HIS DISH AND UTENSILS into the sink, watching them drop below the surface of greasy suds. It would do to let them soak for a while before scrubbing. Breakfast had been a heavy affair, his appetite having returned after weeks of planning and worrying. *All my worries are over now*, he thought, turning away from the sink. The corners of his mouth turned up, his eyes twinkling. He had a newfound energy in his step that he had thought long lost, and he bounded out of the room and down the stairs.

Already packed for the trip to Washington, D.C., all that was left was to reset the switch on the nanos, program them for use, and load the car. The culmination of decades of dreams and plans lay before him. Tomorrow he would meet with his Congressman, who would then introduce him to several others, walking the chain all the way to the President.

From there it is a short hop to every leader of the free world, he thought, the grin refusing to leave his face. Dieter reached the bottom of the steps and turned to the lab, humming Wagner's *Prelude to Parsifal* like a lovestruck teen. Soon he would return to the Zzkritti, bearing in triumph the gift they had grown too timid to take for themselves.

* * *

The long driveway, broken and jumbled in places, lay before Jack like a Lego minefield. *Riley never learned to pick them up*, he thought, his mouth turning down. It was no longer enough to learn who was responsible for their deaths—that someone must now be made to *pay*. Everything he had worked for—all he had *sacrificed* for—was at the end of this driveway. Amber walked behind him, just out of arm's easy reach, holding Bill's gun in front of her like she meant to use it.

"No matter what," he said without turning, "don't show any emotion. Don't even answer his questions."

"Won't he get suspicious?" she said as loud as she dared, her lips barely moving.

"Sure, but if you say anything, I guarantee he'll know right away that something isn't right." Jack stumbled when his toe struck a protruding cobblestone, but he didn't fall. "Careful, Amber," he said. "No one will believe that I wouldn't take advantage if you fell."

"I'm not the one tripping on a pebble," she said. He could actually *hear* the smirk.

For a time the only sound was their footfalls as they shuffled along the drive, not even birdsong penetrating the gloom of the place. The sunlight seemed dimmer inside the walls, without a hint of breeze to rustle either the sparse branches of the timorous trees huddled against the wall, or the desiccated leaves that lay on the carpet of gray grass.

They rounded the side of the main building, their feet now crunching pea gravel rather than broken cobblestone. Twenty yards away, Dieter's dull and battered Mercedes rested beneath a porte-cochère, its trunk lid up. An open doorway invited, drawing them in like they were circling a drain.

* * *

Dieter hefted the duffel from the floor and settled the strap over his shoulder. The bag held the last of the equipment he needed for this trip, and if it hadn't been for his own nanos coursing through his body, he might never have gotten it up the steps to the car. He cast a sidelong glance at the workbench. The little machines hadn't quite finished replicating, though the container was nearly full. Once everything else was in the car, he would come back and shut them down for the drive to D.C.

Everything is coming to fruition, he thought as he climbed the steps. *As long as the Zzkritti remain fixated on Mr. Montgomery.* That was how he had planned it. He regretted having to give the entire file to Jack, but even if the man still had it, by the time he convinced anyone to read it *and* take it seriously, it would be far too late. *In twenty-four hours the world will be mine for the taking.*

It was likely Jack's capture would come too late. He is more adept at capture avoidance than I ever hoped possible.

Dieter regretted the deaths almost as much as the loss of the file, but they were necessary. *Once I have control of everything, that's when the real work begins.* Entire populations needed pruning before implementing his eugenics program—a forced march through evolution's gauntlet, leading to the perfection of man. Only *then* could the human species be ready to not only cross its next Great Filter, but lead the Zzkritti past theirs.

Billions may perish, but the species survives!

He reached the top step, pushing through the door and into the kitchen just as the outer door on the other side of the room slammed shut. The duffel slid from his shoulder as he furrowed his brow, and he tilted his head at the sight of Jack Montgomery standing in front of him, Amber Riley pressing a gun into his ribs.

Dieter couldn't help himself. He laughed and clapped his hands.

"Welcome, Jack!" he said, unable to contain his glee. "I do hope you haven't been followed."

* * *

"He's a Bond villain," Jack had said. "Or at least he sees himself as one." He had looked around the table then, holding each set of eyes with his own, doing his best to convince the group of the necessity of his actions.

Standing in the room, holding a gun on Jack and seeing Dieter's reaction, Amber at last believed the plan had a chance of success.

"He'll monologue," Jack had said. "He can't help himself. And we need him to tell us who else he's infected with the nanos, and if he managed to get them to reproduce."

"Well *I* say we go in guns blazing, and call it a day," Bill had said, wiping his hands in the air for punctuation. "Unless he's got muscle guarding the place, that's the best approach."

Sohrab gave a sad shake of his head. "And if there *is* muscle, as you say?" He shrugged. "It might be best if I take care of the man quietly."

"Or we could take him into custody," Rutger had said, the lone voice of reason.

Bill snorted. "And do *what* with him, exactly?" Bill shook his head. "The man's done nothing wrong that we can prove, and Jack here is on every wanted poster between here and Oahu."

The argument had raged through the night and into the morning, and Amber had remained silent throughout. *Because I didn't want any part of a decision that would get anyone else killed.* "Not choosing *is* a choice," her daddy had told her. *God, I could use my daddy's guidance now*, she thought.

Dieter's eyes bored into her own. "My dear," he said, his voice full of reason, "why did you bring him here?"

Don't respond. Look through him.

She did as Jack instructed, doing her best to focus her eyes past the man while looking straight at him. Her mind was a roiling cauldron of anger, hate, and fear, but she struggled to keep her exterior as calm as the Sargasso Sea.

Dieter took a step closer, narrowing his eyes at both her and Jack. "The more immediate question, though, is *how* you found me."

"Probably has something to do with the nano-machines you infected her with," Jack said, his voice darker and more dangerous than she imagined it could be.

"Hmm," he said, leaning forward to look deeper into her eyes. "I guess that might be possible." He leaned back, pursed his lips and tapped them with a finger. "Yes, of course," he said, eyes widening. "I programmed her to protect me, but to do that, she would have to know where I am at all times." He laughed and clapped his hands again. "Sometimes, I amaze even myself." Dieter removed his glasses and cleaned them with a handkerchief he pulled from his pocket. He placed them back on his face, pushing them up the bridge of his nose with a gnarled forefinger, and tilted his head at Jack.

"Would you like to see how I did it?"

* * *

"We're not gonna get there in time!" Bill hollered for perhaps the fifth time. "Will you please fucking *step on it?*"

Rutger was as anxious as everyone, but Bill was losing control. *And how would I react if it were my brother in danger?* Rutger wondered.

"We are not more than ten minutes behind them, Mr. Montgomery," he said. "Jack did promise to wait."

"And you bought that?" Bill said with a sneer. "You Europeans sure are a gullible bunch."

"Well," Rutger sniffed, "we aren't accustomed to having our friends lie to our faces."

"Welcome to America," Sohrab said. Rutger couldn't tell if he were being jovial or cynical.

More than once he toyed with the idea of having Sohrab pull over to let him out, another Alice to be left behind and out of the game. What stopped him was his loyalty. Not to Jack, but to his *oath*. He couldn't stop them from attacking Dieter, but perhaps he could keep them from killing him. Without a gun, his only real weapon was *reason*, and it was unlikely any of them other than Sohrab would stop to listen.

Somehow, then, I must get Sohrab to support me, he thought. Rutger knew what the Iraqi was, even if the others were unclear, and he didn't completely trust the man. He may not convince him that killing Dieter was wrong, but he might appeal to Sohrab's professionalism. If deadly force wasn't necessary to attain their goal, then its use created more problems than it solved.

There was no way to discuss it in front of Bill, nor in the heat of the moment. Rutger would have to bide his time, seizing the opportunity when—or *if*—it arose. *Until then*, he thought, rubbing the stubble on his cheek, *vigilance is the watchword.*

* * *

Bond villain, Jack thought, willing his face to remain neutral—refusing to smile. *They just can't help themselves.*

"I so enjoyed our little discussion yesterday," Dieter said as he led them down the stairs to basement. "It was a shame our time was cut short." He walked in front of Jack, Amber at the rear still holding the gun.

He's not even afraid I'll try to harm him, Jack thought.

Jack wanted to smile—*needed* to—but used his anger to hold it at bay. The instant he broke character, he was sure Dieter would notice, and that would be the end of the game. *It's fourth down, and only enough time left for one more Hail Mary.*

Jack was never good at football.

"I wasn't lying, you know," Dieter said as they reached the bottom step. His voice echoed off the stone walls, making him seem larger than he was.

"About what?"

"I was truly sorry to have caused the death of your family, but it *was* an unforeseen accident." Dieter pursed his lips, then walked to a heavy door a few steps away from the stairs. He reached for the handle, stopped, and turned to face Jack. "Unfortunate as it was for *you*, it at least brought you to me." Dieter looked up, smiling. "And you have been *most* helpful."

He grabbed the handle and pushed the door open, gesturing for Jack and Amber to precede him into the room.

Jack would have preferred to strangle the life out of the man then and there, but he choked back the bile in his throat and stepped forward. Amber followed close behind, holding the gun with a rock-steady hand. *She's either playing her part better than I expected*, he thought, *or he's regained control of her.*

As soon as he entered the dark and dank room, the smell slapped him in the face like licking a nine volt battery. *Acid.* Either there had been a recent massive spill, or somewhere in the room was a large container open to the air. He didn't have time to search for it, though, his attention drawn to the workbench on the far wall. Specifically, the glass container full of—*something*—resting there.

The mass inside the container flowed and undulated like a living thing. He stopped just inside the doorway, not daring to approach within range of the device. Rather than the "gray goo" of science fiction, the nanos looked more like an oil slick. A deep, light-devouring black, there appeared throughout the mass a shimmer of all the colors of the rainbow, flowing and writhing in a chaotic storm of polychromatic ebb and flow.

"Mesmerizing, isn't it?"

* * *

"There it is," Bill said, pointing. His car was parked near the gate, just off the side of the road, and as he expected, Jack was nowhere in sight. "Asshole went in without us," he said, slapping the dashboard. "I fucking *knew* it."

"He can't have gone in more than a few minutes ago," Sohrab said, pulling next to the Big Cat and killing the motor. "We need to assess the situation before moving."

"Fuck that," Bill said, opening his door and climbing out. "Jack's in there, and probably in trouble. *Again.*"

"Bill," Sohrab said, exiting the car and running around to block Bill's path, "we must be smart about this." He placed splayed hands on Bill's chest, a gentle push against an overwhelming force.

"Listen to him," Rutger said, standing beside the car, his hand on the door ready to close it. "We don't know anything other than Jack is not where he said he would be."

Bill was breathing hard. *Too hard*, he thought. *Fucking arm hurts, too. Shit.* He slowed his breathing and his shoulders slumped, relaxing every muscle he could. "What do you want to do?" he asked Sohrab.

"Give me five minutes to look around and report back," he said. "If I don't signal you before then," he shrugged, "do what you must."

* * *

"What is it?" Jack said. He knew exactly what he hoped it *wasn't.* *Keep him talking*, he thought.

"Those are the means to an end, Mr. Montgomery," Dieter said. "An end to all war, poverty, want, and need. An end to mankind's childhood." His face glowed with the joy of a man on the precipice of attaining his heart's true desire. It was a face most people reserved for the birth of their first child.

Jack clenched the muscles in his jaw and his eyes narrowed. No sight could have sickened him more. Dieter was not only talking about the potential deaths of *billions* of human beings, but the virtual en-slavement of what was left.

And this monster is reveling in it.

"Those are the nanos you use to control people?" Jack said. *Keep the bastard talking.* "People like Amber, here?" he nodded at her.

"Oh no," Dieter said. "These aren't ready for use." He smiled at the tank, then walked over and placed a hand against the surface. "They only know how to eat and make new nanos like themselves." He petted the tank like a cat.

"But if they escape—"

347

"No worries, Jack," Dieter said, shaking his head and waving his other hand. "I have complete control over them."

Just like every other true villain, this one had no doubt in his own infallibility. *And why not? Everything's gone his way so far.*

That was going to change soon, as far as Jack was concerned.

Amber stood at Jack's back, gun in hand, as still as a statue. He could feel the heat from her body, she stood so close now, but he still had no clue if she was still *her*. Worse, he wouldn't know until the time came and she either shot Dieter—or *him*.

"Why do you need so many?" Jack asked. Amber's breathing was louder now.

"That should be obvious, Jack," Dieter said, his eyes twinkling. "I'm not Zzkritti; I can't control minds. To do what must be done, I will need to gain control of more than a thousand corporate leaders and heads of state." He leaned forward and said the *exact* wrong thing. "You could help me immensely with that, you know."

* * *

"That's it!" Bill said, slamming his fist on the hood of the car. "Sohrab's five minutes are up."

Rutger stepped in front of Bill and tried to block him as Sohrab had earlier. "It has only been a few minutes," he said, but Bill brushed him off like a pesky fly. He stalked past and onto the cobblestone driveway. Rutger had only moments to make a decision, and he prayed he chose wisely.

"Slow down," he said. "I'm coming with you."

* * *

"Fuck you, you Nazi son of a bitch!" Jack yelled. He could no longer control himself; he no longer *wanted* to. "You're fucking *delusional* if you think I would ever help *you*." He took one menacing step in Dieter's direction, then froze as the muzzle of Bill's gun pressed against his spine. Jack turned to Amber, his eyes wide. Amber looked back, her face devoid of all emotion. She could have been a robot, for all he knew. Her only motion was a barely perceptible nod past his shoulder.

The device in his pocket was as cold as his car keys.

The air around him was acrid in its pungency, drawing his attention like a siren call. He ignored it for more immediate concerns, though the hair on his neck stood as reminder. *I'm missing something*, he thought.

"What do you think I can do for you?" Jack said, turning back to Dieter.

Dieter smiled. A death's-head grimace of satisfaction. Everything was right with his world, and he knew it. "To begin, you may help me carry this," he tapped the tank full of hungry nanos, "up to the car." He tilted his head and shrugged. "After that, who knows? You may come to believe in my work as much as I."

Not a fucking chance in hell, Jack thought.

"I'm not going anywhere near that thing," he said.

"Oh, not yet, Jack. First I have to turn them off." He turned and grabbed several small dropper bottles from a shelf at the back of the workbench. "Once shut down, the nano-machines will stop moving, coalescing into a monocrystalline solid. The result will be a lump of matter no larger than your fist, though heavier than a comparable sample of gold and harder than diamond."

That's it, then, Jack thought. *Once those things are shut down, I'll make my move.* He was confident the man had told him all he would about his plans, and the only thing left now was to ensure the nanos were inert.

Now if he were only as confident that Amber was still Amber.

In the end it doesn't matter, he thought, every muscle in his body tensing. Either she is or she isn't, but I'll never have a better chance to end this.

* * *

Shit!

Now there was no one at the cars, and Sohrab was sure what had happened. Bill, impatient to do something, had gone to Jack's aid, and Rutger followed to keep him from getting killed.

Sohrab walked to the back of his car, lifted the hatch, then the flooring. It wasn't much of a weapon, but it was all he had. He took the road flare from the emergency kit and shoved it into his shirt.

"Still less dangerous than driving a cab in D.C.," he muttered to himself as he slammed the hatch closed.

* * *

Jack's voice, carried on the wind in anger, was unmistakable, and Bill ran to the stairs as soon as he crossed the threshold. An odd odor drifted up from the basement, but he ignored that. Rutger was close behind, but nothing would keep him from going down those stairs.

As quietly as he could, he descended into the dark, Rutger at his back.

"Please don't do anything rash," Rutger whispered.

Nah, Bill thought. I'm the least rash guy you know.

The going was slower than he liked, but any faster and they would sound like a herd of elephants on a dance floor. He reached the bottom and listened, standing as still as his pounding heart allowed. *Damn, already out of breath*, he thought, rubbing his chest.

Rutger, watching him, started to speak, but Bill held his hand up to cut him off. Jack was speaking again, and he was close. Bill pointed to the open door a few feet away, and they crept as one to the opening.

Bill flattened himself against the wall and peered around the jamb.

There was Jack and Amber, their backs to him. She was holding his gun on Jack, breathing fast and hard.

* * *

Dieter took four small strips of cloth, lined them up on the workbench in front of him, and placed a single drop from each of the bottles onto its own strip. "The programming is pheromone based," he said, like a professor instructing his class. "The machines have chemical receptors that, when activated in the correct order, tell them what to do." His back was to them as he worked, lifting each strip and placing them one at a time through a small opening in the top of the tank. When the last one dropped into the mass, he turned back to Jack and Amber.

"If you look closely, you'll see the change beginning. In a few minutes they will all be in a sleep mode." He stood there, leaning back against the workbench, smiling at Jack.

"That's enough," Jack said, staring straight into Dieter's eyes. "Do it."

The smile melted from Dieter's face as Jack felt Amber shift behind him.

* * *

Not again! Bill thought as his mind raced.

Amber lifted the gun in slow motion. *Everything* was in slow motion as Bill cried "No!" and barreled into the room. He grabbed her arms just as she pulled the trigger, the slug leaping from the barrel and shattering a glass tank beside Dieter. A heavy and solid mass toppled out onto the floor with a dull thud, an oily substance clinging to the tank.

And then the oil *leapt* at Dieter.

"Bill, no!" Jack yelled as he turned, grabbing Bill by his wrists and pulling him away from Amber.

No one was paying attention to Dieter.

Until he screamed.

* * *

Everyone froze as the scream reached its peak. Jack watched as Dieter writhed in agony, as his own nanos fought the invaders to a standstill. It was ultimately a losing battle, since those now devouring him were also making more. Jack spread his arms, pushing everyone back toward the door.

The device in his pocket was so hot now it burned his leg. If he stepped into the fight, the device might shut down all the nanos, but that would leave Dieter alive. There was also no assurances that they wouldn't restart once the device was taken away. Left alone, they would spread to convert *everything* into copies of themselves.

Gray goo. Everywhere. And not a single living thing on the planet will survive, Jack thought as Dieter cried. Jack's breathing was so hard the odor of the basement burned his lungs, and he threw a hand up to shield his mouth and nose. *The air,* he thought. *There's something—*

Dieter screamed again. Not in pain, but in defiance, and he rushed forward, bringing death with him.

"Jack!" he screamed, arms outstretched, stumbling toward the man he had so carefully led to this.

The device will protect me, Jack prayed.

Before he could move, Bill pushed around him and tackled Dieter to the floor. The two rolled there for a couple of seconds before Bill began to scream. He stood, slapping at his clothes like he had fallen into an ant bed. Jack saw nothing there, but when Bill's shirt dissolved he understood. His brother's knees buckled as his skin dissolved, sloughing off to create puddles of nanos beneath him. His eyes, wide and wild, begged for relief. When his ribs, white and clean, peeked through liquefying flesh, those eyes begged for *release.*

"Do something!" Amber screamed.

The device! On instinct Jack moved forward, but powerful arms grabbed him from behind and pulled him back. They held him there, arms locked behind his back. He felt Sohrab's heavy beard brush against his neck.

"Stop, Jack," he said in Jack's ear. "There is nothing you can do."

Bill's screams climbed the scale, reaching a pitch the big man should never have been able to attain. It stopped only when the nanos had chewed through his diaphragm, ending his ability to breath at all. Bill turned to Amber, sweat pouring from his face, and mouthed two words—*Kill me.*

Jack turned to her, her eyes red and swollen, just as she squeezed the trigger on Bill's gun. The sound exploded from every surface of the stone walls and floor, deafening him—the flash from the muzzle blinding him, but the sound of Bill's body hitting the floor would be with him forever.

Somewhere far away, Dieter still screamed, his nanos engaged in a last desperate battle to keep him alive.

Jack shook Sohrab off and took the gun from Amber's limp hand. He turned to Dieter, aimed, and placed two slugs into the man's skull, ending his torment.

"Better than you deserve, asshole," he said.

Jack turned back to the group—his friends, though none were family. He no longer had any family. He shoved the gun into his pocket, then fished the device from the other. It felt like molten metal in his hands, but he no longer cared.

"How do we stop those things?" Rutger said, pointing at the nanos, now furiously converting Bill and Dieter into more of themselves. Those near the solid mass also solidified, but much of the main group was no longer attached, and those continued to spread and *hunt.*

He tossed the device into the center of the pool, and all but a small section outside the range of the thing grew still. The rest continued to grow.

"Looks like I can't," Jack said with a shrug. He lowered himself to the floor and sat cross-legged, waiting for the end. "Get to the other side of the planet. You can probably stay alive for a year or more."

"Look around," Rutger said to Sohrab. "Surely the man had some way of neutralizing a breech."

Soon we'll all be neutralized, Jack thought. Bitter bile rose in his chest, but he bit back the tears that threatened to spill from his eyes. *I won't cry for Bill. He did what he thought best.* He took a deep breath, the air stinging his lungs. *I won't cry for myself, either.*

"Jack," Amber said, her voice soft and soothing. She sat beside him on the stone floor, mere feet from certain death. "There has to be something. Bill died protecting you." She placed an arm around his shoulders, and he stiffened. "Don't let him die for nothing."

"Ah, fuck *you*," he said, his face inches from hers. "You've killed the two most important people left in my life, and now you want to use one of those deaths as *motivation?*" He was breathing hard and fast, warming up for a lifetime of guilt, pain, and regret to spew in her face.

Instead, he coughed.

Fucking acid, he thought.

And just like that, the nagging at the back of his neck turned into a pounding on his head.

"Acid!" he yelled up at Sohrab and Rutger. "There's a honking big supply somewhere in here. I can smell it! Probably hydrochloric or hydrofluoric." He stood, waving his arms. "Look for a large barrel made of HDPE." The looks on their faces was clear, and he spit, "*Plastic.*"

They all fanned out, even Amber, and it was she who found it.

"Over here," she called from far end of the workbench.

Jack ran to her, pulled off the cover, and sniffed. He coughed and covered his nose. "That's it," he said. "Rutger... you and Sohrab help me with this." The two men hurried over, and together they moved it closer to the room's entrance. "All right," he said, "on three we push this thing over into the nanos. Be sure to jump back out of the splash zone."

He looked up into the eyes of each, nodded, then turned back to what was left of his brother. "See you on the other side," he said to Bill. In one last nod to childhood tradition, he leaned into the barrel and yelled "Three!"

The barrel toppled, spilling liquid death over the stone floor, digesting everything in its path. The nanos, solid or liquid, never had a chance as the acid dissolved all creatures, man and machine alike. The sizzling of the breaking molecular bonds was like steak frying, and Jack's gorge rose at the thought. The smell of the acid doing its work quickly overpowered any fresh air that managed to find its way to the basement.

"I don't think there's any ventilation down here," Jack said, looking up at the ceiling. "We better get upstairs before we pass out. This whole room will be filled soon with hydrogen gas from the reaction."

"We need to make sure they're finished," Amber said, her eyes full of fear and guilt.

"I'll come back to check," Sohrab said. "Let's go while we can."

* * *

They sat outside, huddled beside Dieter's car until the coughing subsided. Jack stood and stepped away from them, his back to the group. Sohrab saw the man's shoulders shaking at times, and knew Jack cried for the loss of his brother. Amber sat on the stoop next to Rutger, who draped an arm over her shoulder in a gesture of comfort.

When he judged they had waited long enough, Sohrab entered the building. Before going downstairs, he checked the refrigerator and took out a whole chicken that had been left to thaw. He descended the stairs, and once at the bottom, took several deep breaths, holding the final one. *The door to the lab is intact, so if the nanos are still active, at least they have not reached this far*, he thought.

He poked his head through the door and looked for signs they were active. The acid had dissolved everything with which it came in contact, and there was nothing left of the bodies. There were no signs anything else was happening, but he tore a leg off the chicken and tossed it into the center of the room. When he didn't see anything happen, he ripped pieces from the bird and threw them everywhere he had seen activity before.

Nothing, he thought. His lungs screamed, burning to breath, and he gave in at last. His eyes watered as he coughed, and he walked back to the stairs. Sohrab gave the room one last look, then climbed the stairs back to the kitchen. He pulled the flare from his shirt, struck it, and tossed it down the stairs to the basement.

Then he ran.

* * *

"Run!" Sohrab yelled as he exited the building at a clip. Jack turned, wondering what was up, but the others were already in motion. He watched as Sohrab pulled the others to the opposite side of the car, ducking low. Jack felt a tug, then he, too, was on the ground beside the rest. He started to stand, but the explosion nixed that idea. More of a muffled *Whump!*, the force of the blast blew out the windows on the building and the car.

When he felt it was safe, Jack stood. The building, long dead, was engulfed in flames—a funeral pyre lighting the way to a realm of eternal night. The heat drove them back, and they watched it burn from their cars.

CHAPTER 30

With the others riding with sohrab, Jack drove the Big Cat alone back toward the highway. Two lime-green firetrucks blew past going the opposite direction, rattling his car if not his nerves.

Good luck, guys, he thought. The building would be a total loss before they even finished setting up. *I fucking hate green firetrucks.*

"Where are you going?" Rutger had asked, standing between Jack and the car's door.

"Home," Jack had told him, as if that were all that needed to be said.

"You are still a wanted man, Jack."

"Then arrest me or get out of my goddamn way." He had been in no mood to argue and was more rough than he intended when he pushed past. "I'm going home to have a drink or ten and try to figure out what to tell my sister-in-law." He had looked into each face, daring them to complain.

"The police will arrest you on sight, you know," Sohrab had said, his hand placed with care on Jack's shoulder.

"Good. One less thing on my to-do list, then." He removed Sohrab's hand and opened the Big Cat's door, slid behind the wheel, and left them all there.

He could still see their faces as he drove away.

Especially Amber's.

Eyes half-lidded, he slouched in the seat, one hand on the wheel. He pressed his foot to the floor and the Cat responded with a full-throated growl, chewing up the miles between him and home.

Which Amber pulled the trigger? he wondered. Was it the woman I fell in love with, the one controlled by Dieter, or the one that lied to me in Germany?

Maybe they were all the same person. Maybe they were none of those.

The others would follow—how could they not?—but for now he needed to get as much space between himself and them as he could.

* * *

"I don't understand."

"It is not your job to understand, Inspector," Jeff said. He rolled his eyes like a human would, though the motion required careful consideration. "Your only job is to pay the men on this list the amounts I indicated. After you have completed this task, we will both go see the Bureau's director." Jeff leaned close, and Stirling recoiled. "Are we clear?"

"Yes, sir." Stirling stilled his hands with an obvious effort. "What I meant was, I don't understand the *reason* for this change."

"Your's is not to reason why," Jeff said, nodding and offering a thin grin. "Now run along," he finished with a dismissive flip of his hand.

Stirling nodded and scurried away, leaving Jeff at his makeshift desk in the hotel lobby.

Being in charge is not as much fun as humans led me to believe, he thought. The Zzkritti leaned over the papers there, working out his next moves. His face buried in the data, he didn't notice the shadow fall across the table at first.

"Hello Thirteen," he said without looking up. "I'll be with you in a moment."

* * *

Amber stood at the door to her apartment, one hand on the police tape, the other on Sohrab's shoulder. She had done little more than stare at the tape since they arrived. Sohrab had been patient with her, allowing her to lean on him for support.

He's a good man, Amber thought. She knew there was far more to him than simple cab driver, but at this point none of it mattered.

"Here he comes," Sohrab said, nodding to the stairs. Rutger was unaccompanied, but he was smiling and holding a ring with a single key dangling.

"Your manager was most helpful," Rutger said to Amber. "He did not appear to be alarmed by our presence, so I take that as a sign he is not calling the police at this moment." He reached down with the key, but before he could place it in the lock, Amber closed her hand over his.

"Thank you, boys," she said, her voice a husky whisper. "I've got it from here." She tried to smile up at both men, but all she managed was a grimace.

"Are you sure?" Sohrab asked, leaning closer. "Perhaps—"

"It's okay," she said, managing a smile this time. "I just want to be alone for a while."

She ripped the tape from the door, took the key, and opened her apartment. The door swung inward, light spilling over the devastation of police intrusion, and she turned a wrinkled nose to Rutger.

"Sorry about that," he said, dipping his chin. "I would be happy to—"

"It's fine," she said, patting his arm. "Gives me something to do other than sit and stew."

She took a cautious step inside, then turned to face two men she hardly knew yet trusted with her life. *How much do people have to go through to bond?* she wondered. *At what point do we become family?*

Amber elevated on her toes and kissed each man on the cheek, one hand on each face to hold them close.

"Thank you for everything," she said and turned, closing the door behind her.

* * *

Sohrab pulled up to the curb for passenger unloading and shifted the car into park. He exited the car the same time as Rutger, and both men seemed to race to the rear. Sohrab got there first, opening the hatch and pulling Rutger's luggage from the back. He handed the bag to the Inspector and nodded.

"I wish I could say it has been fun," Sohrab said, then shrugged and grinned.

"No need to sugar coat it, as the Americans say," Rutger said with a half-smile. "This has indeed been no vacation."

"Saving the world never is," Sohrab said. *I would know, I guess,* he thought. *Better than most.* He tilted his head and pursed his lips, considering the professional in front of him. Rutger raised an eyebrow in return. Sohrab nodded, reaching a decision. He fumbled his wallet from his back pocket and withdrew a card, hesitating for a few seconds, then extended it to Rutger. "My number," he said, and winked. "Just in case."

Rutger hesitated as well, then took the card from Sohrab's hand. He took out his wallet, withdrew his own card, and held it out for Sohrab. "Just in case," he said.

Sohrab took the card and shoved it into his pocket. There would be no casual gripping of hands or brotherly hugs for these two. They had each taken measure of the other, filing the information away for when it was needed. Both men nodded in wary trust and no small amount of respect, then each turned toward their futures.

Post 9/11, airport security didn't like people to linger at drop-off or pickup, so when the uniformed officer strolled toward Sohrab, he smiled, waved, and drove away.

"It is going to be a long drive home," he said, shaking his head. He thought of Mason and Bill. *At least I get to go home.*

* * *

Jack sat in the middle of the sofa, his apartment littered with the detritus of a thorough FBI search. Most of his belongings were somewhere in the bowels of the nearest division headquarters, but they had left the large furniture, the TV, and the contents of the fridge.

"Thank the Flying Spaghetti Monster for small favors," he said, opening a bottle of beer with a quick twist and holding it up in salute. "All hail his noodley appendage." He took a long swig, then pushed aside the file—the one Dieter had given him—and propped his feet on the coffee table. Remote in hand, he turned on the TV and channel-surfed, looking for anything to put his racing mind into neutral.

Jack had been home a full day, and still no cops had come knocking. Part of him wanted to turn himself in, but he was curious to see how long it took them to figure it out. He wasn't hiding, having already picked up his mail and made a grocery run, but everyone steadfastly refused to recognize him.

"It's what I get for looking like Jon Hamm," he said, and took another pull on the bottle. He checked the time. *Close enough*, he thought, and turned to one of the networks for the news.

"… as many as eight thousand were killed, the earthquake measuring at least seven point eight in magnitude." The newsreader on the screen was appropriately concerned, her voice tight and hard-edged. The chyron at the bottom of the screen crawled from right to left with interesting tidbits from the day's devastation. "Officials in Nepal also report a massive avalanche in the Himalayas, with as many as twenty people reported missing," the blonde with the perky upturned nose said.

"Yeah," Jack said, waving his bottle at the screen, "don't forget the aftershocks coming May twelfth." He took another drink. "Those are gonna be a bitch, too."

It was all there splayed on the coffee table under his feet. He would be able to predict disasters for years to come if he so chose.

Does Vegas take bets on shit like this? he wondered.

"That's just sick, Jack," he said. *Ah fuck, now I'm talking to myself.*

He saluted the development by finishing off the beer in his hand. He tossed the empty in the general direction of the trash and pulled another from what remained of the six-pack at his side.

Watching the first of a long list of disasters, assassinations, and wars was at once both exhilarating and depressing for Jack. Everything he had been through—everything he had been told—was now confirmed, but that was small comfort to those now dealing with the devastation.

"Fuck!"

He turned the TV off, then threw the remote at the screen. It missed its mark by three feet, which was impressive since he was only ten feet from the thing.

Jack laughed. Long and hard, doubling over and holding his stomach. His laughter rose in pitch, becoming something maniacal. Regaining control, his dwindling chuckle soon became sniffling, devolving into chest-heaving sobs. He dropped the beer bottle to the floor and rocked, pulling his hair and crying for everyone he had lost. Jack sucked great gulps of air and rolled to his side, curling up like a child.

He lay there for more than an hour, his mind recalling his life in bits and pieces—an *amuse-bouche* of tasteless regret. Sleep would not come, and his head ached. He sat up, rubbing his head, and his foot landed in the puddle of beer-soaked carpet. Before he could decide between aspirin or cleaning up the mess, there was a soft knock at the door.

"Jack?" Amber said through the door. She knocked again, louder this time.

Go away, go away, go the fuck away!

He projected his thoughts at her, rubbing his head, but he did not answer. He couldn't. Not now.

"Jack, please," she whispered, then knocked again, each softer than the one before. "I need to talk to you."

You need to talk to me? You *need?* Jack was breathing hard; he could feel the heat rising, and he stood.

Still, he couldn't call out to her, or open the door.

"Have you heard the news?"

Of course I've heard the fucking news! People are dying, and I didn't do a goddamn thing about it!

He couldn't have. He knew that, but it didn't matter. I never had control. Not one fucking time, but it's still all my fault.

Amber brushed her fingers across the face of the door and sighed. "When you want to talk, Jack..." she said, and walked away.

Jack went to the window and peeked through the curtain, but all he saw was the top of her head as she descended the stairs.

* * *

"Will," Jenna called up the stairs, "could you *please* get your sister down here? She's going to miss her bus."

"Okay, mom," her son hollered back. "*Jeez.*"

"Don't start with me," she said, turning away from both the stairs and another argument with the boy. When a child turns 12, he should be kept in a barrel and fed through the bung hole, until he reaches 16...at which time you plug the bung hole. She hadn't thought of the Twain quote in years, but it seemed appropriate now. Will was taller than she, and that fact had put the idea in his head he was not only a man, but her equal.

His daddy's going to have a talk with him when he gets back, she thought.

When he gets back was how she always thought of it. Every morning when he left for work the phrase rolled through her mind like a tank, fading only when he *did* come home. She was used to him not calling when he was working, but the last conversation she had with Bill had been two days ago. His job was no longer inherently dangerous, but this mess with Jack was different.

Jenna bit her lip and looked at the phone on the kitchen table.

He'll call, she thought. He'll call or walk in the front door today.

Two pair of feet pounded down the stairs, threatening to shake the house to kindling, and she turned to face her children with a broad smile that *almost* reached her eyes.

"Get your packs, guys, and get out there!" she said, shooing them to the front door. "Buy your lunches today. I didn't have time to make you anything."

"Aw, mom," Sarah said, wrinkling her nose. "I hate going through the line." Her clothes were cute and picture-perfect, the pink bow in her hair placed just so. *As always*, Jenna thought, shaking her head. *How the hell did we raise such a girly-girl?*

"Just *go*, already."

"Okay, okay," Will said. "Don't blow a gasket."

Jenna sighed heavily, biting back a response, and pushing them out the door. Seeing the kids off to school was one of the few joys left in raising them, and they were quickly souring her on *that*. She had arranged her schedule to allow her the time, and she was now learning to regret that decision.

She walked back to the kitchen table and sat facing the garden. It was Bills chair, but she used it every time he was away. The garden soothed her nerves like nothing else.

The bus squealed to a stop outside, and less than a minute later rumbled away again. Only then did she relax. Jenna marveled at the women who managed careers and kids as a single parent. *I know I couldn't do it without Bill's help.*

She picked up her morning's coffee mug and stood. Before she could walk to the pot to refill it, there was a knock at the front door.

Don't answer it! The thought boomed in her head without warning, and she wrinkled her nose. *Where the hell did that come from?*

Jenna set her cup on the counter, turned and walked to the door, another round of knocks providing a counter-melody to the sound of her heels clicking on the floor. When she reached the door, a wave of trepidation shook her, churning her stomach.

"I'm being silly," she said, and pulled the door open.

Two officers in dress blues stood in front of her, stern and sad expressions on their faces.

Jenna crumbled to the floor.

*   *   *

Light streamed through the curtain, and Jack threw his arm over his face with an angry growl. He lay there pretending he didn't have to pee, but his stomach ended all thoughts of further sleep with a long and low growl of its own. He hadn't eaten anything—not counting *beer*—since breakfast two days ago.

I wonder how Alice is getting along? he thought, then chuckled. *At least she's still alive.*

The TV was still on, the morning news offering stories that someone deemed important. Jack sat up, rubbed his head with both hands, and took stock of the room around him. The mess left behind by the cops was nothing compared to the mess sitting on the sofa, though he had no desire to clean either. He stood, scratched his ass, and took a step toward the bathroom just as knuckles rapped on his door.

She's never going to give up, is she? he thought, eyebrows forming a hairy shelf and mouth tightening into a lemon-sucking pucker. Dark clouds gathered around his head as he stalked to the door and threw it open with a wide sweep of his arm.

Two men stood in the opening. One familiar, and the other definitely *not*.

"Hello Jack," the Shadowman said, an amiable grin splitting his face. "May we come in?"

I can't say I'm surprised, he thought as he stared at the two men. His face relaxed, shoulders slumping, and he stepped away from the door. "It's not like I can stop you," he said, and waved them inside.

The smaller man entered first, looked around the train wreck that was Jack's apartment, and tilted his head, looking up at him. "Does it always look like this?"

Jack ignored the dig, sneered, and turned. "Make yourselves at home. I've got to go bleed the lizard."

"Bleed...?" the little man said, looking up at the Shadowman.

"Pee," the Shadowman said, removing his hat. The little guy seemed satisfied with the explanation, and Jack walked away to take care of business.

When he returned, both men were on the sofa, most of the trash swept away and piled in a corner. Both men sat on the edge of the cushions, backs straight. The little man, though, kept shifting his weight as if he were uncomfortable. The Shadowman waved Jack to sit in the chair to his left. Jack frowned, reached to his end of the sofa, and grabbed the last bottle of beer from the pack. He twisted off the cap, took a long swig of warm beer as he eyed his visitors, flopped into the chair, and crossed his legs on the table.

"To what do I owe the pleasure?" He took another sip, his eyes never leaving the two. "Here to kill me at last?"

"Nothing of the kind!" the little man said, sputtering. "Why, you—"

"We are here to discuss your future," the Shadowman said, placing a hand on the other man's leg to quell him. "This is... my *superior*, Jack. You may call him Jeff."

Jack snorted once, then his eyes narrowed. "Superior?" he asked.

The Shadowman nodded once, a slow dip of his chin.

"You mean, like... Zzkritti? *That* kind of superior?"

"Yes, of course," Jeff said, his impatience growing. He leaned toward Jack and smiled like a fox. "Would you like to see?"

"Nope," Jack said without a thought. "I've seen enough horrors for one lifetime." He took another long drink, then set the bottle on the table. "No offense."

"None taken," Jeff said, still smiling. "Humans are rather ugly to us as well."

"Yeah, well, I don't like humans very much, either."

"Jack," the Shadowman said, "we are here to offer you a... job, of sorts."

"Fuck that idea, too." He picked up the bottle and took another long drink. "The only job I have concerning you guys is stopping your fucking *plan*."

The two on his sofa looked at one another, sharing a thought between them. The Shadowman nodded, and Jeff turned to face Jack.

"At this moment, your sister-in-law is receiving the news of her husband's death," Jeff said. Jack's face clouded at once, his eyes narrowing, and Jeff recoiled. "She will also find out later today that her husband had purchased a sizable insurance policy on his life," he said before Jack could speak.

"*How* sizable?" Jack asked, his voice dark and dangerous.

"Is a million dollars enough?" Jeff said, then turned to the Shadowman as if seeking approval.

"Make it two," Jack said. "Just on general principal."

"Very well," Jeff said, nodding. "The same will apply to Ms. Jackson's husband, of course."

Sally, Jack thought. Until now he hadn't thought of her at all. *What kind of a fucking monster am I?* "Why are you doing this?" he asked, leaning back, one eyebrow raised.

"As Thirteen said, we would like you to work for us."

"We?" Jack swirled the beer by the bottle's neck.

"The Zzkritti," Jeff said. "There have been some... ah... *changes* of late, and I have apparently been placed in charge of all Earth operations."

"I thought you guys only had queens as leaders."

"In normal circumstances, yes," Jeff said. "These are no longer normal circumstances. We are far too few to continue the plan," he tapped the folder on the coffee table, "as formulated."

"How many of you are there, actually?"

Jeff lowered his head, his fingers still brushing the file folder. "Far fewer than there were two days ago," he said, his voice soft and far away.

Does this mean I can rid the planet of these things once and for all? Or does it mean just what he says—their hand has been forced, somehow?

"If you join them, Jack, you'll be given your own nano-machines," the Shadowman said. "All your injuries will be healed, allowing you to effectively live forever." When he said it, it did not sound like a boon to Jack.

Besides, he thought, not all my injuries are physical.

"Pass," Jack said, surprising himself.

"But Mr. Montgomery," Jeff said, "there are still people out there programmed by Dieter, and we don't know who they are or what function they will perform."

The ultimate sleeper cells, he thought. Wonderful.

"Like I said, boys... I pass." Jack stood, finished the bottle, and threw it into the trash pile. "Now, if you'll excuse me," he said, gesturing toward the door. "By the way," he said to the Shadowman, "sorry I lost your doohickey." Jack grinned down at him like an old Eddie Haskell.

"Doo—?" Jeff began.

"It's nothing," the Shadowman said, waving it off. "You'll get another someday," he said to Jack.

Both men stood as one, Jeff looking relieved to no longer be sitting. Jack hustled them to the door, opened it, and showed them out. Before he could close it, the Shadowman turned, a sad smile on his face.

"One day," he said, "when you are old and frail I will visit you again, and you *will* take what they offer." He placed the hat on his head and adjusted it. "They are quite patient," he shrugged and frowned, "and humans are weak."

Jack leaned as close to the man as he could stand. "Don't count on it," he said, and slammed the door in his face.

He listened to their footfalls as they descended the stairs, then walked back to the sofa. Before he sat, he reached beneath the farthest cushion and withdrew Bill's gun, tossing it to the table. It landed with a heavy thud, spun once, and stopped with the muzzle pointing at the sofa where Jack lowered his weary body.

He leaned forward, arms on his legs, one bouncing like a junkie in withdrawal. The now-useless folder stared at him, accusing. He reached for the gun, feeling the weight of it in his hands. The TV news was now all earthquake, all the time, but across the bottom the chyron crawled.

"Doctors in Kazakhstan report the children in the small town of Kalachi waking from their long slumber," it read.

Jack squeezed his eyes, tears forming in the corners, and wiped them dry with the back of one hand.

The hand holding Bill's gun.